I0700897

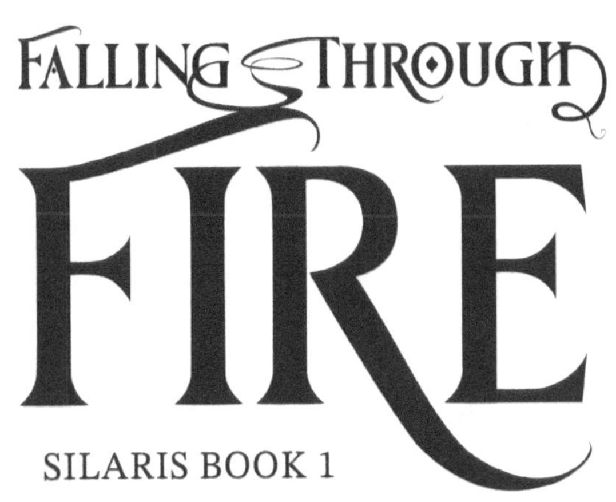

FALLING THROUGH FIRE

SILARIS BOOK 1

BY

LEAH LORE

THROUGH THE RIFT PUBLISHING

Copyright © 2025 by Leah Lore

All rights reserved.

No portion of this publication may be reproduced in any form without written permission from the publisher or author, except as permitted by U.S. copyright law.

This is a work of fiction. Names, characters, places, and events portrayed in this book are products of the author's imagination, and any semblance to actual events or places or persons, living or dead, is entirely coincidental. Likewise, the views expressed herein are the sole responsibility of the author.

Without in any way limiting the author's [and publisher's] exclusive rights under copyright, any use of this publication to "train" generative artificial intelligence (AI) technologies to generate text is expressly prohibited. The author reserves all rights to license uses of this work for generative AI training and development of machine learning language models.

Cover and interior art and design by Sara Copes.

Map art and design by Ryan Tyree and Sara Copes.

Visit: Linktr.ee/LeahLore

ISBN 978-1-966638-04-9 (paperback)

ISBN 978-1-966638-03-2 (ebook)

For everyone searching for adventure and acceptance, family and fortitude, loyalty and love.

May the Forest watch over you,
May your hunt be fruitful,
May your heart be unburdened,
May your head stay clear.

HIREATH PINES

SILARIS

Contents

Content Warnings

This series takes place as society prepares for war. There will be battle, blood, swearing, descriptions of injuries, and death, including parental, child, and sibling death. There will be flashbacks of battles and traumatic experiences, including abuse, car crashes, and (off page) sexual assault. There will be mentions of self-harm, racism, kidnapping, suicide and suicidal thoughts.

Readers who may be sensitive to these elements, please be advised. Stay safe and keep your mental health at the forefront. If you or someone you know needs support, call or text 988 for the national suicide and crisis line, or visit 988lifeline.org.

Prologue

I'M JUST FOLLOWING ORDERS.

Tree frogs chirped in the distance and an owl hooted a few trees away. Fireflies swirled around me, flashing red with the occasional burst of orange or yellow. I pulled the black fabric of my cloak closer, hiding from the Forest's despondent stare. The night creatures were usually my allies, but tonight their judgment weighed me down.

She made her choice. I'm just following orders.

A branch groaned beneath my fingers and I forced my grip to relax around the rough bark. For this to succeed, stealth was imperative. Hidden as I was, perched on a limb high in the canopy, I could afford mistakes. Once on the forest floor, however . . .

I closed my eyes and took a deep breath.

She deserves this.

I stepped off the limb. Wind rushed past my ears as I fell ten feet—twenty—forty.

The tension bled from me, taking with it the sting of her betrayal. In the meditation of the fall, I called my shadows. Darkness momentarily obscured my vision, then the world reappeared. I landed back in the canopy, several trees from where I started. I adjusted my balance, then stepped again, using my shadows to materialize in the next tree. I shadow-walked through the canopy, flitting from one branch to the next with little effort.

The trees grew progressively larger until I arrived at my destination—an ancient oak with lines of decay spidering up its trunk. I reached out my mind to the massive tree but received only silence. That wasn't uncommon. People living this far from civilization were forced to shape roots into homes, as the new growth was the only part of the tree willing to change. Often these giants were impenetrable at this height, already too set in their ways.

I peered down. Far below, a small dwelling was formed from the tangle of roots at the tree's base. My shadows swirled again and my feet sunk into the spongy moss of the forest floor. Blackened leaves scattered the ground around me. I stepped carefully to avoid their crunch.

I crept toward the large, oval window on the east side of the home, conscious of the many holes in the root system that made up the structure. I was familiar with this dwelling, but any of the gaps in those twisting vines could be hidden windows. A glance outside could mean my discovery.

Black tendrils stretched from my feet and up the wall to the oval window. Satisfaction flashed through me as my shadows disarmed the magical wards, and the pane opened with a soft click. I eased into the dark room, not daring to breathe. Blood pounded in my ears as I listened for any movement. I could barely make out the slow, even breaths of someone sleeping in the next room. A quiet coo sounded from the darkness.

I spun, flinging a handful of gray powder toward the noise. Through the cloud of dust, wide green eyes stared at me from an intricately carved crib. Pink hydrangeas climbed the bars and a mobile of brightly colored songbirds spun slowly overhead. The infant smiled and cooed again before falling fast asleep.

I let out a long breath, willing the shadows to conceal me. The powder was just ground gardenia amplified with a spell—harmless, but would keep the baby asleep while I completed my mission. It was for the child's own good. For the good of our people. For all of Silaris. She deserved everything that was coming.

Does she really?

The intrusive thought clanged through my mind like a gong. I froze with my arms stretched halfway to the infant. Did anyone truly deserve this sort of punishment? I'd loved her once . . . was I doing the right thing?

The shadows swirled around my wrists, giving me strength and renewing my splintered confidence. My resolve solidified, and I lifted the sleeping child from the crib.

She made her choice—thus forcing mine.

One

Rose

I was late.

I used to care about things like punctuality, but not anymore. These days, all sorts of heavy emotions buzzed inside me. If I didn't acknowledge them, their constant white noise offered me a sort of numb peace. I clung to that numbness as I navigated the halls of the unfamiliar math building, passing classrooms and lecture halls. Conversations and laughter floated around me, bouncing off without penetrating. The sounds of normal life were muted against the constant crackle of flames in my mind.

It wasn't difficult to find the right room. When I walked through the heavy wooden door to my Calc 1 class, the smell of dry-erase markers and floral perfume assaulted my nose. A middle-aged woman was going over simple derivatives on the whiteboard. She turned and glared when the door slammed shut behind me. The entire class did. I froze.

"Sorry." My voice was flat. Dead. I tried to smile, but it was half-hearted and came out like a grimace.

I stood frozen until the professor—Dr. Winters, according to my schedule—gestured for me to take a seat. Only when the other students turned back to the whiteboard did I force my feet toward the nearest open chair.

I sat and pulled my notebook from my backpack, taking slow deep breaths to calm my racing heart. I had to keep my grades up to keep my scholarship. I had to make my parents proud. I could do this. I just had to avoid people and focus on—

"Excuse me?" A deep voice whispered from behind me. I twisted to meet the warm amber gaze of the man sitting behind me. "Are you Rose?"

I narrowed my eyes but nodded.

"Cool." Color stained his russet-brown cheeks. "Would have been embarrassing if you weren't. I'm Blaine. I was told to keep an eye out for you. My dad works with Martin in the ER."

"Oh." I relaxed. "You know my uncle? Is your dad a paramedic too?"

His black curls bounced around his ears as he shook his head. "Trauma surgeon."

"Small world."

He laughed, earning a glare from the teacher. He grinned sheepishly and waved an apology.

"Small town," he corrected. "Hey, do you need someone to show you around? This is my last class until the afternoon."

"Isn't this your first day too?"

"Yeah, but my dad lectures here sometimes, so I'm pretty familiar with the campus."

"I'm fine, but thanks." I turned around to pay attention to the professor.

"I know the first week of college can be overwhelming," Dr. Winters said to the class, "and I know you just want to make friends." She shot a scolding look at Blaine, who awkwardly cleared his throat. "But I'd like to get a baseline of where you stand before we start the semester. Break up into groups of two or three, and I'll give everyone an equation. Once your group solves the problem, come write it on the board."

I almost jumped out of my seat when I felt a tap on my shoulder.

"Ope, sorry." Blaine grimaced, pulling his hand back. "Do you want to team up?"

"Uh, sure." There was no reason to be so twitchy. "Yeah, that would be great."

Blaine smiled then glanced at something over my shoulder. He blinked a few times, transfixed. I turned to see a pretty blonde girl gliding toward us.

Pretty was an understatement—this girl was gorgeous. Probably a dancer, judging from the grace of her steps. She would be right at home in a ballet company. The girl's soul-piercing green eyes scrutinized me and I forced myself not to squirm under her gaze.

"Hello," she said.

Even her voice was beautiful. Melodic. It matched her vibe—wispy and ethereal. Blaine's brows lifted as she spoke. His lips parted and he stared, obviously starstruck.

"Hi," I said, trying to break the awkwardness.

"May I join your group?" she asked. Her voice lilted in an accent I couldn't place.

Blaine recovered himself.

"Of course!" The smile he gave her lit up his face. "The more the merrier!"

"Wonderful." The girl smiled and pulled up a seat. "My name is Flora."

"I'm Blaine."

"Rose." I tried not to scowl. Wonderful, now I had to be cordial with two people.

"Flora and Rose?" Blaine laughed. "A regular bouquet."

I forced a smile at the joke, but Flora didn't. She just tilted her head to the side. Blaine's laughter choked off at her stoic expression.

I began to relax, despite warnings to myself not to let my guard down. With Flora here, Blaine wouldn't look at me twice. That was good. I could work with that.

Flora's gaze cut to me. I couldn't read her expression before she turned back to Blaine. I was never a great judge of character, but I was extra out of practice reading people.

I hadn't been social in a while. I hadn't even left the house since I moved in with Martin last month. Being around others always made me feel more alone. Even just being here this morning was overwhelming. I only had one more class today, then I could go back to Martin's and hide from the world. It was harder to breathe out here.

Or maybe it was just the overpowering smell of that awful perfume.

I grabbed my inhaler from my bag, shook it, and took a deep pull. Dr. Winters dropped a worksheet between us and moved on quickly. Blaine looked down at the paper and furrowed his brow. He twirled his pencil between his fingers.

"I'm not sure how to start this," he admitted.

"May I?" I asked.

He turned the paper around to face me.

"Oh, I've done this before," I said. "The equation seems tough, but it's pretty straightforward."

I held my hand out for his pencil and he gave it to me without hesitation. I worked through the problem, explaining the steps as I went. Blaine and Flora listened with rapt focus. When I got to the end, I circled my answer. They both leaned forward to study the paper.

"See," I said, "if we break it up into smaller pieces, it's not as overwhelming."

"Wow," Blaine said. "You're really smart."

I shook my head. "Math just comes easy to me."

"Oh!" he exclaimed, as if just realizing something. "That's right! Martin said you're some kind of genius."

"He said that?" I blushed. "It's not true."

"You got a big scholarship, right? That's pretty impressive."

I shrugged. Silence fell over our group. Blaine tapped a nervous finger against the desk. Unable to stand the weirdness pervading us, he gestured to the completed worksheet.

"You did all the work. Do you want to write that on the board?"

I looked at the paper, then up at the whiteboard. Everyone else was still working on their problems. Did we just get an easy one?

The thought of being the first person to walk up there had my hands going clammy. I was already the center of attention once today. I didn't want to be on display again. I swallowed, trying to think up an excuse. Fortunately, Blaine offered me the out I needed.

"Or I could do it, if you want."

I tried not to look too relieved as I nodded.

"Unless you want to, Flora?" he asked.

"No, you may proceed."

Blaine's mouth quirked into a perplexed smile. "Alright, I'll be right back."

He picked up the assignment and walked toward the board, leaving me alone with Flora. We watched as he wrote out the equation in green marker. I thought about asking Flora where she was from but refrained. If I asked her that, she might ask in return. I wasn't ready to talk about my past. I didn't even want to think about Florida. About the humidity and the heat. About the crackle and pop of flames devouring plaster and stucco. About my parents and the people I left behind—

Stop! I scolded myself. *Don't think about that.*

I swallowed my grief behind a wall of indifference. If I didn't feel anything, I couldn't feel pain. Of course, that was easier said than done. Waves of sadness crashed into me over and over again. I was going to drown in it if I didn't get a hold of myself.

"You have very pretty eyes."

Flora's words shocked me out of my own head.

"What?" The word was barely audible.

"I wish mine were blue." She was still watching Blaine. I followed her gaze. He was finishing up the equation and circling the answer. "I'm jealous."

"You're jealous?" She must have been joking. "Of me?"

She met my gaze with an intensity that made me blush. Before she could respond, however, Blaine came strolling back. I looked past him to the professor, who flashed me a smile and a thumbs up. It seemed I was forgiven for my tardiness.

"Dr. Winters said ours was the toughest problem," Blaine said. "Nice work, Rose!"

Our group waited together while the others finished. When everyone wrote their problems on the board, Dr. Winters went over them, explaining what we did right and wrong. I took detailed notes, though I already knew most of it.

When class was over, Blaine led the way out of the classroom. He was taller than me, but only just. He was narrow but obviously fit, with an easy confidence to his gait. Flora was quite a bit shorter than both of us—petite in a way I could never achieve. Her perfect posture had me torn between trying to stand up straighter or slouching to hide at her height.

Blaine held the exterior door open. It was sunny outside, but a cold wind bit through the sleeves of my jacket.

"Well, it was nice to meet you both." Blaine held out his hand for me to shake.

I stared at it for a moment too long before I took it—who shook hands anymore? His grip was firm, but his hand was soft and warm. The sky didn't fall when he touched me. I was fine. Actually, shaking hands with this stranger was weirdly comforting. Especially when I saw something that looked like concern in his deep amber eyes.

I quickly shoved my hand into my pocket. I thought his smile flickered, but it was so fast, I might have imagined it. Flora shook his hand next, if a bit stiffly.

"Likewise," she said.

"I would love to start a study group." He grimaced. "I'm obviously not very good at math, but I'm fair at science. I'm willing to trade tutoring."

"That sounds like an excellent idea," Flora said. "We could meet at my house. I live nearby."

"I'm close, too, but I still live at home, so my parents would drive us crazy. I'm cool with going to your place. What about you, Rose?"

I jumped at the sound of my name. I thought they forgot I was here and was wondering if I could sneak away without drawing their attention.

"Um, what?"

"You cool with going to Flora's?" Blaine asked.

"Oh, I don't know . . ."

"Please, Rose? I could really use your help. I'm seriously not sure how I'm going to pass this class. I need to ace it for a shot at medical school."

"I . . . sure," I said. "I could probably use the extra study time."

And Martin will be glad to see me out of the house.

"Great!" Blaine's face lit up. "Let's exchange socials."

After promising to meet up, Flora glided away and Blaine pulled his half-concealed skateboard from his bag. I tried to squash down the seedling of hope sprouting in my chest. The one trying to convince me it would be okay to be friends with these two.

Blaine hopped onto the board and was soon speeding away.

"Wait!" I called before he could get too far. The back of the skateboard skidded against the ground as he stopped, then he rolled back to me.

"Yeah?"

"Could you show me where the Creative Arts building is?"

Blaine smiled and that hope dug roots deeper into my chest.

Blaine

"Why me?"

Flora looked up at me from our usual table in the back of the Student Union. Mouth full of fries, she tilted her head to one side to show her confusion.

"How did you know it was me?" I sat across from her and tapped the simple golden ring that hung from the chain around my neck. I hadn't taken it off since Flora gave it to me yesterday. I couldn't believe I hadn't thought to ask her then—though, if I was being fair to myself, I had been a bit overwhelmed.

Flora swallowed and took a sip of soda before answering. "I wasn't positive at first, but I knew it was either you or Rose. That first day of class, I was drawn to you both. The ring was guiding me." She shrugged. "I wasn't even registered for calculus."

"Okay, so how did you know it wasn't her?"

"I actually gave the ring to Rose first. Nothing happened." I frowned.

"We can't tell her." Flora told me. Again.

I gave a harsh laugh and took a bite of pizza. My next class was in twenty minutes and I wasn't in the mood to have this conversation. It had been just over a month since I met Flora and Rose that first day of class, but somehow it felt like we'd been friends forever.

"You can't be serious."

"I am serious," Flora said. "Deadly serious. And stop looking at my ears. You've been doing it all day. It's weird."

"Sorry, I just . . ." I shook my head. Flora's quirks made so much more sense now. "She'll be crushed if she finds out we're hiding this from her."

"Rose will be fine." Flora rolled her eyes.

I wasn't so sure. I saw how she looked that first day of school. Sunken. Hollow. Dead on her feet. Even now, weeks later, I would catch her falling back into that depressive trance. She never talked about what happened to her parents, but at least she genuinely smiled now. She even laughed at my stupid jokes.

"Plus, Silaris isn't for Rose." Flora popped another fry into her mouth. "Even if I wanted to take her with us, she wouldn't survive the Rift."

I coughed and had to take a drink of water.

"Wait, what?" I asked. "What do you mean she 'wouldn't survive'?"

"Well . . ." Flora looked abashed as she smiled sweetly. "Humans—*regular humans*, I mean—can't cross the Rift."

"Why not?" My hands went cold.

"There's a spell on the Rift to keep our lands safe. It keeps humans out."

"It keeps your lands safe . . . by killing anyone who tries to come through?"

"Yes," she confirmed.

I couldn't help myself—I glanced at her ears again. Her perfectly normal, rounded ears. I never thought of Flora as callous, but apparently I hardly knew her at all. Maybe her attitude toward danger and death was a common trait of her people.

"Blaine!" She glared at me and arranged her golden hair to cover her ears.

"How did you know I would survive?"

"Well, I couldn't be completely sure."

I stared at her, incredulous.

"Flora!" I barked. "Don't you think you should have told me I might die going through that portal?"

"Lower your voice." Her own voice was calm, while my heart thundered in my chest.

"Lower my . . ." I cast my gaze around the cafeteria. People ate or studied. There was a steady hum of conversation around us. No one noticed my outburst. Yet. I leaned forward and hissed at her. "I could have died!"

"You wouldn't have died." Flora rolled her eyes again and pointed at my chest. "That ring proved it. When it reacted to your presence, it confirmed who you are."

I already wished the stupid thing hadn't glowed when I touched it. I should have known it was more trouble than it was worth.

"The Rift wasn't going to kill you," Flora continued, heedless of my thoughts.

"You still should have told—"

"But it will kill her."

Flora's eyes darted over my shoulder. I turned to see Rose approaching. I clamped my mouth shut—no more talk of Silaris. Not here, where Rose might overhear. I wanted her involved, but I didn't want her dead. An adventure wasn't worth her life.

As much as I hated to admit it, Flora was right. I would keep this part of my life from Rose. I would hide it to keep her from getting hurt.

Just what I needed, something else to feel guilty about.

"Hey, what's up?" Rose asked as she placed her tray next to mine. She sat down and brushed her brown hair over one shoulder. The practiced flip of her hand flashed chipped purple polish over chewed nails.

"Nothing!" I said it too fast. Flora's lips pressed into a hard line and Rose raised her eyebrows.

"We were just talking about the math quiz," Flora covered for me. "Blaine is embarrassed because he didn't do very well."

I felt my face heat. I really hadn't done very well.

"Oh." Rose's shoulders relaxed. "I think I did okay on that one. If you want, we can go over the problems you missed tonight. We're all good for our Friday study session, right?"

Rose doing 'okay' on a math test meant she definitely aced it.

"Yeah, that would be great." I smiled. "I just can't understand what we're doing in that class."

Flora gave me a pointed look.

"Oh, but uh . . ." I cast around for a reasonable excuse. "I can't study tonight. Mom has people coming over for dinner. Can we do it next week?"

Rose looked surprised, but she nodded. "That's okay. Flora, do you still want to get together? We could binge that reality TV show you like."

"Actually, I can't either. I'm going home to visit my parents this weekend." The lie rolled smoothly off of Flora's tongue.

I scoffed internally. I wasn't even sure if Flora *had* parents. I wouldn't have been surprised if she told me she was grown from some sort of plant. Had she ever told us the truth?

"Oh. Okay." Rose looked back at me, penetrating blue eyes stark against her dark hair. Guarded. Calculating.

My face warmed. Did she know I was lying? Probably. She was clever and I sucked at being secretive.

"Well, I hope you both have fun tonight." Rose forced a smile. "We can hang out when you get back."

"Definitely," I said, jumping on that possibility as a distraction. "Monday?"

"Sure." When she thought I wasn't looking, she frowned down at her plate.

The rest of the day passed in a blur. After my last class, Flora and Rose met me in the parking lot, as usual. I dropped Rose off with a promise to text her and was pulling up to the curb outside Flora's house less than a minute later. We got out of the car and walked up the front path amid the colorful flowers that cascaded across the lawn. I followed Flora into the house and a pang of guilt hit me when I glanced at our usual study spot in the living room. The matching red armchairs and the simple black couch judged me with their emptiness as I walked past them into the kitchen.

"You ready?" Flora unlocked the pantry door and swung it open wide, revealing a swirling vortex of light and color. The Rift.

I nodded.

I pushed my guilt over Rose from my head, compartmentalizing it to dwell on later. I needed to focus. I stared at the Rift before me. I watched as Flora stepped into it. Her form wavered, shifting into lines of color, before disappearing completely. I waited a few seconds, then took a deep breath and stepped forward.

Once I was within reach of the Rift, colorful tendrils snaked toward me. They wrapped around my arms and legs, immobilizing me. I forced myself to relax as light rippled over my skin like water. I felt a yank and my stomach flipped. Colors swirled around me as I tumbled through a vortex of light. I plummeted, shattering the colors like glass. The tiny shards scattered in all directions. Wind buffeted against my ears and an uncomfortable pressure squeezed the air from my lungs. I gritted my teeth, focusing on keeping my feet underneath me.

Several unsettling seconds later, I landed on my ass amid vibrant greenery.

I groaned. "When people said college would be a different world, this isn't exactly what I imagined."

"You didn't scream this time." Flora smirked down at me.

"What, like you didn't scream your first time? I didn't realize I was being graded on portal travel."

She shrugged. "You're lucky it's Pass/Fail."

She offered me her hand. I grabbed it to pull myself up, feeling only a little satisfaction when I pulled her off balance.

"Whatever." I brushed grass and dirt from my legs. "It's only my second time here. You've had a lot more practice going through the Rift."

"I wouldn't say 'a lot'," Flora said. "Come on, the Council will be displeased if we aren't punctual."

She strode away and I jogged a few steps to catch up. I didn't want to be alone in this unfamiliar forest. Sure, it was beautiful, but the massive trees that surrounded us were intimidating. I couldn't shake the feeling of being watched.

"Who exactly—" I cut off as Flora spun around to look at the Rift. Her perfect mouth popped open in a gasp.

I turned to see what had her so concerned. I went cold when a familiar form coalesced from the swirling colors. Rose appeared, shifting from a figure made of light into the girl I knew. I watched, frozen, as her feet touched the grass, then she crumpled to the ground.

My mind blanked and my heart stopped, then picked up in double-time as I raced toward her lifeless form.

Two

Rose

I hit the ground. Hard.

Luckily, I landed on springy, pillow-soft grass. I gasped and almost choked on the cleanest air I had ever tasted. Confused, I put my hand to my chest and—for the first time in my life—took in a full, easy breath. The permanent tightness on my ribcage was gone. I inhaled again, relishing the ease at which air filled my lungs. Blaine and Flora stared down at me with mirrored looks of shock. After a few seconds of stupefied silence, they spoke simultaneously.

"Rose? Are you alright?" Blaine asked, kneeling beside me and looking me over.

"You can't be here." Flora shook her head. "That's impossible."

I blinked at them while I tried to make some sense of what happened. Flora's blonde hair cascaded around her ivory face in waves as she bent over me. Her eyes narrowed in confusion. Blaine's radiated concern. The blade of grass sticking out of his black curls reminded me of my own appearance. How disheveled did I look after that nauseating fall? I ran a hand through my hair, attempting to tame it.

"Talk to me, Rose." Blaine half reached out but didn't touch me. "Are you okay?"

"Y-yeah," I managed to stutter.

He released a breath, shoulders slumping. "Good."

I flinched when a hand grabbed my arm but tried to relax when I saw it was only Flora. A weird heat rushed through my body at the unexpected touch. Her grip was tight enough that my flinch didn't dislodge it, but she released me quickly.

"She's unharmed." Flora shook her head in disbelief. "Rose, how did you get here?"

"Well," I said, shoulders curling forward, "I was about to knock on your door, but . . . I don't know why I just went inside. I heard—or maybe felt—something, then there was all this color and I was falling . . ." I shuddered and looked around. "How did I get outside?"

Blaine leapt to his feet and offered me his hand. I stared at it for a moment before taking it. He pulled me up but didn't let go.

"Why were you at Flora's?" Blaine asked.

I pulled my hand from his and looked at the ground. My cheeks grew warm and I was sure they turned bright red.

"I just wanted to . . ." What did I say? That I knew they were lying to me? That I was spying on them?

Flora snorted. When I gathered the courage to look up, I quickly looked away again. Blaine was studying me with a dark expression.

He was mad.

"Blaine, she can't be here," Flora said, drawing my attention to her. "She has to go back."

"Why?" Blaine asked. From the corner of my eye, I could still see him watching me. "She made it through the Rift. There's no reason she can't come with us."

Wait . . . he wanted me here? I blinked. His steady gaze muted the constant thoughts in my head. The ones telling me I didn't belong.

"Because it's not . . ." Flora seemed to flounder for words. "She just can't."

"She stays," Blaine said, finally turning from me and leveling a look at Flora. He didn't wilt under her glare as I would have. "Or I go."

"Blaine, you can't leave. I—" Flora's face grew even more pale. "We need you."

"Well then, there you go. She's coming." Blaine turned to me with a bashful smile, growing uncertain. "If you want, I mean."

I couldn't comprehend the emotions that coursed through me at his words. I didn't understand anything that was happening here, but I wouldn't be left behind. I nodded.

After a few strained seconds between them, Flora closed her eyes. She pinched the bridge of her nose and huffed an exasperated sigh.

Blaine's smile grew.

"Um, where exactly are we?" I almost didn't ask, still nervous they weren't going to let me tag along.

Blaine stepped out of my line of vision, spreading his arms wide for me to take in the scene.

"Welcome to Silaris."

I looked past my friends to the world beyond. An unknowably ancient forest loomed over me, stretching as far as I could see. Massive trees grew for miles in every direction. The trunks of the largest were the size of a basketball court. The foliage grew so dense at the top, only slivers of sunlight made it all the way to the moss-covered forest floor, casting a green tint to our surroundings. Thick roots snaked around patches of grass between the trees. The scale made me feel tiny.

Cicadas and other insects buzzed and chirped, creating a soothing chorus. Small, brightly colored birds swooped between branches. They squabbled amongst themselves, not noticing or caring that there were three intruders in their midst. A doe and her fawn stepped into view. They glanced at us curiously but didn't spook. Their legs were thicker than they should have been, like those of a horse. They began grazing right in front of us.

I spun slowly, trying to absorb everything and make sense of what I was seeing. I came to a stop when the same colorful vortex from Flora's kitchen came into view.

Could breathing too much air cause hallucinations? The extra oxygen flooding my brain must have made me giddy, because the vortex was suddenly the most ridiculous thing I had ever seen. I burst out laughing.

"The Rift clearly fractured her mind." Flora cocked her head.

"Flora!" Blaine hissed.

"That was in your kitchen," I said, still laughing and pointing at the swirling colors.

"Yes," Flora responded, even though it wasn't a question.

"You must . . . have a really . . . good contractor!" I gasped out between fits of laughter.

Blaine laughed along with my stupid joke. Flora didn't.

"You may have traversed safely through the Rift," Flora said, "but your sense of humor did not." She strode purposefully into the forest.

"Give her a break, Flora." Blaine gestured for me to follow him away from the vortex of colors and lights. Once I recovered from my fit of laughter, I complied. "This is her first time in a parallel world. It's a miracle she's joking at all." He leaned closer to me while we walked and lowered his voice. "Though, to be honest, I thought it was hilarious."

"A parallel world?" I tripped on some roots, too busy admiring the forest around me. I felt more like myself with every step. Not myself from the last few months, but myself *before*. I felt light—I was definitely getting too much air. "How did you find this place?"

"Well, Flora's actually from here," Blaine said. "She's an elf."

"There's no such thing as . . ." I trailed off as Flora pulled back her long blonde hair to reveal her ears. Pointed ears. "Oh."

"The Rift revealed itself to me recently," Flora said in a strangely formal tone. "I would often frequent the isolated clearing where it currently resides to break from society. One day, I closed my eyes to meditate and opened them to the Rift. Before I could react, it entangled my limbs and pulled me through." She chuckled. "Needless to say, I was quite confused when I was deposited into a random house in your world. When I returned home and relayed my experience to the Council of Elders, they speculated that the Rift appeared for a reason then tasked me to return and find the Veritace."

"Huh."

It took me a while to process this. Flora was an elf—that was impossible, of course. Then again, so was teleporting to a new world. I glanced at Blaine's ears. Even under his thick curls, I could see they were rounded. That meant he was human . . . right?

"I . . ." I didn't even know what to ask. I wrapped my arms around myself and began chewing on my thumbnail.

"Take your time," Blaine said.

I nodded. It took a few minutes, but I settled on a question. "If you're an elf, why are you going to college in *Ohio*, of all places?"

Flora stood taller. "I was sent by my people to retrieve the Veritace."

"The . . ."

"It translates roughly to 'chosen one'."

I blinked. "Chosen . . . for what?"

"To save the world, obviously."

"Which world?"

"This one." Flora hesitated, then frowned. "Both, maybe? It's unclear."

"So," I looked at Blaine, "*you* are this Veritace?"

Blaine flushed. "That's what she keeps telling me."

"Blaine *is* the Veritace. The ring proves it," Flora said confidently. Blaine's hand went to a simple golden ring hanging from a cord around his neck. "Besides, if he wasn't, he would have died upon traveling through the Rift—"

"Again, that would have been good to know *before* I went through that portal with you," Blaine muttered.

"It opened specifically so he could come through. No mere human is able to pass through unharmed." She studied me. "At least, they shouldn't be able to."

"Oh." *Then how did I get through?* "W-where are we going?"

I lost all sense of direction in this forest. The trees obscured the position of the sun and everything looked the same. I was at the mercy of Flora's navigational skills. I shoved down my discomfort—Flora and Blaine wouldn't lead me into danger, right?

"We are going to Trehilm, my home." Flora grinned. "Then, we adventure."

Beads of sweat were forming on my forehead when Flora finally stopped and turned to us with a broad smile.

"What do you think?" she asked.

"Of . . . what?" I glanced at Blaine's confused expression. The section of forest behind her looked identical to the one we just traversed. I was expecting houses or tents, at the very least. "This is where you live?"

Flora looked confused at first, then understanding dawned on her features.

"Oh, my apologies," she said. "We don't typically bring in outsiders. I forgot about the cloaking spell." She waved her hand in front of my face and my vision wavered as if I was looking up through a body of water. The forest came back into focus and I gaped at the sight before me.

"Whoa." Blaine echoed my thoughts.

The trees had been transformed into living houses. Staircases spiraled the outside of the trunks, leading to doors at various levels. Each tree functioned like a multifamily home or a natural apartment building. Windows framed each story and people occupied the balconies jutting from the trunk. Some hung freshly laundered clothes or tended to plants growing out of the tree bark. Some simply read books in the diffuse sunlight. They were all inhumanly beautiful.

Because they weren't human—they were elves.

As we traveled deeper into the city, elves of different heights, ages, and skin tones crowded the paths. A few frowned as we passed, but most didn't even glance our way. Pointed ears framed delicate features and eyes in shades humans could only dream. The most prevalent was some shade of green, but I noted individuals with violet, cerulean, and even magenta-colored irises. The alien stares emphasized that Blaine and I were outsiders. Distracted as I was by everything around me, it took me a few minutes to comprehend Flora's words.

"Did you say cloaking spell? Magic is real?" Of course, magic was real. I saw it with my own eyes, first at the Rift and then when those tree-condos appeared out of nowhere. "You can do magic?"

"Yes, all elves possess some ability with magic." She reached down to a flower bud on the side of the path. As she gently caressed the bud, the flower burst open, revealing beautiful crimson petals, vibrant against the endless green landscape. "I am not the strongest in the art, but I can hold my own."

"Can humans learn magic?"

"A group of humans discovered magic long ago," Flora grimaced. "Their power originated from a dark source, whereas ours is derived from nature itself. Witch magic is very different from mine and from what I understand it is hereditary, so I could not instruct you on the subject."

"That's too bad," Blaine interjected. "Learning magic would be cool. And probably helpful for—" he waved a hand in the air "—whatever it is we're doing."

"Speaking of that," I said, "are you going to tell us what this adventure is all about?"

"My apologies, but . . . look, I don't really know." Flora sighed. Upon approaching Trehilm she had been stiff and formal, but here I saw a shade of the friend I had known for months. The one I gossiped with about classmates and reality TV shows. The formal speech sounded odd coming from her lips. "The elders are the Keepers of Knowledge, but they do not always share memories that would cause our people pain. They will reveal the information we need and tell us what needs done."

"You don't think it's odd they keep secrets?" I asked, skeptically.

"I have not been in your world long, but even I've observed your leaders keeping things from your people."

I conceded with a nod.

"Plus, look around," she gestured to the homes. "People are happy. The elders know all the horrors of our past. So long as everyone listens to the Council, the dark parts of history will not repeat itself."

"Sure, but aren't you just a little interested?" Blaine asked.

"Most certainly not," Flora answered a little too quickly. Blaine and I shared a skeptical look, but we let the subject drop. "Come, the Harmonious Tower is this way."

We followed Flora to a bustling section of town and stopped before a massive, cathedral-like structure. I craned my neck to stare up at it. The Harmonious Tower was an intricately connected conglomerate of large trees. Branches twined between the trunks, growing into each other and acting as open air walkways. Elves far above us navigated those walkways to travel from one tree to another, disappearing through archways into the trunks. At its base was an ornate staircase that would look more at home in some mansion's ballroom than in a forest.

As we climbed the staircase to the doors of the Tower, I noticed the steps were not carved, or even built, but were growing out of the tree itself. They merged fluidly with the base of the trunk and were covered with bark worn smooth from wear.

"We asked the trees for shelter and they provided," Flora said when I inquired. "Elves do not build the way humans do. We shape nature around us but do not destroy it."

I frowned at the jab. Not all humans destroyed nature. Some of us volunteered at our local wetland cleanups, patrolled for sea turtle nests, and marked Burrowing Owl dwellings for protection. Though, it had been a few years since I did any of that.

"We could learn a lot from the elves," Blaine said.

We followed Flora into the tower, feeling like tourists following their enthusiastic guide. As we passed through the main hall, she emphatically described the mural that flowed along the wall with us, depicting the first elves that migrated to Silaris from across the seas. The pictures began with a simple scene of five figures surrounded by untouched forest, but as we walked, it showed each elf touching a tree. Those trees burst into progressively larger structures, until the city that stood today was pictured.

We climbed to the next level and emerged onto one of the outdoor walkways, high above the ground. I looked over the edge, admiring the unique merge of forest and cityscape. Flora told us there was magic in place to keep us from toppling off, but Blaine stayed close to the middle of the path, refusing to look down.

We passed through an arched opening into a different tree and found ourselves in a museum. Blaine and I admired the artifacts on display as Flora rambled and pointed out some of her favorites. Among them was a towering mural picturing a gigantic, metallic-gray dragon with shining white eyes. The creature's wings were outstretched and its teeth bared against a lone elven figure in a billowing green robe. The strength radiating from the elf was palpable. There was a faint glow coming from him, drawing focus to the figure. The dragon—half of its body hidden in the shadows—was the most menacing thing on display in the room. Malice dripped from the image like the beads of blood off the dragon's yellowing teeth. The elf stared resolute before the dragon, holding a staff that glowed with the same material as the dragon's eyes.

"This is the story of Lutya and the dragon, Argonius," Flora explained. "This mural depicts the famous fight between our first Councilor and the evil dragon that was plundering the land and killing all who stood in his way. Many tried before, from all the races in Silaris, but Lutya was the one to succeed. It is said he single-handedly brought down the dragon and saved Silaris from its evil."

"Is Lutya the first Veritace?" Blaine asked.

"What? No, Lutya is an elf," she said, as though it was obvious. Blaine and I stared at her, confused. She failed to notice. "It is rumored Argonius created the Rift to your world. His claws were so sharp they cut through reality itself."

I eyed the portrayed claws. They *were* excessively long and sharp.

"Where are the swords and bows of ancient elven heroes displayed?" Blaine asked in a hopeful tone.

Flora sighed and led us to a dark corner of the small museum. The cases showed a thin layer of dust, neglected compared to the rest of the displays.

"I expected there to be more here," Blaine commented, dejected. He pointed to a particularly gruesome serrated short sword that seemed out of place among the beautifully carved recurve bows and thin, delicate rapiers. "Can you tell us about this one?"

"No," Flora said, looking at the weapons with disinterest. "The elders don't burden society with this history."

The other artifacts in the room sported name placards with short descriptions, but the weapons held no labels. I admired a pair of delicately curved, metallic green sheaths decorated with a carved leaf pattern. Who would be graceful enough to wield such beautiful weapons? My gaze darted to Flora, then back to the swords. Definitely not me. I didn't know the first thing about—

"Uh . . . guys?" Blaine's voice cracked.

I spun toward him and shielded my eyes from a bright light. The glow dimmed to reveal a thick longsword vibrating in its sheath, trying to escape the brackets restraining it.

Blaine backed toward us, not taking his eyes off the sword as the clattering grew louder and more frantic. There was a shatter of glass as the sword broke free from its display case, sharp tip heading directly for Blaine.

Blaine yelped, throwing his hands in front of his face to protect himself. Before the tip could puncture his palms, however, the sword stopped, rotated midair, and pressed its hilt into his hand. Blaine grasped it reflexively but stood stunned while the sword hummed with power in his grip. After a few seconds, the sword stopped vibrating, and the light flickered out. Blaine scrambled back, dropping the sword. The clatter of metal echoed in the quiet room.

Three

Blaine

"Fascinating."

The three of us turned in the direction of the new voice. A man stared at us from an open doorway. His shoulder length brown hair split around his pointed ears and was topped with a gold circlet resembling vines. He wore long, flowing red robes.

"Elder Siltyn." Flora bowed.

"Come with me," the elder snapped, looking our group over. "Bring Peacekeeper with you."

Peacekeeper?

"In its sheath, please," Elder Siltyn continued. "There's no need to be running about with an exposed blade."

Oh, the sword. I blinked down at the weapon on the ground. Now that it wasn't flying at my face, I could get a good look at it. The sword was simple, but with a crossguard in the shape of sweeping wings. Worn, brown leather wrapped around the handle, and the steel glinted, daring me to reach for it.

Elder Siltyn left through a different hallway. Although he didn't look to see if we were following, he continued speaking as if we were, his voice becoming softer as he got further away. "There will be enough consternation as it is. Imagine a sword being carried in the Tower. That hasn't happened in my lifetime. Though, I suppose a sword following you through the air may cause more alarm . . ."

The three of us exchanged a look. I bent to cautiously pick up the sword while Flora and Rose scrambled to unhook the sheath displayed on the wall. Once Peacekeeper was safely sheathed, we hurried to catch up to the elder. I carried the unfamiliar weight of the sword awkwardly, eyeing it every few seconds to make sure it wasn't going to start glowing and attack me again. It stayed obediently in my grasp as we walked.

We heard the elder's words before we fully caught up with him, still speaking as if we were right beside him.

". . . had hoped this was all a fluke, but I suppose that was too much to ask for." He sighed and glanced at me. "Wait here, the Counsel is still gathering. We will call you when we are ready. Put that on." He eyed the sword before walking through a set of intricately carved double doors.

We stood in a small waiting room adorned with an assortment of chairs. A pretty girl who appeared to be around our age sat at a large desk beside imposing double doors. Her emerald-rimmed hazel eyes widened when we appeared, but she quickly covered the expression with a smirk.

"Impressive, Flora." The girl tossed her red hair over one shoulder. It smoldered like embers when it caught the light. "I always knew you liked to cause trouble, but what have you done to get summoned before the Council?" She glanced at Rose and me then did a double take. "Are those *humans*?"

"Hello, Tisha." Flora's expression was smooth as she ignored the question. "If you'll excuse us."

Flora gestured to some chairs at the far end of the room. Her nose crinkled in annoyance once the girl, Tisha, could no longer see her face.

"Friend of yours?" I muttered under my breath. I was relieved how steady my voice was. I was still pretty shaken from staring down the blade of a sword.

"Hardly." Flora sniffed. "We may have had a *thing* once. I didn't know she was working here. It probably satisfies her need for gossip, being this close to the Council. I suppose this quest won't be very secret anymore."

Tisha scowled at us from where she sat.

"But that isn't important right now." Flora pointed to Peacekeeper. "Blaine, put on that sword belt. An elder's instructions should never be ignored."

I did what she said, feeling uncomfortable as I strapped the belt to my waist, situating the sword so it hung at my left side. I took a few practice steps around the girls, feeling slightly less awkward as I got used to the weight of the long sword banging around my legs.

"I'll probably have bruises from this thing," I said, striding back to my friends. "Is this even on right?"

Both Flora and Rose shrugged.

"Thanks, you guys are so helpful." I rolled my eyes.

The girls flashed me matching apologetic smiles but quickly lost them as the double doors opened on their own.

"You may enter the Harmony Chamber," Tisha said in a haughty tone. As we walked through the doors and they swung shut behind us, I imagined her crouched behind them, listening.

The imagery fled when I entered the vast chamber. The room was circular, with steps on either side of the door leading up to a raised gallery. Dozens of graying elves in deep red cloaks sat, watching us with somber faces. Each one of them wore the same vining circlet atop their heads. In the center of the room was a large, round table that looked to be grown directly from the tree instead of being fashioned with tools.

An elf with long silver hair was studying something on the table. He looked up when we entered the room. His robes—green instead of red—were more ornate than the others and his circlet had blooming flowers on the vines.

"Welcome, Veritace," he opened his arms wide, "to the Council of Elders. I am Head Elder Rhisler and I welcome you to this gathering. May the sun shine upon you, always." The greeting rang with formality and was followed by a pause. Flora nudged me.

"Uh . . . thank you." I swallowed. "I'm honored to be here."

"The honor is mine, Veritace, though not many will see it that way. Your arrival prophesized pain and suffering. You will find we elves have no taste for the atrocities of war."

I was at a loss for words. I opened my mouth to speak but closed it again. Before I could think of anything to say, Rose spoke up, coming to my rescue.

"What about all those weapons in the museum? They look like they were made for elves," she said.

Flora groaned softly beside me.

"Those weapons are but a greasy smudge on our peaceful existence." The elder peered at Rose with shrewd gray eyes. "Youngling, who addresses the Council?"

"The human, Rose, addresses the Council, Head Elder," Flora stated, formally. "She came through the Rift with the Veritace. We beg your assistance . . . is this mentioned in the prophecy?"

A quiet murmur drifted through the elders in the gallery. Elder Rhisler was quiet for a long moment before answering, his eyes narrowed and lips pursed.

"Certainly not as I've heard it recited. However, if she truly traversed the Rift unscathed, perhaps this human has a role to play." He looked down his elegant nose at Rose. "Though I can't imagine what it would be."

I didn't think the elder meant it as a slight, but Rose's shoulders hunched. I shuffled closer to her.

Elder Rhisler heaved a weary sigh. "I suppose it is time to recount the history relating to your task. Know this," —he fixed his icy gaze on us— "what I am about to tell you is guarded knowledge. It is not to be repeated within the elven community, for it will cause unnecessary panic amongst our people. Inciting hysteria will not be tolerated. Do you understand?"

We all nodded.

"Head Elder," one of the elves from the gallery called. "I beg forgiveness for speaking out of turn, but how can we be sure this child is the Veritace?"

"The child carries the sword, but can he wield it?" another voice called from the gallery. The murmur grew to a buzz of whispers until a third voice spoke up.

"The sword recognized this human. It came to him. I saw it with my own eyes." The voice belonged to Elder Siltyn, though I could not see him in the crowd. "Is that not proof enough?"

"He wears Alaric's ring!" another voice called. "Perhaps the sword merely recognized that presence."

"Very well, very well," Elder Rhisler said to the gallery. "To prove himself, the young man shall give us a demonstration."

I stiffened where I stood. A *demonstration*? How could I give a demonstration of who I was? I didn't even know why I was here!

"Oh, I don't know—"

Before I could get the words out, Rhisler raised his hand. A pure beam of blue energy crackled out of his palm and shot directly for us.

Rose

I threw my arms in front of my face, cringing in anticipation of a blow that never came.

I cautiously lowered my hands and looked around. A massive burn mark scorched the wooden floor. Blaine stood before Flora and me, sword held defensively in front of him. Peacekeeper emitted an angry glow in the dim light of the chamber.

Blaine stared at the sword, aghast. He was trembling. I reached forward to put a comforting hand on his shoulder.

"That was quick thinking," I whispered.

"I wasn't really thinking." Blaine watched the radiant light fade in his hands. "It was more of a reflex."

"That should satisfy the Council," Elder Rhisler said, as if he had not just tried to kill us. Even Flora was shaken by the experience. The color drained from her already pale face.

"Head Elder," she said, "you just shot—"

"Enough," he said, waving her off. "We have little time and much to tell. The Council honored you with this task, youngling. If you are too inept for this challenge, you may leave and we will find the Veritace a more competent guide."

He allowed a small pause for Flora to speak. She didn't cower, like I would have, but she also didn't argue. She stood up straighter and schooled her expression blank.

"Very well. Where to begin?" he mused.

Elder Rhisler gestured for us to follow him to the table growing from the floor. We gathered around as he placed his palms on the ringed wood. I gasped as stick figures made of lightning formed on the table, animating the elder's words.

"We elves have lived peacefully in Silaris since the beginning of time. Even the fearsome dragons did not trouble us when they roamed the land, instead choosing to live amongst us."

It was like a TV screen, though the elder's two-dimensional animation was basic compared to what we had on Earth.

"Then, the Rift was opened and the first humans came through." He drew the humans shorter and wider than the elves. Though the stature of the elves we passed outside didn't differ much from a crowd of humans. "Originally, we were overjoyed. We believed another intelligent species from a different plane of existence could advance our society. We feasted with them, we taught them how to survive the dangers of our world, we introduced them to magic.

"The humans aged and died so quickly, we failed to foresee the impact they would have on our lands. We encouraged them to settle here in hopes of establishing trade. We underestimated how . . . fecund your race was." He shot a disdainful look at Blaine and me. The implication brought warmth to my cheeks as the portrayed human population grew on the table. "Or how destructive. They swarmed through the Rift and overran us. Their settlements damaged our sacred Forest, prompting the Council of the time, our forebears, to seal the gateway to the human world.

"That enraged the humans." A sneer flashed across the elder's angelic features before he schooled his face to neutrality. "They claimed we acted to trap them here, but they could not see the pain they inflicted. Our relationship with them strained as their rage simmered for many generations.

"Matters were made worse when disease struck. The humans' rapid breeding reacted with the magic abundant in our world to create a terrible shape-shifting curse. The poor creatures turned into wolves and slaughtered their loved ones."

Blaine and I glanced at each other. My face mirrored his alarm as he mouthed the word that had popped into my head, as well.

Werewolves.

"Shortly thereafter, the humans learned to control the dark magic that cursed the others of their kind. Their lust for power was insatiable, but before we could intervene, they were lost to reason. Infighting rampaged within the three factions of humans. The ruin we beheld . . ." He shook his head.

Rhisler's sympathetic expression stayed in place. Maybe I imagined the earlier sneer? He seemed sincere, if self-righteous.

"Disagreements and skirmishes blossomed into full-out war." Elder Rhisler's lightshow grew fuzzier as more figures joined the fighting. "We were pulled into the fight against our better nature. The battles were bloody affairs with no end in sight—that is, until the first Veritace appeared."

Blaine leaned so low over the table I thought the lightning figures might shock him.

"Alaric Nightstorm, a human warrior and leader, was the bearer of that sword you now carry. With Peacekeeper's power, he fought the evil bred by war. Surprisingly clever for a human, he negotiated a ceasefire, ending the pointless killing. He assembled the leaders of each race and formalized the treaty by which we still abide."

With a flourish of Elder Rhisler's hand, the scenes of war transformed into a long document with flowing script. The only thing I was able to make out were the last four lines.

May the forest watch over you,
May your hunt be fruitful,
May your heart be unburdened,
May your head be clear.

"As you can see," Elder Rhisler waved his hand over the table. The treaty shifted into a three-dimensional map made of light. "The treaty divided our lands, allocating each race their own dominance. We control the northeast part of the continent, the lycans occupy the south of us. The human colonies are to our west and the abomination witches to the southwest."

Elder Rhisler made an elaborate hand motion, and a smokey gray shadow appeared in the middle of the map. The shadow expanded outward until the elder closed his fist. At another hand motion, a pitch black spot formed in the map's center. It spread like a liquid over the terrain, flattening the landscape. Another closed fist halted the spread before it reached the edges of the gray shroud.

"Evil encroaches on all our lands. This area"—he gestured to the gray cloud—"is muted. Life is barely sustained. The center of Silaris, however, is devoid of all life. Any who wander into it are lost to us forever. There is nothing but uninhabitable desert as far as our scouts can see. If left unchecked, I fear this will be our fate." He opened his hand. Gray enveloped the remainder of the map, followed closely by the inky nothingness.

"How did this happen?" Flora asked.

Elder Rhisler studied Flora with narrowed gray eyes before looking at Blaine. I had been momentarily forgotten, which was a relief.

"To our utter embarrassment," Rhisler said, "the cause is a rogue elf who has been infected by evil. She has discovered a power source that devastates the land while feeding her corruption. Her name was once Mika, but no longer. Now, she is the Defector."

"An elf caused this?" Flora stared at the blackened map. She shook her head, but her denial couldn't alter the truth.

"We knew Mika was unstable, but when her lover grew ill, she became dangerous. We should have worked harder to prevent Dorian's death, but nothing could be done. Being so close to Mika's darkness weakened him too much. Knowing she caused his death was what snapped Mika and allowed the Defector to emerge. She fled Elvanar, using her evil magic to break the treaty Nightstorm created. She must be stopped and the treaty must be reestablished. Otherwise, destruction will befall us all."

"How do we stop her?" Blaine's brows furrowed in concentration as he listened intently to the elder.

"In case he was needed again," Rhisler said, "Nightstorm transferred his knowledge into his sword and the four gemstones inlaid into the blade. The gemstones—Alaric called them Argems—held the bulk of his memories. He ordered the Argems removed and split among each race to protect, thus not giving one race his entire arsenal of knowledge. You must travel Silaris and find these Argems. Once you reunite them with Peacekeeper, you will obtain the knowledge to reestablish the treaty and stop the spread of evil."

"If his memories are in the sword, that explains why I was able to use it," Blaine said, looking over the blade. He had not sheathed the weapon. I noticed indentations in the sleek metal where the stones presumably fit. "Are you saying once I collect these . . . *Argems*, I'll know how to fight?"

"You will know more than just fighting techniques. Alaric Nightstorm was also an expert politician and scholar." Rhisler sighed heavily and grimaced. "However, I suppose your fighting skills will be required to fight the Defector."

"If we destroy the Defector, will her corruption recede?" Flora asked.

"That is our belief." Elder Rhisler looked at Flora, and an odd expression crossed his face. "If you can stop her, it will at the very least stop the progression of evil, giving us more time to deal with the consequences."

"How . . ." Blaine swallowed, still staring at the map. "How are we supposed to fight that?"

"That, Veritace, is something you will have to figure out for yourself. Presumably, gathering the Argems will give you that knowledge." Elder Rhisler clapped his hands together, signaling an end to our discussion. "Time is a luxury of which we do not have much. Elder Asish will assist you in your preparations. The closest stone is just north of here, in the Grove of Contemplation." His tone was almost bored as he studied the map on the table. Apparently story time was over. "I suggest you start with that one. Report to us any issues. May the Forest watch over you in your journey."

Four

Rose

MAYBE IT WAS JUST my ignorance of elven culture, but Elder Rhisler seemed a bit . . . arrogant. After his abrupt dismissal, Elder Asish descended from the seating area and guided the three of us out of the Harmony Chamber. Without a word, he led us past Tisha's desk. Flora didn't look at the girl, but I couldn't help but glance back at her perplexed face. When she noticed, she scowled.

We followed Elder Asish out of the Harmonious Tower and into a bustling market nearby. It reminded me of a farmers market from back home, only much larger. There were rows upon rows of merchant booths selling goods. Flowering vines adorned with every color imaginable grew along the tents, decorating them. In some places, those same vines spelled out the names of shops. The voices of criers filled the air as they competed to bring in customers.

"Fresh produce here! Free from growing spells and the only fruit in the market without preservation spells!"

"Unique, local artist! Wild landscapes and stunning views. You won't find anything like it in all of Elvanar!"

"Protection charms, peace amulets, and fertility idols. All spelled responsibly and guaranteed!"

Elder Asish led us through a maze of tents to one labeled Hassen's Blacksmith Shop. This tent was larger than the ones around it and opened to the sky. In the center sat a large forge, unadorned with finery. The tent flaps were drawn up to let the heat of the forge escape, but the tan, shirtless blacksmith inside glistened with sweat. The muscular elf worked hard at the forge, pounding a horseshoe with his hammer. When we entered, a gust of hot air pushed my hair from my face. The blacksmith's broad shoulders initially led me to believe this elf was older, but his face was young. He smiled and bowed to Elder Asish.

"Welcome, Elder." The elf glanced at our group and rubbed his short-cropped beard. His dark green eyes lingered on Flora slightly longer than the rest of us. "How may I help you today?"

"Jallix, please fetch your master. We have business."

The elf, Jallix, nodded and hurried through a makeshift door at the back of the tent. After a few moments, Jallix returned, holding the door for an elf with a short white beard and wrinkled skin. Despite this elf's apparent age, his arms were extremely muscular, likely from many years working metal in a forge.

"Ah, Asish." The older elf smiled. "I was wondering when you would be stopping by. I have those tools in the back for you. Some of Jallix's finest work yet. He will be master of this forge before too long." The young elf went back to his horseshoes, beaming with pride at the complement.

"I shall return for those later, Hassen." Elder Asish lowered his voice and tilted his head to our group. "Unfortunately, I must call upon you for less palatable business."

The old blacksmith looked us over, his face growing solemn when it landed on Blaine—more specifically, on the sword buckled to his waist.

"I see." Hassen rubbed his beard. "So it is time. Jallix, finish up and join us."

Hassen didn't wait for Jallix's confirmation before leading us through to the back room. The space was cluttered. Tools and scrap metal lay haphazardly around half-finished projects. Metal ingots of all shapes and sizes were piled around the room. Hessan didn't make excuses for the mess, just walked a meandering path to the corner. He shoved aside a pile of junk and pulled away some fabric to reveal a safe. Hassen bowed his head and let out a long sigh.

"I had hoped to be dead before you came for these." His gaze fell on Blaine. "How much do you remember?"

Blaine flinched at the hard gaze, but he shook his head. "I don't remember anything."

The blacksmith nodded, as if expecting this.

"I knew you the first time around," Hassen said. "I'm the one that removed the Argems from Peacekeeper for Alaric—for you."

"That means . . . you must be really old!" Blaine blurted. "How long do elves live?"

Flora cleared her throat and Blaine blushed.

"Same old Nightstorm." Hassen laughed. "Always speaking his mind. Welcome back, old friend."

Hassen held out his hand for Blaine, palm facing forward like he wanted a high-five. Blaine frowned, then looked to Flora. She mimed what to do by placing her palms together. Blaine gave a sheepish smile, but pressed his palm into the large elf's hand. At that moment, Jallix entered the room, wiping his hands on an ash-stained rag. He gave Blaine and Hassen's clasped hands a curious look, but didn't comment.

Hassen grinned. "To answer your question, we elves live a long time. Usually a few hundred years, but I'm currently the oldest in the territory. As to why I'm still around . . . That's a long story that includes a vengeful witch and a sleeping sickness. I'll tell you some other time over some mead," he said with a wink. "But it's a good thing I'm still around, since no one else remembers how to forge these."

The blacksmith snapped his fingers and the safe behind him unlocked with a loud click. The thick door swung open, revealing a large cache of weapons.

Hassen and Jallix distributed the weapons among us. After eyeing the sword strapped to Blaine's waist, Hassen handed him two daggers to put on his belt. Flora and I both received daggers along with sheaths and thigh straps. Jallix held a delicate rapier with intricate golden vines inlaid on the hilt. He gazed at it lovingly for a moment, then walked over to Flora. Taking her slender hand in his, he pressed it into her palm. He leaned close and whispered something into her ear. Her expression never changed as she nodded, but her cheeks flushed slightly as he pulled away.

After learning my name, Hassen chuckled and muttered something about fate while he pulled a slender short sword from the safe. There were roses engraved into the hilt and etched down the blade of the sword.

"Thanks." I took the sword. "It's beautiful."

"Deadly, more like," the blacksmith grumbled. He was probably wondering why I was here—that made two of us. "If they become damaged, you bring them back. No one else in Elvanar has the skill to forge these weapons. Do you know how to care for them?"

The three of us shook our heads in unison.

After Hassen and Jallix showed us how to properly care for our new weapons, Elder Asish led us to the north edge of town. There, he gave Flora a map that mirrored the one in the Harmony Chamber, with rough estimations of where the Argems were rumored to be hidden. He warned us to keep our mission secret and to not return to Trehilm unless absolutely necessary.

The day was bright and the sky was a clear, deep blue as we headed to the Grove of Contemplation. Blaine and I unsheathed our swords and mimicked fighting off evil creatures as we made our way among the tall trees. I couldn't remember the last time I felt so upbeat. Flora rebuked our waving of weapons as "irresponsible and childish," trying to maintain a serious countenance. Nevertheless, the three of us had high spirits as Flora led the way to our destination.

Our conversation turned to familiar topics of school gossip and homework assignments. I was listening to Blaine complain about the recent math test when I heard an unsettling noise. It was something between a yip and a growl. I jumped closer to Blaine, my nerves jittering.

"What was that?"

Blaine squinted in the direction I was looking. "I don't see . . . oh!"

A dog-like animal with large antlers darted in and out of the trees in front of us.

"It's just a coyote," Flora said. "Don't worry, they hunt small animals. Not elves—or, uh, humans. You should be safe."

"But it has antlers," I said. "Coyotes don't have antlers, right?"

"Perhaps not in your world." Flora smirked.

The creature growled at us, then scampered away. Once it disappeared, small fox-like animals ventured out on branches high above us. They jumped from limb to limb over our heads, nimble as squirrels. Colorful birds chirped their annoyance at the creatures when they ventured too close to nests made of twigs and fur.

The wildlife here was so similar to Earth's, but there were little differences—one being none of these animals feared us. They didn't even look at us as we passed.

"Have you ever been to the Grove of Contemplation, Flora?" Blaine asked, drawing me from my observations.

"Once, with my father," she replied. "It was beautiful and serene, but a bit boring if I'm to be honest. He brought me there to teach me about some of the plants that only grow in the Grove."

"Oh, so you do have parents."

Flora scowled at Blaine. "Of course I have parents. Well, it's just my dad." She gestured behind us. "He lives on the other side of the city."

"What does he do?" I asked. What kind of jobs did elves have?

"He's an herbalist," she said. "He travels around all of Elvanar and uses his knowledge of nature to help people. In human terms, he is kind of like a . . . healer?"

"Oh, like a doctor?" Blaine asked. "How does he feel about you being on this dangerous quest?"

"He's . . . not thrilled, to say the least." Flora grimaced. "We haven't really talked since the Council's assignment. It feels like he's . . . disappointed?" She shrugged. "I dunno."

The stiff formality Flora spoke with her fellow elves melted away the farther we traveled from the city. I asked about her formal speech, and Flora sighed.

"We elves have a lot of traditions and with our long lifespans, there is not a lot of change within communities. Formal speech is just one way to improve communication and prevent misunderstandings. Imagine having a two-hundred-year feud with someone because you said something stupid. I've fallen a bit out of practice spending so much time with the two of you. It's nice to be able to speak without thinking over your words from every angle."

"Hundreds of years . . ." Blaine shook his head in wonder. "Flora, how old are you?"

"I'm not that old." Flora glanced over her shoulder at us from where she was leading. She turned around to watch where she was going. "Don't get weird."

Blaine faked a scoff. "I'm not weird."

Flora and I both snorted at that, and even Blaine couldn't keep the smirk from his lips.

"I'm forty-three," she said after a short pause, "but humans mature a lot faster than elves. Developmentally, we're about the same age."

Forty-three? She was older than my uncle? My mind fought to grasp the new information as I studied her. We were children compared to her. No wonder she didn't want me to come along—she probably felt like she was babysitting. A familiar weight settled back onto my chest.

"Huh," Blaine said. That was all.

"I told you not to get weird," Flora's shoulders inched toward her ears.

"I'm not being weird," Blaine said, striving for lightness. "I was just thinking about how you try to examine your words before you say them. I don't think my mind works fast enough to do that."

I forced a cheerful tone. "I don't think it does, either."

He laughed and playfully shoved my shoulder.

"I walked right into that one." He rolled his eyes and threw up his hands in mock defeat. "But see? I guess I'm feuding with Rose now."

Flora's shoulders relaxed as she shot us a warm smile. My tension evaporated along with hers.

"Does that mean I get two-hundred years of silence?" I asked.

"Oh no, feuds with me involve a large amount of terrible singing."

The three of us were laughing again when Flora stopped short. She stepped to the side, pulling back a branch to reveal a large clearing.

"Welcome," she said with a grin, "to the Grove of Contemplation."

Soft foliage whispered beneath our feet as we entered. The vegetation around the edges of the Grove were dense enough to form a natural wall, which was situated in a perfect circle around a massive oak tree. Light danced through the branches and filtered through the air, giving the clearing an underwater effect.

"Wow." A steady buzz of energy radiated from the tree and an incredible sense of peace settled over me.

"I feel like I can finally breathe easily, and I didn't know I couldn't before," Blaine whispered.

"Very eloquent, Veritace," Flora said dryly as she approached the large oak in the center of the clearing.

"Something is calling to me." Blaine turned to me. "Do you feel it?"

I shook my head. All I felt was that overwhelming peace. I wrapped my arms around myself. I didn't deserve the feeling—I needed to leave the Grove before I corrupted it.

"Come on." Blaine coaxed me forward. I hesitated, then followed.

Flora sat cross-legged facing the trunk, assuming a meditative pose with her back straight and her hands laying lightly on her knees. She gestured that we adopt similar positions. Blaine struggled to adjust his sword as he sat and my muscles strained to keep the proper posture, but eventually we were all on the ground, facing the tree in a semicircle.

All was silent, save the birdsong and rustling of small animals in the forest. After a few minutes, Flora began to sing in a soft, lilting voice. The language was one I'd never heard, but the tone was pleading and respectful. Flora's singing reverberated around the clearing, echoing back to create a harmony with herself. The buzzing got louder and magic tingled my skin, giving me goosebumps.

Flora's voice amplified as the echoes of her song layered back on itself. The air wavered around her like heat off blacktop on a hot summer day. When she opened her eyes, they burned like green fire.

The song ended with a clear, high note, the echoes fading off around us. The silence held, not even the wind daring to move around us. Then, the fire faded, returning her irises to their familiar bright green. She blinked once and swayed before collapsing onto the soft grass of the forest floor.

"Flora!" Before I could catch her, the buzzing intensified. Energy screamed through my mind and I clutched my rattling head. The ground rumbled and shook, knocking Blaine and I off balance. Deep fissures appeared in the ground around us, separating me from my friends. I watched in horror as Flora's motionless body slipped through a crack in the ground.

Blaine

I lunged forward, grabbing Flora before she could fall into the dark abyss. I pulled her to the relative safety of quaking ground. My breath came in uneven pants and I held her close. I searched frantically for a safe place to—

The fissures stopped widening. Roots appeared, their rapid growth filling the cracks splintering the Grove. When everything stilled around us, I released Flora and got to my feet. I clutched my sword hilt—I wasn't sure what I would do with it, but it seemed like something the Veritace would do. I wouldn't go down without a fight, especially if my friends were in danger.

Rose crawled on hands and knees to Flora while I inspected the roots around us. Everything seemed normal, but I was still wary. Flora woke and wiped blood from her nose as Rose frantically inspected her for injuries.

"That took more energy than I expected." Flora shivered. "I've never been connected to something so powerful."

I examined my friend, concerned by the fatigue in her tone. There were leaves tangled in her perfect hair and dark circles under her eyes, but her focus was on the tree. I followed her gaze. The bark of the massive oak opened to reveal a brilliant green gemstone. The call was stronger now—like someone yelling to get my attention. It pulled me closer.

Emerald light flickered to life inside a perfectly round green stone. It wavered like candlelight, but grew steadier as I approached. When I was within an arm's length, the glow was blinding.

This was it. My last chance to bail. To go home and pretend none of this ever happened. To let my memories fade into some strange dream. To let someone—some future me—come pick up this Argem. To shirk this responsibility onto someone else.

I could walk away . . . but how would I live with myself?

I reached out and grabbed the stone. The light flared between my fingers. Magic rushed from the Argem and blew my hair away from my face like a storm wind. My vision went green as knowledge was shoved into my head. Years of training and practice and teaching were compressed into seconds. I didn't know the first thing about sword fighting, but at the same time, I had always been an expert.

The Argem dulled to a quiet glow in my grasp. I marveled at the stone, then pulled my sword from its sheath, exposing the grooves set into the blade.

Peacekeeper was no longer awkward in my hand—it belonged there. The hilt warmed as I placed the green Argem into its slot. The gem was happy to be reunited with the sword. It was happy to be home.

Could a magic stone be happy?

Above me, the giant oak groaned. Its branches thrashed in a nonexistent wind. I looked up just in time to see a limb hurtling toward me. I scrambled back as it crashed to the ground, leaving a deep groove in the soft dirt. Somehow, I kept my footing and my grip on the sword.

With no time to think, I leapt over the branch and ran for my friends. They were farther from the trunk than I was, but still within range of its deadly branches.

Something—instinct maybe—pulled me up short. I skidded to a halt just as another limb slammed into the ground in front of me. Chunks of dirt and grass flew everywhere as I stumbled. The tree was searching for something—the Argem.

"Get back!" I screamed to Flora and Rose.

Flora was quick to obey. She grabbed Rose's hand and they darted away, leaping over roots as they went.

I brandished Peacekeeper in a defensive stance. I tried not to think too hard about how I knew any defensive stances, having never learned them. The tree shuddered and swayed above me but paused its relentless pummeling. Instead, the tree's smaller branches stretched out to surround me.

One by one, the branches struck quick as a whip. My stuttering parries were slow to deflect them. I wasn't fast enough. Wasn't strong enough. I knew the moves thanks to the magic of the Argem, but had no muscle memory.

No stamina, either. I was already tired and my movements were clumsy. One of the branches smacked my arm, drawing blood. I managed to cut the next one, but the branch after whipped through my defenses. Soon, several thin cuts peppered my arms and legs.

I stumbled backwards, desperate to get away from the tree. The movement was sloppy and just resulted in more cuts and welts. I raised my sword in a defensive position and the tree shuddered again. Its branches retreated for a moment before diving back at me.

That gave me an idea.

Instead of attacking the branches outright, I tried a different defensive pose. The branches paused again and I grinned—it was a puzzle. The tree wasn't trying to kill me, it was meant to stop anyone else from stealing the Argem. I possessed Alaric's skill with a sword. I didn't have to fight the branches—I had to dance with them.

I eased from one stance to the next, running through a standard feather flow. My confidence grew as the branches weaved around me, stretching out beside me, but not attacking. My feet moved almost on their own, circling around the great tree as I danced with Peacekeeper. My footwork needed some fine tuning, but the sword hilt was warm in my grasp as the blade sang through the air. I felt graceful. Powerful. Content.

Too soon, I completed my revolution around the tree. I found myself out of reach of the branches and next to Flora and Rose once again. The tree calmed and its limbs returned to their normal positions watching over the Grove.

My friends stared at me with wide eyes. I sheathed Peacekeeper, hiding the sparkle of the green Argem as I did. As soon as the sword was sheathed, I felt unsure of myself again. Had all my confidence come from the stone?

"Well, I wouldn't call this grove boring." I wiped the sweat from my forehead and grimaced at my friends.

"What on Earth was *that*?" Rose asked.

I grinned. "Technically, we aren't on Earth anymore."

When Rose continued to stare at me, I cleared my throat and shrugged. "It's a series of exercises to improve strength and precision with a blade."

"Did you know how to do that before today?" Flora asked, cocking her head to the side.

"No." I looked down at the sheathed blade. While the sword was out, I felt good. I felt whole. Now I just felt . . . incomplete.

"I suppose the more Argems we collect, the more you will remember of your past life."

And the more of myself I'll lose.

"However you learned or remembered it," Rose said, "can you teach us?"

Flora's eyes widened. "Yes, that would be quite useful."

I nodded, but my arms chose that moment to quiver. "Can we wait until tomorrow? I'm weirdly exhausted."

"It's been a long day." Flora's smile warmed my insides. "Come on. It may take the remainder of daylight to return to the Rift."

I pulled out my phone to check the time, shocked that I hadn't thought to look at it sooner. The time displayed was 6:53 pm. Had it really only been a few hours since we came through the Rift?

"Time moves a little differently here," Flora said when I voiced my confusion. "One day in your world is roughly equal to one and a half days here. Your phones keep moving at Earth time while we speed up."

"How'd you figure that out?"

"I did some experiments when I first found the Rift."

"Does that mean we're aging slower while we're here?" I asked. "Or faster?"

"Neither," Rose said. "Time is relative."

I pretended to gape at her. "You're related to time?"

Rose groaned at my joke, but I caught her smile. Flora's eyebrows lowered and she pursed her lips.

"That extra time will be handy during the week," I said, pushing through a yawn. "We can pop over here to do our homework."

"Do you think we'll get extra credit for saving the world?" Rose asked.

"We'll be lucky to get any time to do our homework," Flora said.

I perked up at her words. "Does that mean you'll still be coming to school with us, Flora?"

"I have to keep an eye on you two." She smiled. "Plus, I enjoy learning about your technology."

"Meaning you're addicted to those games on your phone?" I teased. Flora blushed.

"And who got her addicted to all those games, Blaine?" Rose chided.

Our banter continued as we made our way home, but I didn't think I was the only one longing for my pillow as we trudged through the forest—not to mention dinner. Despite my grumbling stomach, I was proud of what we had accomplished today. I spent the entire walk pushing down my worries, and my spirits were unusually high when we stumbled through the Rift.

Five

Rose

I CRUMPLED ON THE floor of Flora's kitchen with a thud. Instantly, it was hard to breathe—but that was normal. Flora came through the Rift gracefully, staying on her feet with an inhuman litheness. In retrospect, it was obvious Flora wasn't human. How had I not seen it before?

Looking around the kitchen of the perfectly ordinary house sent my mind reeling. I had just stepped out of a movie set and quite literally crash landed back to reality. Perhaps I woke up from a fever dream and my friends were here at my hospital bed to welcome me back to the land of the living.

"Was that real?" I pushed myself onto my knees, still trying to recover my breath. Blaine offered me his hand, and I gratefully took it to pull myself to my feet. He squeezed my fingers once before letting go.

"I asked Flora the same thing." Blaine grinned and I felt my face mirror the emotion. We both started laughing.

"You guys, this is serious. We have a lot of responsibility. We need to do this right," Flora closed the pantry door, hiding the Rift within. "Go home and pack for tomorrow. We should get started early so we can get back for class on Monday."

"Class?" I laughed. "Who needs school when you get to watch the Veritace save the world?"

"Or when you can just learn stuff by putting rocks in a sword." Blaine added, gesturing to Peacekeeper.

Flora scowled.

"Oh, come on, Flora," Blaine said, taking her shoulders. She tried to keep her expression serious, but the corners of her mouth twitched upward. "This is going to be awesome!"

"I suppose I must admit," Flora said, "today was pretty awesome."

We succumbed to fits of exhausted laughter. When our hysterics finally died down, Flora led us to her spare room and instructed us to leave our weapons. We didn't need to be carrying swords around on Earth. They would just call attention to us. Blaine reverently laid his sword on the twin bed and hesitated before backing away. I placed mine beside his and Flora propped hers haphazardly against the wall.

Blaine drove me home to pack and get permission to go on our 'camping trip' with Flora's family. He dropped me at the end of the driveway and I waved to him while I pulled my keys from my pocket. The house was dark, but there was a flickering light coming from the living room as I entered.

My uncle Martin lounged on the couch, engrossed in some reality show with beer in hand. Only ten years older than me, we had always been close, even before my parents' deaths. He was my role model. My favorite birthday present when I was nine had been a medical playset—complete with a fake stethoscope—because Martin had just started training to be a paramedic. My parents came home from work one day when he was babysitting to find him covered in medical wrap and bandages.

"Hey Rosie." Martin was the only one still allowed to use that nickname. "How was your date with Blaine?"

I blinked at him. My overstimulated brain stalled, taking several seconds to remember that I should have just returned from my friend's house—not a whole different world.

"It wasn't a date!" I wrinkled my nose. "Blaine is a friend. Plus, Flora was there."

"Mhmm." The disbelief was clear in Martin's tone.

I rolled my eyes. "Flora invited me camping this weekend. The plan is to leave early tomorrow."

"That sounds like fun," he said. "Do you need a tent and stuff? I think we still have some gear in the garage."

"Uh, yeah. I probably do," I said. He laughed and pushed himself off the couch.

"Well, let's go see what we've got."

Martin's old camping gear obviously hadn't been used in years. When he wrestled the sleeping bag down from the top of the shelving unit in the garage, a sizable puff of dust came with it. After a prolonged bout of coughing—followed by several puffs of my inhaler—he helped me pull down a tent and carefully brushed the dust from it.

"Me and your dad used to go camping all the time. I haven't even looked at this stuff since . . ." He trailed off, lost in thought. He shook his head. "Maybe the two of us could go sometime soon. If you want, I mean."

My parents' deaths had been hard on Martin, and now at only twenty-eight years old, he was stuck in his childhood home with his older brother's teenage kid. Instead of trying to speak through the newly formed knot in my throat, I nodded.

After throwing some essentials in my backpack—my inhaler, a flashlight, a lighter, some snacks and a few changes of clothes—I set my camping gear by the door. I got ready for bed and set an alarm on my phone for early the next morning. After a few restless hours, I finally drifted to sleep.

I couldn't breathe. Smoke filled my room. Ash scratched my throat in place of oxygen. My lungs refused to expand, sending me into a new coughing fit with each attempted breath. Fire leapt around my room, devouring seventeen years of my life in a flash.

Tears blurred my vision as flames licked at my fingers. Heat pressed over me like a weighted blanket, shackling me to the floor. I forced myself to crawl, fighting for every inch.

Escape.

Windows shattered and wood groaned over the roar of the fire. Distant pounding and the crashing of falling beams reverberated through my chest. Screams sliced my heart like the glass digging into my forearms.

Shattered glass means an open window—there!

Freedom beckoned behind a wall of crimson flames, hot enough to burn through stucco. Acrid black smoke cut off my vision. If my options were to sit here and suffocate or burn to death for a chance at survival, my choice was clear—I would go out in a blaze.

I gathered my strength and the dregs of my courage. Pulling my legs beneath me, I blasted into a shaky crawl-run, staying low to avoid the worst of the smoke. I squeezed my eyes shut and leapt into the flames.

I woke up coughing.

Blankets tangled around me and sweat coated my skin. I kicked free and reached for the inhaler on my nightstand. It took two puffs before I felt any relief from the iron bands constricting my chest. I huddled in bed and willed away the nausea threatening my stomach.

Just a dream. It can't hurt you.

But it did. Not physically, but each night, one of two dreams gouged apart my heart and fractured my soul. I pressed the heels of my hands against my eyes, trying to block out the screams still echoing inside my head. Logically, I knew I hadn't heard them that night over the roar of the house burning down around me. That didn't stop my brain from torturing me with their voices.

I sat like that for hours, watching a beam of sunlight inch across the plush cream carpet. When my alarm blared beside me, I didn't move to turn it off. Why would I? Every day was the same as the last. What was the point of getting up? Of leaving this room? It wouldn't bring my parents back. I listened as the shrill tone grew louder and louder.

The memories from yesterday trickled through my dissociative haze. Every day wouldn't be the same—I had a whole new world to explore. I latched onto the thought like it was a life raft. I grabbed my phone to send a text to Blaine, but he had beaten me to it.

Blaine

In case you were wondering, yesterday wasn't a dream.

Warmth chased the numbness from my chest and a smile tugged at my lips.

Me

Meet you at the Rift!

I took a deep breath and got out of bed.

After a quick shower, I grabbed some granola bars from the kitchen and headed to the front door with my gear. Martin was passed out on the couch when I left, more empty beer bottles on the table than usual. Some nights were harder for him than others. Was last night's binge due to the memories I'd brought up of him camping with my dad? Guilt sliced through my chest—I needed to do better. For Martin.

The sun was just starting to rise as I made my way to Flora's house. There was a chill in the air and the scent of rain on the wind, so I pulled my jacket tightly around me. The difference in weather from the day before was astounding, but I had been told that was typical of weather in the Midwest. I would take sun and humidity over the cold any day.

I made it to Flora's just as Blaine did. We knocked then walked inside together. Flora was packing up supplies for our trip as we entered. We quickly recapped the plan and looked over the map Elder Asish gave us. It felt surreal studying a map of a fairy tale in the same place we usually did our homework.

"This is the Rift." Flora placed her finger on a hand drawn star on the map. Then she pointed south to a rough circle etched into the paper. "And this is the closest of the Argems. We'll have to cross into lycan territory. I've no idea what to expect when we cross that border. The mark on the map covers a few square miles, so we might need to do some searching."

"Hopefully when we get close enough I'll know how to find it," Blaine said. "Like how I could hear the green Argem calling to me in the Grove of Contemplation."

"It astounds me you can hear anything considering the volume you listen to that racket humans call music."

Blaine chuckled.

With one final check of our gear, including the map and our new weapons, we stepped through the Rift one at a time. Blaine went through first to scout any potential dangers. As he stepped into the small closet, the vortex of light seemed to recognize him and coiled quickly along his shape. Soon he was totally engulfed by swirling colors. I waited ten seconds before taking a deep breath and stepping into the Rift.

The familiar feeling of immobility struck me first, followed by a falling sensation that pushed the air from my lungs. I jumped off a thirty-foot cliff at a mountain lake in Tennessee once—the fall felt similar to that, only much, much higher. When I plunged into Silaris, my feet hit the grass, then my knees gave out.

The soft, green grass that cushioned my fall splayed between my fingers. An outstretched hand offered assistance. I looked up to see Blaine, attire and hair rumpled from the trip. I looked down at myself before taking Blaine's hand.

"Well, that was graceful," I said as he helped haul me to my feet.

"It gets easier the more you do it. Just take Flora for example." He gestured at the Rift behind me as a colorful, light-bound shape floated lightly to the grass. When the swirling light retreated, Flora was as flawless as she had been on Earth, not a single blonde hair out of place.

I ran my fingers through my messy hair and brushed the grass from my knees. Blaine reached toward my face and I flinched.

He froze, hand still raised between us. "May I?"

"Oh, yeah." I forced out a nervous laugh and held still as Blaine plucked something from my hair. "Sorry, I'm a bit jumpy today. Excited but nervous, you know?"

"I get it." Blaine smiled and pulled away with a strand of grass. "Don't worry, you'll be safe with us."

When we made eye contact, the understanding written across his features made my breath catch. I quickly looked away. "Thanks."

"If you two are done playing with each other's hair," Flora called, "we're on a tight schedule to get home in time. By my calculations, we have roughly three days here to Earth's two. Meaning, we have one day to get to the area, one day to search, and one day to get you home."

"I thought you wanted to learn some swordplay." Blaine smirked.

Flora hesitated, and I nodded enthusiastically.

"Okay." Flora sounded eager at the prospect. "Just the basics now in case we run into trouble, but we can do more when we set up camp tonight."

"Draw your weapons." Blaine brandished his sword. "The first thing I'm going to show you is a solo exercise called the feather flow."

"The *feather* flow?" Flora tilted her head. "That doesn't sound very scary."

"Swordwork isn't just smashing your opponent with brute force." He crouched and held Peacekeeper up near his head, then shifted his footing and swung, twirling the sword in an elegant loop to end in a different position. "The feather flow is named for the delicate movements necessary during a duel and the flexibility required by the duelist."

Blaine went through the steps, frequently stopping to correct our stances as we followed along.

"It's important to switch up the order of the movements every time," Blaine said. "That way, you don't get caught up in muscle memory when you're in a real fight. It helps me to imagine someone is coming at me with different moves and I have to defend myself."

"Wouldn't it be better to practice against each other?" Flora asked.

"*Yeah . . .*" Blaine drew out the word. "That's not going to happen. I don't want you hurting each other. Or me. Let's stick with imaginary foes for now."

Flora huffed indignantly, but I agreed with Blaine. These swords were heavy and sharp. There was no way I could make it through an actual fight.

"It's also a good idea to vary your speed as you go from one movement to the next. The slower you move, the harder your stabilizer muscles have to work to keep the correct form." Blaine demonstrated moving from a high parry, as if an attack was coming from above his head, to a low thrust toward his imaginary attacker. The movement crept so slowly that a tremor went through his arm as the muscle strained. "Going faster—" he flicked his blade upward in a quick, sweeping attack before bringing it close to himself in a defensive stance "—creates elasticity in your muscles and helps with stamina."

He went over the basics of defense, telling us to try to incapacitate our opponent just enough to get away. Flora and I laughed at the silly names of the defensive moves he showed us. Rabbit in the Hutch was a technique to be used in tight spaces, when you didn't have room to fully swing your blade. Fox in the Henhouse was a series of rapid thrusts meant to surprise your attacker and throw them off balance.

"You're more likely to hurt yourself with your swords right now if you choose to stay and fight. There is no shame in running from danger when you're outmatched." Blaine paused to let that sink in. "Also, try to get in the habit of drawing your sword at the first hint of danger—it could save your life. Once it's out, remember to breathe and wait for the danger to come to you so you can use the defensive techniques we just went over."

After practicing with the swords for long enough that my arms were burning, we set out towards the south.

"It's weird to me how there's no vegetation getting in our way," Blaine said. "Back home, the undergrowth obscures the forest floor. People need to constantly be trimming away honeysuckle to maintain trails through the woods. I wonder if it would look like this at home if the settlers didn't come in and cut down all the old growth trees."

"Your town's vegetation is quite young," Flora said. "Is it like that all over your world?"

"I don't really know." Blaine shrugged. "I've lived in Ohio my whole life and haven't traveled much. You traveled a lot with your parents, right Rose?"

My heartbeat stuttered. Could I speak about my past without falling back into my depression? When I shot Blaine a questioning look, he grimaced. "Your uncle gossips."

"I moved all over the country with my parents, but I've never seen anything like this. Our last house was in Florida." I sighed to combat the tightening of my chest. "It was warm all the time and we lived within walking distance of the beach. It was my favorite place to be."

"No wonder you were so tan when we met." Blaine laughed, then grew more somber. "Did your parents move for work?"

I shook my head. "Mom didn't like to settle in one place for very long. She said she got it from her parents. I never met them, but they called it wanderlust." My voice strained as my throat tightened. This was the most I'd spoken about them since their deaths.

"I'd love to see more of the country," Blaine said, changing the subject and shaking me out of my thoughts. "I don't know if I could take the Florida heat, though."

"That's why the beach was nice," I said, thankful for the subject change. "There was always a breeze coming off the water and you could jump in the ocean if you got too hot."

"What's a beach?" Flora asked.

Blaine and I stared at her for a second, taken aback.

"It's the area where the land meets the ocean," Blaine said.

"Where Elvanar hits the sea, the land is not hospitable." Flora frowned. "I've never seen the ocean."

"Well, we're going to have to change that," Blaine said and I nodded. "Maybe when all this is over, we can take a trip to the coast."

"Maybe over winter break," I agreed. "Then we can get away from the Ohio winter."

"Ohio's winter isn't even that cold." Blaine laughed.

I rolled my eyes. "And Florida isn't all that hot."

We bickered and laughed as we traveled, making the hours pass swiftly. I was glad I wore my sturdy hiking boots, but my feet were still sore by the time we stopped for lunch. Flora picked some berries from a bush she swore wasn't poisonous. We ate them along with the lunch meat sandwiches Blaine's mom packed in a cooler for us, then continued on our way.

After another hour or so of walking, the birdsongs quieted and the animals that were so abundant before were nowhere to be found. Even the light that filtered in through the leaves to illuminate the forest floor dimmed.

"We've reached the corrupted land," Flora whispered. "Be on your guard."

We stepped into the unknown together.

Six

Rose

"THE TREES ARE THINNING."

Blaine's voice rang too loud in the quiet forest. Less than a minute later, we found the edge of Elvanar. We paused behind the last of the trees to stay hidden.

The boundary was stark. Elvanar ended abruptly, opening up to a barren stretch fifty meters across. Even the trees avoided extending their branches into the nothingness. On the far side of the path, sloping rock walls jutted from the landscape.

"What's it called?" I whispered, gesturing to the rocky landscape. The terrain reminded me of the Grand Canyon. Large pillars of red stone reached into the sky, ending in a series of outcroppings and plateaus of all different levels and sizes. Some of the rock shelves were connected, forming a makeshift path high above us. I shuddered to think what kinds of creatures used those paths. In the distance, rusty mountains climbed from the horizon, casting long shadows in the setting sun.

Flora shook her head. "We never talk about it."

The three of us studied the new land in silence, each lost in our own thoughts.

"We should camp in Elvanar tonight," Flora said. "It's getting dark and I don't know what sort of danger to expect."

Somewhat reluctantly, Blaine agreed with her logic. I was just relieved to be tagging along and didn't complain when Flora sent me to gather firewood. We set up our tents far enough from the border that our firelight would be hidden from any scouts on the cliffs. Blaine made us perform a feather flow before bed, even though we were all still tired from this morning. We agreed on a rotating watch—first Flora, then me, then Blaine.

I wasn't used to sleeping in a tent. The unevenness of the hard ground kept me tossing and turning to get comfortable. Whenever I drifted to sleep, the night sounds of the forest would crescendo and I would jolt awake. In those moments, I had to reorient to where I was and start the process of falling asleep all over again.

It was still dark when I woke in a cold sweat, huddled on my side and clutching my knees to my chest. It was *that* dream again.

The nightmare was so vivid—so real. My fingers tingled as I wrestled to shove down my panic. I focused on my breathing and willed away my nausea. At least the dream didn't trigger my asthma this time.

I'm not there. I looked through the mesh opening of the tent at the forest around me. Blaine tended our tiny fire while he kept watch. *I'm in Silaris. I'm with friends. I'm safe.*

I repeated the mantra until my heartbeat slowed. I must have fallen back to sleep because I jerked awake to the clatter of cookware. Blaine was packing up supplies and must have dropped them. The dark circles under his eyes and slumped posture indicated he hadn't slept well either. From the palpable nervous energy he exuded, I was surprised he waited for Flora and me to wake up before tearing the tents down around us. He bounced on his toes, backpack already on, as we got ready to leave. To save time, I scarfed down a granola bar while I followed Blaine back to the border.

"We should just make a run for it," Blaine said, looking at the barren land in front of us.

"I disagree. There could be any number of enemies hiding in those cliffs," Flora countered. "We should search for some cover."

"I think we'll be walking a long way before we find any cover." I looked up and down the boundary line. It was barren for as far as I could see.

"Exactly," Blaine agreed. "We don't have time to find cover. We have to find the Argem."

Flora looked at Blaine, then at me, then frowned at the boundary.

"I don't like it," she said with a resigned sigh. "But I suppose you're correct. Do you see that rock outcropping?" She pointed to an overhang that jutted out, forming a shallow cave. Blaine and I nodded. "That's where we run, as quickly and quietly as we can. Are you ready?"

As soon as we left Elvanar, a chill ran down the back of my neck. Anyone could be watching us from those cliffs. We sprinted across the boundary line, the only sounds our footsteps and breathing.

When we reached the relative safety of the outcropping, we paused to catch our breath. The sudden, dry heat that bombarded us when we passed under the stone shelf felt like the blast of hot air from a preheated oven. The sounds of our ragged gasps echoed against the rocks and made obvious our inadequate fitness levels. Flora recovered first and peered around the unfamiliar landscape, eyes scanning for any danger. Only when she took a deep breath did I allow myself to relax a little.

"I've never been outside of Elvanar before," she said. "The treaty must be truly broken; otherwise, we wouldn't have been able to cross that boundary."

Blaine rested a hand on her shoulder. "We'll fix it."

She gave him a grateful nod and led the way into the unknown.

We traveled through tunnels and valleys of stone, colorful striations running through the rocks beside us. We walked for hours, climbing over boulders and along the maze of raised platforms, toward the spot indicated on the map. My legs were tired and my feet were sore, but I refused to be the first one to complain.

Blaine came to an abrupt stop.

"I feel something," he said.

Flora and I turned to him in excitement, all fatigue forgotten.

"The Argem?" Flora asked.

"Maybe," Blaine said. "I think so."

"If the feeling gets stronger or weaker, let us know."

We continued on for about a mile when Blaine spoke up again.

"It's gone," he said, stopping. He took a step backward, then a step forward again. He furrowed his brow. "It didn't get any stronger or weaker, it just started and then stopped. It must be back the way we came."

"It's time to start searching methodically," Flora said. "Let's mark where we are now and search for the Argem in a grid pattern. With all these loose stones and caverns, we could walk right next to it without seeing it."

We set off side by side, staying about ten feet from one another and marking the places we already searched with distinct piles of rocks. It was slow going, but at least we had a specific area to search instead of an entire territory. About fifteen minutes into our search, a shallow pool blocked our path. The pool was filled with an oily gray liquid—like molten metal. I got the sense it was watching us. Waiting.

"I don't think you should touch that," I said as Blaine crouched and stretched his hand toward the shiny surface. He halted inches before his fingers brushed the sinister pool.

"You sound like my dad." He chuckled but pulled his hand away.

The liquid surged and cascaded toward us. Before anyone could do more than flinch, it splashed onto us. Then there was nothing.

Darkness enveloped me. I blinked rapidly, desperate for my eyes to adjust. It was so dark that I couldn't tell if my eyes were even open. Before I could make out anything in the void, a tiny spark appeared. It grew into a roaring flame, briefly taking the shape of a tall, broad-shouldered man before spreading into a wall of fire.

I cringed from the heat and coughed on dry air. I tried to run, but flames surrounded me. I flung my arms up to protect my face and heard the sizzle of my skin as it blistered. I had to find a way out. I searched as best I could, but the ring of fire wouldn't let me move. Smoke tore at my throat. I couldn't breathe. I couldn't think.

I fell to my knees, coughing and retching.

This is how I would die. It was fitting, really. I wasn't meant to survive the first time. At least I would see them soon.

Peace settled over me. It was okay. I was ready.

Then, the darkness faded. I could breathe again. Flora crouched with her head in her hands. Blaine panted, sword rammed into the center of what used to be the oily pool, a wild look in his eyes. The echoes of long dead flames still burned into my retinas.

Without thinking, I ran—from those flames, from my friends—but most importantly, from the past.

I ducked into the first cave I could find and collapsed against a rough stone wall. I slumped against the cool rocks in the darkness, gasping for breath between sobs. The steady drip of water off a stalactite in the distance acted as a metronome to coax my breathing back into its normal rhythm. The damp air and chilled stone gave me goosebumps and helped banish the flames engulfing my mind. By the time my tears stopped, I had chewed the remainder of nail polish off my left hand.

A vision. It wasn't real. It couldn't hurt me. I wouldn't break—

Rocks clattered nearby. My head snapped up and I bolted to my feet. The sound came from deep within the cave. I peered into the darkness and a shiver of fear ran through me.

"Hello?" I croaked softly.

Nothing answered, but I heard the soft padding of approaching footsteps. Something was coming—and it had four feet.

I drew my sword, berating myself for not doing it sooner, and held it out in front of me. The tip shook as I took up the defensive stance Blaine showed us earlier. Fox in the hutch or rabbit in the henhouse or . . . whatever it was called. I breathed in and out, trying to steady my hands. Goosebumps erupted on my arms as I felt a wave of heaviness sweep through me. I could almost hear Blaine's voice in my head repeating the mantra he had drilled into us: Legs bent, back straight, wait for them to strike.

"If I wished you dead, human, you would already be so." A soft voice rumbled from the darkness, deep as a growl. A pair of yellow-orange eyes glinted from the darkness of the cavern. "Put that toothpick down."

I didn't move my sword an inch.

"Smart human." The eyes seemed to laugh. There was a soft sniffing sound. "You are human, aren't you?"

"Who are you?" I rasped out, voice tight but surprisingly even.

"Nobody important. Who are you?"

I didn't answer.

"How are you still human? The disease . . . are you immune? What pack are you from?"

I still didn't respond, too busy figuring out how to run away.

"Unless . . . you aren't from a pack." There was a pause. "The Howling Peaks are dangerous. That toothpick won't protect you. Not from us."

I focused on my stance, not even daring to look toward the cavern exit.

"Run home, *little human*." The last sounded like a sneer. "This mountain is deadly. Go too much farther and you won't make it out." The eyes faded into the blackness and footsteps—two beats now—retreated. "Don't say I didn't warn you." The voice sounded from deeper in the cave.

I waited until I could no longer hear the pacing of footsteps before I scurried outside. I felt those orange eyes burning into me the entire way back to my friends.

Seven

WHEN I FOUND BLAINE and Flora, they were in a heated discussion.

"I already told you, Flora, I don't know. That thing . . ." Blaine wiped the sweat from his forehead. "I felt so . . . empty. Are they all like that? All the things corrupted by the Defector's evil magic?"

"I'm not sure." Flora shook her head. "I felt powerless. Alone. Saw the bars of a cage." She shivered from the memory and hugged herself. "It was inside our heads. It knew what we feared most."

Blaine reached out to her. "Flora—"

"Blight!" Flora hissed the word like a curse when she spotted me. "Rose, where were you? It's dangerous out here!"

"I'm sorry," I said, glancing behind me toward the dark opening. "I just . . . I needed a minute."

"We've been looking everywhere—"

"It's fine." Blaine cut a sharp look to Flora, who rolled her eyes. They both looked paler than usual. "As long as you're okay?"

His comment tilted up at the end, forming a question. He looked me over as if expecting me to be missing a limb.

"I'm fine." I crossed my arms in front of myself.

"We stay together from now on," Flora said, her glare flipping back and forth between Blaine and me. We both had the good sense to nod.

"Come on," Blaine said. "Let's keep looking. The sooner we find the Argem, the sooner we can get out of here."

We combed our grid for hours with no luck. We were tired, sore, and quickly losing hope of actually finding the Argem. Flora's mood soured further each time she pulled out her phone to check the clock. The hours ticked by, bringing us closer to our time limit. Frustration mixed with hunger until we were all sniping at each other enough for Blaine to call a halt to our searching to eat a quick meal.

Maybe the smell of food drew them to us—or maybe they had been watching us for a while—but we all froze when a harsh growl sounded from across the section of flat rock where we sat. Blaine leapt to his feet and drew his sword.

At the edge of the plateau stood a petite girl in worn, ripped clothing. She looked about twelve years old and had long, silver-blonde hair that curled into wild ringlets. She stood with her head cocked to the side. At first glance, she looked human—even innocent—but her blood-red eyes and predatory smile quickly shattered that illusion. Behind her, a massive gray wolf emerged from the rocks and padded up beside her, teeth bared. The wolf's head came up to the girl's shoulder, dwarfing her already petite form. She put her hand on the wolf's back, quieting the snarling creature.

"It looks like we found some new play things, Toreth." The little girl's shrill voice sent a chill up my spine. She sniffed at the air and a wicked grin spread over her face.

Flora and I scrambled to our feet. Before I could draw my sword, a deep, bored voice floated down to us from an adjacent cliff.

"They're under my protection, Cora."

He sat about ten feet above, his legs dangling from the side of the cliff. He looked down at us, elbows on his knees and head propped in his hand. He looked our age, with a thin build and brown, shaggy hair. His frayed clothing was even more threadbare than the girl's. A leather pack hung over one shoulder, torn and dusty from repeated use. His yellow-orange eyes met my curious stare and he winked. I gasped—those were the eyes from the cave. "I'm afraid you'll have to find your fun elsewhere."

"Asher?" The girl's eyes widened at the newcomer. Her mouth twisted into a sneer, disgust transforming her features as she studied him. "What are you doing with outsiders? Finally lost your mind wandering solo?"

"Our plans are our own," Asher said with a smirk. "Why don't you run along to your master."

"Don't presume to give me orders, pup!" the girl spat. The angry furrow between her brows aged her several years. "If your pets are too stupid to stay out of our territory, we get to play with them."

"If I'm not mistaken, Cora," Asher's bored voice held a hint of a growl, "they're not in your territory."

"Perhaps not yet," Cora purred, her head tilting from one side to the other. "But territory lines are changing. And they want to come play, isn't that right, Toreth?"

The giant wolf drew my attention as he looked from Blaine, to Flora, to me. When his black eyes locked on mine, a numbness spread through me. I tried to look away—to blink—but I couldn't move at all. I couldn't even breathe. I was frozen in place.

Until I started walking.

I took a step toward the wolf, then another. I tried to stop—to dig my heels into the dirt—but my legs weren't listening.

What the hell?

Something slimy coiled around my muscles, forcing me forward. There was another presence in my body, an oil that squirmed its way under my skin. Someone else was controlling me. I wanted to scream.

Help me!

It was no use—I was already out of my friends' reach. My lungs constricted even as my heart pounded against my ribs. I walked closer to my inevitable death with each unwavering step. I couldn't even look away from the wolf's eyes to see my friends one last time. That cold, metallic black was the last thing I would ever see.

I almost preferred the fire.

Strong arms looped around me, preventing me from taking another step. As hard as my body fought to get away, those arms held like iron bars. Relief cut through my panic even as I struggled against my protector. I never thought I'd be so happy to be grabbed unexpectedly. Safe. I was safe.

Blaine had rescued me. I was going to be okay.

The arms spun me around so I was no longer looking at those terrible, cold eyes. As soon as the contact was broken, I could breathe. I gasped a ragged breath like I just surfaced from deep underwater. I flexed my trembling fingers and sobbed in relief—I was in control of my own body again. I sagged against Blaine, using him for support as my breath rasped in and out. My eyelids fluttered as a wave of exhaustion crashed over me. I clasped the sturdy arms and fought to stay conscious as dark spots swam in my vision.

Wait . . . when did Blaine get so muscular?

"Don't worry, little human. I've got you." The quiet voice in my ear made me stiffen. That was *definitely* not Blaine.

Because Blaine and Flora were standing in front of me. They were in the same spot, arms half stretched toward me as if to grab me. They weren't moving. Were they frozen as I had been?

I tensed again as I looked over my shoulder. Brilliant orange eyes gazed down at me. No, not orange. Gold. Gleaming gold with flecks of silver. They stood out, wild and bright against the tanned skin of his narrow, almost sunken face. I hadn't noticed how thin he was from a distance—much too thin for someone of his build. His brown hair had streaks of dark red running through the messy locks. Everything about him screamed *feral*.

Why was I just . . . looking at him?

"Are you alright?" His gaze flashed to my trembling hands, still clutching him for support. My nails dug into his skin, but he didn't comment. Didn't pull away. He spoke calmly, as if we had all the time in the world. As if there wasn't a demented child and her murderous wolf just yards away. As if my friends weren't frozen by the same power that previously held me captive.

"My friends!" I snapped out of whatever had frozen my brain. "They need help!"

I tried to pull away, but I was too weak. Too tired. Without the support of his arms, I would have been a pile on the ground. I was helpless—at the mercy of this stranger. My whole body shivered uncontrollably.

"They're fine." His arms didn't budge. I wasn't sure if he even registered my movement. "We're just moving a bit faster than they are. I figured you might need to catch your breath after Toreth's assault." A soft growl crept into his words. I would have shuddered had my shivering not already grown violent.

I looked around him to see Cora and Toreth frozen in place—just like Blaine and Flora.

"I . . . w-what?"

"Breathe. You'll feel better soon."

My lungs obeyed. I focused on breathing in and out and not on the stranger that was studying me so intently. Even as I leaned on him for support, I felt my strength returning, my heartbeat slowing, the shaking in my limbs calming. I studied the arms wrapped around my waist, counting the faint white scars that peppered his skin. He smelled like the sea. His warmth radiated into my back like sunshine on a clear day. Against my better judgment, my body began to relax.

"What happened?" I asked, looking back into those burning gold eyes.

"I'll explain later." He glanced back at Cora and Toreth. "I can't hold us at this speed for much longer. Can you stand?"

I tried to get my legs underneath me, but it took a few tries to stand on my own. Eventually, I was steady enough to take a small step away. He still held my hand, like I might fall at any moment and he was ready to catch me.

"Are you ready?" he asked.

I wasn't.

"Wait," I said. "Who are you?"

"You are terrible at answering questions, little human." He huffed a laugh. "I told you before, I'm nobody important."

He turned around to face Cora and Toreth, stepping in front of me to act as a shield, hand still holding mine.

"I'm ready," I lied.

He squeezed my fingers, then released my hand.

A wave of heaviness swept through me—was that magic?—and Blaine and Flora scrambled up beside me, swords drawn.

"What the hell, Rose?" Blaine hissed, but his eyes were still on Cora and Toreth. "You can't just stroll into danger like that."

"I didn't—"

A growl from the wolf cut off any further discussion. I peeked around Asher's large form. The girl was no longer smiling.

"You'll regret this," she snarled in her child's voice. "You better keep a close watch on your *pets*." She spat the word, then glanced at me and smirked. "We'll be waiting."

Asher's quiet growl vibrated through me as Cora and Toreth melted away into the scenery. Once they were gone, Asher faced us and held his hands up, palms toward us. He took several steps back, distancing himself from our group. I was confused at his actions until Blaine advanced, putting himself between Asher and me, sword raised and eyes hard.

"Blaine, stop." I grabbed Blaine's arm. "He just saved my life."

"He what?" Blaine lowered his sword a few inches but didn't put it away.

"He . . ." I swallowed. Asher *had* saved my life—that wolf would have killed me. I wrapped my arms around myself to hide my trembling hands and forced myself to take slow, even breaths. I felt all three sets of eyes on me while I pulled myself together.

"He's a lycanthrope!" Flora hissed, as if I didn't realize. Blue energy crackled at her fingertips and a strong wind picked up around her.

"And you're an elf," I said more calmly than I felt. If only I could get my hands to stop shaking.

"You don't understand, we can't trust him."

"Are we just supposed to distrust people who aren't like us without giving them a chance?" I asked, standing up straighter. "If so, Blaine and I shouldn't be here. Really, Flora, you're being extremely small-minded."

The three of them gaped at me as I pushed past Blaine and walked up to Asher. I stopped a few feet away and extended my hand to him, proud that the tremors were barely visible anymore. He was taller than I realized and I had to crane my neck to look up at him. He had about eight inches on me. He looked at my hand and cocked his head. I blushed.

Of course he didn't know what a handshake was.

I hesitantly took his right hand in mine, then shook it up and down once.

"My name's Rose," I said. "I'm a human. It's nice to meet you."

"Asher. Lycan. The pleasure is mine." He studied me, tilting his head in the other direction. The expression was still animal but less predatory than Cora's had been. "You aren't from these lands."

"What makes you say that?"

"I expected that," he looked pointedly at Flora, who was actively glaring at Asher, then to our still clasped hands. "Not this."

I blushed deeper as I pulled my hand from his, but I didn't back away. He flashed me a crooked smile.

Blaine put his sword back into its sheath.

"Blaine!" Flora hissed, sword still drawn.

"Rose is right," Blaine said with a shrug. "He deserves a chance. He did scare the others off—I got some weird vibes from them. We wouldn't have made it away from those two without a fight otherwise." He looked at me. "Why did you just walk off like that?"

I shivered, remembering that helplessness, and wrapped my arms around myself again.

"I couldn't control myself. When I made eye contact with that wolf, I . . . I was trapped. I couldn't look away. I couldn't stop. I . . ."

I looked into Asher's burning eyes and knew he could read what I couldn't say.

I would have died.

"What happened?" I asked.

"Some of us have . . . certain skills." Asher's lip curled in disgust. "Toreth has the ability to control those without strong mental shields. It's a vile power. One of the most corrupt. Cora can change her outward appearance. She isn't as young as she appeared."

"Do you have a skill?" Blaine asked, genuine interest on his face.

"I'm very fast," Asher said. In my opinion, that was quite the understatement. "That's how I got to . . . Rose so quickly." His gaze briefly flicked to me when he said my name. "From there, it was easy to break the eye contact necessary for Toreth's control."

Blaine sized Asher up for a moment, then he stepped forward and extended a hand toward the lycan. Asher looked him up and down but awkwardly took Blaine's hand and shook it once.

"Thank you," Blaine said, "for helping my friend. I'm Blaine."

Asher cocked his head.

"He just wants to kill her himself," Flora muttered.

"I could have done that hours ago," Asher said with a tight smile. "You're exposed along these cliffs. Why are you in the Howling Peaks, anyway?"

"We're looking for something," I said. Flora gave me an exasperated look. "What? He knows this place better than we do. Maybe he can help."

"That's a great idea!" Blaine agreed. "We're looking for—"

"Blaine!" Flora hissed. "Don't tell him what we're doing! We were ordered to secrecy."

"We were ordered to keep this quest from the *elves*," I countered. "And, as you already mentioned, Asher is not an elf."

Flora glared at me. I crossed my arms and stood my ground.

"Flora," Blaine said, "we've already been here for hours. We're no closer to the stone than when we got here. We can't go home empty handed."

Flora shifted her glare from me to Blaine. There was a long silence before she finally rolled her eyes.

"Whatever. You're the Veritace." Flora threw up her hands. She stalked away, muttering 'stupid idea,' but stayed within easy earshot.

"We're looking for a gemstone," Blaine said, turning to Asher and drawing his sword enough to expose the green Argem. "It's about this size. Do you have any idea where it might be hidden?"

"That sword . . . that's Peacekeeper." Asher's eyes went wide. "Are you the Savior?"

Blaine frowned. "The Savior?"

"The one who will travel the land to collect the Argems, overthrow a great oppressor, and unite the land to bring peace?"

"Unite the land?" Flora interrupted. "He's meant to reestablish the treaty. That's the only way we'll have peace."

Asher's gaze narrowed on Flora.

"Call me Blaine," Blaine said with a chipper smile, trying to relieve the building tension.

Asher blinked a few times. He opened his mouth to speak, then closed it again. "No title?"

"Nope. Just Blaine."

"You . . . aren't what I expected." Asher shook his head. "I can bring you to the Argem."

Eight

ASHER ALLOWED BLAINE TO walk in front of him, showing deference to his 'Savior' even when it would have been easier to lead the way. After guiding us through a hidden cave with twisting passages breaking off in countless directions, Asher pointed us to a massive underground cavern. The space was so large, our flashlights—which Asher kept looking at strangely—couldn't illuminate the opposite wall.

Asher gestured to an ominous looking path that descended into darkness. "Legend says the Argem is at the end of this trail, but I've never been past this point."

Flora huffed. She had watched Asher with mistrust for the past hour.

"It's down there." Blaine kept a hand on the cave wall as he frowned into the dark cavern. "I can feel it."

My legs screamed at me after hiking the uneven terrain all day, but we were so close to our destination. I was pushing myself to the limit to keep up. Perhaps that's why when my foot snagged on a crack, I couldn't recover and ended up sprawled on the ground.

"Rose!" Flora kneeled beside me and checked me over.

"I'm fine," I said, embarrassed with the three of them circling around me. "I just tripped."

I tried to stand, but my sluggish legs betrayed me. This time, I landed hard on my knee.

"Let me help you." Flora offered me her hand. With her assistance, I was able to stand, although I was still wobbly.

"You're exhausted." Asher's golden eyes narrowed at me. "You haven't recovered from earlier. You should rest."

"We're almost there." I pulled away from Flora. "I'll rest when we find the stone."

"And what if we need to fight or run after we get the stone?" Blaine ran a hand over his dark stubble. "It's dangerous to push yourself too far when we don't know what's ahead."

"We're running out of time. If we don't get the stone soon, we'll have to turn around empty handed." I wasn't even supposed to be here—I refused to slow them down.

"We can always come back here if we can't find it this time."

"It might not be that easy now that people know what we're looking for." Flora glanced sidelong at Asher.

"I'm not worth risking the fate of multiple worlds," I said. "Let's go."

Blaine's gaze narrowed. "Rose—"

"I'll protect her here," Asher interrupted. "She can rest while you two get the Argem."

Flora scowled. "You think we'd just leave her with you?"

"I'll keep her safe. You have my word."

"Your word means nothing, you—"

"Flora!" Blaine admonished. He looked at me with a grimace. "Up to you, Rose. You comfortable staying here with Asher?"

"Yeah." I sighed, resigned. The longer we stood here, the more exhausted I felt. "Just don't do anything stupid."

Blaine smirked, but Flora glared at Asher for a long moment with narrowed eyes. Asher nodded once and Flora stalked down the path without another word.

Asher and I watched the bounce of the flashlights playing over the walls as they left. I settled down against the cave wall, facing the expanse of the cavern. Why was I so tired?

"You're bleeding." Asher was probably annoyed to have to stay behind. I bet the weak didn't live very long here.

I blinked, then rolled up my pant leg to examine my stinging knee. Just a scrape—nothing that would hinder me. It wasn't bleeding *that* much.

"How did you know?" I looked up at Asher. He studied the dark passageway, a wary look on his lean face. He didn't look dangerous. What was Flora so afraid of?

Asher's gaze fell to the scrape on my knee then traveled to my face. "I have a good nose."

"Oh." He could *smell* my blood? I shook my head. "We should've brought a first aid kit."

"A what?"

"Um, it's a kit," I said, lamely, "with, like, bandages and wound cleaning stuff. You know, in case we get hurt."

"Oh." Asher's eyebrows pulled together. "Yes, you absolutely should have brought one of those. You're lucky you haven't needed one yet."

I started to pull my pant leg back down, but Asher stopped me. He reached into his bag, pulling out a strip of frayed, off-white cloth, then gestured at my leg.

"May I?"

I nodded, but held my breath as he approached and knelt in front of me. His deft fingers were gentle as he wrapped the fabric around my knee and tied it.

"Thank you," I breathed as he finished and pulled back from me.

The tension around his eyes softened for a moment when he smiled at me, but then it was back. "We don't want anyone else scenting your blood. If they know you're weakened, they'll attack."

He sat beside me, not too close, but within reach. I closed my eyes and leaned my head back against the rough wall.

"I don't understand why I'm so tired." I sighed. "I'm not as fit as I used to be, but I should be able to at least keep up with Blaine."

"You fought Toreth pretty hard. I'm surprised you made it this far without needing to rest. It requires a lot of energy to fight a wolf's skill. You're stronger than you look."

I cracked an eyelid to glance at him. He seemed relaxed, but his eyes scanned the darkness around us. I had so many questions but didn't know the best place to start. I didn't want to make him mad. What was the etiquette of asking about one's race in this world?

"So . . ." I began, "you're a werewolf?"

"A what?"

"Sorry, a *lycanthrope*?" The unfamiliar word sounded odd as it left my mouth. His ever-observant eyes slid to mine and he raised his brow, wary.

"Yes."

"How long have you been a lycan?"

"My whole life," he said, looking a bit confused. "Do people just change races where you're from? That's not how it works here."

"There are no lycanthropes where I'm from." That I knew of, anyway. A week ago, I would have bet there wasn't a portal to another world in my friend's pantry. "But there are stories about werewolves—sorry, lycans—that say if one bites you, you turn into one on the next full moon."

He burst out laughing. The sound echoed through the cavern before he could clamp a hand over his mouth to muffle it.

"I'm sorry," he said, still snickering. "That's just so ridiculous."

"It's just something I've heard!" I couldn't help but smile at his laughter.

"Unfortunately," he said, getting himself under control again, "we're stuck in the race we're born into."

"I see. But you can transform into a wolf?"

"Yes."

"Any time you want? Or just during a full moon?"

"Any time, though it does use quite a bit of energy." He looked at me oddly. "What's this about the full moon?"

"Probably just another thing the stories got wrong." I pulled my knees up and put my arms around them.

A comfortable silence settled over us as we gazed into the dark abyss together. A bouncing light along the far wall pierced the darkness. Blaine and Flora were making quick progress without me to slow them down. We watched the light until it disappeared again.

"Any more questions?" Asher's voice was soft.

"Loads, but I didn't want to be rude."

"Ask away," he said, eyes back to scanning the darkness for any danger.

I pursed my lips. "How old are you?"

"Eighteen, I think." He frowned. "Maybe nineteen. I haven't needed to keep track."

"We're about the same age then, though time works differently here than it does on Earth."

"Earth? Is that what your home is called?"

I nodded. His eyebrows shot up.

"What?" I asked.

"Nothing," he smirked. "I'm just shocked you actually answered one of my questions."

"This isn't an interrogation." I smiled. "You're welcome to ask me questions too."

His smirk deepened. "Am I?"

"I just may not answer if I don't like the question." I shrugged. That caused him to chuckle.

"Well then, I'll start with something easy." He thought for a moment, then nodded toward the descending path. "How did you meet those two?"

"School. I moved to the area recently and met them on my first day. You have school, right?"

"Yes," Asher said. "We aren't total barbarians. Though, I'll admit I haven't been in a while."

"Is the wolf transformation . . . painful?"

He shrugged. "It's nothing I can't handle."

"That sounds like a yes."

"Yes," he conceded. "The shift is painful, but it's worth it. What's on your nails?"

I held up my right hand, splaying my fingers to reveal the remnants of purple paint on the chewed nubs. "Nail polish. Why, do you want some?"

He held out his own hand beside mine. "I don't think purple claws would make me very menacing."

I laughed. His finger brushed mine and I pulled my hands away, trying not to think about the strength coiled in the muscles of his exposed forearms. My smile slipped away. Toreth had forced me to use all my strength to get away from Asher on that plateau. As much as I struggled, I couldn't budge from his grasp.

"Asher . . ." I wrapped my arms around myself. "How did you know we needed help?"

"I . . ." He hesitated this time and gazed into the cavern. "I followed you." He glanced at me. "You really shouldn't be running blindly into caves. Anything could have been waiting inside."

"Yeah, I know." I grimaced. "I was . . . distracted. I'm glad I ran into you, though."

He studied me with a curious expression. I jolted, realizing what I said.

"Instead of something bad, I mean!" I blushed, and he raised a brow.

"I was only going to make sure you made it out of the Peaks in one piece, but when I caught scent of those two . . ." His fingers arched against the ground, nails scraping the rock. "I figured you might need a hand. I was hoping to scare them off from a distance, but when Toreth tried to take you I . . . I couldn't just let that happen."

"You knew them?"

"We used to be in the same pack. I . . . had disagreements with the alpha, so I broke out on my own."

"What about your parents?"

"I never knew my dad. My mom was killed when I was young." His eyes took on a faraway look. "They killed her. I left."

"Toreth and Cora killed her?"

"No. Though, they didn't do anything to help her. It's . . . complicated."

"I'm so sorry about your mom. You must be lonely."

"I'd rather be alone than be part of a pack like that." His lips turned up into the ghost of a smile. "Though, it is nice to speak to someone. It's been a few years."

"I was alone for a while, too, before I met Blaine and Flora. My parents died. Recently."

His gaze slid to me. I looked away, but continued. Why was it easier to speak to this total stranger than it was to my friends?

"A few months ago, there was a fire at our house. I got out, they didn't." I stared at the cool expanse, but flames danced in my vision. My eyes stung with tears, but I refused to cry. Asher already thought I was weak.

"I'm sorry," he said. The silence stretched between us. When I still didn't respond, he asked, "Can I show you something?"

I nodded.

"Put out your torch."

I did as he asked, flipping the flashlight's switch and throwing us into the complete, pressing darkness only found deep underground. Several moments passed and nothing happened. I looked to where I thought Asher sat, my eyes uselessly straining against the darkness.

"If you're gonna kill me, please make it quick."

"I'm not going to kill you." His voice was soft.

I smiled. "Just a joke." *Though it might be something of a relief.*

Just as I was about to ask what we were doing, I saw the outline of Asher's face. It faded into view, staring at me with concerned eyes. I looked away, only then noticing little patches of light.

The rock behind us was glowing. Not the entire wall, but a network of splintering channels within the stone glowed yellow with some sort of bioluminescence. I ran my fingers along the pathways on the wall between us. The longer I stared, letting my eyes adjust, the farther the glowing pattern extended. If I focused hard enough, I thought I could almost see the far edge of the cavern.

"This is so cool!"

"You're cold?" Asher's nocturnal eyes glowed in the darkness.

"Oh, it's just an expression." I smiled. "It means it's beautiful, or awesome."

"I see. I suppose it is both of those things. I used to come here a lot when I was a kid. My mom showed me this place the first time she told me of the Savior. She made me promise to keep it secret. I thought it was just a legend. After she . . ." He swallowed. "I sat here for hours studying these stones. I felt drawn to them. Like I was meant to be here. I tried finding meaning in the light patterns. I never did."

After a few minutes in the comfortable darkness, I gained the courage to ask the question pestering me.

"Asher, why did you save us? You could have just let us die. Instead, you made trouble for yourself."

"Is that how I come off? As a coward who would just let someone die right in front of me?"

"I mean . . . I didn't mean it like that. I just . . . I'm sorry."

His silence was deafening. I hugged my knees closer to my chest. *Nice going, Rose.*

"You asked."

My breath caught. "What?"

"You asked for help."

I did?

In the darkness, his reflective eyes were all I could clearly make out. I thought their glow might be creepy, but they were strangely comforting.

"Thank you." My throat was tight. "I don't know how to repay you. I really thought I was going to die." I closed my eyes to force back the sudden tears blurring my vision, horrified as the traitorous moisture ran down my cheeks. Was his wolf vision good enough to see my momentary breakdown?

A gentle, calloused finger brushed my cheek, wiping away the stray tear. My skin heated at the unexpected touch, but I didn't pull away. It happened so fast, and then his hand was gone, leaving me unsure if it actually happened.

"You owe me nothing, little human," he said. "You're safe now, you should get some rest."

Was I safe? I didn't know this man. He had saved me, sure, but did that mean I could trust him?

Could I ever trust anyone again?

He wouldn't have bothered wrapping my leg if he meant to kill me.

I nodded, settling in to try to make myself comfortable, and closed my eyes. After a few minutes of silence, the exhaustion pulled me toward unconsciousness. Before sleep claimed me completely, another question popped into my head.

"What do you eat?" I blurted.

Asher barked another laugh. "Similar things as you, I expect. Just a bit less cooked."

He was still chuckling as I drifted off to sleep.

Nine

Blaine

*T*HANK GOODNESS *I* ALREADY *got the green Argem. This descent is insane.*

The path down was treacherous, with its uneven ground and steep drop to one side revealing the massive cavern. The balance I gained from the Argem had already saved me from falling—twice. I still surprised myself with my reactions, even after a few days with this knowledge. What new piece of the puzzle would I get from this stone?

Would I still be me when the puzzle is complete?

"I don't trust him," Flora said, breaking our silence. She glanced up to where we left Rose with Asher about an hour ago. I could barely see the faint glow of the flashlight as we looped around the outside of the cavern.

"Why not?" I asked.

"Lycanthropes are tricksters. They play the long game to get what they want."

"Have you ever actually met one?"

"Well, no," she admitted, "but, Blaine, we can't rely on someone like him. Our task is too important."

"He led us here, Flora," I said, gesturing around. "Do you think we could have found this place without him?"

"If the Argem is even here!" she hissed. "What if he's leading us into a trap?"

"I already told you, I can feel it." The pull was getting stronger the farther down we went. "And if he wanted us hurt or dead, why step in when those other two tried to attack us?"

"Like I said, maybe it's part of the long game."

"Rose said he saved her life," I said. "I don't know if you noticed, but it takes a lot for her to open up." She still never talked about her past. "We should give him a chance."

"I can't read him," Flora said, "and I loathe the way he looks at her."

I rolled my eyes and continued toward the cavern floor, following the pull of the Argem. We reached the bottom of the cavern without issue and crossed the rocky floor. I looked up to search for Rose's flashlight but couldn't see anything. We must have been really far below them. It was going to take us forever to climb back up the trail.

"There it is!" Flora said, pointing ahead as a lone pedestal came into view, yellow gemstone glinting in our flashlight beams.

I hurried closer as Flora swept her flashlight around, looking for any potential threats or traps. The pedestal was shoulder height, the Argem delicately perched on top. I reached out to the stone but paused about a foot away.

"What's wrong?" Flora asked.

"I just feel like I'm going to pick up this stone and a giant boulder is going to come falling from the ceiling to crush us."

"What makes you say that?" She looked around. "I don't sense any magical traps here."

"I've watched too many movies, I guess." I shrugged and drew my sword. This close to the Argem, there was an almost magnetic attraction between it and Peacekeeper.

I reached out and grasped the stone. I hesitated for only a moment, but when nothing happened, I placed the Argem into the blade. The stone clicked into place and a wave of yellow light broke away from the sword, ruffling my clothes in a phantom breeze and briefly illuminating the cavern.

I blinked. One moment I was in the large cavern, the next I was in a rustic log cabin. The smell of firewood perfused the air and old, handmade furniture adorned the room. I sat at the table, eating a meal with my family. But wait—these people weren't my family. Why were my hands so small and pale?

I blinked again. I was in a half-plowed field, my horse refusing to take another step until she ate her dinner. Smoke was a good worker, but she definitely had a mind of her own. I stood there, holding her bucket of grain while she happily munched away. At this rate, I wouldn't be finished with this field by nightfall. I frowned up at the storm clouds on the horizon.

I blinked again. I was at the university—in astronomy class—when the pretty brown-haired girl beside me leaned over to pass me a slip of parchment. Her smile was sweet, but she had a mischievous glint in her eye. I opened the note.

Dinner tonight? -Alora.

I grinned, compiling a list of the best taverns in Kelmoran.

I blinked again and my vision blurred. I was seeing through tears. I cradled Alora in my arms. I held her tight as grief coursed through me. She was older, but not by much. She was still devastatingly beautiful—even in death. Blood soaked her clothing, making the fabric dark. Sorrow ripped open old wounds in my chest. It was too soon, she was too young. I slipped the golden ring from her finger with trembling hands.

I blinked again. My sword cut cleanly through my opponent, splattering his comrades with sticky red blood. The beauty of the invading elves did not protect them from death by my blade. My Alora was more beautiful than any of them. They were the reason she was dead. I screamed my rage as I sliced into yet another foe, blood splashing into my face.

I blinked again. This year's Warriors Academy class was a sorry lot. Not only had these young men never fought in a battle, but they had never even held a sword in their short lives. I had a difficult task ahead of me this time. The war effort needed every able-bodied soldier, so no willing volunteer was rejected. My job was to give them the skills to make it home to their families. I picked up my sword.

I blinked again. I was too old for battle. Perhaps this meeting would accomplish something, unlike the others. There were too many deaths on all sides. I glanced at Silva across the table from me. The witches were almost wiped out after the last skirmish. If we couldn't establish peace now, I didn't think their race would survive.

I blinked again. Hassen was examining the Argems set into Peacekeeper's blade. I hated to dismantle the sword, but no single race should hold its powers. The blacksmith nodded. He'd only just started this forge, but he was the only elf I trusted for this work. I glanced at his shifty-eyed apprentice who watched from a distance.

"I can do it," Hassen grumbled, his disdain over dismantling such a magnificent sword apparent. "But it will take some time if you still want the blade to be usable."

I nodded. "Work your magic, Hassen. I have more important things to do than watch you sweat."

The elf smirked.

I blinked again. I was holding the yellow Argem in a huge underground cavern in the newly formed lycan territory. Arturo assured me the stone would be safe here. He promised only his direct lineage would know its location.

Whatever happens, I thought, presumably to my future self, *have faith in yourself. You'll find a way.*

Have faith.

I blinked again. I was in that same cavern. No time had passed, but the stone wasn't on the pedestal. I looked at Peacekeeper. Why were two of the stones in my sword? Why . . . why did my hands look so delicate and dark skinned? These were the hands of a young man. Hands that had never worked a plow. Hands that had never fought a battle. Hands that had never taken a life.

I collapsed.

"Blaine!" Flora's panicked voice echoed off the stone walls.

Blaine. That's me. I'm Blaine.

"Yeah," I groaned, sitting up from where I had fallen. Her hands touched my face as she checked me over for wounds. "I'm fine."

"What happened?" she asked, sitting back on her knees.

"I . . ." I shook my head, trying to organize my racing thoughts. "I just got a bunch of Alaric's memories."

Ten

Rose

I WOKE TO THE sound of footsteps and heavy breathing. I opened my eyes to veins of yellow crystal glowing in the walls around us. Artificial light from a flashlight bobbed and bounced from not far away. My heart skipped a beat when I realized what—or who—I was using as a pillow.

"Sorry," I mumbled, pulling away from Asher.

"It's no problem, little human." He turned on my flashlight, illuminating his smirk. I scooted farther from him and ran a hand through my hair. He stood and paced away just before Flora and Blaine came into view, breathing hard. Blaine walked over and plopped down beside me.

"I'm so out of shape," he panted. "Next time I'll rest and you can go get the stone, yeah?"

"I'm not the *Veritace*." I laughed. "You found it?"

Blaine nodded and pulled his sword far enough from its sheath to show off the yellow Argem.

"What did you get this time?"

"Mostly memories." He frowned. "I'm still trying to work out what they mean. It's weird remembering things I didn't do. It's even weirder remembering myself with a different face."

"Was it a cute face, at least?" I asked.

Blaine looked thoughtful and wobbled his hand in a 'so-so' gesture.

"It can't be any worse than the current one," Flora piped in. Blaine put a hand to his heart in mock hurt and Flora huffed. "I'm only joking. Your face is acceptable, for a human."

"Such high praise," Blaine deadpanned, but he quickly changed the subject. "Unfortunately, there was nothing in this stone as useful as the sword skills from the last one."

"Better luck next time." I elbowed him. "Maybe the next Argem will give you the power of flight."

Blaine's eyes widened. "Or invisibility."

"Or—"

"We should head back." Flora put her hands on her hips and glared at where Asher stood a few steps away.

"Are you ready?" Blaine asked me, eyes growing serious.

"Yep." I got to my feet. I was feeling much better after that nap. I offered my hand to Blaine, who sighed dramatically, then took it to pull himself up.

"You good enough to carry me?" He draped his arm around my shoulders. "I'm exhausted."

I grimaced. "I don't know if I've ever been that good."

Good people didn't burden everyone around them.

"Do you need to be carried?" Asher asked. There was a strange glint in his eyes as he looked between Blaine and me.

"Nah, man." Blaine stood up straighter but kept his arm around me. "I'm only joking."

"Um, should we get going?" I pushed Blaine's arm away and walked past Flora, where she stood watching the guys with a thoughtful expression. I heard them follow me up the path.

When we got to the mouth of the cave, the sun was beginning to set. Asher made us wait while he did a sweep of the area to ensure there would be no ambush. Thankfully, the way was clear and we made it back to the edge of the Howling Peaks without any trouble. Once at the border, Blaine, Flora and I waited yet again while Asher scoped out the surroundings for danger.

"He's pretty useful to have around, isn't he?" I murmured to Blaine.

Blaine cocked an eyebrow and Flora narrowed her eyes. Both of them looked in the direction Asher had disappeared.

"He did help us find the yellow Argem." Blaine rubbed his chin. "He might be a valuable asset to the team."

"You can't be serious." Flora's voice dripped with disdain.

"I think I trust him," Blaine said. "He reminds me of someone from Alaric's past. A lycan that he knew."

Flora glared at me for a moment. The look penetrated my soul.

"I want it noted that I don't approve. Just because he hasn't betrayed us yet doesn't mean he won't."

Blaine snorted. I turned away to hide my grin. Asher soon returned from his self-appointed scouting mission.

"You should be safe to cross," Asher said, "but move quickly. We may have been followed."

"Thanks for all your help, Asher," Blaine said. "We couldn't have done it without you."

Asher smiled and nodded to Blaine. The motion was almost a bow.

"May your hunt be fruitful, Savior," Asher said in farewell. The sincerity of the formal statement hung in the air as Blaine studied the lycan.

"Asher . . ." Blaine hesitated, as if fearing rejection. "How would you like to come with us?"

Asher froze. "Really?"

"Yeah." Blaine shrugged. "You've been nothing but helpful. I'd love it if you'd give us a hand with this quest. We may have . . . underestimated the danger involved."

"I . . ." Asher glanced at me, then at Flora. He narrowed his eyes and nodded to Blaine. "It would be my honor, Savior."

"I thought we agreed—no title, please." Blaine smiled. "Come on, let's get out of here."

Blaine led the way, striding back to Elvanar with confidence. Asher only hesitated for a second. He spared one glance behind before taking a breath and following us into the openness, then into the forest beyond.

We walked as far as we could through Elvanar before night fell and we were forced to make camp. By the time we had a fire going, the darkness laid around us like a woolen blanket.

I handed out some granola bars to everyone from my pack. Asher looked at the colorful wrapper in confusion, so I showed him how I opened mine on the perforated end. He followed my lead and took a bite, grimacing a bit.

"That's . . . different." He took another bite.

"Yeah, sorry," I said. "We didn't come very prepared."

"Dad's got a stockpile of emergency rations in his bug-out bag." Blaine stretched out by the fire. "I should have borrowed some."

I frowned. "Your dad has a bug-out bag?"

"Yeah, he's a bit of a doomsday prepper." Blaine smiled. "Mom makes fun of him for it. She says if she can't eat an actual meal, she'd rather starve. She's a great cook, though." Blaine's stomach grumbled. "Gosh, I can't wait to eat something warm."

"You know," Asher began, "I could hunt for some food."

"I wouldn't turn that down," Blaine said, sheepishly looking at his granola bar.

"Really?" I asked. "Aren't you a picky eater?"

"I've eaten a lot of weird stuff here." Blaine shrugged. "Or, at least, I remember eating things. It's strange, I don't know."

Flora and I stared at Blaine, but Asher grinned. He shoved the rest of the granola bar in his mouth and stood to walk into the forest.

"I'll see what I can find." He pulled off his shirt as he went and dropped it on the ground.

"Do you need any help?" Blaine called after him.

"No thanks." Asher paused, turning partially back toward us. Flora and I glanced at each other and quickly looked away. Flora's pink cheeks mirrored the heat I felt in my own. That half-naked wolf was *fit*—no wonder he thought I was weak.

"I'm faster on my own." He disappeared into the darkness. A moment later, I felt a faint shudder go through the air.

Blaine frowned as he cobbled together a makeshift spit for the fire. Once done, he drew his sword and began a feather flow. He opted to do the movements slowly, focusing on building strength over stamina. It seemed Flora and I weren't the only ones to notice our new friend's fitness level far exceeded our own.

Flora and I joined Blaine in the flow. My arms were shaking with exertion when I felt that same shudder again. Shortly after, Asher entered the clearing holding two dead rabbits. He left his shirt on the ground while he lay the rabbits on a rock. Digging in his pack, he pulled out a knife and began skinning one of them.

"You two keep going." Blaine sheathed his sword. "I'm going to help with dinner."

We dutifully continued our exercises while he joined Asher and pulled a knife from his pack. Blaine took over preparing the other rabbit as if he had done it a million times. Before I completed my flow, the meat was cooking over the fire.

When Blaine returned, he scrutinized our stances. After making an adjustment to Flora's feet, he took my aching arm and turned it slightly.

"You'll be less fatigued if you hold it like this. Your bicep is bigger and stronger than the muscles in your forearm." He touched the muscles in my arm as he named them. It was purely instructional, but I still forced myself not to shy away. The weight of another set of eyes made me glance at the campfire. Asher leaned against a tree in the firelight, his attention fixed on us.

"Dude, can you put some clothes on?" Blaine called, following my gaze.

"Am I making you uncomfortable?" Asher raised a brow.

"You're distracting the ladies."

"Am I?" He smirked.

Those predator's eyes slid to me, reflecting the light of the fire. I forced my gaze to my sword and continued the exercise.

I heard him chuckle as he stood up and walked to where he left his shirt. I was determined not to look in his direction.

"I don't think I've ever seen you blush so much," Blaine said, so quietly only I could hear.

I wrinkled my nose, but didn't respond. After a few minutes, I finally finished the feather flow and put away my sword. Blaine caught my shoulder before I could walk away. When I tensed, he pulled his hand back quickly.

"Sorry . . . I—" He scratched his chin. "I just . . . never mind."

I frowned. "Blaine, are you—"

"Smells like the food is ready," Flora said as she strolled by us toward the fire. "Will you two love-doves be joining us?"

"Love . . . doves?" Blaine asked, blinking at her.

"Isn't that the phrase?" Flora frowned. "Maybe I got it wrong."

Blaine chuckled. "I think you mean *lovebirds*."

"Don't even joke about that in front of Martin." I groaned, rolling my eyes and starting towards the fire. "He's already got wedding plans in his head for Blaine and me."

"Yikes," Blaine said with a laugh. "Too bad for you, I've got my eye on a certain cheerleader."

"Blaine, you know Krista Winchester does not even know you exist," Flora stated, bluntly.

"Maybe not yet," Blaine whined, "but I'm the Veritace."

"I'm not sure she would know what that means, even if you could tell her," I teased.

"She's not the brightest flower on the bush, is she?" Flora smiled.

"She doesn't have to be smart," Blaine complained, sitting down and taking a rabbit off the spit. "I have enough brains for the both of us."

"If you say so." I sat down next to him, across the fire from Asher, who was watching our interactions with perplexed amusement.

Flora took a seat to my other side while Blaine and Asher dished bits of rabbit onto some flat rocks we were using as plates.

"So none of you are . . . mated, then?" Asher asked.

Blaine choked on his rabbit at the question.

"No," Flora said. "We're all just friends."

"I thought maybe you two . . ." He gestured between Blaine and me.

"Why does everyone think that?" Blaine asked, exasperation clear in his voice. "Does Krista think I'm taken?"

"You act like being with me would be torture," I said flatly. Blaine's eyes widened and he froze with his food halfway to his mouth.

"N-no, th-that's not what I meant!" Blaine stuttered out, obviously trying to backpedal. "I just . . . oh." I couldn't help the smile that broke through my mask and Blaine huffed a laugh. "You got me."

He elbowed me softly in retaliation. I chuckled and elbowed him back.

"That right there," Flora pointed between the two of us, "is why people think you're dating. That, and the fact Rose doesn't let anyone else within five feet."

My laughter withered in my throat. Was I that obvious?

"That was uncalled for." Blaine shot Flora an icy glare.

"What?" Flora asked. "You asked a question. I was just answering it."

"That's enough," Blaine commanded.

Flora's brows knit together, but she shrugged one shoulder. Asher's narrowed eyes met mine. I glanced down at my food rather than hold his gaze.

"What are you doing?" Flora's affronted tone made me look up. She glared at Asher.

"Shielding her. What are *you* doing?" Asher glared right back. "It's taboo to invade another's mind, not to mention rude."

"What's happening?" Blaine looked back and forth between them.

Asher raised his eyebrows. "They don't even know?"

"I was going to tell them, I just . . ." Flora flipped her hair over one shoulder. "I didn't want to overload them all at once."

"Is that what you tell yourself to justify it?"

Flora's face reddened. "I've been shielding them."

"Not well enough," Asher growled. "Toreth almost took her."

"That was a momentary lapse—"

Asher cut her off with a dark laugh. "How dare you invade their privacy and not even protect them properly."

Flora huffed. "I wouldn't have to protect them if mongrels weren't so deceitful."

Asher flinched, then bared his teeth. "Stay out of people's heads, elf."

"Whoa, guys." Blaine held out a palm to each of them, acting as the mediating force. "I don't know what's going on, but I don't love where this argument is heading."

"She's been listening to your thoughts without your consent," Asher snarled.

"She's been *what?*" I stiffened.

"You can do that?" Blaine narrowed his eyes at Flora. "You've *been* doing that?"

"I . . ." She frowned. "Yes."

"Why?" The hurt resonated clearly through his voice.

"You humans are so different, I just wanted to understand you." Flora looked down. "I wanted to fit in. I'm sorry. I shouldn't have invaded your privacy like that."

Blaine stared at her for a few heavy seconds. When he spoke, his voice was hard. "Don't do it again."

"I promise." Flora flashed him a grateful smile.

I didn't comment. A weight formed in my chest at the thought of Flora barging into my head. How often had she heard my thoughts? How much did she know? I suddenly felt exposed. I gripped the rock-plate on my lap, trying to hold it together. My knuckles went white. I didn't want to break down in front of my friends, so I pushed my betrayal down. I'd deal with it later.

I cast around for a safe topic but came up blank. The silence between us grew unbearable. Tension tightened my chest and

I shrank in on myself. I blinked rapidly to push back tears. If I couldn't distract myself soon, I'd—

"Aren't elves vegetarians?" Asher interrupted my thought spiral.

Blaine tensed, obviously ready for the fighting to start up again.

Flora scoffed. "Where did you hear that?"

"Stories, I guess." His gaze found mine and the knot in my chest loosened. I took a deep breath and offered him a grateful smile.

"I thought all lycans traveled in packs," Flora accused.

"Most do," Asher said.

"It's interesting that we've all heard stories about each other's races, but they're all pretty stereotypical." I sniffed at my meal. The smokey meat made my mouth water.

"Hey, what have you guys heard about humans?" Blaine asked through a mouthful of rabbit. Asher and Flora exchanged a look.

"Mostly that you're rash," Flora said at the same time Asher said, "Herd mentality."

It was mine and Blaine's turn to look at each other.

"I mean, they aren't wrong." Blaine shrugged and took another bite. "This tastes almost how I remember, but it's missing *something*."

Flora and Asher were already eating, so I took a bite. The taste was similar to chicken, but gamier. It wasn't too bad, and it was nice to eat something warm. The rabbit thawed the pieces of me that froze up today.

An easy silence fell over us. I was staring into the campfire, lost in my thoughts, when Flora spoke up.

"Thank you for the meal," she said, nodding to Asher and Blaine. "It's time we got some sleep. Since we're still in an infected section of Elvanar, we should rotate keeping watch. I can go first, who wants to go next?"

I volunteered to take the next watch, then Blaine, then Asher. Still exhausted from the day's events, I said goodnight to everyone and slipped into the tent I would be sharing with Flora. I settled into my sleeping bag and was asleep before my head hit the pillow.

It felt like I just closed my eyes when Flora woke me for my shift. It took me a minute to drag myself out of bed, but once I stepped out of the tent, the cool night air rejuvenated me a bit. I walked over to the fire where Flora was sitting. It was mostly embers, but as I approached Flora threw a log onto it to keep it burning. A camping kettle sat in the embers, keeping warm whatever had been brewed inside it. I yawned and sat beside Flora.

"You can't fall asleep," she said.

"I know. Is that tea?" My voice was rough with sleep.

She picked up the kettle, poured some into a mug, and handed it to me. I took a sip and sighed at the pleasant heat.

"Mmm. Peppermint. My favorite."

"I know." She hesitated. "That wolf, today . . ."

Any residual sleepiness fled at the memory of Toreth. I shivered and clutched my mug tighter. I tapped my toes inside my shoes to prove to myself I was still in control.

"It was terrible," I squeaked, almost inaudibly. "It was like there was something under my skin—something slimy—and I couldn't do anything about it. I had to do whatever it wanted." I pulled my knees to my chest.

Out of the corner of my eye, I saw Flora shiver. She reached out slowly and took one of my hands in both of hers. There was a soft glow between her palms and a gentle feeling of warmth spread up my arm, then through the rest of me. Peace settled over me.

"Any skill that a lycanthrope thinks is bad must be terrible to experience." Flora shook her head. "I can't even imagine what you're feeling right now."

I gave a bitter laugh. "Haven't you been in my head? Seems like you could imagine pretty well."

"Rose, I—"

"How much have you seen?" I glared at her, but couldn't hold her gaze for very long. The look on her face told me everything I needed to know. As much as I wanted to let go of her hand, I wasn't ready to give up the glowing peace it provided.

"I'm so sorry for invading your mind," she said. "For bringing you into this. For everything. Once we get you home, if you don't want to come back, we will understand."

"Just sit at home knowing you guys are in danger?" I asked with more bravado than I felt. "Not a chance."

"Why am I not surprised?" she asked wryly. The glow faded and I pulled my hand from hers. "I'm exhausted. Wake Blaine in a few hours. And yell if you see anything strange."

"I will." I hesitated. "Goodnight."

"Goodnight," she mumbled as she slipped into our tent.

My watch passed without incident, though I jumped at every strange noise. When the time came, I woke Blaine by tapping the fabric of his tent. I heard a groan from inside, then a muffled, "Be right out."

I returned to my spot at the fire to wait for him. Blaine came out of the tent and made his way over to me, yawning. He sat next to me and stared groggily into the fire.

"There's tea in there if you need it," I said, pointing to the kettle.

"Da'rett," he said, then he shook his head, seeming to wake up. "Uh, I mean 'thanks'."

"What was that?"

"I'm pretty sure I can speak a different language now," Blaine said, rubbing his face with his hands.

"You . . . wow."

"Why would Alaric put an entire language into the stone?" he asked, staring into the fire. "And all those memories . . . we've only gotten two Argems now, but there was a moment in that cave when I had trouble differentiating my memories from his. What happens when I have all four stones? Will I stop being me when I have all his memories?" He fiddled with his sword belt. "And if I do become him, will I be able to hide it from my parents? I don't think they would handle losing me very well."

Here I was, wrapped up in my own silly problems, while my friend was struggling with something huge. How could I be so selfish?

"Hey, that's not going to happen." I bumped my shoulder against his. "You have us here to ground you back into yourself if you need it. I won't let you lose yourself. I care about you too much for that."

"I know you do." He opened his arm and I scooted closer to let him pull me into a hug. He held me there for several moments, obviously needing reassurance, so I squeezed him back. His lowered voice sounded softly in my ear. "But can we be sure about Flora? I mean, her whole mission was to find me so I could do this quest. Wouldn't she want me to turn into him?"

"I don't know." I thought back to Flora's comforting hand around mine. If she didn't care about me, she wouldn't have bothered wasting magic, right? "She's still our friend. I'm sure she doesn't want to see you get hurt."

"You're right, I have to believe that. What other choice do I have?" Blaine sighed and I felt the tension drain from him. He pulled back abruptly, releasing me. "Oh, shit, Rose. I'm sorry. I know you don't really do physical contact."

"What? N-no, you're okay," I stammered, weirdly more uncomfortable with this line of conversation than I was with the hug. "It was actually nice."

"If you don't stop blushing like that, I'm going to think you're into me, too." He joked, trying to lighten the conversation. He opened his arm to me again, offering, but not pushing.

"Whatever, Blaine, you're like my brother." I rolled my eyes, but I did lean into him, letting him put his arm around me. "Wait, what do you mean 'too'?"

He looked pointedly at the tent where Asher was sleeping and then back to me, raising his eyebrows.

I shrugged, blushing deeper.

"Thought so." He chuckled. "Thanks for listening. You know, if you ever need help with anything, I'll be there for you, too."

"Thanks," I said, resting my head on him.

"Any time, sis," he said, squeezing me gently. After sitting like that for several moments, he asked, "Are you still awake?"

"Barely."

"Go to bed, Rose," he said, pulling me to my feet. I complied and walked back to my tent, passing out quickly.

I dreamed that I was still talking to Blaine around the campfire, laughing and joking. I threw a log into the flames, and when I looked at Blaine, it was a stranger's face looking back at me. I jumped to my feet and backed away. The stranger, face lined with age over a graying beard, stared at me with icy blue eyes before fading back into the darkness.

"You were supposed to ground me, Rose." Blaine's disembodied voice sounded weak. "Why weren't you there for me?"

I'm here! I tried to shout, *I'm right here!* I screamed the words, but no sound left my mouth. The darkness surrounding the circle of light cast by the fire turned sinister as wisps of shadow crawled toward me.

No, no, no, no, no. . .

I was surrounded. The first oily tendril to reach me wrapped around my ankle. It was the same slimy evil from earlier, the one that had taken over control of my body. I tried to yank my foot away, but it held strong. The shadow was hard as iron as it pulled me to the ground and into that inky blackness.

I bolted upright, struggling to escape my restrictive sleeping bag. I could still feel that shadow tendril wrapped around my ankle. It was so dark, I didn't know where I was until a soft light from behind me illuminated the inside of the tent.

Flora watched me from within her blankets as I tore away at my bedding. Her hand was open with a small orb of white light floating over her palm. I only relaxed when I uncovered my ankles. They were bare, with no sight of those shadows anywhere.

"Just a dream," I breathed as I fell back onto my pillow, heartbeat still thundering. When the light began to fade, my breath hitched involuntarily. Flora's light orb was gone, but now her hand itself was glowing. She extended it towards me, and craving the warmth from earlier, I took it.

Peace floated through me and my heart rate slowed. I might forgive Flora for the mental intrusion if her presence could chase away the darkness clouding my dreams. This time when I fell asleep, I didn't dream.

Eleven

Blaine

I woke from a fitful sleep in an empty, sunlit tent. My dreams had been a strange mix of Alaric's memories and my newfound fears. Talking with Rose had helped calm some of my nerves, but it hadn't solved anything. What could she actually do to keep me from losing myself? I could save this world, but who would save me?

When I emerged from the tent, Asher and Flora were already sitting by the fire and talking quietly to each other. The smell of roasting rabbit made my stomach growl.

"Good morning," I said cheerfully. Their somber faces looked like they could use some cheerfulness. "That smells delicious."

They both stared at me. Asher with confusion, Flora with outright shock.

I sat down with them around the fire. "Is everything okay?"

"I'm sorry," Asher said. "I'm not very good with the old language."

Damn, I did it again. "I didn't realize I was speaking a different language." I hesitated. "That was English, right?"

"It was something I could understand. So it was probably whatever you call your language."

"Wait, what? Aren't you speaking English?"

"No." Asher smirked. I looked at Flora. She shook her head.

"We're from completely different worlds, Blaine," she said. "Did you really think we all evolved the same language? Even Asher and I speak different dialects."

"How can we understand each other?" I asked.

"It's an old magic from the time before the treaty granted each race their own land."

"Banished us to our own prisons, more like," Asher muttered.

Well, that was a new take on the treaty.

"This magic is so powerful that it spans all of Silaris," Flora continued. "Everyone here is affected. It acts as a translator in your brain, so you can understand any other language."

"That doesn't explain why I could understand you when we first met," I said, "before I came here."

"Yes, well . . ." Flora looked a little uncomfortable. "I may have mimicked that spell on anyone I came into contact with so they could understand me. So your parents, Martin, anyone in my classes . . ."

"Spelling people without their permission?" Asher chuckled darkly. "I thought elves were supposed to be above such tactics."

"I wouldn't have done it if it wasn't necessary." She lifted her chin and glared at him. "I got permission from the Council of Elders."

"Just another example of a bunch of old elves telling us what's okay and what's not, without concern for the people their decisions affect."

"The Council may not be perfect, but they are the only thing between civilization and *savagery*." Her lip curled in disgust as she shot the word at Asher.

"Yes, because *I'm* the savage here."

Flora sniffed. "Anyway, the magic translation doesn't work on the ancient language. My people still use it for highly complicated spells, but no one speaks it colloquially."

"So now that I've been here in Silaris," I said, "am I going to start getting A's in Spanish class?"

"Maybe if you'd actually do your homework," Flora said and I chuckled. "You'll be able to understand people speaking in different languages. However, they will not be able to understand you."

"I'll have to be careful not to slip up and speak in the ancient language around my parents."

"Why don't you tell them what's going on?" Asher asked. "I would think your parents would be proud for their son to be the Savior."

"You don't know my parents," I said. "They're extremely overprotective. If they knew I was out here doing anything remotely dangerous, they would ground me for a year."

"Ground you?"

"Essentially locking me in my room for my own safety."

"They would imprison you for following your fate?" Asher frowned. "*That's* savage."

"It's not as bad as you're probably picturing." I shrugged. "They just don't want me to get hurt . . . so yeah, telling them is not an option. I'm a legal adult and I barely convinced them to let me go away for the weekend. They think we're staying at some safe campground with Flora's parents. I would never be able to get away if my parents knew I was practicing with a sword or running into lycans. No offense, Asher."

Rose emerged from her tent while I was speaking. I waved a greeting as she took a seat. She flashed me a brief smile, but lost it as she stared into the campfire, absently chewing on a nail. Was it my imagination, or was she even paler than yesterday?

"I get it." Asher's brows pulled together as his gaze tracked Rose's movements. "We're dangerous."

The four of us ate our small breakfast then broke down the tents. After we cleaned up our camp site, the girls and I went through our morning feather flow. My muscles were sore from trekking up and down all those hills yesterday, but the stiffness soon faded from my awareness as I focused on the movements.

When I finished, I gave the girls guidance on their forms. They were both pretty awkward with their swords, but I knew in time and with more strength they would get the hang of it. I had trained plenty of students in the sword . . . well, Alaric had, anyway.

After the girls completed their solo flows, the four of us set off for home. We walked in relative silence until we left the tainted section of forest. When we finally emerged from the gloom, the birds sang louder and the colors appeared brighter. I sighed, and some of my tension melted away in the bright sunlight.

Flora and Rose showed similar reactions, but Asher paused. He looked around with narrowed eyes and cocked his head.

"It's very green here," he said as a pair of brightly colored birds flitted past him. "I've never seen anything quite like it."

"We don't have anything like it in our world, either," Rose said to him. She was quieter than usual. Maybe she was still tired. "We saw some deer the other day that didn't even run from us when we got close. I think we could've reached out and pet them."

Asher smiled ruefully. "That won't happen while I'm with you. Most animals see me as a predator. They can sense the wolf."

"As do most elves," Flora said. "We will have to be careful not to frighten anyone as we approach the city." She glanced at him. "On second thought, you shouldn't go too near the city before we can warn the Council. Your presence could indicate that the treaty has been broken."

"Your people don't know?" Asher raised an eyebrow.

I saw Rose attempting to hide a smirk in her palm before Flora could notice. From the clipped tone Flora responded with, I didn't suspect she was successful.

"Most do not," Flora said, then her shoulders fell as she deflated, "but that wasn't my decision and there's nothing to be done about it."

"We know, Flora." I offered her my elbow as a show of support. Flora twined her arm through mine. She flashed me a rueful smile when I managed to catch her gaze. I tried to ignore my body's response to her being so close. How could someone still smell so good after not showering for three days?

I led her onward at a quicker pace, letting that conversation lapse. I didn't want another fight to break out. Not when we were all so tired. In Alaric's experience, that's when someone was most likely to say something regrettable.

I glanced back to where Asher and Rose walked, confirming I had put a little bit of distance between us and them. Asher had mirrored my chivalrous pose and he and Rose were walking arm in arm. I wasn't sure how to feel about that.

"Are you doing okay?" I kept my voice quiet so the others couldn't overhear. When Flora finally answered me, her voice was rough.

"I don't know what's right anymore," she said, matching my volume. "I had a long talk with *Asher* this morning." I noted the grimace at his name, but at least she didn't call him *the lycanthrope* this time. "I still don't trust him but . . . maybe he isn't the monster I was led to believe. He saved Rose's life back there. I can't believe I let my prejudices cloud my judgement." She closed her eyes and let me lead her as she used her free hand to massage her temples. "The flaws he pointed out in our current system . . . I thought I was doing the right thing bringing you here, but what if I'm wrong about that too? I don't want you or Rose to get hurt."

"We might get hurt." I thought back to Alaric's more painful memories. "Heck, we probably will, but we'll be careful." Flora narrowed her eyes. "We have to fight this evil, Flora. If not us, who? I would rather be the one who gets hurt than shirk the responsibility onto someone else."

Flora sighed. "I just need some rest and things won't seem so dire anymore. I spent a little too much energy last night taking away Rose's nightmares."

"Nightmares?" I glanced behind us again. Rose and Asher were deep in their own conversation, not paying us any mind.

"The poor thing woke up in a panic last night. I'm not surprised with what she went through with that lycan."

Flora shivered and I felt my lip curl. I had asked Asher for more details about those wolves when we switched shifts last night. How dare Toreth try to take my friend? If we met him again, I would be prepared. I'd—

"Now that she has her own personal bodyguard," Flora pulled me from my thoughts, "she should be okay. Lycans are protective over their packs, and I'm pretty sure that's what Asher sees us as now."

"What makes you think that?"

"The way he looks at her. I thought it was predatory before, but now . . . I think he just notices things. He noticed when she was under that other lycan's control and grabbed her. He noticed when she was exhausted and offered to protect her for us. He said that's what wolves do for their packs—provide safety for the weaker members."

"Rose isn't weak." I frowned. *Damaged, sure, but who wasn't?* "I just thought he might be attracted to her."

Flora stiffened and almost missed a step. She looked over her shoulder, then ahead again, eyes narrowed.

"I hadn't considered that possibility," she said. "That might cause some issues going forward. Though, it will all but guarantee her safety."

"As long as she's safe and happy, I don't see an issue with it," I said. "We all deserve some happiness."

"I don't disagree, but is an interworld relationship something any of us are ready for?" Something in my chest panged at that statement and she heaved a weary sigh. "It's been a long weekend. I'm ready for a break."

Rose

My legs refused to pick up the pace, even as the distance between my friends and me widened. It was all I could do to keep the same speed. My legs ached from all the hiking and I had blisters from my boots.

To my surprise, Asher stayed by my side. He studied my friends, then offered me his arm, just as Blaine had for Flora. I hesitated, then took it with both of mine, grateful for the extra support.

The position brought us close as we walked. I laid my head against his arm and took a deep breath, closing my eyes and allowing him to lead me. He smelled like saltwater and sunshine, like a day at the beach. Like safety.

I looked up to see him studying me. His soft eyes were brimming with questions.

My cheeks burned. *What was I doing?*

"Sorry!" I tried to pull away, but he placed his hand over mine before I could.

"Don't be sorry, little human. You can use me anytime you need support." He looked down at his hand covering my rigid fingers. "I'm sorry I made you uncomfortable yesterday."

I narrowed my eyes. Uncomfortable? Asher had saved my life then sat with me when I couldn't keep up with my friends. I felt safe around him. Too safe.

"We lycans don't find nudity shameful," he continued, "but I will respect your culture and shift out of sight."

Oh.

"That's not . . . I mean . . ." I didn't know what I was trying to say.

He raised an eyebrow and waited for me to continue. I looked away, cheeks burning again.

"I just . . . I didn't expect . . . you're very . . ." I exhaled. Just spit it out, already. "You look good without a shirt on. That's all."

"Oh, is that all?" There was humor in his voice, but I was too mortified to even glance up at him. "Little human, look at me."

I bit my lip and stared at my boots.

"Please?" At his plea, my gaze snapped to him like it was pulled by a string. His expression wasn't self-satisfied or mocking, as I expected. It was . . . sincere. "I think you're very cool."

I blinked. "I'm cool?"

"Yes. You know, awesome and beautiful."

There was a weird flutter in my chest. Alarm bells rang in my head—whatever I was feeling, it was dangerous. I didn't really know this man. For all I knew, he could be just as bad as—

"W-what?" I forcefully cut off my train of thought.

"You paid me a compliment." He cocked his head. "Am I not allowed to return the favor?"

He was just being nice. No one was beautiful after all the hiking and camping, except maybe Flora. Three days without a shower—or a mirror—and I was genuinely afraid of how my hair looked.

So why was I disappointed?

"I said something wrong." Asher shook his head and sighed. "I'm out of practice speaking with people. I offended you."

"You didn't." I looked up at him and forced a smile.

He frowned at me for a moment, then turned his gaze forward with a contemplative look.

"I'm bad with words. Wolves don't often use verbal communication, just thoughts or physical touch. I must admit, it's been a while since . . ." He looked down to where I held his arm. He ran a gentle finger along my knuckles before covering my hand again with his. "I didn't realize how much I craved contact. Not until I put my arms around you on that plateau and you just felt so . . . perfect."

I tripped over my own feet. Asher steadied me, then scowled ahead with narrowed eyes and a clenched jaw. I looked up too, just in time to see Flora checking up on us.

Nosey elf.

I felt that wave of heaviness hit me again. It swept over me, raising goosebumps on my arms. Asher halted, pulling me to a stop beside him. I tensed until I saw Blaine and Flora frozen mid-stride in front of us. This was his magic—his speed. I relaxed again.

"I asked Blaine what Flora meant yesterday about you not letting people get close to you." He faced me, holding my hand between both of his. Did his spell require contact? Or did he just want to hold my hand? My heart stuttered at the thought. "Blaine said you don't like to be touched."

I didn't know how to respond.

"I can see it. You flinched when Blaine grabbed your shoulder yesterday. Even when you see it coming, you're still tense. It's obvious you aren't comfortable. Then, other times . . ." Asher looked down at our joined hands. "Other times you lay your head on my shoulder and fall asleep beside me." His golden eyes were piercing when he looked up. "Why?"

"I don't know." I felt my cheeks warming again and cast around for a new subject. "What else did Blaine tell you about me?"

"That he thinks of you like his sister, so not to even *think* about hurting you, or else he will kill me."

I snorted, and Asher's lips quirked up at the sound. His smile faded, however, as he spoke his next words.

"He also speculated that someone must have hurt you because you rarely trust people."

"I—" My gaze drifted to the grass. I thought I was hiding it better.

"The one who hurt you . . . are they still . . . are they in your life?"

"No." I shivered and my fingers curled into his without conscious thought. "Not anymore."

"Good," he growled. I felt him exhale, tension draining away. We stood like that for several moments. I couldn't bring myself to look up at him yet. I wasn't sure I wanted to see what emotions he wore.

"You can trust me, little human," he said. "I know you don't have a reason to, I know you don't know me, but I promise you can. I would never do anything to hurt you."

I dared a quizzical glance up to find him studying me. He looked so sincere. I wasn't ready to believe the words—I probably wouldn't ever trust anyone so completely again—but I appreciated the sentiment.

I felt one side of my lips pull up into a half smile. "That means a lot."

The smile that bloomed across his face was soft. Gentle. So at odds with the rest of him, all angles and hard lines.

"We lycans are protective." He placed my hand on his arm again and let go of his magic. The heaviness swept through me as Flora and Blaine started moving. A smirk played at the edge of his lips. "Some consider it a character flaw."

I couldn't help but laugh.

"That's not the worst flaw in the world."

Twelve

"YOU SHOULD REMAIN HERE," Flora said to Asher when he and Rose caught up to us. We had slowed our pace considerably as we approached the Rift. "I'm not sure you will survive the journey."

Asher raised his brows, eyeing the swirling vortex of light.

"There was a restriction put on the Rift," Rose clarified for him. "Apparently Blaine and I risked dying on our first trips here."

I threw a pointed look at Flora and she rolled her eyes, exasperated.

"I see," Asher said slowly.

"I'd offer my loft," Flora said, "but it's pretty close to town . . ."

"No problem," Asher said. "I'll set up camp here and await your return."

"Here, take this tent." I handed him the one on my back.

"Thanks, though I probably won't use it."

"Better to have it and not need it than to need it and not have it," I said, using my dad's favorite preparedness quotes. "We'll come back tomorrow after school. I'd like to practice more with my sword."

"It will be mid-morning here when we return," Flora said. "Don't let anyone see you."

Asher shot her a scathing smile. "I know how to be discreet."

Flora frowned at him. With a sigh, she strode into the Rift. Her form flashed into pure color, then she disappeared.

"Whoa." Asher stepped back.

"Yeah, best not to get too close. It likes to pull you in." I demonstrated by standing next to it and letting the light tendrils reach out and grab me. "See you later, alligator!" I managed to say before the familiar feeling of falling through nothing surrounded me. Then I was stumbling into Flora's kitchen, the sunlight through the windows much dimmer here than in Silaris.

"You left her there alone?" Flora asked, incredulously. Her hand was outstretched, obviously expecting Rose to need the support when she came through.

"She's fine," I said, moving out of the way. "She was right behind me."

As I said it, the vortex swirled into the shape of a person. Rose laughed as she stumbled forward, but Flora caught her before she hit the hard kitchen floor. Rose's breathless laugh turned into a cough. She took a few labored breaths before reaching into her pack and taking a puff from her inhaler.

"I had to explain to Asher what an alligator was." Rose giggled, once she could breathe again.

I smiled. "You're welcome."

I dug my phone out of my backpack and powered it on. After the start screen, notification after notification sounded. All of them were texts from my mom with messages varying from "I hope you're having fun" to "Text me as soon as you get service." I rolled my eyes and typed out a text.

Not thirty seconds after I pressed send, my phone chimed again.

I shoved my phone into my pocket and grabbed my keys from where I left them on the counter.

"It's getting pretty dark outside," Rose said, glancing at the clock on the stove that read 8:24 pm. "Martin is probably wondering where I am."

"I'll give you a ride," I said. "Flora, we'll see you at school tomorrow."

"Sounds good," she said, stifling a yawn and locking the door behind us.

I pressed the unlock button on my key fob and slid into the driver's seat of the red sedan, throwing my pack in the back seat.

I reached over to unlock the passenger door for Rose. There was something wrong in that door mechanism that I hadn't found time to fix yet. She slid in with a sigh and dropped her pack on the floor at her feet.

"I'm exhausted." Rose laid her head back against the headrest and closed her eyes.

"Same." I pulled out into the street. "I feel like I could sleep for a week."

"I feel like I could shower for a week."

Laughter bubbled up my throat. I totally agreed.

"I noticed you needed your inhaler back there." I looked at her sideways. "Did something in Silaris take your breath away? Or someone, perhaps?"

She rolled her eyes. "When I first got back here it was just . . . hard to breathe. I must have gotten used to the clean air in Silaris."

"Did you use the inhaler at all while we were there?"

She grew thoughtful. "I don't think so."

"Interesting." I pulled up to the curb in front of her house.

"Thanks again, for the ride," she said, reaching for the door handle.

"Hey, Rose?" I asked. She looked back at me, eyebrows raised in question. "Call me if you need anything, okay? Anytime."

She smiled.

"Right back at you, Veritace," she said, opening the door and getting out of the car.

"Mom, Dad, I'm home!" I called when I walked into the kitchen.

"Hey, hun!" Mom called back over the music drifting out of the living room. "There's some pizza in the fridge if you're hungry!"

I grabbed a piece of homemade pizza from the refrigerator and ate it cold. Processed pepperoni was *much* better than unseasoned rabbit. I stuck another few pieces on a plate and warmed them up in the microwave. Once I had my plate of pizza, I walked into the living room.

"We missed you this weekend. Did you have fun?" Mom asked. Her long, dark brown hair, only a shade or two deeper than her skin, was tied in the same loose braid as it always was in the evenings. She sat cross legged as she relaxed on the couch with a romance novel. "Tell me everything."

"It was a blast," I said. "We wanna go back again soon."

"Can I see pictures?"

I froze mid bite but recovered before she noticed.

"I actually didn't take any. I think Rose did, so I'll get them from her tomorrow at school. I had my phone turned off all weekend since there was no service anyway." I made a mental note to fabricate some pictures of our camping trip.

"We should do a family camping trip without phones some time." Dad rubbed a hand over his buzzed hair. His brown eyes were hidden behind the glare of thick glasses as he stared at the case files on his lap. "We can test out some of the bug-out bag gear."

"I'll stay here with my shower and my bed, thank you," Mom scoffed. "You two can go right ahead."

After finishing my plate, I bid my parents goodnight and jumped in the shower, ready to scrub off the grime of the last few days. The hot water was heavenly on my tight muscles and I had to shampoo my hair twice before it finally felt clean.

I stepped out of the shower and wrapped a towel around my waist. My reflection stared back at me from the large mirror on the wall. I looked the same as I always did, except something felt off. I was different somehow. Was it the reflection of Alaric in my new memories staring back at me? I almost expected to see his blue eyes instead of my own.

Maybe I'm just crazy.

I shook my head and finished getting ready for bed. I went to my room with the intention of texting Flora and Rose, but sleep claimed me before my head hit the pillow.

I woke the next morning to my alarm blaring. I rolled over and hit the snooze button, then laid in bed, trying to enjoy five more minutes of rest. When I heard my alarm again, what felt like seconds after the first one, I knew I had been successful. I noticed a text from Rose before I could hit snooze again.

Rose

Could you pick me up this morning?

Me

Yeah. Be there in 20.

I pressed send and heaved myself out of bed.

When I pulled up to Rose's house, she was already waiting on the front steps, her school backpack over her shoulders. She pushed herself off the steps, somewhat stiffly, before shuffling to my car. I reached over to open the passenger door and she slid into the seat.

"Thanks for the ride." She looked better today, but the dark circles under her eyes matched my own. "I have blisters from my boots and my legs are killing me."

My whole body was sore when I got out of bed, but it was loosening up as I moved. I wanted to do another feather flow this morning, but I left my sword at Flora's. I couldn't carry a sword through a small college town. My parents would think I had lost my mind.

"No problem," I said. "Your text made me get out of bed."

"Happy to be of service."

We pulled into the school's main parking lot just in time to rush to our respective first classes. Flora didn't have a class this early, so she wouldn't show up for a few more hours.

The morning passed in a blur, classes melding from one to the next. I kept to myself and didn't interact with people, barely following the lectures. That wasn't my typical attitude, and I heard some of my classmates snickering and looking in my direction. I thought I heard the word "hangover" and smiled to myself. Let them think I was at some rager last night. A frat party, maybe. That was a better excuse than any I could have come up with at this point.

I didn't feel fully awake until lunch time, when I was due to meet Flora and Rose in the Student Union. I sat down at our usual spot to wait for them as other students filtered past.

"Hey, Owens!" someone called from nearby. I looked up at the sound of my last name to see Brad, Tyler, and Rylin passing my table. The three guys graduated with me last year. They were on the high school football team, so I rarely spoke with them, but we were on friendly enough terms.

"It looks like you had a good time last night," Brad laughed.

I nodded with a grimace, and they chuckled as they continued on to their table. Unfortunately, Rose and Flora arrived as the guys passed.

"Give me a call next time you plan on getting drunk with pretty girls, Owens," Brad winked and gave the girls a crude once-over. Flora arched a scathing eyebrow, but Rose stiffened. "I could show you how to have a *really* good time."

"Dude, inappropriate." Rylin pushed Brad past the girls before I could even rise from my seat. "Sorry," he said, continuing to push Brad away. "He's an idiot, sometimes."

"Try all the time," Tyler interjected.

"Man, shut up!" Brad shoved Tyler. They moved past, leaving Flora and Rose to make their way to the table.

"I don't like that guy," Flora said as she and Rose sat down.

"Yeah, he's a piece of work," I agreed.

Rose

Brad's comment was just a teenage boy's stupid attempt at humor, but those eyes . . . something had flashed in Brad's eyes—something cruel. It reminded me of *him*.

It's because Asher asked about him. I was thinking about him yesterday and my mind is playing tricks. That's all.

"Rose?"

I blinked, pulled from my thoughts. Blaine and Flora were staring at me.

"Sorry, what?" I asked.

"Are you not hungry?" Blaine asked.

"Oh," I looked down at my plate to where the food sat untouched. "Right, yeah. I must still be tired from the weekend." I shoveled the food into my mouth. When did I get so famished?

"Do you still want to come tonight?" Flora asked. "It's okay if you would rather get some rest."

"I know where the Rift is now. You just try to keep me away."

Blaine smiled and Flora rolled her eyes.

"Then it's settled," Blaine said. "Rose, tell Martin we're studying at Flora's and I'll do the same with my parents. Meet at my car after class?"

Flora and I nodded. I bid goodbye to my friends and took one last bite before standing to throw my trash away. I took the back door out of the Student Union to head toward the Creative Arts building. On entering the classroom, I was greeted by the usual exuberance of the art teacher.

"Welcome, welcome!" Mr. Engle said happily as students filed into the room. "I hope your day has been fantastic so far! Are you ready to work on some calligraphy?"

I smiled and made my way to the back of the room to grab my oversized work folder, then went to my assigned seat to start working. We were practicing the alphabet so we could write and mount a poem for our midterm assignment. I was looping a 'C' when I heard someone behind me.

"Hey, you're Blaine's friend, right?"

I started and looked around to see who was speaking. It was one of the guys from the group at lunch. Before I could do anything more than tense up, he continued.

"I just wanted to apologize for what happened earlier. What Brad said was not cool. He's not really my friend, but we're on the same football team, you know? He's not usually like that."

"It's fine," I lied. "Already forgotten."

"Cool," he said, relieved. "My name's Rylin, by the way."

"Rose."

"Wow, your calligraphy is *way* better than mine. Have you done this before?"

"Nope, this is my first time," I said, looking back to my page. "I think it's all about patience. You can't just scribble through like you can with a pencil."

"Do you think you could give me some tips?" he asked.

"Sure, though I'm hardly an expert."

Rylin brought his supplies to my table and set up across from me. Our conversation was easy, if a bit awkward at first. Soon I was laughing along with him as he told me who—in his *humble* opinion—were the most attractive guys at our college. I didn't know most of the names, but to my surprise, Blaine was in the top ten.

"Wait," I said, "where are you on the list?"

Rylin had an easy confidence that I envied. "Oh, I'm number one, obviously."

Art class passed quickly and Rylin and I walked to the parking lot together. Flora was already waiting by Blaine's car, eyes glued to her phone. She looked up when we approached.

"Thanks again for the help, Rose." Rylin kept walking when I stopped beside Flora.

I waved to him, then I leaned on the hood of Blaine's car. I looked over Flora's shoulder as she resumed a game on her phone. We weren't waiting long.

"Hey, don't scratch the paint!" Blaine called as he approached. I looked at all the scratches already on the car and raised my eyebrows. Blaine was a careful driver, but the car's previous owner had already done a number on it. "Nah, I'm just kidding. Hop on in."

"Can we just get out of here, please?" I asked, still a little on edge from the day. Flora rolled her eyes as she climbed into the back seat.

"Someone is eager to go hang out with our new friend," Blaine said, getting in the car and starting it up.

"I'm just ready to leave before we have any more run-ins with Blaine's high school buddies," I said. Blaine was right, though. I was excited to go back to Silaris.

"Speaking of that," Blaine said, "did I see you walking with Rylin Spears?"

"Oh, we're in art together," I said.

"So everything was cool?"

"Oh, yeah. Rylin's nice. He even apologized to me for Brad being so weird today."

"Good," Blaine said. "I've known Rylin for a while and always pegged him to be one of the good guys. I'm glad to know I wasn't wrong."

Thirteen

"**D**O YOU THINK I should have ordered Asher's burger rare?" I asked as we got out of the car at Flora's house.

Blaine snorted. "Probably."

"Next time we go by the diner," Flora said, "we'll just tell them to add a scoop of uncooked meat to the bag for our pet wolf."

"I'm sure he'll prefer the burger," Blaine assured me.

Blaine grabbed an extra backpack and a picnic blanket from the trunk of his car and we hurried inside. After grabbing our weapons from the spare room, we went through the Rift.

Blaine went first. The colors surrounded him and he disappeared. Flora nodded for me to go next, so I followed Blaine through. I tried to force myself to relax this time as I fell. Swirling colors shifted to flashes of Elvanar and my feet slammed into the ground . . . followed by the rest of me.

"Ugh!" I exclaimed, propping myself up on my elbows. "Will I ever get this right?"

"You're getting better." Blaine offered me his hand.

I grabbed it, pulling myself up and out of the way with a laugh. Now that we were back in Silaris, I felt lighter. Like there was a weight off my shoulders. I took a deep breath, inhaling the pollution-free air of Elvanar, as Flora made her way gracefully through the Rift.

I looked for Asher but didn't see him. Did he leave already? Did he realize how broken I was and run for the hills? A familiar, depressive weight settled into my chest until Flora spoke.

"It sounds like he's over here." Flora walked into a grove of trees. I followed, trying to keep my relief from my face.

We walked for a few minutes before coming upon the tent and the smoldering embers of a campfire. There was a pile of gathered firewood and kindling set to one side of the campsite and two large logs were arranged as seats around the fire. Asher was sitting on the ground, leaning on one of the logs. He used a claw-tipped index finger to whittle a stick as we approached.

"Wow," Blaine said, "you've been busy."

"I had plenty of time." Asher threw the stick into the fire. His dark brown hair was damp, making it look almost black and hiding his red streaks. He was wearing a different set of clothes, but these were just as ragged as the ones he was wearing the last time we saw him. When his gaze fell on me, his lips twitched upward. My stomach fluttered.

Stop it, I told myself. *It's just a smile. It doesn't mean anything.*

"We brought dinner—er, lunch maybe for you," Blaine said, looking at the position of the sun directly overhead. He laid the extra backpack over by the tent before taking a seat on the unoccupied log. "And some extra supplies in case you need them."

Flora handed Blaine his burger and fries and took her grilled chicken wrap from the bag before handing the rest of the food to me. She went and sat on the log next to Blaine, leaving the only open seat next to Asher. I walked over, a little self-consciously, and perched on the log.

"We didn't know what you liked, so we just got you a burger and fries. I hope that's okay," I said, handing him a foil wrapped burger and cup of fries.

"Thanks, you didn't need to do that." Asher took the food from me and inspected it.

I pulled my burger out of the bag and unwrapped part of it, leaving the foil on as a handhold. Asher mimicked my actions and took a bite. His eyes widened as he chewed.

"This is much better than whatever was in the crinkly wrapper you gave me the other day," he said. "What is it?"

"Cow," Flora said. "Wrapped in vegetables and bread."

"I don't think I've ever heard of cow," he said thoughtfully. "It's delicious."

"Agreed," Blaine said, already halfway through his burger.

As we ate, we discussed our next steps and tried to come up with a plan. We had two more Argems to gather—one from the humans and one from the witches. The map was marked with a circle on the western coast of the witch territory, but there was no indication of where the humans might be keeping the stone.

"I guess we should probably try for that one, since we know where to start looking," Blaine said, pointing at the southwest quadrant of the map. He shrugged. "Maybe the knowledge I gain from that stone will tell us where the next one is."

"I wonder how the Council knew where the others were but not the one in the human territory," Flora pondered.

"I think the more important question right now," Blaine said, "is when can we make the trip? I don't think we're going to be able to travel across all of Silaris in one weekend."

"Good point," I said. "This stone looks way farther from the Rift than the one in the Howling Peaks."

"I don't understand the issue," Asher said. "Why can you only go on certain days?"

"We have school on five of the seven days of our week with only two days off on the weekends," Blaine said. "We can skip a few classes here and there, but not very many."

"I can't skip classes," I said. "I'm on scholarship, remember? If my grades slip, I'll lose the money and have to drop out."

"So no skipping classes." Blaine nodded.

"What about fall break?"

"Oh, yes!" Blaine exclaimed. "Of course, how could I forget? That's only three weeks away."

"How many days do we get off?" Flora asked.

"The entire week," Blaine said. "Plenty of time for an extended camping trip. Plus, that gives us a good amount of time to prepare for the trip and for me to get stronger. Speaking of preparation, I've got some swordwork to practice."

Blaine brandished his sword and walked out of camp, just far enough to find an opening in the trees wide enough to go through his feather flow. After completing it once, he reset himself and started at the beginning again, switching up the movements as he went. Flora and I joined in beside him, but I only made it through the movements once. My arms were exhausted. Flora continued to practice with Blaine, the two of them flowing gracefully from one movement to the next, while I claimed a seat on the ground next to Asher and pulled out my homework.

He looked over my shoulder at the math problem I was working through. After I solved the twelfth equation on the page in about as many minutes, Asher interrupted me.

"You're good at mathematics."

I jumped a little at the words. I had fallen into a rhythm and forgotten he was beside me. That wasn't like me, at all.

"Oh, yeah," I let out a nervous laugh. "I mean, it's not hard stuff yet."

"It looks harder than the basics I was taught," he said. "My old pack didn't put emphasis on things like that. They were more interested in making sure we knew how to survive."

I finished another problem. "I don't know anything about survival."

"You've already survived monsters, little human."

I glanced up to find him focused on me. I swallowed and closed my math homework in my textbook.

"I had a thought last night . . . about something you said." I hesitated, but he just cocked his head and waited for me to continue. "You said Toreth's power affected me because I wasn't strong enough."

"No," he corrected, "I said your mental shield wasn't strong enough."

"Right. Can you . . . is that something I could learn? The mental shield?"

"Of course."

"Would you teach me?" I wasn't sure why my stomach tied up in knots.

"Absolutely. Want to start now?"

"Really? Yes, please!"

He stood, offering me his hand. I took it and he pulled me to my feet. We only walked a few yards away from the campfire when he stopped and laid on his back on a particularly soft-looking bit of grass.

"Lay down with me." He gave me a lazy smirk when he saw my doubtful expression. "I promise I won't bite." He hesitated. "Not today, anyway."

When I still made no move, he propped himself up on his elbows.

"This is an important part of the process. It's the only way I know how to teach it. Flora might know a different way. If you prefer to ask her, I won't take offense." The sincerity in his golden eyes convinced me to lower myself to the ground and lay beside him.

"Okay," he said, lying back on the grass again. "Make yourself comfortable and close your eyes."

He put his arms back, hands cradling his head, and closed his eyes. I laced my hands together on my stomach and laid my head back, looking up at the canopy above. A gentle breeze stirred the leaves, causing the filtered sunlight to dance around us.

"Are your eyes closed?" he asked, not opening his own.

I squeezed them shut before I answered. "Yes."

"Good. Now just breathe in," —He inhaled, and then he exhaled— "and breathe out. And again."

I let the deep breaths and his soft voice relax me into a trance.

"Feel the ground beneath your body. The grass and the soil below, all the way down to the rock underneath. Let it be your anchor."

I pictured the layers of the ground below me based on images I remembered from my science textbooks, imagining a tether grounding me to the strongest, most base layer.

"Feel the sky above you," he continued. I felt the slight breeze on my face and the gentle warmth of the sun on my skin. "Now, imagine expanding your consciousness to fill up the sky."

I pushed my mind forward into the distance while staying aware of the ground at my back. We laid there for several minutes. At first, nothing happened. It just felt like I was meditating. Like I was expanding my awareness. I heard the birds chirping and the insects buzzing. I felt the soft grass brushing the sensitive skin of my neck. Then I felt something—something distinctly not me.

Wow, you're good at this too.

"What was that?" I gasped and sat up.

Asher still lay on the ground, blinking up at me. A smirk pulled one side of his mouth up.

"*That,*" he said with some incredulity, "was *you,* reaching into my mind. Are you sure you've never done this before?"

I shook my head.

"I didn't expect you to pick up mind manipulation so quickly," he said. "Try again. I'll put up my shields this time."

I laid back and started the process over again. It was more difficult this time since I didn't want to intrude on his thoughts, but after a minute of listening to him tell me to breathe, I was able to expand my mind again. This time, I felt him lying in the grass beside me. I sensed his mind as an orb, but if I looked closer, my thoughts just slid off of him as if it was a frictionless substance.

"Don't panic and don't pull away," he said. "I'm going to let you into my head."

A crack appeared in the orb and my mind slipped through without meaning to. I saw a few flashes of recent memories through Asher's eyes. Images of the campsite, images of me frowning down at him lying in the grass. Then there were no memories, but I could *hear* his voice in my head.

Impressive, little human. Now for the hard part. You felt my shield, right?

Yes. I projected the thought toward him.

I want you to make your own shield just like that. I want you to pull your consciousness back and separate us with a barrier so you can no longer hear my thoughts.

I'll try. I imagined a sphere around myself, and I imagined his thoughts sliding off my barrier like mine slid off of his.

Can you still hear me? he asked in my head.

His voice was quieter this time. I must be doing something right.

Good, he said.

Hmm. He must be able to hear my thoughts because I didn't purposefully send him that message.

Yes, I can hear your thoughts. I could have sworn I heard laughter in that thought. *Keep trying, imagine a thicker wall.*

I tried not to think of anything embarrassing, like how distracted I had been when he had strolled into camp that day without his shirt on.

Focus, Rose. His voice was louder that time and there was definitely amusement in it. Crap.

I imagined adding layers to the wall of the barrier until it was several feet thick. Only then did his voice in my head go silent.

"Well done," he said aloud. I opened my eyes to look at him, but immediately lost the shield. His consciousness brushed across mine before it pulled away. The sensation made me shiver. "It took me several sessions of just breathing before I could find someone else's mind."

"That's really hard," I complained. "Do you keep your shields up all the time?"

"I do. If you practice enough, it becomes second nature."

"Can we try again?"

Asher smiled. "As many times as you want."

Fourteen

Blaine

MY LIMBS SHOOK WITH exertion as I swung Peacekeeper. I was simultaneously amazed and frustrated with how much I could do with the sword—the knowledge was there, but I was too weak.

I needed to push myself harder—needed to get stronger. I couldn't shake the feeling that however long I practiced wouldn't be enough. *I* wouldn't be enough.

The physical exertion of the feather flow calmed me and gave me an opportunity to think. Back on Earth, Alaric's memories were muted. When I came through the portal this time, it was all I could do to keep standing as the onslaught of memories crashed through my mind again. Was that because of the other Argems in this world? Were they calling out to me, even from this distance, making my connection to Alaric stronger?

I didn't know the answers, so I moved from guard position to parry, parry to lunge, lunge to guard until my body was screaming at me to stop. When I finally sheathed my sword, I looked around. Flora was sitting cross legged in a meditative stance, eyes closed. I stretched my sore shoulders as I approached her.

"What are you doing?"

"Listening," she said. "Grounding myself to the life of the Forest. It's hard to be away from it for so long in your world. Earth drains my energy."

I sat beside her and continued stretching.

She cracked an eye to look at me sidelong. "You need a shower."

"Yeah." I wiped the sweat from my forehead. "I should have brought extra clothes. Tomorrow I might take a shower at your place before I go home."

"Good idea." She closed her eye again. We sat like that for a few moments. "You're getting better with that sword."

"I have all the memories," I said, a slight bitter note in my voice. "It's just about getting the strength back. I wish I could practice more."

"Don't push yourself so hard that you break."

"Yeah, I know. I can't save the world if I'm broken." I sighed, laying back in the soft grass.

"That's not . . . I care about you, Blaine." Flora shook her head. Did she notice how my breath caught in my throat? "I'd rather you not get hurt. Part of me wonders if I should have brought you here at all."

I sat up and bumped her with my elbow. "Whatever happens to me, I'm glad you brought me here. This," I gestured to the forest around us, "is worth the trouble. I can't even imagine going back to before I met you." I reached out and took her delicate hand in mine. "I wouldn't want to."

"I wouldn't either." She smiled. "I've learned a lot in your world that I hope to bring back here eventually. The machines you humans create, the technology, it's amazing. I need to discover a way to integrate them here without poisoning our air."

"If you figure that out, we could really use that technology in my world. Maybe we could help each other."

"I'd like that." She squeezed my fingers. "Come on, we have homework to do if we're going to fix your world."

"After we save yours, you mean?" I laughed as she pulled me to my feet and back to camp.

Rose

As many times as I wanted ended up being three times. On the fourth attempt, I couldn't even summon a barrier and accidentally sent Asher some of my memories instead. When I realized what I was doing, I panicked. Asher closed off his mind to prevent me from sending him anything I didn't want him to see.

"Sorry," I cringed. "I guess I'll have to keep working on that."

"The best way to get better is to practice." He rolled to his side and propped himself up on one elbow. I quickly sat up. The exposed position put me on edge, especially when he was no longer in the same pose beside me. "For now, we should probably head back. We can work on this more tomorrow."

As we made our way back to the campsite, we found Flora and Blaine stretched out on the picnic blanket. Homework was spread out around them in haphazard piles.

"There you guys are," Blaine said with a wave. "Rose, I don't think I'm getting the right answer on this math problem. Have you done number seventeen?"

"Not yet, but I can take a look." I grabbed my textbook and settled down next to him. Asher picked up someone's discarded fantasy novel from the blanket and flipped to the first page. The four of us worked in companionable silence in the soft light of the forest.

"Oh shoot." Blaine suddenly pulled out his phone. "I forgot my mom asked for pictures of our camping trip. Do you guys care if we take some staged shots?"

After showing Asher how to take pictures with a phone—as well as explaining what a *camera* was, and then what a *picture* was—the three of us staged a camping trip. Flora and I acted like we were setting up the tent, and then we posed together next to it with big cheesy grins. Blaine held up some firewood to the camera and then got a picture of him holding a thin stick over it like he was cooking something. Asher took a picture of the three of us together in front of the fire, arms linked together. They were all pictures Blaine's mom would love.

My chest tightened—My mom would have loved them too.

"Anything else?" Asher asked, holding out the phone like it might bite him.

"Actually, yeah." Blaine took his phone back and flipping the camera to the front screen. "Get in here, we'll get one of all of us. You show up in pictures, right Asher?"

"You're thinking of vampires, Blaine," I said.

"Oh, right." Blaine laughed as he stretched out his arm.

Asher hesitantly stepped in next to us as Blaine held his phone out at arm's length. He was still half out of the shot, so I grabbed his arm and pulled him in closer. He raised his eyebrows but gave a half smile to the camera.

"What's a vampire?" he asked through his teeth.

Blaine snorted. "Keep reading Flora's book and you'll find out." He took several snaps of the group from various angles. "That should be enough."

"Can you send me those?" I asked. "Martin might ask, too."

"Of course, as soon as we get some service."

Later that night, after we had said goodbye to Asher and Blaine dropped me off at Martin's, I slid into bed and opened my phone to look again at the pictures from today. Even though they were staged, it was obvious we were having a good time. I swiped to the last few group pictures that Blaine sent. One photo in particular drew my attention. Blaine had snapped it before we were all ready, while I was pulling Asher toward me. I zoomed in on the two of us. I looked genuinely happy. The way Asher's eyes focused on me sent a rush of warmth through me, even now.

I reached for the strip of tan fabric tied around my headboard. It was the bandage Asher tied around my knee when we first met. I had washed it and tied it there as a reminder of our adventure. I smiled as the soft fabric ran through my outstretched fingers. I fell asleep that night with a smile on my lips.

The next few days passed just as the last. The three of us labored through our classes until we were free to go to Silaris in the evenings. On the fourth day, we teleported into darkness. Night had fallen and the stars were shining overhead. Multicolor fireflies flashed intermittent patterns around us. I reached out to catch one. It flashed blue in my hand, then red, before it crawled to the tip of my finger, lifted its wings and took flight.

"Hopefully Asher isn't asleep," Flora said.

"Are you saying we should let a sleeping werewolf lie?" Blaine asked, deadpan.

"That's not bad advice," Flora said. I rolled my eyes at Blaine.

A campfire crackled and cast long shadows around the site as we approached. A massive, furry form slept in the light of the fire—a wolf. The wolf was curled up with his tail covering his nose. The streaks of auburn running through his dark brown coat reflected in the firelight.

My heart stuttered and my body froze.

Predator! My instincts screamed at me. *Run!*

Before I could flee, the wolf opened his golden eyes. He wagged his massive tail once, then twice, scattering any leaves and kindling that got in its way. Just like that, I could breathe again. It was just Asher. I knew he had a wolf form, but it was hard to reconcile this creature with my friend. My instincts still told me to run.

The wolf-Asher stood up and stretched. When standing, he was even bigger than I thought—at least five feet at the shoulder. My brain could hardly comprehend that a wolf could be so large. He yawned, showing off his sharp teeth, then shook himself and sat. He stayed preternaturally still as he waited for us to approach.

Blaine and Flora were frozen beside me, wide eyed. I forced myself to take a step forward and the wolf wagged his tail again, giving me the encouragement to continue.

The wolf's eyes were level with mine. When I stopped a few feet away, he laid down and rested his head on the ground, staring up at me with a familiar gaze. It was surreal seeing the eyes of my friend on the head of a massive animal. Could he hear my thundering heart?

"You're beautiful," I whispered. "Can I . . . do you mind if I touch you?" I reached out my hand. He scooted closer and met me halfway, rising just enough to place his head under my outstretched palm.

His coat was coarse on top, probably waterproof, but the undercoat was soft between my fingers. His golden eyes closed as he leaned into the touch. When I pulled my hand away, he whined. It sounded involuntary. He had been alone for so long, starved for physical contact. My heart broke for him.

He did so much for me, it was my turn to help him. I sat on the ground, back against one of the logs, and stretched my legs out in front of me.

"Come on, then." I patted my lap.

Asher chuffed, then slowly placed his head on my thighs. He stared up at me, watching for any sign of discomfort. As I ran my hand down the back of his neck, I was surprised to find that I was fine. I had no problem touching the wolf. After a few strokes, Asher closed his eyes and sighed.

"Well, that's a sight I never expected to see," Flora said, staring at the wolf. She sat delicately on the other log.

"I think it's awesome," Blaine said. "I wish I could turn into a giant wolf."

"Isn't your mom allergic to like . . . everything?" I asked.

"Yeah, they probably wouldn't let me in the house," Blaine said. "Though, I guess I'd have an excuse to move out. Asher, can you communicate in that form?"

Asher's ears twitched, but he didn't open his eyes.

"Not to you," Flora said to Blaine. "It seems Peacekeeper shields your mind too strongly. Rose, he said you could try."

I nodded and closed my eyes, breathing in and out. I hadn't reached out with my mind while sitting, so it took me a bit longer to get into the right mindset. Eventually, I was able to expand my mind. I brushed against Asher's familiar presence, but I also felt the alien consciousnesses of my friends. Flora's shield gave the mental impression of thorny brambles, while Blaine's was a steel wall. Before I could think too hard about what I was doing, Asher opened his shield for me and I was pulled inside.

Hey there.

My hand stilled on his back. This was Asher, not a dog. Was it weird that I was petting him like this?

Not at all, he thought, sending feelings to me through our mental link. Pleasure and contentment were at the forefront, but uncertainty was hidden there too. I wasn't sure if he meant to share that last feeling with me. My own amazement and wonder drifted to him through our connected minds. *It's still just me, little human.*

I didn't realize your wolf form would be so big.

He exhaled what sounded like a chuckle as I stroked the fur on the back of his neck. *Why do you think I call you 'little'?*

I didn't get my homework done that night as Blaine, Flora, and I talked around the fire, Asher drifting in and out of sleep on my lap.

Fifteen

Blaine

M Y FIRST ALARM WENT off and I silenced it quickly. I got out of bed and crept to the closet to retrieve my makeshift sword. I had tied some bits of scrap metal to a long stick and snuck it up to my room. The balance was off, but it was close enough to the weight of my actual sword that I could practice before school started. I went through what movements I could in the small space until my second alarm sounded. This one I let go off for a while longer to muffle the sounds I made hiding the makeshift practice sword back in my closet. Pretty soon I heard my mom call through the door.

"Honey, you better wake up or you'll be late!"

"I'm up," I said to her, doing my best to make my voice sound groggy from sleep. "I'll be down in a few minutes."

I listened to her footsteps retreat downstairs before I darted into the bathroom. I jumped in the shower to erase the signs of my work out. When I was clean and dressed, I headed downstairs to grab a quick breakfast. Mom sat at the kitchen table, reading something on her tablet, a plate of half-finished eggs before her. A platter of bacon was ready on the counter, so I shoved a few pieces into my mouth.

"You're going to have to get up earlier if you are going to keep taking morning showers," Mom said, glancing up from her tablet to note my still wet hair. "You won't have time for a proper breakfast, otherwise."

"Sorry, Mom." I slid my feet into my shoes and grabbed another slice.

"Wait a minute, Blaine," Mom said as I started toward the garage. She placed her tablet on the table and turned her attention to me.

"I'm gonna be late," I said, still backing up toward the door.

"Are you feeling okay? I heard you talking in your sleep last night."

I froze. I had dreamed of Alaric's memories last night. How much was audible?

"You haven't done that in years." She frowned. "Are you stressed about something? Is this about—"

"I have a big calculus test right before break. That's why I've been over at Flora's studying so much. We're all pretty nervous about it, but Rose is really good at math, so she's been helping."

Mom's shoulders relaxed. "That school puts too much pressure on you, if you ask me. Worrying about your upcoming tests so much that you get bad dreams? It's ridiculous."

"I've got to go, Mom. I'll see you later."

"Blaine, we should—"

I slipped out the door and jogged through the lawn to my car. I spared the passenger door a glance before sliding behind the wheel—I needed to get that fixed.

I sat for a moment, lost in thought. I really had to get control of these memories. If they kept appearing as dreams, I was going to slip into the ancient language around my parents. Pushing the memories down to suppress my past life obviously wasn't working. Tonight in Silaris, I needed to try something different.

We went through the Rift that evening and arrived in Silaris at sunrise. As we came upon the campsite, we saw Asher's wolf form slip into the trees. He came out a few minutes later in his human form wearing one of the outfits I had slid into the backpack for him. We were about the same size, so I donated a few shirts and jeans to him. I was relieved he didn't feel weird wearing the stuff I gave him. I wasn't sure if lycans actually wore underwear, but I went to the store to get him a new pack, just in case. I know *I* wouldn't have worn somebody's used underwear.

"Hey, all," he said with a yawn. "Good morning."

I pulled out the breakfast food we brought to cook over the fire. I stacked up some logs and retrieved the cookware stashed in the tent. Soon the bacon was sizzling in the pan, releasing its savory scent.

"I need to find a way to deal with these memories," I said to my friends. "I've tried to trap them in the back of my mind, but they keep popping out at random times. The other day in my history class, the professor was lecturing on the Civil War and I almost asked which side the humans were on."

Rose raised an eyebrow at me.

"How can a war be civil?" Asher frowned.

I ran a hand over my face. "It was essentially a race war, not too different from yours."

Asher cocked his head.

"In our world," Rose explained, "we're all human, but we still find things to divide us. We've divided ourselves into races based on skin color. Then we divide ourselves further into things like gender, nationality, and social structure."

"For having such a herd mentality, we really like being divisive," I muttered.

"You two are different races in your world, even though you're both humans?" Asher asked.

"Their world is a strange place," Flora said to him.

"That's something we can actually agree on." Asher smirked at Flora.

"You guys, I really need help. Pretty soon my parents are going to be wondering what I'm shouting in my sleep. I need to figure out how to stop it. Does anyone have any ideas?"

I looked at their thoughtful faces. My hope dwindled with their silence.

"You need to create a hatch between your memories and Nightstorm's," Flora said, "so you can open and close it whenever you need. Have you tried to access the memories?"

"No," I admitted. "I've been ignoring them. They haven't been particularly useful. Mostly life experiences."

"Why don't you try now?" Rose asked. "Better to practice with us than around your parents."

"Alright." I closed my eyes, trying to remember my dreams. They slipped away before I could grasp them. I opened my eyes to see my friends watching me expectantly. "I'm not actually sure how to start."

"They come to you in your sleep?" Flora asked. "Perhaps if you can achieve a meditative trance state, it will allow you to open the door to your dreams."

"Worth a shot," I said. "How do I meditate?"

"Close your eyes," Flora said, closing her own. "Start by thinking about your breathing. Inhale—"

"Wait," Asher interrupted. My eyes, which were in the process of closing, snapped open. He pointed to Rose. "You, stop."

Her shoulders hunched and she paled. "S-stop what?"

"Stop casting out your mind." Asher softened his tone. "Your shields aren't ready. If he pulls you into his other half's memories, it may not be easy to get you out."

"I didn't even realize . . ." She trailed off, eyes widening.

"She'll be fine." Flora waved him off. "Meditation isn't dangerous."

"Maybe not for someone well practiced," Asher snapped at her. "But these humans are not from this world and are wholly unfamiliar with magic and mind manipulation."

"They aren't completely helpless," she retorted. "You said yourself Rose is progressing exceptionally quickly."

"Going headfirst into this with both of them would be reckless and irresponsible," he snarled, clearly getting upset.

"They aren't unprepared—"

"Not unprepared? You didn't teach them how to shield before throwing them to the literal wolves!" He stood, claws sprouting from his fingertips. Flora opened her mouth, then closed it again. Asher took a deep breath, visibly trying to calm himself. His claws retracted before my eyes. "I will not risk her safety. Rose and I will go a safe distance to work on her shielding while you two try this. Let us know if you need any help, we won't be far."

He stalked off, not looking back. Rose glanced nervously between us and Asher's retreating figure. She gave us an apologetic shrug before hurrying after him, scrambling through the undergrowth with considerably less ease than the lycan. Once they were out of sight, Flora deflated.

"He's right." She groaned. "We rushed into that journey thinking it would be as easy as recovering the green Argem from the Grove of Contemplation. I should be preparing you more."

"We survived. We learned, and next time we'll be more prepared. Now tell me how to do this magical meditation."

She nodded and set her lips. Guilt shifted to determination as she switched into information mode. It turned out, meditation was just a lot of breathing. Flora instructed me to clear my mind, then imagine a door at the edge of my consciousness. Beyond that door was Alaric's memories, the key was to figure out how to open and close that door on command.

I pictured a towering red door with black symbols scattered around its arching frame. There was a giant gold knocker in the shape of a snarling dragon's head, but there was no handle.

"This would have been much easier if I had imagined a handle," I grumbled to myself, inspecting the door in my mind.

"We don't get to consciously choose what our door looks like." Flora's disembodied voice was projected through my head like an intercom system. "Your door really doesn't have a handle?"

"Nope," I said, feeling around where the handle should have been.

"I feel like you're purposely making this harder on yourself."

"I thought I didn't 'consciously choose' my door," I muttered under my breath.

Flora huffed an exasperated breath. "Maybe try knocking?"

I knocked. Nothing happened. Try as I might, the door stayed shut and locked. I sat there for an hour before I was too frustrated to make any progress.

"Ugh," I groaned, leaning back onto the ground with a huff. "I thought meditation was supposed to be relaxing. I'm just getting angry."

Flora opened her eyes and looked at me.

"I wonder why you can't get into the right mindset," she mused. "Maybe if you hold your sword?"

"Oh, is that the mindset I need to be in?" I said with a smirk.

"Possibly." She either missed the joke or simply chose to ignore it. "You may need to be touching the yellow Argem, since that's where the memories came from."

I sighed and pulled Peacekeeper from its sheath, laying my hand over the yellow Argem set into the blade. I imagined the door again. This time, it *was* different. The black symbols shifted within the wood. They splintered and swirled, changing shape and color, until they formed legible words in a golden script.

Accepted is the path.

"There's something here," I said aloud, repeating the words to Flora.

"Can you open it?" she asked.

I tried, but the door didn't budge.

"No."

Flora hummed. "Continue trying whenever you have time."

"Okay." I wanted to melt into the ground. I was a failure.

"Hey, cheer up." Her delicate hand squeezed my shoulder. It made me feel a little better. "We have all weekend to figure this out."

Hopefully the weekend was enough. Hopefully I was enough.

Sixteen

Rose

FEELING ASHER SLIP THROUGH my shields was weirdly intimate. When he was in my head, I couldn't read his thoughts, other than the ones he sent me, but I could feel his emotions. Did that mean he could feel mine, too? At least I was certain that his earlier annoyance at Flora hadn't been redirected at me.

It was taking me progressively less time to get into the state of mind to put up my shields, but I still tired quickly. When I got tired, I lost focus. When I lost focus, Asher slipped through a crack in my defenses. When he was in my head, I would panic and my shield would crumble.

Each time, Asher was rewarded with a snippet of a memory. Luckily the memories were recent, as he wasn't purposely digging through my head.

Whenever he realized my shields were down, he pulled back and shielded his own mind. The reprieve let me reset my defenses, but I was still letting too much through. After one of my failed attempts, he rolled onto his side and propped himself up with his elbow.

"Can I ask you a question? It's about the memory I just saw."

The last memory I accidentally sent him was the one of Brad in the Student Union. I hadn't run into Brad since and had almost wiped the encounter from my mind. Seeing it again made me uneasy.

"Sure." I mirrored Asher's pose. The movement brought us close together. His golden eyes were thoughtful as he studied my face.

"That man . . . I didn't like how he looked at you."

I waited for a question, watching Asher struggle with some emotion I couldn't place.

"You were afraid," he continued. "Are you in danger in your home world?"

I shook my head. "Brad is just a stupid guy who thinks he's funny. I'm not afraid of *him*. For a moment, his expression just reminded me of . . ." I swallowed the sudden lump in my throat and forced a smile. "It doesn't matter, I'm fine."

Asher hesitated. "Please, don't do that."

"Don't do what?"

He reached his hand toward me, then caught himself and placed it back on the ground.

"Don't smile when you aren't happy," he said. "You don't need to pretend everything is alright just for my peace of mind. Don't lie to me."

"Oh." I let the false smile fade from my lips. "I'm sorry, I didn't . . . I guess it's just become second nature."

He narrowed his eyes. "How did that happen?"

"I think . . ." I rolled onto my back and gazed up at the light filtering through the dancing leaves of the canopy. It was easier to talk when I wasn't looking at him. "I don't like to make people uncomfortable. It hurts me to cause others pain."

"Who do you think you're hurting?"

"My uncle, Martin, for one. He just lost his brother and I . . . I was suddenly thrown into his life. I don't want him to think I'm not grateful. I had nowhere else to go."

"You just lost your parents." Asher's voice was gentle. "Would he have thrown you out?"

"Probably not." I almost left it at that, but I made the mistake of meeting Asher's gaze. He looked at me with so much open concern, the truth tumbled unbidden from my lips. "It actually started long before my parents died. I did it a lot for—" I swallowed and looked away again. I couldn't even say his name, too afraid it would send me spiraling back to that memory.

How pathetic.

"For the person who hurt you," Asher finished for me in a flat voice. "You were afraid to upset them, so you smiled. You pretended to be happy."

"I guess so," I said in a small voice, embarrassed how dumb it sounded.

"There's nothing wrong with that, little human. You did what you had to do to survive, but you don't have to do that anymore. You're safe with me."

I looked at him. He gazed into the distance over my shoulder, lost in thought.

"My mother was the same," he whispered. "I was too young to do anything about it. I wasn't strong enough to protect her. When I see you smile like that . . ." He shook his head as he trailed off. I placed my hand over his. He flipped his palm up to hold mine, absently tracing circles on the back of my hand with his thumb. The unexpected motion made me shiver, and he stopped.

"Rose, you never have to fake happiness for me." His eyes focused back on me. "If I do something wrong or say something stupid, I want you to tell me. Tell me if I ever start to go too far. I won't be angry with you. I would *never* hurt you."

I swallowed at his intensity. "That's not been my experience with men."

He nodded. "Good thing I'm a wolf."

"I think I'm more comfortable with the wolf part," I said with a half smile. My tone was playful, but there was a terrifying amount of truth in the statement.

Asher pulled my hand up and pressed my palm against his cheek, warm and rough with stubble. He inhaled deeply and closed his eyes. His breath tickled my wrist as he exhaled. "You know, that night you came into camp while I was in my wolf form, I thought you'd be afraid of me. I was convinced you would run away screaming when you saw me." He smiled at the memory. "Imagine my surprise when you walked up and asked to touch me. You are so brave."

He opened his eyes in time to see my blush. I didn't dare move my hand from where he placed it, though his hand had slid down to rest lightly on my wrist. He wasn't holding me there, just keeping contact. Was he afraid I would disappear if he let go?

"That was the best night's sleep I've had in years." He closed his eyes again, a contented smile lingering on his lips.

"Even with us talking over you all evening?" I asked, rolling back to face him. Asher took my free hand and placed it on his chest. I could feel his steady heartbeat through his shirt. For some reason, the feel of it relaxed me, and I found myself inching closer to him.

"Yes, even then," he said, voice growing rough. "Being so close to you . . . feeling your touch. I can't describe how it felt."

I wondered if he could hear the stutter in my heartbeat as well as I could feel the increase in his.

"Is this okay?" he asked, eyes half opening to study me.

"Yeah." The word came out shaky.

"You can tell me if it's not." He released the gentle grip he had on me and laid his hand deliberately on the grass between us.

I didn't remove my hands from him. Instead, I grazed my thumb over his cheekbone, smiling when he closed his eyes again and leaned into my touch. How long had he been alone? How long had it been since he felt a friendly touch like this? A hug? He had said *years*.

What would that do to a person? A child . . . he had only been a child.

"It's okay, Asher," I said, more confidently this time. I slid closer to him and rested my forehead against his chest. His heartbeat thundered erratically before stabilizing into a steady rhythm. He slowly put his arm around me, giving me plenty of time to pull away. I didn't. The gentle rise and fall of his chest and the feel of his fingers stroking my hair slowly coaxed my tension away.

I was . . . comfortable.

I couldn't remember the last time I was comfortable in a hug. Especially one as intimate as this. I inhaled deeply, letting his sea salt and sunshine scent envelop me. As I exhaled, I relaxed further into his warmth. I stopped thinking and just existed in the moment. I wanted time to slow around us so we could stay like this—peaceful and content—forever.

"Who hurt you, Rose?" Asher breathed into my hair.

That shattered my peace.

"Just some guy," I whispered. Ice crackled over my heart like frost on a still lake. I breathed in Asher's warmth, using it to banish the chill growing in my fingers. The numbness that threatened to overwhelm me whenever I thought too much about the past. "No one worth talking about."

Asher's fingers halted in their gentle movements when I failed to suppress a shiver. I scooted closer to him, and he started again.

"Will you tell me anyway?"

"I—" My voice broke, so I took a deep breath.

No one had ever asked me outright. I'd never talked about it. I could have made something up, could have deflected, but Asher was my friend. He gave me this moment of comfort. This moment of relaxation and safety that would shimmer like an Argem among my collection of darker memories. He gave me one of his truths, so I could give him one of mine.

"It was . . . a while ago," I said before Asher could explode from tension. "I was young and naive. He was older than me. I didn't know what love was or how a relationship was supposed to work and he . . . took advantage of that. He took advantage of me." Asher's hand paused on my back, and a light prick of claws dimpled my skin. I vaguely noticed that I was scrunching up his shirt where my hand was still on his chest, but I couldn't let go.

"I'm so sorry that happened to you, little human."

"I was stupid." I sighed into him. "I . . . I don't trust people. I have trouble letting them get close to me . . . but I'm trying."

"So brave." Asher breathed the words so quietly, I wasn't sure if he wanted me to hear them. Then, louder, "I'm not sure what I can do to get you to trust me, Rose, but I am going to prove it to you one day."

I found myself hoping he would.

That weekend and the following week was spent preparing and training. Classes crawled by, but we spent every evening in Silaris. We were there as much as possible without drawing suspicion from Blaine's parents and Martin. When Blaine wasn't meditating to unlock his memories and I wasn't working on shielding with Asher, I was practicing swordplay with Blaine and Flora. My stamina was increasing, and I was able to go through more repetitions of the feather flow with fewer corrections from Blaine.

After several rounds one day, Flora and I both collapsed from fatigue. Blaine was somehow still going. He called to Asher, who was reclining against a tree, watching us sweat.

"You know, you could benefit from knowing a few moves with the sword, too, Asher!"

"I prefer my weapons to be a little more close range." He wiggled his fingers in the air. "But I do have some training, in case I'm stuck in this form."

"Well then, come on," Blaine said, gesturing Asher over. "Show us what you got!"

Asher grinned.

"Are you proposing a duel?" He stood, holding two wicked looking daggers. They were curved slightly, like claws, and about the length of my forearms.

Blaine's eyebrows pulled together. "Uh . . . where did those come from?"

"Magic." Asher smiled. He spun the blades once in his hands, then held them vertically in front of his face.

"Alright . . ." Blaine's tone was uncertain now, but he mirrored the motion with Peacekeeper. With the regular meals over the last few weeks, Asher had filled out and now cut an imposing figure. "Let's duel, but stop short before any blood. I'm still a little rusty."

"Rusty?"

"Yeah, not as good as I once was," Blaine clarified.

"You have some weird expressions," Asher said, then he attacked.

He was fast, but Blaine was able to get his sword up in time to parry the two quick knife thrusts that were coming at him. Asher jumped back out of reach, and the two circled each other like predators, trying to find a weak point in each other's stances. Blaine lunged and Asher blocked, then Asher struck and Blaine parried. It went back and forth like that, their blades moving so fast I could hardly tell what was happening save for the loud clash of metal on metal. After a particularly hard blow, both guys stumbled backwards. They glared at each other, breathing hard. Sharp blades pointed toward fragile, exposed flesh.

My heart jumped into my throat and a stab of fear shot through me—I couldn't handle one of my friends getting hurt. I would break if I lost either of them. This duel was getting out of hand. Maybe I should step in and—

The guys grinned at each other, wicked excitement mirrored on their faces, then dove back into the fight. My tension eased at the sound of their endorphin-fueled laughter.

The cloud of swirling blades continued for what felt like hours. I didn't know how they had the energy for all this fighting. I was proud of how many times I made it through the feather flow before collapsing, but watching the guys . . . I was still so weak.

Eventually, Asher and Blaine came to a sudden stop, blades held against each other's throats. My breath caught until the guys simultaneously disengaged and stepped back. Both men held their weapons vertically in front of them again in some sort of salute.

"Man, that was awesome!" Blaine said, sheathing his sword and rubbing his shoulder. "I'm going to be feeling that tomorrow."

"You almost had me a few times," Asher said. "Usually the daggers have a bit of an advantage over the sword if I can get in close enough," —he spun the blades in his hands again and sheathed them— "but you're quick."

"Coming from you, that's a huge compliment." Blaine grinned. "Can you show me again how you deflected that second thrust I attempted? I've never known that one to fail."

"Sure." Asher nodded. "If you show me how you got out of my attack on your right side. I almost lost my dagger in that move."

The two of them spent the rest of the evening deconstructing each other's attacks and defenses. The conversation being too far over our heads, Flora and I decided to warm up some food. By the time the guys put away their weapons and came back to the campfire, we had a whole pile of hot dogs ready. Blaine grabbed one and barely finished shoving the first into his mouth before he picked up his second.

"Slow down before you choke," Flora said, deadpan.

I laughed. "Seriously, Blaine, were you raised in a barn?"

"Sorry." He shrugged, mouth full of hot dog. He grabbed a third before Flora pushed him away from the food. "I'm starving."

Asher picked up a hot dog and examined it. He took a tentative bite, chewing and swallowing before speaking.

"You have weird expressions *and* weird foods," he said, but he finished his hot dog and took another.

The four of us sat around the fire as we devoured the food. Some time ago, we had established a camaraderie—a team—and it was finally starting to feel like one. The four of us laughed and joked around the fire for hours that evening, neglecting our homework for the night. The crackles and pops of the dry logs were a soundtrack to our conversation as the night grew dark, and the firelight cast a comforting bubble around us.

Blaine

Today's the day.

I sprang out of bed and performed my usual routine of exercises with my makeshift sword before sneaking down the hall to take a shower. As I slipped out of the bathroom to head back to my room, towel around my waist, I collided with my mom in the hallway.

"Mom!" I gasped, clutching my chest. "You startled me."

"*I* startled *you*?" she asked, indignantly. "I didn't think you were even awake yet! I was coming up to make sure you were getting ready. You don't want to keep the Smiths waiting."

"I know, I'm getting my things packed."

"You look skinny," she said, looking me up and down. "Have you been eating enough?"

"Yes, I've been eating." I slipped past her. I had actually been eating more than usual. I was just burning a lot of calories in Silaris. My excess fat was slipping away, slowly revealing toned muscles. I actually looked pretty good—almost good enough to ask Krista out.

If I had time to date.

"I know school has been stressful," she continued as if I hadn't spoken. "This camping trip will be good for you to relax, but make sure you're getting enough food."

"I will, Mom," I said, slipping into my room and closing the door behind me.

Moments later, I was rushing down the stairs and out of the house. My backpack bounced on my back as I went, packed full of clothing, a small cooler, and food supplies, such as salt and other spices. We were traveling a bit more prepared this time around.

"Bye, honey!" Mom called from the living room. "Have fun! We love you!"

I paused halfway through the doorway. I usually didn't say it back, thinking it was embarrassing or something, but I didn't know what would happen to me in the coming weeks.

"Love you, too!" I called, not looking back and continuing out of the house.

"Our nine-day break from school is going to feel much longer while we're in Silaris," I said to Rose as we walked through the front door of Flora's house. "It will probably be more like three weeks."

"Just over thirteen days, actually." Rose smirked. "Maybe we should keep up with our math homework while we're there. It seems like you could use the practice."

"I don't think we could practice enough!" Flora called from deeper in the house, coaxing a chuckle from Rose.

"Honestly, why do I hang out with you two?" I asked in mock hurt.

"Because you love us!" Flora called again.

"Where are you, Flora?" Rose called out. "Are you ready to go?"

"Oh, calm down." She walked out of the bathroom wrapped in a towel. Her hair was still wet and there were tiny droplets of water on her shoulders. It looked like she just stepped out of the shower. My mouth went dry and I stared for longer than I should have before averting my eyes. "Your puppy will be waiting where you left him. I'll be going too long without a shower this week to not thoroughly enjoy the one this morning."

"Just get dressed, please," Rose said as she nudged me the other direction. My feet needed the extra push to start moving. "We'll meet you there." Then she lowered her voice so only I could hear it. "Unless you want to stay here?"

"No, that's okay." I felt myself turning red.

Rose laughed. "Liar."

When we stepped into Silaris, Asher was already waiting with the campsite packed. He greeted us with a smile and a wave as we approached.

"Where's Flora?" he asked.

"She's taking her sweet time in the shower," Rose said, rolling her eyes.

"Shower? Like, rain shower?"

I walked away, chuckling. Rose could explain what a shower was to Asher. With the campsite packed, I figured I could probably make it through one or two rounds of the feather flow before Flora got here. Plus that would give the 'love-doves' time for a proper greeting.

I pulled out my sword and flowed through the first movements. They were pretty much muscle memory after weeks of training, day and night. I went through the entire flow twice and had only just started to sweat when Flora came through the Rift.

Flora's appearance reminded me of our meditation sessions to access Alaric's memories. Thinking of the red door that locked the memories away made it appear in my mind. I froze—it was more solid today. The words *Accepted is the path* were clearly legible on the arch.

In the very center, an obsidian handle sparkled.

Without thinking, I lunged for the handle and turned it. The door burst wide open, throwing me back and bathing me in a light so bright, I had to cover my eyes. Once the light faded, I was in a memory.

This time differed from when I first grabbed the stone. I still saw out of Alaric's eyes and knew what he was thinking, but the thoughts in my head were still mine.

Alora looked so beautiful tonight, Alaric thought as he walked to his dormitory. It was dark, but the street lamps illuminated his way. The college town was safe enough for someone of Alaric's stature, though he had insisted on walking Alora to her residence. Kelmoran was well fortified against an attack from outside, but Alaric wasn't naive enough to think evil only existed outside those sturdy walls. He couldn't get the image of Alora's amber eyes out of his head. She had laughed loudly at the joke he had made about their astronomy professor, almost getting them both into trouble during class. It had been worth the risk. Alora's laugh had been musical. It made him smile, even now.

The memory shifted, leaving me reeling and trying to comprehend what I was looking at.

"Charge!" Alaric screamed from atop a gray warhorse.

Men surged around him as they responded to the call of battle. The sounds of clashing swords and screams echoed as the front line crashed into the approaching witches. Blasts of magical forces crashed into his lines, scattering bodies in their wake. Caderafel bombs were fired from the trebuchets in the midst of Alaric's forces. The bombs were engineered to explode in the air, scattering the magicbane to affect the greatest number of magic wielders. Half-casted spells skittered out when the oil hit the witches, giving the human troops a chance to cut down their closest opponents.

The memory sped up, as if someone had pressed the fast forward button, only to slow again to normal speed at the conclusion of the battle. From the state of the battlefield, it seemed both sides had taken heavy losses through the night, but the witches had turned to retreat when the sun began to rise. It was the first battle against the witches that the humans won. Alaric opted to call off his troops, choosing to let the survivors flee rather than slaughtering them as they ran. It seemed the right thing to do, but he would probably get yelled at by command for the decision. This was war, there was no room for doing the right thing.

Alaric had been thrown from his horse when the poor creature was struck by some blast of energy. As he trudged back toward the war camps through the battleground, the reek of blood and vomit in the back of his throat, he contemplated the field of the dead surrounding him. Humans and witches lay scattered everywhere, sightless eyes already being scavenged upon by the bravest of birds. In his fatigue and state of battle shock, Alaric couldn't distinguish witch from human while they lay intermingled on this field, body parts missing or torn apart. Weren't we all people? Why were we fighting?

The chanting began as Alaric made his way back to his battalion. His feet dragged over the slippery, blood-soaked ground. His helmet hung from his fingertips. It had saved his life several times that day and it didn't deserve to be dropped haphazardly in the mud. He didn't notice at first, but eventually the chanting grew too loud to ignore. He lifted his head and forced the fog from his mind. His soldiers, the ones who survived, were chanting *his name*.

"Alaric! Alaric! Alaric!"

He could do nothing but stare at them as they yelled, mind blank from shock or grief. He wasn't sure which.

"Did you see him fight?" One of the younger soldiers yelled above the din. "He was like a storm in the night, fighting off those emotes in the front lines and blowing them back to where they came from!"

"Alaric the Nightstorm!" Another soldier called, prompting the soldiers to pick up the word.

"Alaric Nightstorm! Alaric Nightstorm! Alaric Nightstorm!"

Well, at least it sounds impressive. Alaric thought, tiredly. He struggled to lift his helmet high in the air. The sounds of cheering erupted around him.

The memory shifted again. My stomach, already churning from the gore of battle, flip-flopped as I settled into a new vision.

"Alaric," the haughty voice of the elf intoned as he looked over the map laid out in front of the group, "you can't seriously mean to give the lycanthropes and witches *that* much land."

Alaric suppressed a groan as his frustration flared at the elf's tone. Bryony was a good man, but he was an elf, and as such had an inflated ego. At least he hadn't used the derogatory terms *mongrels* and *emotes*. This time. Alaric found himself again wishing the elves had sent Saerwen, instead. A soft growl emanated from deep in the chest of the lycan at the other side of the map table.

"Why not, Bryony?" Silva hissed. Sparks skittered along her fingers as she fidgeted with the quill in her hands. "Are you saying the elves deserve more than the rest of us because you're the more *superior* race?"

"I never uttered those words." Bryony glared at Silva with unfettered disgust.

"You don't have to say them." Arturo growled, hackles rising. The alpha was reasonable and reliable, unlike his predecessor, but he was fiercely protective of the lycans. "They're written all over your face."

Alaric agreed with Arturo, but he kept his expression carefully impassive.

"Why do you think the elves deserve more land, Bryony?" Alaric asked.

"We elves have a much larger population size," Bryony declared. "We need more space."

"You have a much larger population size because you slaughtered the rest of us," Silva muttered under her breath, well aware everyone in the room heard.

"Elves don't reproduce as quickly as the rest of the races," Alaric said, ignoring the challenge in Silva's tone, "so I don't think that's a valid argument. The human population, alone, will surpass the elven one in fifty years."

"If we're going by population, perhaps the elves should have the smallest territory," Arturo mused. There was a heavy silence as tension gathered between the elf and the lycan.

"Perhaps the lines are acceptable as they are currently drawn," Bryony said, reluctantly.

"Agreed." Arturo flashed Alaric a friendly smile before turning to Silva.

"Agreed," she said, though embers still danced around her fingertips, seeking to ignite the tension filling the room.

"Fine." Bryony sighed. "Agreed."

"Agreed," Alaric said with a feeling of great relief. "Now for the matter of resources . . ."

The voices in the room warped and undulated as they continued arguing, but I was pulled out of the memory by a familiar voice.

"Blaine?"

I opened my eyes, the green forest surrounding me a shock after being in Alaric's memory. Flora was in her usual hiking clothes and sturdy boots, but she was staring at me with her lips pressed into a thin line. Behind her, Asher and Rose were watching from a few yards away. To my surprise, I was in a different guard position than when I first saw the door handle. I felt a thin sheen of sweat beading on my skin. Did I continue the flow while in the memories?

"Yeah?" I sheathed my sword and stretched my shoulders.

"Are you okay?" Flora asked. "You seemed like you were somewhere else."

"That's because I was." I rubbed sweat from my forehead. "I was in Alaric's memories again, but it was different this time. I couldn't control them but I at least knew I was in a memory. There was a handle on the door today, so I opened it."

"The meditation practice must be working!" Flora beamed. "As much as I want you to try again, maybe we should wait until we set up camp tonight."

"Sounds good." I wasn't ready to see more bloodshed, anyway.

We distributed supplies and set off to the south. We followed a similar path to the one we took to get to the Howling Peaks, then branched off to the west after walking for most of the day. Doing this, we skirted the majority of the infected areas in the middle of the continent. We didn't want to alert the Defector of our presence.

We stopped to set up camp in Elvanar before we hit the tainted areas. When we sat around the fire to cook the rabbit Asher snagged along our way, I took off my boots to rub my feet.

"I know hiking boots are good to protect your feet on the trail," I complained, "but they are exhausting to lug around."

"Maybe you should get some new ones," Flora said, admiring her own boots. "These are pretty light."

"Yeah, I probably should. I hope I won't have blisters by the end of this trip." I glanced at Rose. "Did your feet heal okay from last time?"

"Oh yeah, they're good now." Rose pulled her own boots off and wiggled her feet in my direction. Cartoon avocados smiled at me from her toes. "I packed more reasonable socks this time."

I laughed. "Those are reasonable?"

"I didn't know you were injured," Asher said to her.

"'Injured' is a strong word," she said. "It was just a blister. Anyway, we have more important things to deal with."

"You are important, Rose." I frowned. "When we get home, we'll both go shopping for new boots."

"Yeah, maybe." Her tone was noncommittal.

"No really, my treat."

"Your . . . treat?" Asher cocked his head.

"He's offering to buy me boots." Rose clarified for him. "You don't have to buy me boots, Blaine."

"I do, though. You wouldn't be here, needing boots, if it wasn't for me. Just let me buy you boots."

"You could buy *me* boots," Flora said.

"What? You have nice boots already!"

"Yeah, but I could do with another pair," she said.

"*What* could you do with another pair of boots?" I asked.

She smiled. "I still have room in my closet."

I rolled my eyes, but couldn't help but laugh alongside my friends at the ridiculous statement. When our laughter died down to a comfortable silence, I ventured to ask what had been on my mind for the last few hours.

"If you guys had the power to rearrange the world order, what would you do?"

There was silence as the weight of the question settled around the campfire.

"Or what would you do to make this world a better place?" I tried again.

"Reestablish the treaty," Flora said. "It worked for several thousand years, who's to say we can do anything better than that?"

I didn't particularly like the idea of putting this burden onto someone else's shoulders a few thousand years down the road, but I didn't speak up. I asked, now it was my turn to listen.

"The treaty may have 'worked' for some," Asher put in, "but certainly not all. An entire race being exiled to a harsh terrain where food is hard to come by is not exactly what I would call *ideal*."

"We could do it better this time," Flora argued. "They were actively warring when the treaty was created, there was bound to be some bad blood and some manipulation between the races. This time, we know more. We can create better borders and a more equal distribution of land."

"You really think your Council will give up *this*," Asher gestured to the lush woods around us, vibrant with life, even in the late hour, "in exchange for some rocks? Flora, this is a *paradise* compared to what I've known."

Listening to Flora and Asher argue was weirdly parallel to hearing Bryony and Arturo fight over the creation of the treaty. I was about to cut in, but Rose beat me to it.

"We know from our history on Earth that 'separate but equal' is not truly equal." Rose said, placing her hand over Asher's momentarily. I was surprised by the casual touch from her. Those two were getting pretty close during their mind shielding lessons. "We tried that and it didn't work. One race is always going to have better resources and better options."

"Your races are integrated now. Has it fixed all your problems?" Flora asked.

"Well, no."

"We still have to fight for what we believe in." I nodded. "It doesn't just end when we get what we want. There's always going to be someone else out there that wants something different."

"Is it better?" Asher asked. The reluctant hope in his eyes made me grimace.

"It's better than it was," I answered him. "Equality is a work in progress."

"I don't know that we have enough information or experience to be having this conversation," Flora said. "Hopefully the knowledge trapped in the rest of the Argems will make it clear what should be done."

"It's always worth having the conversation," I countered, "but I agree. I don't know enough to make any sort of decision, yet."

"The fact that this decision lies in the hands of someone who barely passed their last history test is troublesome," Rose said, coaxing a giggle from Flora.

"I don't disagree," I said, giving her a wry smile. "I'll be happy when I'm done with these gen eds and can focus solely on biology."

We went to bed early that night, anticipating an early morning to continue our trek. We decided against setting up the tents, opting instead to set out sleeping bags around the fire. Sleeping under the stars was a new experience for me, and I rather enjoyed the sleepover-esque quality of speaking to my friends in hushed tones until we all drifted to sleep.

Being used to my secret, early morning routine, I was the first to wake up the next morning. I quietly slipped away from the others to wash up in a nearby stream, then grabbed my sword to go through my exercises. The cascade of the movements from one to the next lulled me into a meditation of sorts, and before long, I was envisioning the red door. I stopped in front of it, reading the inscription along the top.

Accepted is the path.

I looked down at the sword in my hands. The door had opened for me while I was doing the feather flow. I felt so much more myself while I was practicing with the sword. Perhaps that small acceptance put the handle on the door in the first place. If so, would that mean if I accepted Alaric and I were the same, another part of the door would unlock?

Only one way to find out.

I reached out and grasped the handle. The door opened and I was thrown into Alaric's memories again.

Peacekeeper stopped the attack of the elven blade inches from my throat. The elf snarled at me, even as I pushed him away and gutted him with my own sword. The family heirloom in my grasp worked as well now as it did the day it was forged, cutting through flesh and muscle as it would butter. The draconic magic in the blade kept it from dulling or tarnishing, even after centuries of disuse. I sent up a quick prayer of thanks to my ancestor for accepting the sword from one of the great dragons in the days before they were hunted down.

Wait, not my ancestor, I thought. These were Alaric's thoughts. I needed to keep myself separate from his memories. If I didn't distance my mind from Alaric's, I'd lose myself.

After dispatching several more elves stupid enough to put themselves in the way of his blade, Alaric noticed the horde approaching the old church. Wickedness gleamed in the elves' faces as they reached the church and attempted to open the locked doors.

"No!" Alaric yelled in a raspy voice. He bolted for the church. The children were inside, hiding from the bloodshed. The elves couldn't truly mean to attack children. His mind wouldn't accept that *anyone* would purposefully go after the innocent, but something withered in his chest at the sight of the battering ram. The old doors wouldn't stand a chance, even coated in the magicbane infused lacquer to keep the elven magic from penetrating the wood.

Alaric cut down anyone who stood between him and the church. There was no way he would get there in time, but he tried nonetheless. In Alaric's battle-shocked brain, between one step to another, the memory skipped. His vision swirled with color and he was suddenly in front of the church, standing between the elves and the children. The elves dropped the battering ram and pulled out their swords to attack. Alaric was able to hold the elves off until help arrived. Together, he and the other townspeople defended their homes against the invasion.

The memory faded from the sounds of clashing swords, only to materialize into the sounds of raucous laughter and the smell of pipe smoke.

"Look, boys." A low-ranked elven commander sneered at a lycan entering the tavern. "Someone let a mongrel in. Better not give your disease to the bartender. This is the best place to get a drink in this shithole of a town."

The human bartender glared at the elf but cast a wary eye toward the lycan. It was common knowledge that lycanthropy was a genetic disease that couldn't spread to others, but there was still little empathy between humans and lycans.

"You should have locked that cat flap if you didn't want his kind coming around," another elf called from somewhere else in the tavern, earning a guffaw of laughter from the elves in the room, and a few reluctant snickers from the humans.

The lycan barked out a laugh at the words, though there was no humor in the sound. His eyes were dark. They looked as if the weight of all they had seen—the killing, the injustice, the suffering—had worn them down until they would never see happiness, or true laughter, ever again. They reminded Alaric of the eyes he saw whenever he was unlucky enough to glimpse himself in a mirror.

"This tradition is honored by *all* races on the eve before battle," Alaric growled at the room in general. "Get him an ale and leave him be."

The laughter quieted down as the patrons noticed Alaric. Much to his dismay, people knew who he was and feared his skill with the sword. The lycan's wolfish orange eyes met Alaric's blue ones and held them. The lycan nodded his thanks and prowled to the bar to take the ale waiting for him, eyes scouting for danger in the tavern around him. He left a silver mark on the bar and retreated, making his way to Alaric's otherwise empty table.

"May I sit?" The lycan asked. His voice was smooth and soft, belying the power that Alaric knew lurked beneath. When Alaric nodded, the lycan pulled out a chair and sat opposite him.

After a few moments of silence, the other patrons of the tavern returned to drinking and gambling. It seemed clear that Alaric and this lycan weren't going to do anything exciting, so they went back to their drink and conversation.

"Thanks, stranger," the lycan said under the buzz of the crowd.

"Call me Alaric."

The lycan raised a brow and inspected Alaric more closely.

"Alaric Nightstorm? I've heard of you. I'm Arturo. Second in command to the Alpine Legion of Lycans."

"I've heard of you as well. I've heard you're an honorable opponent on the battlefield. I've also heard your alpha is hard to deal with." Alaric grimaced. "Sorry, I mean no offense."

"Oh, no." Arturo waved away the apology and took a swig of his ale. "You're right. That's why I'm here tonight. He is in a dreadful mood. Best to steer clear."

Alaric's mouth kicked up on one side and Arturo's expression mirrored his.

The memory blurred and shifted again.

"You should listen to us, human," the head elder chided, as the rest of the Council looked down their elegant noses at me—at Alaric. I recognized the room as the Harmony Chamber. I had been there just weeks ago with Flora and Rose. It looked exactly the same as it had then. "You are very young. We have much greater experience in this area than you. Perhaps you should follow our command."

Alaric bristled at the thought. He was here to broker a treaty among the races, not to be a pawn to a bunch of self-serving *puppets*. After taking a deep breath to settle himself and to try not to do anything irrational, Alaric answered.

"Yet," Alaric said, unable to keep the scowl from his features, "it was under your rule that war broke out. At least I can claim innocence in that."

Every single elf on the Council stiffened. Some even bared their teeth in a feral gesture, but the old elf before Alaric just smiled slowly, his eyes so cold Alaric expected to be frozen to the spot any minute. He continued speaking in a more confident voice than he felt.

"I believe, however, we will all benefit from a treaty assembly. I am asking you to supply one elf to argue the treaty on the behalf of your race. All races represented in the assembly will have the opportunity to change the treaty, but the wording will have to be agreed upon by all."

"What if our steward will not agree, young human?" the elder asked. "We are winning this war. We could continue fighting, if we wished."

"The other members of the treaty assembly will have the power to expel someone if they are being intentionally obstinate. That race will therefore be excluded from writing the treaty with no option of sending another candidate. You could continue fighting, but you would be fighting a unified force." Alaric smirked as the smile slipped from the elf's haughty countenance. "I will be awaiting your decision."

Without another word, Alaric turned on his heel and left the Harmony Chamber. He breathed a sigh of relief when the double doors slammed shut behind him.

I emerged from the memories on my own this time and froze in my feather flow stance, gazing at my sword. Alaric believed it was made by dragons. Actual *dragons*. I shook myself and continued my flow until the end of the routine, attempting to process what I saw. Why did *those* images come to my mind? Was there a reason, or were they just random thoughts clamoring to get into my head?

When I finally sheathed my sword, the smell of roasting mushrooms hit me. I returned to the group to find Asher and Rose sitting by the fire. Most of our stuff was already packed away.

"You guys didn't have to clean up my stuff," I said, snatching a mushroom from the cookware on the embers.

"It was no trouble," Rose said. "We figured you'd want to get going as soon as you were finished."

I nodded. "Where's Flora?"

"She's meditating over there." Rose pointed to a thick patch of trees where I could just see the glimmer of golden blonde hair.

I nodded, then grabbed another mushroom and made my way over to Flora, trying not to disturb her. I entered the thicket of trees and stared. Flora sat on the forest floor with her legs crossed. She was illuminated by a soft light. It highlighted her pointed ears and delicate features, making her look more ethereal and otherworldly than ever. As I settled down close by to wait for her to finish, she peeked at me with one eye. The light around her dimmed slightly, but her eye glowed the most brilliant green—it was the green of fresh spring grass poking through a field of snow. A lump formed in my throat at the sight. How could someone be so beautiful?

"I'm almost finished," she said, closing her eye again. Her voice held a strange musical quality to it and the glow around her intensified.

"Take your time." My voice was rough and grating compared to hers.

After a few minutes, the glow faded and Flora heaved a deep sigh. When she opened her eyes this time, they were their normal shade of green. When she smiled, joy radiated through her features.

"I've been meaning to replenish my power for a while," she said, lying back into the soft grass, a smile still playing on her lips. "I'm glad I got this chance before we left."

"Is that what you were doing?"

"Yes." She actually *giggled*. "The Forest was kind enough to give me a little extra strength, since we might be gone for a while."

"It was beautiful," I whispered. "You're beautiful."

The admission warmed my cheeks. She looked at me, golden hair spilling along the soft grass, and laughed again. The sound was musical.

"The beauty you see belongs to the Forest." She reached her hand up to the canopy, as if she could touch the leaves fluttering softly in the breeze. "I am only their conduit."

I wasn't so certain of that.

"Flora," I asked in a mock serious tone. "Are you high?"

"Sort of." She laughed, running her fingers through the grass. "It won't last much longer. Let me enjoy it."

I chuckled, but let her ride out the rest of her high in peace. When she sat up a few minutes later, brushing the grass from her otherwise perfect hair, I couldn't help but smirk.

"I don't think I've ever seen you so relaxed."

"You weren't really supposed to see that." Pink colored her pale cheeks. "It's how I recharge my magic. The endorphins that come with it are just an added bonus, but it's not something we share with outsiders."

"Your secret is safe with me." I stood and offered her my hand. She took it and stood gracefully.

"Thanks." She pulled her hand free from mine. "We should get going. We have a long way to travel."

I nodded and followed her back to the others. I could almost see the stress of our task weighing down her shoulders more and more with each step.

Seventeen

Rose

S HORTLY INTO OUR SECOND day, we arrived at the three-way boundary separating Elvanar, the Howling Peaks, and the desert. We sat, scoping out our options for a few moments.

"Looks like we have a choice." Blaine looked back and forth between the territories. He scratched his chin. "Thoughts?"

"We should travel through the desert." Asher's answer was immediate. "I don't want to run into other lycans."

"There's no cover in the desert. I don't like it," Flora said.

"Exactly," Asher argued. "No cover means they can't sneak up on us."

"But we might draw the Defector's attention. We aren't ready to face her."

"What do you think, Rose?" Blaine asked.

I released a long breath. "I honestly don't like either option."

Blaine was silent for a moment, then he sighed.

"We can't risk the Defector finding out what we're doing, and I don't see anyone keeping watch on those hills. Let's go through the Howling Peaks and cut across there to the west."

Asher's shoulders slumped, but he nodded. His gaze focused on me.

"Keep your shield up the entire time we're in there," he ordered, tapping his temple with his pointer finger. "Don't try to communicate with me, even if I have to shift."

I nodded, putting up my mental shield.

"Good." He gave me a strained smile. "We will stay together, we will stay quiet, and you will follow my lead while we're in there."

Asher's gaze cut to Blaine, expecting an argument from him. Blaine just nodded his acceptance of the plan.

"Asher, we've been there before. We'll be fine." Flora rolled her eyes.

"I honestly don't know how you lasted so long without my help."

"I'm sure," Blaine interrupted their bickering, "that we will appreciate having the help of someone familiar with the area. Now can we get going?"

Asher was tense as he led us across the barren boundary into the rocky mountains. When we crossed into the Peaks, the familiar dry heat hit us. My heartbeat hammered in my chest. Visions of our last trip here flooded my mind: the gray wolf, the oily magic, the complete loss of control over my own body. As if sensing my distress, Asher eyed me and tapped his temple again. I nodded, reinforcing my shield. At least I had that defense, now.

We paused in a shallow cave for cover. Asher sniffed the air outside the cave. He cocked his head, contemplating, then gestured for us to follow. We trailed him in silence for what felt like hours, climbing over boulders and through tight crevices in the red rocks. The sun beat down on us. The heat was stifling and the exertion it took to traverse the terrain had us all sweating. When Asher led us into yet another cave, I leaned against the dark rock wall to catch my breath. Hidden from the bright sun, the rock here was still cool to the touch.

"Maybe we should take a short break," Blaine whispered. They were the first words anyone had spoken since entering the Howling Peaks.

Asher nodded and moved to the mouth of the cave to keep watch. The rest of us sat, taking this time to recover. My pulse hadn't yet settled when a chorus of howls sounded in the distance. Goosebumps formed on my arms and a shiver went down my spine. Asher backed deeper into the cave, still keeping his eyes locked on the surroundings. A quiet, deep growl emanated from him. He shook his head as if to dispel water from his ears and the growling ceased.

"We should keep moving." He glanced back at us. "We—"

"Aaaasher . . ." A childlike voice sang from outside the cave.

Fear flashed in Asher's eyes before they hardened. Blaine shot to his feet and drew his sword. Flora jumped to a crouch, her hands emitting a soft green light. I cowered further against the cave wall.

Asher was beside me in a flash. He pulled me to my feet then tapped his temple. I checked my shield, nodding to him when I was sure it was solid.

"I know you're here, pup," Cora called. "We can smell your little friends. Why don't you come out to play?"

"If this goes poorly," Asher whispered in a rush to Blaine, "run. Get everyone out of the boundary. They won't follow you there."

"Asher—" Blaine started.

"Please." Something unspoken passed between the guys, and Blaine nodded. "Draw your swords. Shield your minds. Be ready to run."

Asher drew himself up. He plastered on a confident facade and sauntered out of the cave. Between one step and the next, he became a different person.

"Cora," I heard him say in a too-casual voice, "to what do we owe this pleasure?"

"We've been looking for you, pup." Cora's voice drifted in to us. "Where have you been? We've been so worried."

"Around."

"Where are your friends? Don't they wanna play with us?" Cora giggled. The sound made me shiver.

"You don't want to play with them. They have claws of their own."

Taking that as his cue, Blaine left the cave with Peacekeeper resting on his shoulder, Flora and I on his heels. I tried to keep the tip of my sword steady as I took in the lycans. The first thing I noticed was Cora's expression. Her childlike face radiated loathing, though her voice was still deceptively light. The massive gray wolf crouched beside her. I triple-checked my mental shield as an oily tendril snaked along it. The gray wolf met my eyes and growled. I gasped, realizing he just tried to control me again, but this time found no purchase on my mind.

"We're passing through. You will leave us alone," Asher said to them.

"Listen to the itty-bitty puppy, Toreth." Cora laughed. "He thinks he can give us orders. I think Galbraith will be interested to hear about that, don't you?"

The wolf barked a cruel laugh. Asher went very still.

"You don't want to say that name to me, Cora," Asher growled, his voice deadly quiet. All pretense of boredom was gone.

"Why not?" she asked, too innocently. "I bet he'd *love* to meet your new friends. You know more than anyone that he has a thing for pretty girls that are too weak to put up much of a fight."

A violent tremor wracked Asher's entire body. Claws protruded from his fingertips as he strained to remain human.

"You will pick your next words *very* carefully, if you want to continue living."

The growled threat made the hair on the back of my neck stand up. I had never seen this side of Asher before—the deadly side of him. Sure, I knew he was powerful. Dangerous, even. But knowing was somehow different than seeing.

"Oh, pup," Cora smiled, but there was a bitterness in her voice. "Do you really think this time is going to end differently? You can't beat him. No one can. He's going to have his fun with these ones, just like he did with—"

A feral growl ripped from Asher's throat as he leapt forward. He exploded into a whirlwind of teeth and fur as he shifted midair into his wolf form, shredded remains of clothing falling to the ground. A blur of deep-brown and auburn fur charged Cora's slight form. Before my eyes, Cora's shape changed, and she was no longer a little girl. She grew taller, thinner, and her hair darkened to a sleek black. Her facial structure narrowed, casting an unexpected resemblance to Asher in his human form.

Asher stumbled and slid to a stop before the woman, still snarling. I was surprised to see Asher was larger than the gray wolf, at least by half. Cora's newly golden eyes opened wide at the sight of the giant wolf. The two stared at each other, frozen.

Before either of them moved an inch, Toreth jumped and sank his teeth deep into Asher's shoulder. With an enraged growl, Asher broke eye contact with the black-haired woman. He snapped his teeth at Toreth but couldn't quite reach the gray wolf. Toreth held tight, raking his claws down Asher's side. The crimson blood that seeped through Asher's fur made me dizzy.

That was strange. I had never been bothered by the sight of blood before. With a start, I realized I was holding my breath.

Stupid! I scolded myself. *I can't help Asher if I pass out.*

I forced myself to breathe as Asher rolled to the side, dislodging Toreth. The two wolves lunged at each other, clashing in a fury of teeth and claws. The splatters of bright red blood on the wolves made my breath catch as reddish brown and gray fur blurred together. They were moving so fast, I couldn't tell who was injured.

How do I help?

I glanced at Blaine, who was obviously struggling with the same issue. His muscles were straining where he stood as he tried to decide what to do. When he met my glance, the resolve in his eyes solidified and he advanced toward the battling wolves. Before Blaine could do more than take a step, however, Cora was running for us.

Snow white fur sprouted from around her hairline and covered her features. The long black hair on her scalp shortened and lightened in color as her face became more angular. Teeth sharpened and fingers sprouted into claws as she ran. She either couldn't shift as quickly as Asher or didn't want to shift completely. When she engaged with Blaine, she remained in that strange half-wolf form.

Sharp claws met Peacekeeper as she attacked. Surprise flashed across her features at Blaine's deft use of the sword. Cora danced back and directed her next attack on Flora.

Flora was ready in her defensive stance, but Blaine again stepped in to easily block Cora's attack. Cora's eyes flashed dangerously as she skipped back again. She glanced at me with calculating eyes, obviously debating if I would be worth attacking next.

"Try it," Blaine snapped. "I dare you."

Cora grinned and darted toward Blaine. They exchanged a few blows, then Cora jumped back to reassess. That happened several times. Each time, Blaine would fend off the lycan, but he wouldn't advance toward her. He stayed close to us, waiting for his opportunity.

Before Cora could dart in for yet another attack, she was distracted by a garbled yelp. A few yards away, Asher was standing over a prone Toreth, razor sharp teeth clamped around his neck. Both wolves were covered in smears of blood from their multitude of bites and scratches, but Asher had Toreth pinned down.

The relief that swept through me at the sight made my knees wobble. Asher was alive—bloody, but alive.

A panicked whine came from Toreth as he struggled helplessly, gaining no purchase against Asher's strong jaw. A slow growl sounded from Asher as he lifted his eyes to meet Cora's. She retreated several paces as the white fur reabsorbed into her skin and she shifted back into the image of the young girl. Toreth stopped struggling but continued to whine.

"Well, someone certainly has grown up," Cora breathed, shakily. She lowered herself to her knees and prostrated herself on the ground. "I'm sorry, we won't bother you again. Please . . . please let him go."

Asher growled again.

"We won't tell Gal—" she swallowed. "We won't tell him we saw you."

Asher didn't move.

"*Please.*"

The large wolf finally opened his bloodstained jaw. Toreth didn't move until Asher stepped off the gray wolf and turned away. The moment Asher wasn't looking, Toreth slunk away to where Cora was still bowing. The two of them turned tail and ran, not looking back. Asher prowled to us at a leisurely pace.

"Asher, that was awesome!" Blaine jumped and punched the air. "Man, I wish I could do that."

"You're bleeding," I gasped, reaching for the open wound on Asher's shoulder. He flinched away and nodded his bloody muzzle west.

"We need to keep going," Flora said. "They might return with reinforcements."

Asher nodded and led the way to the west. We didn't stop, even when we crossed the border into witch territory.

Cool, damp air made me shiver as we wove through the trees. The forest was mostly conifers. Among the pines, a few scraggly deciduous trees clung to bright red and orange leaves that fell as we passed. The thick foliage above our heads blocked most of the daylight from penetrating to the forest floor. Trunks reached skyward in weirdly parallel lines and mist swirled at our feet, giving the forest a spooky quality. Beds of pine needles lay scattered around straight trunks that stretched into the sky around us.

By the time we were deep inside the forest, Asher's limp was obvious and he was panting heavily. Blood dripped down his right leg until he left a trail of red paw prints. He pushed on, showing no sign of slowing his pace. I couldn't take it anymore.

"We need to stop," I said. My friends paused. "Asher needs to rest."

Asher shook his head.

"Yes, you do. Can you even shift back?" I raised my eyebrows. He lowered his head. "You're covered in blood and I think a good deal of it is your own. If you can't shift back, I'm going to help you clean those wounds before they get infected. Flora, can I please have the medical kit?"

"I highly doubt you're getting out of this, Asher." Flora smirked as she grabbed our first aid kit from her pack and handed it to me. "Rose can be pretty stubborn when she sets her mind on something. Blaine and I will scout the area and keep watch."

"Just don't . . . bite her or something," Blaine said as he followed Flora out of sight.

Asher's shoulders heaved with each breath. He stared at me with his golden eyes, then huffed a sigh and settled down on the ground. I knelt beside him and pulled the alcohol and gauze from the first aid kit. I dabbed the bloody bite wound on his shoulder. After a moment, a soft whine escaped him and I hesitated.

"Sorry, I know it hurts. I'm trying to be gentle but this gash looks pretty bad."

I tensed when a presence brushed against my shield.

"That's you, right? Is it safe?"

Asher nodded, so I opened my mind to him. I heard his familiar voice in my head.

It's not as bad as it looks. He got in a lucky bite while I was distracted.

That woman, I asked. *The one Cora turned into. She looked like you. Was that . . . ?*

I received a flash of an image in my head. The woman smiled down at me, backlit by sunlight. Her shiny black hair framed her delicate face. Her gold eyes, just a shade lighter than Asher's, sparkled with love. She held my tiny hand as she taught me to hunt for dinner.

I blinked. She was holding Asher's hand, not mine. This must have been one of Asher's memories growing up.

My mom, yeah. He sighed. *I knew Cora would use her form against me, but I still couldn't bring myself to . . .*

He trailed off as I received another memory. This one was darker. Rain fell in droves outside the mouth of the cavern and thunder rumbled in the distance. Asher's mother looked shorter in this memory than in the last, meaning Asher was probably older. Her face was drawn and her shoulders hunched as she curled against the arm of a worn couch—the only furnishing in the cave dwelling. I felt Asher's concern as my own as I studied her. When she saw me looking, she smiled. The expression still lit up her face, even through her exhaustion. At a glance behind me, her real smile fell away, only to be quickly replaced by an obviously forced one.

A recognizable smell entered the cavern, making me tense and spin around. The storm outside had covered up the sound of his entrance, but a flash of lightning illuminated the outline of a man.

"Hello, Seraya."

Galbraith. The alpha's voice sent chills down my spine. Anger and helplessness flared in me. I could scare off the others, but Galbraith . . . how could I even begin to fight the alpha?

I snarled and stepped in front of my mother. My hands shook, but I held my chin high. The shadowy form cocked its head. He could kill me in seconds, but I had to try. I couldn't just stand here while he hurt her. Not again.

A gentle hand squeezed my shoulder. My mom took my hand and pulled me to face her. I did, even though putting my back to the threat went against all my instincts. Dread welled in my chest at the fake smile plastered on her face. Stars, I hated that smile.

"It's okay, Dash," she said softly. She knew I could smell the lie—she was the one who taught me how to do it. "Why don't you go out for a while?"

I shook my head. I wouldn't leave her alone. Not with him. I couldn't.

"Listen to your mother, Asher." The deep voice rumbled through the cavern, making me cringe.

I bared my teeth. How dare he come into our home. How dare he disrupt what little peace we carved for ourselves in this wasteland. How dare he act like she had a real choice when all he had to do was open his mouth to rip away her freedom.

He reached for her and my vision went red. I swiped at Galbraith before I realized what I was doing. My claws tore through the air—fast—and shredded the skin on his forearm.

He jerked his arm back with a growl. He studied me, then the wound on his arm. The scent of his rage rolled off of him like rot, and his teeth formed sharp points.

But I hurt him. I drew blood. I didn't even know that was possible. Maybe it was enough. Maybe he would—

His malicious laughter echoed off the cave walls. I went cold. Stars, what was I thinking? Did I just kill us both?

He advanced, but Mom grabbed my hand and jerked me back. She shielded me with her body. A tiny, scared part of me was relieved. A much larger part of me was ashamed by my cowardice.

She snarled. "Remember our deal, Gal."

The alpha halted, but his eyes flashed at me. His next words were laced with power. "*Go for a run, pup. Don't come back.*"

No. My feet moved without my permission. Her hand slipped from mine. *No, no, no!*

I ran out of the cave and into the rain—abandoning her. Cold water stung my cheeks and soaked through my clothes. I shook with fury. My very soul vibrated in desperation to turn back. After everything I tried, I was still so useless. I wasn't strong enough. I failed her. I would have torn myself apart with my own claws to be able to turn back and help her. I shifted into wolf mid step and howled my emotions into the sky, fighting the alpha's order every step of the way.

Asher's shields forced me out of his head and my mind snapped back into my own body. I reeled, disoriented as I knelt beside the giant wolf in the cold pine forest. It took me a few gasping breaths to get my bearings. A tear slid down my cheek, but I wiped it away before Asher could see. He was pointedly not looking at me. I felt him brush against my mind, and I let myself be pulled through his shields again.

Sorry. A tremor went through him. *I didn't mean for you to see that one.*

It's okay. You've seen plenty of my memories that I didn't mean for you to see. Your mom . . . was she—

She was dead by the time I broke through his compulsion.

I placed my hand on his back, trying to be comforting. I didn't know what to say. 'I'm sorry' never quite felt like enough. With a sigh, I continued cleaning his wounds. The minutes ticked by in silence. I felt glimpses of the storm of emotions he was trying to hide from me. They beat against his defenses like a caged animal, but as I worked, the animal quieted. Settled.

Dash? I finally asked.

He snorted. *Just a nickname. It started as 'Ash,' but when we discovered how fast I could be, it turned into 'Dash.'*

It's fitting.

He didn't respond, just looked at me with solemn eyes.

My uncle, Martin, is the only one allowed to call me 'Rosie.'

Amusement flitted through our connected minds.

You don't look like a 'Rosie.'

Agreed. I nodded. *I'm not into nicknames. My name is short enough.*

Do you not like when I call you 'little human'?

I like that one. Heat flooded my cheeks when I sent the thought, then again at the warmth Asher sent in response. I tried to steer us back to safer conversation. *Can you really smell lies?*

Yeah. I can.

Interesting. I tried to remember if I ever lied to him. I didn't think so, but I'd have to be cognizant in the future. I didn't want to hurt him. *When do you think you'll be able to shift back?*

After I get some rest. He flinched when the alcohol hit a deep cut. *I assume you are putting this liquid fire on me for a reason?*

I blinked at him. *The alcohol? It kills any bacteria that may have gotten into the wound. If we keep it clean, it won't get infected.*

How do you know how to do this?

Martin's a paramedic. That's a sort of . . . healer in our world. I picked up some basic first aid training growing up. It's been useful . . . in the past.

Lucky me. He gazed at me with an unreadable expression. *You scared me back there, you know.*

Rose, I . . . I'm sorry. I didn't want you to see me like that. It's still me, just . . . a different side of me. He settled his head on his paws and looked away.

I wasn't scared of *you, Asher. I was scared* for *you.* I blushed when his eyes flicked up to meet mine. *You ran into that fight all by yourself. When I saw all that blood I . . . I couldn't tell who was injured.*

I was afraid for you, too. His thought brushed my mind like a caress.

Whatever, you aren't afraid of anything. I scoffed, wry smile on my lips. As soon as I said it, I knew it wasn't true. I was in his memory moments ago—I literally just felt his terror of the alpha.

I'm afraid of many things. Losing you is at the top of the list.

My hands stilled against his wound again as his eyes drifted shut.

You're important to me, Rose. I can't get you out of my head.

My lips pulled up at his words. He opened his eyes and gazed up at me.

You have the most beautiful smile.

My breath caught. I was at a loss for what to say. Even my mind went blank.

Sorry. He looked away. *I'm having trouble controlling my thoughts. I may have lost more blood than I realized.*

Asher, I ran my hand through the soft fur on the top of his head. *I don't know what I'd do without you.*

He looked at me again, golden eyes half lidded. *I will protect you. Always.*

An unexpected surge of warmth went through me. *Let me protect you, for now, Asher. Get some rest. Recover your strength.*

Anything for you, little human. He yawned and settled his head on my lap. I ran my fingers through his soft fur as he drifted to sleep. *I will do anything for you.*

Our minds were still connected as he started to dream.

Blaine

When Flora and I returned to find Rose trapped under a sleeping Asher, we decided to set up camp early that day. Rose shushed us when Asher stirred in his sleep, so Flora pulled me away to practice meditating. Unfortunately, it wasn't working.

"There isn't even a handle, anymore," I said. "I can't get in. I think I need to be doing the feather flow."

"You shouldn't have to hold your sword every time you want to access the memories," Flora said.

"Well, apparently I do." I groaned and laid back on the forest floor. The grass here was sparse and brown compared to the grass in the Elvanar. The pine needles that coated the ground poked into my skin, but I welcomed the physical distraction. The mental pressures of this *Veritace* business had a dull pain pounding behind my eyes. I breathed deeply, bringing the cool air into my lungs and holding it there before blowing out a great sigh. "Is meditating supposed to give me a headache?"

"No." Flora's eyes narrowed. "Maybe we should take a break."

"We just started," I muttered.

Flora leaned forward and placed a finger on my temple. I felt a spark of warmth travel from my temple to my shoulders and eventually down my spine. I was too shocked to move before she pulled her hand back.

"Tension headache," she said. "You'll survive."

"You can tell?"

"Healing magic," she said, waving away my question.

"Why didn't you heal Asher?"

"I offered." She rolled her eyes. "He said no. Besides, his wounds weren't that bad. I need to save my magic for an emergency. I can't replenish it in this forest." She looked around at the darkening trees surrounding us. "I'm on a limited supply from here on out."

"I see. But you have enough to check my headache?" I could have sworn she blushed, but it was already too dark for me to be certain.

"That doesn't take as much magic." She shrugged. "Anyway, tell me about the memories you've seen so far."

It took longer than I expected, but I tried to include everything as I relayed the memories to Flora. Any detail could be important. When I finished, she sat in contemplative silence. After a moment, I had to ask the question buzzing around my brain.

"Flora, are dragons real?"

"Of course they're real," she said. When she focused on my stunned expression, she amended, "They're extinct now, but they used to own the skies. I told you one created the Rift, right? That was long, long ago. I've seen hides, though, and artifacts such as your sword. They have a different magic signature than the things we elves create."

"Wow." I looked up at the darkening sky. "I'd love to see a real dragon."

She shook her head. "The stories claimed they were hunted to extinction because they terrorized the inhabitants of Silaris. I don't think I would want to meet a creature like that."

I laughed. "I guess we have enough to worry about without a massive flying lizard popping out of nowhere and attacking us."

Flora's laugh was musical.

The next morning, I powered through my feather flow then built up the fire before anyone else woke. I pulled some bacon from a cooler Flora had spelled to stay cold. It was sizzling in the pan by the time Asher trotted into the woods with his backpack in his mouth. He emerged a few minutes later in human form, fully dressed and with his pack over one shoulder.

"Good to see you back on two feet," I said, handing him some bacon.

"Thanks," he said with a smile, raising the bacon to me in a mock sword salute, then putting it in his mouth. He walked over and sat beside Rose as she sat up in her sleeping bag. Asher aimed his next words at her. "And thank *you* for cleaning me up yesterday."

"How's your shoulder?" she asked through a yawn. She looked him over as if she could see the damage beneath his clothes.

"It'll be healed in no time." He rolled his right shoulder to test its mobility. "It already feels better than I expected."

"Can I see?" The pink blush on her cheeks was visible from where I sat by the fire. "I mean, can I check the wound?"

He smiled and pulled off his shirt—if a bit stiffly—to expose the injured shoulder. I looked too, curious to see how the shredded flesh I saw on the wolf's shoulder yesterday translated to Asher's human form. I expected to see a gory gash, or at least an angry scab, but all I saw was smooth skin. Two thick pink lines trailed from his right shoulder halfway down his back. The fresh scar stood out brightly against his tan. Other, less visible scars peppered his back. I never noticed them before. Were they from yesterday's fight, too? They looked much older.

"It's . . . healed?" Rose leaned forward to probe the fresh scar. Her careful fingers ran over the smooth skin. The wonder in her expression turned to confusion and then to surprise when she glanced up at Asher's face. She had leaned in *very* close.

"Mostly." Asher didn't move a muscle as she stared up at him. He just watched her.

"At least you have a cool battle scar, now," she said.

Asher tilted his head and a strange look passed between them. Rose blushed and pulled away. She clasped her hands together on her lap and stared at them.

"Rose, I . . ." Asher frowned and slid his shirt back on. "I said things yesterday that were a little forward. I'd like to apologize if it made you feel . . . weird or—"

"It didn't! Make me feel weird, I mean." She didn't look up from her hands. "Did you mean what you said?"

"Do . . . you want me to mean what I said?" It was the most awkward I'd ever seen either of them. It was adorable. I tried to focus on the popping bacon grease but couldn't help but watch the exchange out of the corner of my eye. "Or would you rather me . . . not mean it?"

"I want the truth."

Asher put a finger under her chin and lifted her face until she finally looked at him.

"I meant every word," he whispered.

A small, hopeful smile bloomed on her lips. Asher returned her smile. They sat there for a moment, gazing into each other's eyes.

"Ahem." Flora cleared her throat from where she was lying in her sleeping bag. Asher jerked his hand back, and Rose flushed bright red.

"Yeah, we're still here," I said, trying to keep a straight face. "Get a room, you guys."

"Oh, shut up." Rose rolled her eyes before diving back into her sleeping bag to hide her embarrassment. I chuckled at the response.

"Seriously though," Flora said, a muffled voice coming from inside her sleeping bag. "It took you two long enough."

Asher looked at Flora, bewildered. Rose groaned from her sleeping bag. I burst out laughing.

Eighteen

Blaine

THE WORLD AROUND US felt sick. We hiked at a brisk pace for the majority of that day, staying alert for any signs of danger. The forest we walked through was draped in corruption. The animals were quiet and the needles drooped on their branches. At every foreign sound, we took cover. Most of the time we were only hiding from a small forest animal, but it was better to be safe than to be eaten by some evil creature.

About halfway through the day, we crossed out of the corrupted forest into a healthier version. When I stepped off the infected soil, I heaved a sigh of relief and the weight on my shoulders lightened. The sky transformed from dusky gray to bright pale blue and the trees became a vibrant shade of green. There was a life to the forest that hadn't been there moments prior.

Squirrels the size of cats scurried around the trees, jumping from branch to branch over our heads, chittering our arrival. Birds sang more openly now. I caught sight of a few brightly colored feathers, but these birds weren't as friendly as the ones in the Elvanar. They stayed high up in the canopy where they were safe.

When the wind shifted directions, Asher caught the scent of some sort of predator tailing us. He couldn't describe what it was, but it must have decided we weren't worth the trouble because soon after, he couldn't smell it anymore. We stayed vigilant after that, though. We weren't out of danger, just because we were outside the ring of evil.

We stopped to make camp that evening beside a large, moss-covered boulder. I climbed to the top while Asher scouted the area for danger. I watched him slip through the trees from my vantage point high above. When I could no longer see him—or anything else of note—I slid down the rock. When Asher returned, Flora and I broke off from the group to practice my meditation. Before we could get too far away, Asher called us back.

"Can you help us with something for a moment?" he asked Flora. When she nodded, he smiled at Rose. "You impressed me back there, shielding yourself from Toreth. As an elf, Flora's much stronger than I am. Let's see if she can get through your shields."

Rose looked surprised, but she nodded. She sat down on the ground and closed her eyes. After a few seconds, she nodded again.

"I'm ready." She flinched and put her hand to her temple. "Or maybe I wasn't."

"I didn't mean for you to attack her." Asher's voice was clipped.

"Sorry," Flora grimaced. "Try again. I won't push as sharply this time."

"Isn't that the point though? If someone is trying to break into my mind, they aren't going to be gentle about it." Rose took a deep breath and closed her eyes again. "Okay, ready."

She held out longer this time, maybe thirty seconds, before she grimaced and opened her eyes.

"You *are* really strong," Rose said.

"You lost focus that time," Flora said to her. "Up until then, you were keeping me out. That was excellent for how short of a time you've been practicing."

"Think about adding a thicker layer to your walls," Asher said, kneeling next to Rose. "Don't lose focus, no matter what. You've got this."

Rose nodded. Flora's lips pursed, and she tilted her head to the side. How often had Flora done this before we knew she could read our thoughts? How deep did she dig into our heads? I put my hands in my pockets and shifted my weight from one foot to the other. What secrets did she uncover? Should I be learning to shield my mind too, or was having Peacekeeper enough protection? Did she have to be looking at Rose to break into her mind? Flora shot me a quick glance before focusing back on Rose.

Well, that answers one of my questions.

Rose squeezed her eyes shut and furrowed her brows in concentration. Minutes passed. Beads of sweat formed on her forehead and her breathing grew labored. Asher watched her with concern, gaze flicking between her and Flora. He reached up to rub his right shoulder—the injured one. He opened his mouth to say something, then closed it. He did that twice.

"Maybe we should—" At Asher's words, Rose yelped.

"Blight!" Flora darted forward. Her hands fluttered in the air above Rose, looking for the source of her pain. "I didn't mean to go that far."

Rose winced and laid back on the grass, closing her eyes. "You've got some thorns in there."

Flora grimaced. Her upheld hands started to glow. "Can I check you out? I want to make sure I didn't hurt you."

"Sure, no problem," Rose mumbled.

Asher's brows lifted incredulously and Flora's gaze flicked to him before settling back on Rose. She put her hand on Rose's temple, then nodded.

"Thank the Forest," Flora breathed. "No damage."

"I appreciate you not damaging my head more than it already is." Rose's words sounded like a joke, but she didn't rise from where she laid on the ground. What the hell just happened?

Asher ran a hand through his hair and glared at Flora. He stood and walked past me, expression thunderous. After a final look at Rose, still resting on the ground, Flora got to her feet and followed Asher. I knelt beside Rose and took her too-pale hand in mine.

"Hey." I kept my tone soft. "You okay?"

"Mhmm." Her lips quirked up in a small smile, but her eyes stayed shut.

"You look pretty rough, Rose."

"Just what every girl loves to hear."

"Shit, no. I—"

She squeezed my hand. "I'm fine, Blaine."

I wasn't so sure.

"You did an excellent job teaching her," Flora said to Asher a few yards away. "Not many people could have withstood that kind of force."

"I asked you to test her, not incapacitate her," he growled in a low voice.

"That wasn't my intention." Flora bristled. "Like I said, there was no damage."

"What did she mean by 'thorns'?"

She hesitated a beat. "Offensive spears."

"What!?" Asher's fingers shifted into claws. "By the stars, Flora, she's only learning!"

"That's how I learned," Flora snapped.

"She's not an elf! She shouldn't be subjected to your barbaric methods."

"You, of all people, are throwing out the term *barbaric*?" She sneered.

"Uh, guys . . . ?" I called, trying to diffuse the argument. Their volume was steadily climbing.

"Very nice, accuse the people unable to *magic* themselves into civility of being a lower class." Asher's hands trembled as his claws disappeared into fingers, just to sprout back into claws. "Offensive spears, Flora? You could have killed her!"

I flinched and tightened my grip on Rose's hand.

"Wait, really?" I asked. "She could have died?"

"Of course not!" Flora spat. When she looked at me her temper faltered. "I wouldn't have let her die. I'll admit, it was a mistake. It's automatic for me to use them. I didn't think about them until—"

"Until she collapsed?" Asher accused, gesturing to Rose on the ground beside me. Flora narrowed her eyes but didn't respond.

"Asher," Rose said from where she lay. She pulled her hand from mine to prop herself up on her elbows. "I'm fine."

Asher was kneeling by her other side in a flash. Flora stayed back, but I saw the guilty look that crumpled her face.

"Don't lie to me, Rose," he said, "That had to be incredibly painful."

"I mean, it wasn't pleasant, but I feel fine now. No harm done."

"You promise?" Flora asked. "No pain anywhere? I can heal it if you tell me about it."

"Honestly, I'm not even tired." Rose got to her feet and spread her arms out, palms up. "See? Fine."

"I am sorry, Rose," Flora said to her. "I really didn't mean to hurt you."

"I know, Flora. All is forgiven. Though, someone is going to have to teach me how to do that one day."

"You are incredibly strong, little human," Asher said from where he still knelt. "Has anyone ever told you that?"

Rose rolled her eyes, but I didn't think he was joking.

After I was certain Rose had recovered, Flora and I walked a short distance away to practice meditating. I sat cross-legged in the sparse grass and lay my sword beside me on the ground. I still hadn't been able to open the door without holding Peacekeeper, but I tried. After a few moments of nothing, I sighed and picked up the sword. Just like that, the handle appeared.

I opened the door and was swept into Alaric's memories yet again.

"I'm sick of it, Alaric," Arturo spat over the rickety table of the tavern. "Sick of the bloodshed. Sick of the violence."

He closed his eyes and shuddered, as if reliving some battlefield memory. It was rare that they saw each other these days. Arturo replaced Tornuc as alpha several months ago and Alaric was thankful they hadn't yet clashed on the battlefield. Tonight, however, they sat at the same table, drinking an ale and dreading the following morning.

"Me too," Alaric muttered.

"Will it ever stop?" Arturo asked. Alaric didn't have an answer for him.

Someone began playing a string instrument in the corner and a round of cheers went up at the rhythm. Soldiers welcomed any distraction on the night before a battle. Even Arturo tapped his fingers to the beat.

"Do you see who else is here tonight?" Alaric asked, gesturing to the table on the other side of the room. Arturo followed his gaze.

"By the stars, is that Saerwen?" Arturo asked.

Alaric nodded. The elf was among the highest ranked officers in the elven army. She was as deadly as a dragon and as quick as a ridge viper on the battlefield. Alaric wasn't looking forward to tomorrow's fight with her leading the charge.

"You know what? I'm going to ask her to dance." Arturo was up and striding away before Alaric could reach across the table to stop him.

When Arturo approached the table, the two elves on either side of Saerwen stiffened and reached for their weapons. She, however, just drained her ale. Her eyes were shadowed, as if she too was tired of the relentless bloodshed.

Arturo gave an elaborate bow and asked Saerwen for a dance, drawing everyone's attention. Silence swept over the room like a cloak. Even the music stopped playing momentarily, while the elf looked the lycan over.

Slowly, so slowly, Saerwen stood. She walked elegantly around her table and, to the disbelief of her companions, placed her hand in Arturo's. The music frantically started again, missing a few notes before finding its rhythm. The rest of the tavern stood frozen while the elf and the lycan began their dance.

The memory shifted to a battle.

Alaric had been scouting enemy elf territory when they came across the skirmish. The lycans apparently had the same idea, as several wolves were locked in battle with a small elvish force. The lycans were severely outnumbered, just barely holding their positions as the elven guard surrounded them.

Alaric watched from the sidelines as a large wolf—though not quite as large as Asher, I realized—jumped in front of a spear meant for their smaller companion. The chivalrous act cost the lycan a gory slice to the shoulder, but the whimper of pain drew Alaric's attention to the individual. The wolf, reddish in color with blond streaks through its coat, wasn't familiar, but those orange eyes, heavy with pain . . .

He knew that lycan.

Before Alaric could second guess his decision, he was moving. He blocked the killing blow that would have ended his unlikely friend, and efficiently dispatched the elf who tried to deal the damage. Alaric spared a glance to the wolf, who collapsed to the ground, no longer able to stand. The smaller wolf snarled at Alaric, but the wolf on the ground stared with wide eyes.

"Didn't expect to see you here, Arturo," Alaric said.

The wolf blinked his orange eyes once, as if in disbelief. Then, he barked an oddly familiar laugh. A shudder went through the wolf as he shifted into his human form. I found it odd that the man's nudity didn't register any sort of embarrassment in Alaric as he continued to fight. Arturo's face was younger than it had been in the last memory, and when he spoke, his voice was laced with pain.

"Thanks for the aid, brother," Arturo gritted out, holding the wounded arm to slow the heavy flow of blood. "I owe you my life."

"Nah," Alaric said, taking down another elf that foolishly charged him, "just the first round of ale at the next tavern."

Alaric hadn't ordered his small band of scouts to team up with the lycans and join the fray, but they saw their commander's actions and followed suit. Together, the humans and lycans fought back the elven guard, leaving no survivors to report on the temporary alliance.

The memory faded and swirled into a new one.

Seated before Alaric, hands and feet tied to a chair, was a man. The pointed ears led me to believe he was an elf, but that was the only tell. Bruises and swollen skin covered his body. He sagged against his bonds, unconscious.

"What have you learned?" Alaric asked.

"Unfortunately, not much, Lord Nightstorm."

Too engrossed in the horror of what I was seeing, I hadn't noticed the greasy looking man in the dark corner of the room. His black, beady eyes gleamed with madness when he looked toward the elf.

"I'm not your lord, Belan," Alaric grunted. He kept his face expressionless as he spoke to the man, though he obviously thought the situation distasteful. If Alaric was a lord, he would not condone such practices. His stomach turned at the thought of this madman down here alone with anyone. War was war, however. The information Belan obtained had saved countless human lives. "Wake him up."

"Yes, m'lord," Belan crooned. Alaric tried not to grimace at the man as he shuffled closer to the elf, bucket in his hands.

The elf gasped awake when he was doused with the caderafel-laced liquid. The oil had been diluted just enough to cut off his magic without clouding his mind. The elf shivered involuntarily. There was no warmth in this dark cavern, save the flickering candlelight. Alaric had to ball his hands into fists to keep the pity from his face.

"P-p-please," the elf stammered. He was younger than Alaric had first thought. "I've told you everything I know."

Alaric's gaze slid to Belan, who blinked back at him innocently. Had the little man lied?

"Start from the beginning," Alaric said in a cold voice.

"I-I will . . . please . . . don't leave me alone with him again." The young elf glanced at the slimy little man, terror in his eyes. "P-please, sir . . . just kill me."

The *pleading* in the elf's voice as he asked for death . . . I was going to be sick. Alaric thought the same, but he allowed nothing in his expression to change.

"Belan," Alaric said sternly, "fetch me a warm meal."

The beady man jumped to follow the order and scurried from the room.

"Alright, son." Alaric's tone softened. "Why don't you start from the beginning?"

The young elf broke down in tears as he ratted out his companions.

My stomach roiled at the memory. The only thing that kept me from getting sick was the knowledge that Alaric let the young elf go as soon as he got the information. Before I could get a solid footing, the memory shifted again.

This time, Alaric was tied to a chair. A wrinkled woman stood before him. She twirled an iron bar in her hands.

"Well?" she asked. "You know how this ends. Tell us what you know and we'll let you go."

If the witch knew she had Alaric Nightstorm in her clutches, he would never escape. He just had to bide his time and play the game. Resist as much as a low-level soldier, then 'break' and feed her false information. He had been trained for this, but the real situation was much more panic inducing. And painful. His body hurt from the initial beating of his capture. He eyed the bar apprehensively, dread growing at the soon to be inflicted pain.

Here we go, Alaric thought to himself, gathering his courage.

Alaric spat at the woman's feet. Saliva mixed with blood splattered her shoes. She looked down at the mess and disgust curled her lips.

"I see." Her hands sparked where they curled around the bar. The sparks danced up the bar until the metal was glowing red. "Perhaps this will change your mind."

The white-hot sear of the heated iron against the inside of Alaric's forearm jolted through me as well. I was thrown out of the memory, Alaric's scream of pain still bouncing through my head. Nausea gripped me and I heaved the contents of my stomach into a nearby bush, not entirely certain how I got there. A moment later, comforting hands gripped my shoulders.

"Deep breaths," Flora said, "it will pass. I know, it can be a lot to take in. I'm sorry you have to go through this."

She knelt there with me, rubbing my back as I trembled and heaved again. After a few moments, I was able to get my breathing under control. When I felt I wasn't going to get sick again, I spit the taste from my mouth and leaned back.

"Ugh. That was not pleasant." I wiped the thin sheen of sweat from my face and checked my arm for the burn. There was nothing there, of course—not even a scar. Though, I still felt the phantom pain.

"I'm sorry." Flora didn't pull away from me. She just kept rubbing soothing circles onto my back.

"I . . . I think I'm done for today."

"I have some herbs to ease nausea," she said. "I'll make us some tea."

I nodded, but didn't stand. Flora stayed beside me until I was ready to move. I was eternally grateful for her calming presence as I pulled myself back together.

Rose

"Are you sure you're up for more practice today?" Asher asked as he settled on the ground. We found a small clearing, far enough from Blaine and Flora to not disturb their meditation. "Those offensive spears are rough. We should just take it easy tonight."

"I want to practice." I sat cross-legged, facing him. Realizing how easy it was for Flora to get into my head put me more on edge than I was willing to admit.

"Fine. We can review what we've already done so the mental strain doesn't fatigue you—"

"Asher, I'm pretty solid on the shield part. What's the next step?"

Asher stared at me for a moment, searching my face. Eventually, he nodded. "Pockets."

"Pockets?"

"It's what I've been pulling you into in my head so you're not bombarded with all of my deep thoughts and memories," he explained. "You see, a person's thoughts are more than just an internal dialogue running along the surface. Some people think in words, some in images. Either way, the deeper you go into someone's mind, the more truthful they become, but also the more difficult they can be to interpret."

"What do you mean truthful? Can people lie in their thoughts?"

"Yes, someone experienced can lie even through connected consciousnesses. In the outer layer of thoughts, it's easy to think whatever you want. For example, I could think 'the sky is green' and that's what you hear, even though we both know it's not true. People also unintentionally lie to themselves in their own minds. They repress memories they would rather not remember or they choose to believe things happened in a different way, but the true memories are still in there if you go deep enough."

"What does this have to do with pockets?"

"It's another form of protection," he said. "Another shield you can use if someone is trying to break into your head. Imagine your mind as a sphere. Then imagine a tiny half sphere clinging to the inside edge of that sphere. If someone is trying to break into your mind and succeeding, form a pocket. They still get into your head, but you can control what they see. If you're good enough, they might not realize they're in a pocket."

"That's how we've been talking mind to mind?"

"Yes," he said. "You don't want everyone you connect with receiving every memory and emotion that comes into your head. Say, for instance, you're communicating with Flora and a very attractive lycan walks by without a shirt on. I can't even imagine the inappropriate things that would be going through your mind at the sight."

I laughed, rolling my eyes. "Okay, I get it. How do I form this pocket?"

"Pull up your shield. Good," he said when I had done so. "Now create a second shield within the first. It doesn't have to be very big, just a little pocket. Keep the walls thick everywhere. Don't neglect the rest of your shield."

It was difficult to focus on creating the pocket while still maintaining concentration on my shield. After a few tries of either dropping one or the other, I finally was able to picture both shield and pocket clearly in my mind.

"Okay, I think I have it," I said, concentrating hard. "What now?"

"Your outside shield still looks great. Now all you need to do is let me in. You do this by . . ."

Just like that, those words transported me into another time and place, pulling me into a nightmare. Instead of the otherworldly forest, dirty beige walls scattered with crinkled movie posters and chipped paint surrounded me. A hand restrained me by my wrist. Another hand hooked into the waistline of my shorts.

"Come on, Rosita, let me in."

Nausea hit me like a truck and I squeezed my eyes shut. He said we'd only watch a movie tonight, but when I walked through the front door to his crappy, one room apartment, something was off. He must have had a really bad day for him to be acting so rough already. I usually had to do something pretty stupid to set him off.

"Wait . . ." I managed through my fear. "Cal, no—"

His eyes flashed like dull tungsten in the dim light of the room. "What did I tell you about using that word?"

His grasp on my wrist grew painful as he deftly unbuttoned my blouse. The stupid, fashionable shirt fell open, letting the cool apartment air brush my bare skin. The exposure made me shiver.

I flinched from the feel of his fingers drifting down my stomach. I didn't want this. I didn't want his hands on me. I pushed at him, but he was bigger than me. Stronger. He captured both my wrists in one hand and held them above my head. I struggled, but we both knew I didn't have a hope of fighting him off.

He removed my shorts, barely letting them fall to tangle around my feet before shoving me down on the rumpled bed. I scrambled away from him, but his fingers locked around my ankle. He jerked me back toward him, hard, and pinned me to the bed.

I was trapped. I couldn't move. I could barely breathe. Tears stung my eyes as his hands moved up my thighs. I felt the bile rise in my throat as my knees were forced apart—

A ferocious growl ripped me from the memory, pulling me back to Silaris. Green filled my vision. Pine trees towered over me. I curled up, pressing my thighs together and clutching my knees to my chest. I reached out with one hand, burrowing my fingers into loamy soil, feeling the scratch of pine needles against my palms. Grounding myself in reality. I gasped in hiccupping breaths through uncontrollable shivers.

Just a memory. I'm not there anymore. It was just a memory.

My trembling lessened as I wrestled back control of myself. I must have scrambled backwards until I hit the tree I cowered against. Nausea twisted my stomach, but at least I hadn't thrown up this time. Yet. I took deep breaths through my nose, focusing on the smell of the damp forest air. Not on the acrid smell of body odor and bile.

Asher was on his hands and knees several feet away. His fingers dug into the soft ground. Tremors ran through his body as he held himself in place. The growl that yanked me from my nightmare was still emanating from him. From the look of the disturbed pine needles, he had followed me a few steps before collapsing. His eyes were locked on the ground and his lips curled into a snarl. He was deliberately taking slow, deep breaths.

Before he even looked up, my shivering was under control. My features were masked into something less panicked. My heart rate slowed from its thunderous pace. Heat flooded my face as the embarrassment set in. How much of that memory had he seen? How much of *me* had he seen? My shield had shattered when confronted with the ghost of that experience. I must have shocked Asher out of his shield too, because I could see into his mind. He was remembering every sign I gave him. Every clue. He replayed every conversation. Saw every flinch . . . I felt the heat of his anger grow with each memory. His desire to rip apart flesh flooded into me.

I consciously slammed my shield back into place.

Asher leaned back to a kneeling position, removing his hands from the ground. Claw marks raked deep grooves in the dirt. His hard gaze met mine and his fury burned through my shield.

"Rose . . ." he breathed, his voice ragged. "I . . ." He trailed off as another tremor wracked through him. He rubbed the back of his neck hard enough that blood welled where his claws pricked his skin.

"How much did you see?" I whispered.

He didn't say anything, but his rage flared again. I dropped my gaze to the ground.

"I'm sorry," I said in that same small voice. "I didn't want you to see that."

"Rose, don't apologize." He stood on powerful legs and strode toward me. I watched him approach, not sure what to do. Asher was strong—much stronger than *him*—and he was mad. I cowered, pulling into myself as he drew nearer. He froze, eyes going wide. "I'm not going to hurt you."

"You're angry." My words were barely audible.

"Not at you," he growled, dropping to his knees. "I am beyond angry. I am *furious* that he . . . that he hurt you." His shoulders slumped and he ran a hand through his hair in frustration. "I'm mad at myself for making you relive it. I promised to protect you. I can't protect you from your own memories, but the least I could do is not send you spiraling back into them. I failed you. Stars, Rose. I'm sorry."

I took a deep breath to steady myself. Then another. Asher was my friend—he wouldn't hurt me. He was safe.

Right?

I shook my head. "You were talking about surface thoughts and deep thoughts. Well, that memory is never really far from the surface." Another deep, shuddering breath. "It's always waiting for something to remind me and throw me back there."

Asher's gaze never strayed from mine as he crawled toward me on hands and knees. He stopped beside me, leaving his hands on the ground between us. I watched as his claws retracted, forming again into human fingers.

"It's been happening less and less." I caught myself chewing a nail and forced myself to stop. "This was actually the first time I was able to come out of it before . . ." I swallowed. Asher closed his eyes and a muscle twitched in his jaw. I reached forward and grasped one of his hands. His eyes snapped open. "It was because of you. You pulled me out of it. *Thank you*." My voice broke on the words.

He opened his arms to me, and I hardly hesitated before leaning into him. It was awkward at first, but grew more comfortable as my tense muscles relaxed. My head rested against his chest, listening to his steady heartbeat. The sound comforted me as his fingers stroked gently through my hair and down my back.

"Rose, even if I do get angry at you, I will *never* hurt you . . . and I will never be angry with you for telling me 'no'."

I shivered. Asher's sigh tickled my hair and his arms tightened around me.

"You are safe with me, little human. Stars, that I even have to tell you that shatters me. What did he do to you?"

"I think you saw." The tears I tried to suppress burned behind my scrunched eyelids.

"Please, Rose." He was hardly breathing. "Talk to me."

"I . . . I've never told anyone." I swallowed. My voice was barely audible to my own ears. I breathed in Asher's scent, letting it give me strength. "He made me feel like I was nothing. That I was worthless. That if I did tell someone, they wouldn't care. He got so angry over little things. He was . . . physically rough with me." Asher's hands stilled on my back when he saw me unconsciously rubbing my wrists. I clasped my hands together to stop myself. "I know you aren't him, Asher. I *know* that." I took a shaky breath. "I want to trust you, it's just hard to . . . I trusted *him* and . . ." I trailed off, unable to continue past the tension in my throat.

Asher held me for several breaths. "Rose, please look at me."

I tilted my head back to look him in the eye.

"You are not worthless. You are so important. To Blaine and Flora, to this quest, to this world." He tucked a lock of hair behind my ear. "To me. You are amazing, and beautiful, and brave."

When my gaze dropped back to the ground, he sighed.

"If I can help it, little human, you will never feel worthless again." He pulled me against him and rested his chin on my head, his fingers tracing soothing circles down my back. "If I ever meet that monster, I will rip him apart for what he did to you. As for trusting me, I'm in no hurry. I will prove myself to you as many times as you need."

I couldn't hold in my tears any longer.

I didn't know how long we sat there together, Asher wiping away my silent tears while I listened to the steady rhythm of his heartbeat. I was too grateful for the comfort he brought me to be self-conscious at how close we were sitting. He learned about my nightmares and didn't run away. Something inside of me clicked into place. I didn't realize how scared I was that he would leave. That he would think my friendship wasn't worth wading through my mess.

He saw my deepest regret first hand, and he was still here, holding me.

Eventually, my tears ran out and I opened my eyes to a beautiful burning sunset. The colors in the sky ranged from sky blue, to deep purple, to burning orange, and crimson red. The wispy white clouds cut slashes across the sky, fracturing the colors and making them seem brighter. I looked from the vibrant sky to Asher. His gaze fell to mine and warmth blossomed in my chest. His golden eyes were bright in the light of the setting sun. His hand was gentle as he placed it lightly on my cheek to wipe away the final tear.

Nineteen

I DIDN'T HAVE MY usual nightmares.

After yesterday's episode, I expected scenes from the assault to play again and again in my dreams. That's how it always happened in the past. Eventually, I would stop trying to sleep. I would lay there awake all night. I would be groggy and irritable the next day—prone to another lapse into that memory.

This morning, however, I woke up feeling refreshed. I opened my eyes to sunlight streaming into our campsite like a waterfall. Flora was still curled in her sleeping bag, but Blaine was up practicing with Peacekeeper. His puffs of breath were visible in the chilly morning air. Where was Asher? I rolled over, and my heart stuttered.

A giant, fuzzy form lay stretched out beside me. He was awake, resting his head on his paws, scanning the forest around us. Keeping guard over me while I slept. Had he been there all night? An unfamiliar warmth filled my chest.

"Good morning." My voice was thick with sleep.

His tail wagged. He stood, bumped his nose against my shoulder, and trotted away to shift. When Flora woke, we ate a quick breakfast, then packed up camp and set out again. Blaine and Flora took the lead, while Asher and I followed.

The sun was directly overhead when Asher jolted to a stop beside me. Flora grabbed Blaine and pulled him away the same moment Asher hooked an arm around my waist and spun me behind the nearest tree. My back pressed against rough bark and he leaned into me, arms on the trunk to either side of my head. My breath caught in my throat. I was trapped between an unyielding wall and hard muscle. I knew he was providing cover, but it was too similar to the memory. It was too soon. I was going to fall back there. I wasn't strong enough to—

Asher pulled back to put space between our bodies. He was still close, but we were no longer touching. I let out a shaky breath and made myself look at his face. He grimaced down at me.

Sorry. His voice was quiet, even in my head. *Stay with me.*

I took another breath, this one steadier than the last. Asher. This was just Asher. He wouldn't hurt me. He—

Dry leaves rustled nearby. The sound was so soft, I wouldn't have heard it over my own footsteps. Asher caught my gaze. He held a finger in front of his lips then tapped his temple. I pressed my lips together and reinforced my shield.

Out of nowhere, grief overwhelmed me. I was glad for the support of the tree at my back as I sagged against its rough bark. The feeling was so strong, so *raw*, that I couldn't breathe. I didn't know I was crying until Asher wiped away one of my tears with trembling fingers. This was the second time I'd cried in front of him in as many days. I should have been embarrassed, but I wasn't. His eyes were rimmed with red, too. His brows furrowed as he scanned the woods around us. When his gaze locked on something, I peeked over his arm to get a look.

A translucent figure moved in the distance. It was humanoid, but I couldn't make out any details. It floated smoothly over the rough terrain, but its forward movement was jumpy. It was only visible in the shadows of the trees, disappearing in columns of light and reappearing in the next shadow. It passed so close to us I could have reached out to touch it. I bit back a whimper, clutching Asher's shoulders to keep myself upright.

The grief was a boulder on my chest. Tears streamed down my cheeks. I wanted to break down. I wanted to bury my face in Asher's shirt and sob, but I refused to take my eyes off the creature. It paused beside us. The familiar, acrid reek of smoke and burning stucco hit me, and my stomach churned. Faraway screams sounded in my mind, overshadowed by shattering glass and the crackle of flames.

The creature continued on its way and disappeared from my sight. My mind cleared—had I imagined all that? I looked up at Asher, but he shook his head before I could speak. His entire body was vibrating. His fingers shifted into claws, digging into the tree to either side of me. I squeezed his shoulders in a way I hoped was comforting. I was afraid to do more than that.

Several minutes later, the crushing grief faded. Asher took a deep breath and released a sigh. His hands were fully human again when he took a step away from me, but deep grooves scarred the trunk.

"I think it's gone," he whispered.

"What was it?" I asked, matching his volume. Flora and Blaine emerged from their hiding place.

Blaine shivered. "It gave me the creeps."

"I've never seen anything like it." Flora looked shaken, but she was obviously trying to hide it. She looked to Asher, who shook his head. He didn't know what it was either.

"Did you guys feel . . ." I didn't know how to finish that question. I put my hand to my chest, reveling in the fact that I could once again take a deep breath. I hadn't felt grief like that since the night my parents died.

"Yes," Asher breathed. We locked gazes. He looked away first.

"I felt hopeless." Blaine gripped Peacekeeper's hilt. "Empty. Flora?"

Flora wrinkled her nose. "Anxious."

Blaine shook his head. "I feel a lot better now with that thing gone."

"Let's keep moving," Asher said, looking into the distance where the creature had disappeared. "I don't want to be here when it comes back."

The atmosphere of the group was colder than the weather. We navigated through the forest without speaking, each of us wrapped in our own thoughts. We broke for a quick lunch of ham and cheese sandwiches from Flora's magic cooler, as lighting a fire would attract unwanted attention. The usually satisfying lunch meat tasted bland in the dismal atmosphere. Blaine tried to break the tension a few times with some jokes, but I could tell his heart wasn't in it.

After lunch, I walked alone at the back of the procession while Blaine grilled Asher on lycan pack dynamics. Asher kept nervously glancing back at Flora and me. I noticed he liked to travel at the back—most likely because he could protect us from something sneaking up on us. I wasn't concerned. He was so quick, he'd have no trouble getting to us in time if something attacked. Directly in front of me, Flora trudged on, scuffing her feet along the ground and leaving trails in the fallen pine needles.

"Flora?" I asked. "You feeling okay?"

"Of course." She barely turned her head to look at me.

"You just seem . . . distant." They all seemed distant. They had been pulling into themselves during our hike—pulling away from me.

"Don't be ridiculous." She rolled her eyes as she faced forward. "I'm fine."

Right, ridiculous. Because I wasn't helpful to anyone here. I was just in everyone's way. The words hit me hard and my thoughts spiraled to that familiar dark place. I dropped back a bit behind the group, feet suddenly heavy. A familiar iron weight formed in my chest and my lungs worked harder to take in a full breath. I reached into my pack to grab my inhaler—

—and ran into a wall.

I stumbled backwards. My hands flew to my nose as the pain radiated out behind my eyes. I squinted, looking for what I hit. I didn't see anything, so I reached out my hand. There was an invisible barrier there, separating me from my friends. I was dazed long enough to notice the unnatural quiet. The birds stopped singing and the bugs stopped buzzing. Even the wind blowing through the branches didn't make a sound.

That's when the panic set in.

Blaine

"Rose?" Asher's tone made me glance back. Rose was standing a few yards behind us, hand stretched in front of her, waving. Her mouth was moving, lips forming words, but no noise was coming out. She shook her fist in the air like she was pounding it against a wall.

It took my brain too long to comprehend. Only when Flora pressed her palm against the barrier opposite a wide-eyed Rose did I understand—she was trapped. I ran to Rose, slamming my own fists against her invisible cage. Asher used deft hands to feel for a way in, reaching high and low on the invisible wall. He sprinted a wide loop around her with no luck. Rose's brows furrowed and she beat both fists against the barrier.

Flames burst to life behind her and I went cold. She spun around and pressed her back to the invisible wall. Smoke rapidly filled the space as fire burned away foliage. Trunks blackened and needles curled as the flames enveloped them. The smoke got thicker, but it had nowhere to go. It climbed as far as it could, but it was trapped in some sort of invisible dome.

Rose threw her arm over her face, breathing into her sleeve to protect herself from the acrid smoke. Her body wracked, coughing silently. My pounding fists left smears of blood against the dome before I thought to use my sword. I sliced at Rose's prison with Peacekeeper, but the metal bounced off uselessly. Beside me, Flora's hands were glowing against the shield, and Asher was attempting to rip apart the barrier with long, sharp claws.

A wave of power blasted the three of us backwards. Darkness swept over the dome, hiding what was happening inside. Asher was the first one up, slamming himself against the wall again and again before I could even scramble to my feet. A single hand pressed against the inside of the dome where Asher kept attacking. As the seconds ticked by, the hand slid downward. Then it fell away. It didn't reappear.

"No . . ." I choked out. This couldn't be happening. I couldn't lose her. Not again.

Asher slammed his shoulder into the wall with a growl. He stumbled back, strength faltering, then gathered himself for another attack. Before he could hit the wall again, it vanished. The darkness lifted and the smoke dissipated into the air. Rose lay on the edge of a charred circle, pine needles smoldering into ash around her.

I bolted for her, but Asher beat me there. He slid to his knees, stirring clouds of ash. He tried to feel for her pulse, but his fingers were still tipped in claws. He snarled at his own hands and dropped his head to her chest instead, pressing his ear against her sternum. After what felt like too long, he breathed a sigh of relief and sat up to study her.

I crumpled on her other side, gaping. She was completely untouched by the fire. Her clothes were intact; she had no burns that I could see. She just laid there, breathing evenly, like she had just fallen asleep.

Everything else trapped inside that dome was obliterated.

"What the hell?" My voice was hoarse and I cleared my throat. Had I been screaming?

Asher tore his gaze from Rose to meet mine. His eyes were wild with the same panic I felt. Flora knelt at Rose's head and placed a hand on each of her temples. When she made contact, Asher snarled in warning. Flora shot him an annoyed look and closed her eyes. After a moment, her brows furrowed.

"She's not physically injured but she's shielding," Flora said. "I . . . huh. I can't get in." She looked at Asher. "You try. She might recognize you."

Asher nodded, focusing on Rose. A tense moment went by before his expression softened.

"She's dreaming."

"Thank the Forest," Flora muttered under her breath.

Relief washed through me, sapping my strength. I slumped where I knelt. Asher reached out with now-human fingers to wipe a soot smear from Rose's cheek, deftly pushing away Flora's hands in the process.

"We were loud." Flora got to her feet. "That may have drawn some unwanted attention. Are either of you able to carry her?"

Asher nodded and scooped Rose up like she was a small child. The sight of her limp arm dangling from her shoulder made me nauseous. I darted to grab her hand, reassuring myself with her strong pulse as I folded her arm across her stomach. Asher nodded his thanks to me and set off after Flora, who was already slipping silently through the trees. We hadn't traveled far when an eerie yipping sounded from where we had been. What kind of animal was that?

"Come on, we have to keep going," Flora urged.

I helped as much as I could by ensuring Asher's path was clear for him to carry Rose through, but the going was still slow. At one point, Asher stumbled over some uneven footing. I reached out to steady him before they both ended up on the ground.

"Thanks," he muttered.

"Do you need a break?" I asked. "I can carry—"

"No." He spoke through clenched teeth. "I've got her."

It was for the best—I didn't think I was strong enough to carry her for very long anyway. That yipping sounded again, closer this time. We picked up the pace.

"Flora . . . that dome," Asher asked between breaths, "was that by any chance . . . a trap we set off without realizing?"

"No." Flora paused for Asher to catch up. Her calculating gaze landed on Rose, asleep in Asher's arms. "I don't think it was."

He nodded.

"If it wasn't a trap . . ." I said, stating out loud what my friends had already concluded. I had seen power like that in Alaric's memories. The witches would use those domes as protective shields during battle. He saw some that were so powerful they could cover entire battalions. "How is that possible?"

No one had an answer for me.

Rose

The first thing I saw when I awoke was Asher's face. His golden eyes, soft with concern, stared into mine. His arms wrapped around me, just like in my dream. Was I still dreaming? The red streaks that made his hair so distinctive were hardly visible in the dimming light of the forest. This close to him, I could see stubble on his cheeks and the crinkle of skin at the corner of his mouth as his lips moved. His face had filled out some since we met—he looked good. I reached up and trailed my fingers along his cheek, feeling the coarse hair scrape against my skin. His lips turned down in a frown.

"Rose," he said gently, "can you hear me?"

"Y-yeah." Heat flooded my face and I pulled my hand back. "Sorry, I—"

"How do you feel?"

"I'm okay . . ." I frowned, remembering that invisible wall and the encroaching flames. I clutched at Asher's shirt. "I'm okay? How am I okay? What happened?"

"We think—" Asher glanced behind me "—*you* happened."

"What?"

"We think you created that dome." Asher's words were clear, but their meaning wasn't clicking.

"Created it?"

"With your magic," Flora clarified from behind me. I blinked at her.

"You're sure there are no witches in your world?" Asher asked.

"You think I'm a witch?" My head spun. "Blaine, tell them . . ." I trailed off because Blaine was grinning at me. "I'm not a witch, I don't have magic."

"Well . . . but how would we know?" Blaine's excitement was palpable. "What if there are witches on Earth that we don't know about? I mean, we didn't know about Silaris before literally falling through a hole in space."

"It's likely there were witches caught on Earth when the portal was sealed who had to integrate into your society," Flora mused. "Perhaps one of Rose's relatives passed down this power and it's only coming out now that she's in Silaris."

"No way," I scoffed. "What are the odds?"

"You're the math genius. You tell us." Blaine shrugged.

"Infinitesimal. Nonexistent. There's no way I'm a witch."

"You made it through the Rift. Flora said ordinary humans wouldn't survive."

I just shook my head. Blaine wasn't listening.

"Those flames demolished *everything* in that dome, Rose," Flora said. "Everything, except you. The only explanation I can think of is that *you* created them. They were your flames, so they couldn't hurt you."

The flames didn't hurt me . . . just like before when . . .

"We couldn't get to you until you lost consciousness," Asher said, interrupting my thoughts. There was an edge to his voice that I couldn't quite place. "If it hadn't been your magic, I don't think it would have let you go unharmed."

I gaped at my friends. Me, a witch? Impossible. A bubble of laughter broke unbidden from my throat. I covered my mouth with my hand to muffle the hysterical sound, but I couldn't stop. My friends stared at me, wide-eyed.

Then I was sobbing, breaths coming in ragged bursts, tears streaming down my cheeks. I covered my face with my hands. God, they probably thought I was crazy. Asher's thumb caressed my back in a comforting sweep. Elation filled me and I heard myself giggle—actually *giggle*. I leaned into Asher, feeling light. Maybe I *was* crazy.

"Rose . . .?" Asher said, bewildered.

"Mood swings are normal after the first significant release of power," a woman's gruff voice said from behind my friends. Blaine and Flora spun to place themselves between me and the stranger, drawing their swords. Asher's grip on me tightened. I couldn't stifle my laughter.

"At least, I assume this is her first, although she looks a bit too old for that," the woman continued, not bothered by my friends' defensive stances. "Typically, they snap around fifteen, but there's always one or two late bloomers. Come with me, I'll get her fixed up."

When no one moved to follow, the woman put her hands on her hips. "That girl needs to feel safe."

"What makes you think she doesn't?" Flora asked.

"See those storm clouds above you?"

I felt Asher look up, but the hiccupping sobs started again. I buried my face into his shoulder to keep them quiet. It didn't work.

"The creatures in this forest know how to hunt a scared witch," the woman said. Her words were punctuated by strange, high-pitched howls.

"Shit." Blaine pointed Peacekeeper toward the woods behind us. "Those things caught up again."

"A scared witch is a vulnerable witch." She scowled. "You need to calm that girl. And we need to move."

"We can't stay here," Flora muttered. "We should follow her."

"Seems like that's our best option," Asher grumbled. He gave me a reassuring squeeze and lifted me into his arms. The cadence of his hurried steps added to my anxiety, and I clutched him. His voice lowered. "Blaine? Maybe . . . maybe you should carry Rose."

"What?" Blaine's voice sounded startled. "Why?"

"She trusts you."

Did I? Did I trust anyone? My heart constricted painfully in the time it took for Blaine to respond. I wasn't sure if that was part of the mood swings, or if the feeling was real. A few raindrops broke from the clouds above.

"She trusts you too, Asher. Just . . . I don't know. Talk to her."

"What do I say?" Asher sounded panicked. "I don't know how to make someone feel safe."

Blaine snorted. "You think I do?"

"I . . ." Asher sighed. I felt his exhale on my damp cheeks. "Okay. Rose, if you're listening . . . don't be afraid. You're . . ." His voice lowered to a soft murmur in my ear. "You're safe with me. I've got you. Nothing is going to touch you. Let's consider this step one to earning your trust, okay? Step one of one-hundred. Or one-thousand. Or five-thousand. Whatever the number, this can be step one. I will get you out of this safely. I promise."

"Whatever you're doing," Blaine's voice was more distant now. "Keep doing it. I think it's working."

I must have drifted off to sleep, because the next thing I knew I was waking up on a soft couch with a splitting headache. I cracked my eyelids to slits and saw exposed wooden walls—a log cabin? I bolted upright. The sudden movement caused the pain to flair, making my head spin. I groaned as nausea ripped through me. A bucket was thrust into my hands before I could get sick all over the floor.

I retched until there was nothing left in my stomach. Gentle, calloused hands pulled back my hair to keep it out of the way. I was too mortified to look to see who it was. A cold sweat broke out all over my body. I leaned over the bucket for a few moments with my eyes closed, trying to regulate my breathing.

"The first one always comes with a doozy of a hangover."

My eyes snapped open at the unfamiliar woman's voice, and I had to fight through another bout of nausea. I vaguely remembered seeing her in the forest, but everything was fuzzy. I couldn't think past the pain in my head.

She pulled a kettle from the fire and poured its contents into a mug. There was a strange, wispy blue aura surrounding her, but that could have been the migraine. She flourished her hand and I gasped as the bucket I was holding disappeared.

The woman was middle-aged. Her black hair fell around her shoulders and was turning silver in places. She wore a plain beige shirt, dirt-stained brown pants, and soft moccasins, but it was the blue of her eyes that captured my attention. They reminded me of my mother's eyes—of the eyes that peered back at me from the mirror every day. She hesitated, blinking back at me, then handed me the steaming mug. I took it automatically, too dazed to do anything else.

"Drink this," she said. "You'll feel better."

I looked to the steady presence beside me. Asher's hand was still on my back, lending me support. An aura of wispy white clouds lined with gold surrounded him—definitely the migraine, then.

I raised my eyebrows at him and pain shot through my temples. He shrugged one shoulder. That meant it was probably safe, right? Regardless, I was willing to do anything to get some relief. Every little movement sent stabs of lightning through my eyes.

I took a small sip and waited for any ill effects. I grimaced when the hot liquid hit my tongue. The drink tasted nothing like what I expected. It was somehow both extremely bitter and overly sweet. The intensity of my headache did lessen, though. I took another, larger drink, confirming the concoction truly was helping as my splitting headache dulled into a constant pounding in my temples. The auras around Asher and the woman faded. The sudden relief brought tears to my eyes.

I didn't want to risk vomiting again, so I paced myself with the rest of the mug. No longer distracted by pain, I looked around the room. The couch I sat on faced a wide fireplace with cookware off to one side. A small kitchen with a sink and some cabinets were off to my left and two closed doors were to my right. A wooden dining table with four chairs sat near a large window behind me. Flora and Blaine slumped in two of those chairs, looking exhausted. I caught a glimpse of green around Flora before the aura faded completely from my vision, but I didn't see anything around Blaine. Red marks matching the woodgrain of the table marred both of their faces. The curtains on the window behind them were drawn tightly shut, so I couldn't see what time of day it was.

"Who . . ." My voice was thick with sleep. I cleared my throat and tried again. "Who are you?"

"My name is Loretha," she said. "Welcome to my home. You've got a well trained guard wolf here." She looked at Asher curiously. "He hasn't left your side for hours. I'm not sure he's even blinked since you've arrived."

Asher's eyes narrowed at Loretha, but he didn't say anything. He didn't look at me when I peered up at him.

"Loretha." The name felt strangely familiar on my tongue. "Why do you have my eyes?"

"I could ask you the same question, child." Loretha sighed. "Finish your tea, then drink another full mug. Take tonight to rest and feel better. You must be exhausted. We'll talk in the morning. I believe we have a lot to discuss."

With that, she strode through one of the doors and closed it behind her, leaving the four of us alone. A pile of blankets and pillows suddenly appeared on the ground, making me jump. I barely avoided spilling my tea.

In an instant, Blaine was sitting beside me and Flora was perched on the arm of the sofa. She reached over top of Blaine and placed her hand on my forehead. A growl rumbled from Asher, but Flora ignored him.

"Your fever is gone." She sighed in relief. "I can't believe I'm saying this, but you should drink more of that tea, whatever it is."

I nodded and took a long drink, finishing the mug. Flora took it from my hands and filled it up again using the kettle beside the fire. She handed it back to me and raised her eyebrow when I didn't immediately take a drink.

"Give her a second to breathe, Flora," Blaine admonished softly. "She'll drink it."

Flora nodded and perched back on the arm of the sofa, still staring at me. They were all staring. It was getting weird.

"I'm fine," I said. "You can stop looking at me like I'm about to collapse."

"We're just worried about you," Blaine said with a small smile. "You can't blame us for being a bit overprotective after what happened back there."

"I guess there's no sense denying that I'm a witch now, is there?" I took another swallow of my tea. The more I drank of it, the more I felt like myself. I looked around at my friends, they all looked so exhausted. "Are you three okay? Did I hurt anyone?"

"You didn't hurt us, Rose," Blaine said, glancing past me at Asher. "Though, I thought Asher was going to break something trying to get through that dome."

Asher placed a hand on his shoulder and rolled it, wincing. "Nothing a good night's sleep won't fix."

"Then rest." I wasn't sure how I felt about him hurting himself to get to me. I was too tired to process that right now. "You should all get some rest."

"We will," Asher said, but he made no move to do so.

"So . . ." I said after a few moments of silence. "How much do we tell Loretha?"

"Everything," Blaine said. "We were sitting ducks out there. We need her help."

"I don't know much about human magic," Flora admitted. "She may be able to teach you to use your powers."

"You think I should learn it?" I frowned. "I thought you said human magic was bad."

"The Council teaches that it's an abomination but . . . we need every advantage we can get."

I looked at Asher. He was so close I could see the silver flecks in his golden irises as he studied my face.

"She smells like you," he said. "That's why I followed her in the first place. The coincidence is too great to overlook. And she helped you."

"Okay, then it's settled." I drained my tea. "Tomorrow, we'll tell her everything."

Twenty

I WOKE TO THE sounds of a fire crackling in the hearth and the smell of freshly baked bread. My head rested on Asher's chest and his arms wrapped around me. He sat mostly upright with his head leaning back against the couch, eyes still closed. His deep, even breathing suggested he was still asleep. I lay there for a few moments, enjoying the calming effect of listening to his heartbeat, before I carefully extracted myself from his arms. Flora and Blaine cuddled on the couch too—none of us wanted to go too far from the others—and I was surprised my movement didn't wake them.

I shuffled to the little kitchen where Loretha was whisking eggs in a bowl. I shifted my weight from one foot to the other, unsure what to do, until she pointed at the loaf of bread on the cutting board. Relieved at having a job, I started slicing. When I finished, she gestured for me to follow her to the fire. We sat on the ground in front of the fireplace as she dumped the eggs into a preheated pan. I gaped as she levitated the slices of bread into the slots of a strange metal object. Once the slots were full, she placed the contraption on the side of the flames.

It's a toaster, I thought, bemused.

"Your friends were very worried about you," Loretha said as we sat there. "You gave them quite the scare with that shield."

"I didn't mean to," I whispered. "I don't even know what I did."

She pursed her lips. "You may be a late bloomer, but you should still know the theory of how to control your magic by now. Didn't your parents ever teach you?"

"My parents are dead."

"I see." Her eyes softened. "I'm sorry to hear you lost your parents. Would it be comforting to know that we are related?"

"We are? How do you know?"

"The familial magic called to me when you used your power. A lot of things probably felt it, actually—it was strong. You're lucky I was in the area gathering herbs. We witch families have to stay together. There are some nasty things out in those woods, especially recently."

"Yeah, we ran into something earlier." I shivered at the memory. "It seemed to suck out all the happiness from me."

"Ah yes, the mournwraith. They won't actually hurt you unless you get in their way. Some of the more reclusive witches have started using them to patrol their borders, so it's good you avoided the one you saw. It's the sentient pools of darkness you really have to watch out for. People don't always come out of those." Loretha studied me. "But why don't you already know that? And why don't I know you?"

"I'm from Earth—a different world. I came through a portal to get here. I didn't even know magic existed until a few weeks ago, let alone that I could do it."

"A portal to a different world?" Her eyes widened. "My great grandmother once told a tale of a tear in the world created by an ancient dragon. A distant ancestor fell though, never to be seen again. Perhaps your existence proves the story true. It's conceivable she survived and ended up in your world.

"If your parents never taught you how to control your magic, it's possible they didn't have any themselves. Power can skip one or several generations. Where should I begin . . ." She paused for a moment, thinking. "You will have to excuse my disorganization. I haven't taught for many years, and our children are usually much younger when they are learning."

"The elves said human magic was bad," I said. "They called it an abomination. Is it dangerous?"

"Dangerous?" Loretha scoffed. "No, the elves just don't like that we can do magic. From what I'm told, elves draw their power from nature and the natural world. Our powers come from within ourselves, from our emotions. That's why the first time a witch experiences their power, the effect is based on what they were feeling at the time. For example, you created a shield to keep people out. What were you feeling prior? Perhaps unsafe? Vulnerable? Isolated?"

"Isolated, I think," I said, trying to remember. "My brain knew it was stupid to feel that way but . . ." I shrugged.

"Strong emotions don't always coincide with what your brain knows." Loretha smiled. "Your friends seem to care about you very much. You know, that lycan actually *growled* at me when I tried to take you from him."

"Yeah, he does that." I smiled, the thought making me feel warm.

"Be careful." She laughed. "*That* emotion is a tough one to control."

I blushed, and she laughed louder.

"Your friends told me there is no magic in your home world, but I find that difficult to believe. The magic comes from within you, so if you have magic here, you have it everywhere."

"Why am I only experiencing it now?" I asked. "If I had magic on Earth, why couldn't I use it there?"

"Most people experience their powers for the first time in their fifteenth year." Her voice softened. "In my experience, when people don't manifest at that age, it's because they encounter something that stunts their emotional maturity. Some sort of emotional trauma or abuse, perhaps."

"Oh." I stared into the cookfire, unable to meet her gaze. The toast was beginning to brown on one side, so I pulled it out and flipped the slices in the slots before pushing it back into the hearth.

Loretha flipped the eggs in the pan.

"It's hard to control magic if you can't identify healthy emotions. The good news is, magic tends to manifest for those witches when they finally begin to heal from that trauma. However, the older the witch, the harder it is to learn control."

"How can I learn to control my powers?"

Loretha smiled. "Practice."

When the others woke, we gathered at Loretha's table for breakfast. She pulled a fifth chair to the table, muttering about how it had been so long since she had proper company. She told us she was part of the Shellborn witch family, meaning our ancestors were beach settlers who used seashells to aid their spells.

"We know now that talismans, like seashells, aren't necessary for spells. However, that doesn't stop us from clinging to the beach." She gestured around her home. I hadn't noticed right away, but the walls were bordered with old and crumbling seashells. A few of them were unrecognizable as shells.

"If you love the beach so much," Flora asked, "why don't you live closer?"

"We don't have much of a beach in the Hiraeth Pines, unfortunately. After the treaty, we were isolated here without knowing what the terrain would be like. My ancestors tried to settle near the water, but the Cedarclan witches wanted that area for themselves. There was a battle, but with my family being cut off from the beach, we were weakened, and we lost.

"Truthfully, I have never even seen a proper beach. Perhaps, if you four are here, that means the treaty is no longer keeping the border locked. I can't imagine a lycan and an elf also came from Earth." She cast a wary look at Flora and Asher.

"That's a long story," Blaine said.

"In honesty, I can't believe a lycan and an elf are sitting at a table with a witch and a human," —Loretha smiled at me— "but if my cousin trusts you, then so shall I."

A thrill went through me. She said 'cousin' as if I was an equal, not just some kid. It was hard for me to believe that we were related, even though the proof was all around me. I didn't want to get my hopes up, just to have them shattered.

"I have the time if you do," Loretha prompted.

So we told her our story with as many details as we could remember. Each of us jumped in when someone forgot something—other than Asher, who didn't speak, but instead absorbed every detail. When we finished, Loretha looked at Blaine, expression serious.

"I do not envy your task, son," she said. "There are many here who will not be happy this day has come. The young witches trying to gain power will surely resist the change you bring."

Blaine frowned and his shoulders slumped, but resolve tightened his jaw.

"We witches have a legend." Loretha's gaze went unfocused and she held her glass frozen halfway to her lips. "It's told around campfires. A fantastical tale . . . but perhaps not. It claims the Bringer of Change will be our undoing and our salvation. They will come from a distant land to reclaim their once lost home, bringing with them a resurgence of empathy amongst us, therefore cultivating our power."

"And you think I'm this Bringer of Change?" Blaine asked.

"Perhaps, but it is not for me to say." Loretha looked at the glass in her hand as if just noticing she was holding it. She took a drink, then cleared her throat. "Did you bring any ropes?"

"Uh . . . some." Blaine gestured to his pack on the ground by the door. "About ten feet of paracord."

"I'll get you some from the shed before you leave. You're going to need quite a bit to make it down the cliffs."

"Cliffs?" Blaine asked. His voice jumped up an octave. "What cliffs are those?"

"The cave that holds the Argem sits within the seaside cliffs. You'll have a hard time climbing up the rock, so I recommend rappelling down."

"Oh." Blaine paled.

"Do you know the location of the cave?" Flora asked, hopefully.

"I've never been," Loretha said, "but, it's rumored to be within sight of the Dragon's Horns."

"The what?" Blaine asked at the same time Flora muttered, "Ominous."

"A rock formation off the coast." Loretha clarified. "Two spikes jut from the water like horns. It isn't really a dragon. I recommend you start your search there."

We all nodded in agreement.

After breakfast, Loretha brought me to a clearing at the front of her cabin. She shooed away some of her chickens—which were larger and more colorful than any I had seen on Earth—and created a shield around the two of us. I looked around in awe as the shield cut off the sounds of the forest around us and plunged us into almost complete silence.

"Catch this on fire," she said, picking up a stick and stabbing it into the soft ground so it pointed towards the sky.

"How?" I asked.

"Feel it."

"What?" I blinked at her.

"Feel it," she repeated.

"Feel . . . fire?"

"Yes."

Okay, I guess I wasn't getting any more instruction than that. Dumbfounded, I stared at the stick on the ground, willing it to burn. After a minute, I looked up at Loretha.

"It's not working," I said.

"Well, you aren't feeling it."

I narrowed my eyes and focused on the stick, feeling ridiculous. This wasn't any way to teach something. Any sort of explanation would be helpful.

"Come on, Rose, dig deep. Feel the fire," Loretha said.

"I'm trying." Frustration flashed through me. How was I supposed to—"Oh!"

I jumped back as a small flame leapt from the solitary stick. The flame quickly extinguished, but it had definitely been there.

"Good," Loretha said. "What did you feel to create that?"

"I was . . . frustrated."

"Yes, good! Fire is the easiest of elements to start with because it is based on hot emotions such as frustration and anger. The other elements are more abstract. Air is another easy one, as it is based on happiness. Let's try that one next. Think of the happiest memory you have and let's see what happens."

I nodded, casting my mind out for a happy memory. I settled on one from when I was young—the first time my parents had brought me to the beach. We played all day in the sun, making sand castles and running through the shallow water. I could almost smell the salt and feel the wind tugging at my hair. I opened my eyes. The wind actually *was* tugging at my hair. The wind stopped blowing as the memory faded.

"Very good. Now water needs tranquility and earth needs groundedness. Let's try those next."

I tried and failed to summon earth and water. When my head began to pound and flames started coming to me unbidden, Loretha suggested we take a break. She dropped the dome around us to the sharp sounds of clashing swords. I looked across the yard to see Blaine and Asher sparring with each other, Flora watching raptly, trying to learn by observation.

"How do I make that protective dome?" I asked Loretha.

"You've already made a shield. Don't you remember how?"

"Not really," I said. "I just felt so alone, I pushed everyone out. How do I make one, but include my friends?"

"That's a little trickier." Loretha thought for a moment. "To create a shield, you must isolate yourself in your mind. To include others inside that shield, they have to be included in your isolation. Think of what you have in common to the people you are trying to include. For example, you and I are family, so that's how I isolated the two of us from the others. The stronger the bond, the easier it is to erect a shield."

I thought for a moment. "Then how do you drop the shield? I was trapped before. The magic didn't drop until I passed out."

"I would think the answer is obvious. Just don't feel so alone."

I pursed my lips. Easier said than done. "Can I try it?"

"Let me move out of the way first. I'm too old to be getting clobbered by a shield wall." She stepped several feet away, leaving me on my own in the yard. I closed my eyes, reaching for that feeling of loneliness. It didn't take me long to find it, and the sudden stillness of the dome made me open my eyes. Loretha was smiling and nodding. I was pretty sure her lips formed the words "good job" before tapping on the barrier. I walked forward to where she was standing and put my fingers against the dome. The barrier felt a little like glass, smooth and strong. I stepped back into the middle, closing my eyes and trying to feel less alone.

It wasn't working. The absolute quiet built as pressure in my head and my heartbeat pounded in my ears. My breathing, extra loud in the silence, hitched as I fought down the emerging panic. I opened my eyes and they fell on Loretha. She mimed for me to take a deep breath, then pointed over to my friends. Asher and Blaine were still sparring, but Flora noticed my gaze and waved. Just like that, I could hear the sounds of the swords crashing off one another once again.

The barrier was gone.

I took a deep breath and crumpled in the grass. I was exhausted and a sharp pain was forming behind my eyes. Loretha called over to me from where she stood.

"Good job, Rose. Why don't you try again?"

I nodded and closed my eyes, reaching for isolation once more.

Blaine

"Wanna spar, Asher?"

"Hmm?" He tore his gaze away from where Rose was training with Loretha and frowned at me. "Oh, I'm not sure—"

"Come on." I unsheathed Peacekeeper and strode to a patch of level ground nearby. "I need to clear my head." *And so do you.* "Sparring helps."

Asher had been quiet that morning, lost in thought, only responding when someone asked him a direct question. It worried me. Blowing off some steam with exercise would be beneficial for both of us, and I was eager to test myself against him again.

"Fine." Asher shot Rose one more guilt-laced look before pulling his knives from his pack and returning my salute.

He was tense, distracted. His head wasn't in the fight, and I saw several places where I could have disarmed him. I didn't take advantage of the openings, however, and let him keep fighting. After a particularly weak display of parries on his part, I disengaged, taking a step back.

"What's going on, Asher?" I asked with a sigh. His gaze drifted over to where Rose was training. "She's okay. She was never in any real danger."

"But what if she was?" His eyes narrowed, back on me. "I couldn't help her."

"None of us could get past that shield. Why is it affecting you so badly?"

He came at me with a few blows, but his heart wasn't in it and I parried easily. I knew that look—he was thinking things through. Processing.

"When I was young," he said when we broke apart, "people hurt my mother. Repeatedly." His lip curled into a snarl and fury danced in his eyes. "I was too small, too helpless to do anything about it, but I could see it killing her. I started exercising to get stronger, training with the knives, anything to give me an edge over her attackers."

He lunged again, the flurry of blows much faster this time. I cursed internally while I struggled to keep up, just barely staying in front of his blades.

"I trained so hard to get stronger," he gritted out through the clashing of our swords, "but I was too late. One night, my pack's alpha—" he huffed out a frustrated breath "—I was only eleven, no match for an alpha. Had it been anyone else, I could have protected her. Had it been anyone else," he growled the words, "she would still be alive."

Peacekeeper spun through the air as he disarmed me with a powerful twist of his daggers. It flipped end over end until it stuck blade down in the soft ground. Asher let his arms fall to his sides and stepped back, looking up at the sky.

"When the alpha gives a command, no one in the pack can disobey. The purpose of the alpha is to protect his pack, but he *ordered* me to leave. So I did, and I hated myself for it. Still do. I fought the magic the whole time, but when I finally overcame the compulsion, it was too late."

I didn't know what to say, so I just stood there, listening. The pain of his loss was so familiar, it threatened to overwhelm me.

"I failed her." He let his knives slip from his hands and they stuck in the ground, hilts protruding into the air. Asher may have disarmed me, but he was the one who looked defeated. "I buried her myself. Then I packed a bag and ran away. I survived on my own until—"

Asher looked over to where Rose practiced with Loretha. They were far enough away that I couldn't hear what they were saying, but a flame burned in the air between Rose's palms.

"I told myself I wouldn't let her get hurt again. I promised I would protect her, but then yesterday . . ." He curled claw-tipped fingers into tight fists. My stomach lurched as a drop of blood rolled down his knuckles. "I was just as ineffective with that barrier as I was with the alpha."

"Listen bro, I'm sorry about your mom, but you know that wasn't your fault, right? You were *eleven*. Rose is . . . you can't protect her from everything." I lowered my voice. "You can't protect her from herself. Everyone has to fight their own battles eventually. The only thing you can do is make sure they're prepared when that time comes."

Asher stared at the two witches. After a moment, his hands relaxed into human fingers. He wiped his bloody palms on his jeans without inspecting the damage.

"Bro?" he cocked his head at me.

"Short for brother." I offered him a smile.

Asher's brows rose, then he nodded. He retrieved my sword and handed it back to me, hilt first. "Can we try again?"

I took up a defensive stance while Asher retrieved his own blades. I wasn't sure if anything I said to him had helped, but he did seem more focused on our practice after that.

We sparred until we were both sweaty and my muscles were heavy. When Asher and I finally broke apart, Flora, who I thought was meditating nearby, bombarded us with questions regarding our bout. We tried our best to answer before Asher excused himself to go clean up in the stream nearby. Before he got too far away, he paused.

"Hey, Blaine?"

"Yeah?"

"Thanks," he hesitated before adding, "bro."

I nodded to him as he slipped through the trees, leaving me alone with Flora. She stared after him with a thoughtful expression.

She crossed her arms in front of herself. "I can't imagine a leader taking advantage of someone like that."

"It happens more than it should." I looked at her. "Does it not happen among the elves?"

"I've never heard of something so horrible." She looked back at me, tears making her eyes an even more vibrant shade of green. My chest ached at the sight of her pain. I opened my arms and she hugged me, burying her face in my shirt. "No child should have to bury their mother."

We stood there for a few moments and I breathed her in. My shoulders relaxed as her citrus and lavender scent enveloped me. Eventually, Flora pulled away, wiping her eyes.

"Sorry," she said. "The thought of something like that happening . . . maybe we shouldn't reestablish the treaty."

I raised my eyebrows, surprised.

"I don't know the right answer, Blaine. I thought I did, but if corrupt people can take power, there must be something wrong with the system."

"I agree."

"I'm going to watch Rose." She wrinkled her nose. "You should go clean up."

"Yes, ma'am," I said with a mock salute. A smile ghosted her lips.

Asher and I didn't speak much as we cleaned up in the cold river water. I moved as fast as I could then bolted for dry land. I couldn't put into words how much I missed indoor plumbing. Violent shivers wracked my body, making it hard to shrug on my jacket.

"Hey." Asher hesitated. "About Rose and me . . . are you . . . okay with it? With us, I mean."

"I'm not her keeper. She can make her own decisions."

"I'd still like to know what you think."

Was I okay with it?

I thought about how Rose looked when I first met her, sunken in and withdrawn. A ghost wandering the campus, her body on autopilot as we moved from one class to the next. Physically going through the motions of living but mentally checked out. Seeing her in that state of living death terrified me—it hit too close to home.

I knew about her parents' deaths, even then. Martin had told my dad, and my dad asked me to keep an eye on her—but I didn't expect her to be so nervous around people. The more time I spent with her, the more my suspicions grew. I worked hard to get her to be comfortable with me. To let her know she was safe. To get her to open up. And she had, if only a little, in the time before we had fallen into Silaris.

Even that girl, though, had been worlds away from the person she was now. Since coming to Silaris and meeting Asher, she had opened up so much more. She was smiling easily and a lot more frequently. There was a light to her eyes and a spring to her step. Maybe I was a little jealous it wasn't my influence that pulled her out of her shell . . . but what kind of friend would I be if I condemned the relationship that had done so much to help her?

So was I okay with Rose and Asher being together? The answer was obvious.

"Of course I am."

"It's just . . . I'm not exactly . . . human."

I snorted. "Like I care about that. She's safer with you than she would be with any human. Plus, Asher, you're my friend—my brother. I'm all for this."

"But we're from completely different worlds." He frowned. "Where can this go? I can't travel through the Rift to your world, and I would never ask her to leave what little family she has left to stay here with me."

"I don't know the answer, Asher." I placed a hand on his shoulder. "But these things tend to work out in unexpected ways. What I do know is that you're helping her heal from whatever she went through." I held my palms up toward him when he cocked his head. "No, I don't know the details and I'm not going to ask, but I do hope knowing her is helping you heal, too."

Asher looked back in the direction of Loretha's cabin. His mouth twitched up in a wistful smile.

Rose

My head was pounding and I could barely stay on my feet, but I kept pushing. After countless times raising and lowering my shield, I was getting much faster. I was also getting better at conjuring fire and wind, but the other elements still eluded me. I grew distracted when Flora came over to watch and ask questions. I grew even more distracted when a freshly bathed lycan with damp hair sprawled on the grass beside Flora, Blaine in tow shortly behind.

"Ah, wonderful." Loretha smiled. "Who would like to help Rose practice shielding someone else?"

"You said that could be painful," I argued. "I don't want to hurt anyone."

"You have to learn, dear." Loretha waved my concerns away. "Besides, it's not truly painful. It's just . . . unpleasant. Blaine, how about you?"

"Uh . . . how unpleasant are we talking?" He obviously didn't want to participate. I wasn't going to force him. This was insane. I wasn't—

"I'll volunteer," Asher said. I bit my lip.

"Wonderful." She smiled. "Come here. Stand close, but don't touch each other." As Asher stood and made his way to us, Loretha turned back to me. "Think of what you have in common with him. What sets you two apart from the rest of the world? Make it a good, strong connection."

With that, she stepped away. Asher offered me an encouraging smile.

"You don't have to do this for me."

"Anything to help you get stronger, little human." He cocked his head to the side. "I guess I should say *little witch*."

"I don't want to hurt you.' My voice wavered.

"You won't."

He said it with more confidence than I felt, so I nodded and closed my eyes. What did we have in common? We were both trying to help find the Argems. Was that a strong enough connection? We were both trying to better the world we lived in. We shared a common goal. We were on the same team.

I opened my eyes, focused on my connection with Asher, and put up my shield.

His eyes flew open wide as he was propelled backward by an invisible force. His impact with the ground probably made an audible thud, but I couldn't hear it through my soundproof shield. He propped himself up on his elbows and said something to Loretha before I could drop my shield. The first sound I heard was her laughter. I wasn't sure if it was at what he had said or at his expense.

"I'm sorry!" I ran to him as he climbed to his feet. "Are you okay?"

"Yeah, just . . . surprised."

"That was awesome, Rose!" Blaine called from a safe distance away.

"You should try again," Loretha said. I gaped at her, but Asher took my hand and led me back to our original starting point.

"She's right," he said, letting go of my hand. "You need to practice. I'll be okay."

"Are you sure?" I asked, to which he nodded and gave me another encouraging smile.

I took a steadying breath and rubbed my temple to alleviate the growing pain. I racked my brain for a stronger connection. We were both orphans—both subjected to grief beyond what a child should ever feel. That *had* to be a strong connection. I put my shield up.

Asher flew backwards. This time he bounced once before skidding to a halt in the grass. He put a hand to his head for a brief moment, but he was up and shaking it off before I could drop my shield to reach him.

"I'm fine." He was already pulling me back to the middle of the clearing. "Try again."

"Asher, I—"

"Try again," he repeated.

The back of my throat burned and I pinched the bridge of my nose to relieve the pressure building in my sinuses. I was beyond frustrated. We had been inside each other's *minds*. I *knew* Asher. We already had a strong connection. I didn't need a specific reason because our bond was already tangible. I threw up my shield.

Asher flinched. He tried to hide it, but there was no mistaking the tightening of his muscles just before he was hurled backwards. My frustration and anger left me in a quick burst of flame inside my isolated shield, leaving only sorrow in its wake when the flames subsided. When I collected myself enough to lower my shield, Asher was hauling himself up from the ground.

"Asher, I'm so sorry." I reached out and put a steadying hand on his arm. "Are you . . ." Of course he wasn't okay—I just threw him across a field three times. Guilt clawed at my stomach. Why was I always hurting people?

Asher forced a smile. "I can go again."

"Maybe you guys should take a break," Blaine suggested from where he sat.

"I'm fine, really."

"I can't . . ." The horror at what I had done tightened my throat.

"You aren't going to hurt me, Rose," Asher said.

"I've already hurt you!" I snapped at him, pointing to the bloody scrape on his arm. His eyebrows pulled together, then he looked down as if just noticing the injury.

"This"—he held up his arm—"is nothing. My own claws cut deeper." He showed me his palm, where four round puncture holes were beginning to scab. When did that happen? "You won't do any lasting damage. You need to practice. My short-term discomfort is worth you mastering the skill. I can take it."

"I *can't* take it," I breathed, so quiet only he could hear. His eyes softened. I swallowed and forced the next words out. "No. I won't do this again. Not today."

He nodded. "Okay."

I froze. "That's it? You aren't going to argue or convince me to try again?"

"You said no. I heard you." He took my trembling hand. "And I'm not mad."

My breath left me in a rush and a strange warmth coursed through me. Did Asher know how much those words meant to me?

"You sure?"

"I promise." He smiled. "I'm so proud of you."

I blinked back the inexplicable tears his words summoned and squeezed his hand in silent thanks. I didn't trust myself to speak.

"You really should try a few more times," Loretha called from across the field.

"She's finished." Asher's face hardened when he looked at Loretha. "You will not push her further than she's willing."

Loretha raised her eyebrows and stared at Asher. I swayed where I stood as the exhaustion caught up with me.

"Fine," she conceded. "I suppose it's time to get dinner started anyway. Rose, drink some more tea before you pass out. You'll get used to the energy toll required to cast, but it takes time and practice."

Loretha sent Asher to retrieve some salted venison from her cellar while she and Flora picked vegetables from her abundant garden. Blaine stoked the fire while I grabbed the cookware and set five places at the table. Our dinner conversation was easy. Loretha told us about her life, and we in turn told her about our world.

"Thank you for your hospitality, Loretha," Blaine said to her. "You were very kind to take us in when we needed help."

"A witch that turns away family is a poor witch indeed," Loretha said, waving away his thanks. "Besides, I get to enjoy the most wonderful tales. Do people really learn folklore by staring at squares on their walls where you're from?"

We laughed at her bewildered expression.

"I wish we didn't have to leave so soon," I said. "I feel like I have so much more to learn from you."

"Oh honey, you are welcome back here any time." She placed a hand on my shoulder. "For now, though, you have an important task. I don't think it's a coincidence that the four of you represent the four races of Silaris." She looked at each of us in turn. "Fate has brought you together. Look out for each other. If you can work together on this, then you can show the rest of the world it can be done."

We spoke with Loretha late into the night, knowing the next morning we would leave the safety her home offered. Eventually the older woman retired to her room, leaving us to spend our last night indoors for a while together. I knew I should sleep, but I felt safe and warm surrounded by my friends. I tried to memorize every firelit detail of the night, yearning to stay in this moment forever. We stayed up talking late into the night, until our exhaustion finally got the best of us.

Twenty-One

Blaine

WE ATE A QUICK breakfast with Loretha before we said our goodbyes. Rose asked if Loretha wanted to accompany us, but she declined, worried her presence might attract rival witches to complicate our journey. So with farewells and a promise to return as much and as quickly as possible, we finally departed.

"Come back soon!" Loretha called after us. We waved at her one last time. "There will always be a meal and a safe place to stay for you here! Be careful, and may your hearts stay unburdened!"

We followed Loretha's directions to get to the coast. The path took us farther south than what our map suggested, but Loretha advised us it was safer to have to backtrack up the coast than to barge into the middle of Cedarclan territory. She didn't expect them to mind us being there, as long as we didn't do anything to antagonize them. That being said, she did tell Rose to hold off on practicing her magic until we were well away from the cedars.

Our moods were light, which I attributed to having a couple days of solid rest in a safe place. The land was flat and the undergrowth was sparse, making for easy travel. We saw a lot more wildlife on this leg of our journey than we did previously, though the animals still fled if our path took us too close. Even so, Asher didn't have to work hard to catch some game for dinner that evening.

We walked most of the day before coming to a small pond. The sun was setting when we decided to stop to set up camp. The evening buzzed with the sound of chirping insects, so loud that we had to raise our voices just to hear each other. I wondered if we were going to be able to sleep as I gathered firewood from the immediate area.

The weather in the Hiraeth Pines reminded me of late autumn as the nights here were especially chilly. Some of the trees even displayed red and orange leaves. Rose and Flora, not yet used to the frigid winters back home, were already shivering in their jackets. I was comfortable, though. This was my favorite weather. I relaxed, waiting for the quail-like bird Asher caught to cook over the fire. Once it was done, we sat on the ground to eat.

"You know, I think I like this forest better than Elvanar," Asher said, looking up at the night sky.

Flora snorted and dug into her food, but Rose looked at him curiously.

"Even with how cold it is here?" Rose asked, suppressing a shiver.

"It's not that cold," I cut in, earning a glare from both girls.

"Oh, it's cold." Asher chuckled. He wore one of my old jackets. "But the trees here . . . they feel more . . . peaceful. Plus, we can see the constellations. The leaves in Elvanar cover most of the sky. It makes me . . . uneasy."

"Are you claustrophobic?" I looked up at the stars twinkling over the small pond.

"Hmm. Maybe," Asher admitted. "I have this feeling—this concern—that if I can't see the constellations, they can't see me."

"Oh, that's right," Flora said, as if realizing something. "Lycans believe the stars are their gods."

She said it as if it were the most ridiculous thing in the world. I raised my eyebrow at her, hoping she would notice and apologize to Asher for discrediting his religion.

"Flora!" Rose hissed. "Don't be rude. Asher is allowed to follow whatever religion he wants."

"Oh." Flora shook her head. "My apologies, Asher. I misspoke. I mean no disrespect to your religion. It's just . . . difficult for me to understand."

"Why?" Asher smirked. "Because you believe in a singular forest god that you can actually commune with and who gives you powers?"

Flora opened her mouth to speak, then closed it abruptly.

"Don't worry." Asher shrugged. "I don't blame you for being skeptical. I don't know if I completely believe it either. It would just be nice if it were true. Believing got me through some difficult times."

"So, you didn't name your stars after the gods," I asked, "but you believe the stars are actually your gods watching over you?"

"Not the individual stars, but the constellations."

"That's pretty cool." I looked up at the sky.

"Can you show us a few?" Rose asked.

Asher raised his eyebrows at her but nodded. He leaned closer to her and pointed at a cluster of stars.

"Do you see that one in the shape of a lizard?" Asher asked. "It has five bright stars that make up the body, the rest are dimmer."

"I think I see the bright ones," she said, squinting up at the sky. "My eyes aren't sharp enough to see the whole thing."

"I don't see a lizard either," I said.

Asher took Rose's hand. "This is what I see."

Rose gasped as she looked at the sky.

"It's so beautiful," she said in awe. "There are so many stars."

"Would you like to see, too?" Flora asked.

I smiled. "Absolutely."

I felt a soft presence in my mind as an image popped into my head. The night sky exploded with light as stars burned across my vision. It wasn't that my eyes were actually seeing the stars, more like my brain filled in the gaps with Flora's image. There were easily three times the amount of stars than usual, even with the light of the moon shining as bright as the sun.

"Whoa . . ." I breathed. "This is how you two see? How do you walk around in the daytime?"

Asher chuckled.

"I see the lizard now!" Rose said. "But . . . where's the tail?"

"That's Scalesea," Asher said, "the god of healing. Lizards can regrow their tails, but hers stays broken because she chooses to regenerate others over herself."

"Well . . ." Flora said, "I suppose that makes sense."

"I think it's beautiful," Rose said, coaxing a smile from Asher.

"Do you see that one over there, in the shape of a rabbit?" Asher pointed through a group of trees to another constellation. "That's the fertility god, Leporina. She also symbolizes the hunt. My people pray to her for a bountiful year. That one over there in the shape of a stag—" Asher pointed in another direction "—is Certemus. He loses his antlers every so often. He symbolizes the passage of time."

"Wait," Rose said, "how does he lose his antlers?"

"They kind of . . . drift away." Asher shrugged.

"Huh," I pondered aloud. "I wonder if the antlers are made up of planets."

"Oh, maybe," Rose agreed.

"Planets?" Flora asked.

"Yeah, you know . . ." I looked at her. Maybe she didn't actually know. Did Silaris natives not know about other planets? What did they know of their own planet?

Rose seemed to be having the same thoughts.

"So, stars are actually . . ." Rose hesitated, "They're either burning balls of gas—like the sun, only much farther away—or planets . . . like the one we're on now."

Flora and Asher stared at her. She swallowed uncomfortably, so I jumped in.

"Yeah, so Silaris is a continent on a larger world." I paused. I was just assuming Silaris was a piece of the larger world based on our map, but I guess it could be the entire thing. "And that world is a ball hurtling through space at incredible speeds." I pointed to the sky. "Along with the rest of the planets up there."

Flora and Asher stared at me.

"You're saying," Flora said, "there are entire worlds out there that are just like this one?"

"Well, not just like this one." I shrugged. "But there could be some that are similar."

"Is your world out there?" Asher asked.

"Maybe," Rose said, "though, it would be so far away . . . I wonder if we could even see it."

"How can you know all this?" Flora asked. "You humans can't even see half of the stars!"

"We have tools and machines to help us see things like that," I said. "They even take pictures. I can show you when we get home, if you want."

Flora didn't answer. The silence stretched out, feeling heavy. Maybe we shouldn't have said anything about the planets. We might have just toppled Flora and Asher's world views.

"We must seem so stupid to you," Asher said, "with our made-up religions and our petty wars."

"We don't think that, Asher," Rose said. "We've had a bunch of petty wars on Earth, too."

"Most of them over made-up religions," I added.

Rose shot me a wry look. "I think you mean *religious differences.*"

I shrugged. Faith was fine, but I had little patience for organized religion. In my experience, it was just an excuse for people to be bigots.

"Just because we may know more about one subject doesn't make us smarter than you," she continued. "You know much more about magic than we do. On Earth, people don't believe it even exists."

"Honestly," I conceded, "just because it's true in our world, doesn't mean your constellations aren't actually your gods. Things could be very different here."

That seemed to put them both at ease.

After dinner, the four of us arranged our sleeping bags around the fire before setting a watch. Rose offered first, so I closed my eyes and was quickly pulled to sleep by the white noise of the forest around me. I was enveloped by dreams that meshed my current life with my past life, leaving me unsure of which one was which in the haze of the dream. I wasn't sure if it was a normal dream or some sort of memory when I was shaken awake. I opened my eyes to see a giant wolf gazing down his snout at me in the darkness. I jumped when my eyes registered the unexpected sight.

It's just Asher. I told myself, giving him a sheepish smile.

"My turn?" I asked.

He nodded before padding away. To my surprise, instead of settling into his own sleeping bag, he prowled to where Rose slept and laid down beside her. She shifted in her sleep to put her arms around the massive wolf, threading her fingers into his fur and snuggling herself closer like he was a big teddy bear. I smiled wistfully at the two of them, but I looked away when Asher's reflective eyes met mine over the fire, daring me to comment. My gaze fell onto Flora's dark form, huddled against the cold in her own sleeping bag. Should I see if she wanted to share body heat as well? I blushed and pushed the thought from my mind. She wouldn't want that.

Would she?

I thought of how I woke up that first night at Loretha's cabin. Flora had practically been sleeping in my lap with her head resting on my shoulder. I had woken before her but pretended to be asleep. I didn't want to disturb her and it felt nice to be close to someone.

It didn't mean anything.

I pulled my gaze away from Flora and pulled my mind from the past. I needed to pay attention to the surroundings, not think about my friend like that. Nothing exciting happened on my watch, and I was able to wake Flora for her turn before trying to get some sleep. It felt like I had just closed my eyes when I opened them to see bright sunlight streaming through the pine needles above. I groaned and pulled my blanket over my head, hoping to get another few minutes of rest before I was forced to get out of the warmth of my sleeping bag. That's when I heard them.

Waves.

I jolted upright, listening hard and earning a confused look from Flora. Waves crashed in the distance. They sounded angry, like a storm was brewing over the water. They must have been too calm to hear last night. Or more likely, the soundscape created by the nighttime insects overshadowed the sound of the waves. Either way, I hadn't realized we were so close to the coast.

"I can hear the waves," I whispered to Flora, who was the only one awake. "We must be really close to the water."

"Could you not hear them last night?"

"No," I responded, incredulously. "Could you?"

She nodded.

"Well, that's one point for elf hearing over human hearing, I suppose."

She smiled and stared off into the woods, in the direction of the waves. She sat, peaceful and serene, reminding me of one of the old Roman statues with her perfect features and unnatural stillness.

"You said you've never seen the ocean, right?"

She shook her head.

"I'm impressed at your willpower to not go running off to look at it," I said. "I don't know that I wouldn't have, if I were in your shoes."

"Oh, Blaine," she laughed, sending warmth down my spine, "your feet wouldn't fit into my shoes."

I smiled. She didn't understand how true that statement was.

When Rose woke, Asher disentangled himself from her arms—not that he'd been trying very hard—and trotted into the forest to change back to his human form. Then we set out toward the sound of the waves. The forest ended in a sudden drop and the ocean loomed before us, gray in the morning mist. As my friends walked up to the very edge, my heart rate kicked into double-time. I took several steps back to keep from going into a full panic. My hands went sweaty at the thought of walking closer to that ledge.

"Well, it's a good thing we stopped when we did," Rose said. "We might have walked right off this cliff in the dark."

My pulse kicked up again and my lungs felt too tight. I couldn't suck down a full breath.

"We would have noticed the edge," Asher said with a smirk. I wasn't so sure. "But that *is* quite the drop."

Pins and needles stabbed my fingers. My hands curled reflexively into fists as the tingling crept up my forearms.

Get a hold of yourself.

"It's so nice to smell the ocean again," Rose said, closing her eyes and taking a deep breath. "I wonder what the marine life is like here. Like, can we go swimming or will we be eaten by a sea monster?"

Flora stared into the distance, hypnotized by the ocean as the sun rose behind us, casting light down on the gentle swells of the water far out to sea. I inched closer to the edge to look down. This early in the morning, the angle of the sun cast the water below in darkness. The waves crashed against the cliff face, as if the ocean was angry about being denied access to the land. I barely glanced at the roiling waves below before a bout of dizziness swept over me. I stumbled backwards, catching myself on the nearest tree before my legs could give out completely.

"We're going north now, yeah?" I said, hoping the others didn't notice my momentary lapse. I looked up the coast to avoid their gazes. "At least until we see the rock formation Loretha told us about."

"Yes," Flora nodded. "Let's keep moving. It's already taken us a week to get here. If we don't find the stone soon, I fear we won't make it back in time for school."

We continued our trek to the north, sticking close to the coastline. I tried my best not to look out at the ocean. Instead, I kept my eyes on the forest to our right, scanning for any danger. There were a few sections of coast that jutted inward, blocking our path with deep chasms. We were forced to travel inland to skirt these formations. I was happy the chasms were too wide to jump. I wouldn't be able to make it across without my legs turning to jello.

It was approaching noon when we saw the first grove of cedar trees that were home to the Cedarclan witches. We traveled quietly from that point, trying to draw as little attention as possible. Our journey continued uninterrupted, and it was midday when we saw the Dragon's Horns.

The formation appeared abruptly as we rounded a densely packed grove of cedars that jutted into a peninsula. The four of us stopped to admire the massive rock formation that resembled two curling horns. The rock was thicker at the base and slightly curved, tips almost touching and weathered to sharp points at the top.

"I can see why they named it what they did," Rose said. "I've never seen anything like it, and I've always lived near some sort of coast. I wonder how it was formed."

"We need to look for the cave," Flora said, walking to the edge of the cliff and peering over. Rose and Asher joined her in searching. Just the sight of them looking down made me sweat, so I stayed where I was and tried to control my breathing.

"There," Asher said, pointing at an angle that was too steep for my liking.

"That has to be it," Flora agreed. "I don't see any other caves."

"It's a good thing we borrowed that rope from Loretha," Rose said. "I think we'll have to rappel down to get in. It doesn't look like we could climb up to it, even if we were able to get down to the beach."

Just look at it, Blaine. Get over this stupid fear and look down. It's probably not even that high.

I took a deep breath and walked forward, feigning confidence more to convince myself than my distracted friends. When I got to the edge and finally looked at the cave, the air left my lungs in a huff. I couldn't inhale. My vision warped at the shear drop. I swayed on my feet. Images of tumbling forward into nothingness flashed through my mind. I stumbled backwards to keep myself from lurching into the abyss. The others looked back at me in alarm, then they were gone. All I could see was the dark water of the past churning below me.

Pain bit my palms as I gripped the shattered glass of the car window with my tiny hands. Dark blood made my grip slick, but I refused to let go. I watched as red droplets pooled around my fingers before dripping off my knuckles into empty air. One drop succumbed to gravity, growing smaller and smaller until I could no longer make it out against the water below. Then another drop fell. Then another. In my shocked state, I didn't know if they were hitting the waves or disappearing into thin air. I heard the car creak around me as it tottered on the edge of the suspension bridge.

"Blaine!" My mom screamed. I heard the shouts of the men holding onto the car and I felt hands yanking at my seat belt, trying to rip it off. Didn't they know that was the only thing holding me back from falling to my death in the cold water below? The car lurched forward.

"Blaine," I heard my mom say again, more calmly this time. But no . . . that wasn't my mom's voice, though it was familiar.

It was speaking out loud and being projected into my mind. *"Blaine, come back to us."*

I felt a pressure in my head as my panic lessened, and I resurfaced to reality. Flora knelt in front of me, her hands on either side of my head. Her green eyes were vibrant as she studied me. Rose and Asher hovered over her shoulders, staring. I must have actually fallen because I sat with my back propped up against a tree. My vision spun and I was covered in a cold sweat. After a few deep breaths my heart rate slowed, but my hands still shook as I ran them over my face, trying to collect myself.

"Shit," I breathed.

"What was that vision?" Flora's glare pierced me, seeing all my flaws and weaknesses.

"I . . . I was in a car crash when I was little." I averted my gaze. "The car almost went off a bridge and now . . . I don't do heights."

There was a beat of silence.

"Well, that may prove to be problematic," Flora said.

"How did we not know this?" Rose asked.

"There aren't a lot of cliffs where we live." I shrugged. "It never came up."

"But we're your friends. You can tell us anything."

"Do you tell us all your secrets, Rose?" I immediately regretted the words when I saw her flinch. I dropped my head into my hands. "I'm sorry, I just . . . I-I don't think I can do this."

There was another beat of silence. I couldn't bring myself to look at my friends while they contemplated the cost of my failure. My eyes were trained on the pine needles that covered the ground, so I was surprised when I heard Rose's voice from right beside me.

"It's okay, Blaine." She grasped my shaking hand and gently tugged it away from my face. "You don't have to."

"Rose," Flora said, "if he doesn't—"

"If he doesn't want to, he doesn't have to." She glared at Flora. Flora sat back on her heels, obviously at a loss for words. Asher smirked at the exchange. "I'll do it."

Asher's smirk fell.

"Rose," he said, shaking his head, "that's not a good idea . . ." When she shifted her glare to him, he trailed off.

"I've rappelled down cliffs loads of times," she said.

"What if there are protections on the Argem?" Flora asked.

I shook my head. "Alaric figured the witches could easily break a protection spell. There's a different form of magic on this one."

"What kind of magic?" Asher growled.

"The kind that won't let you take the stone if your intentions aren't pure. One of you could get it." I ran my free hand over my face again. Rose still held the other. "But it should be me. I'll try again when we get closer."

"You will not. That would be silly," Rose said. "If you got over the edge and passed out, it wouldn't do us any good."

"I'll go," Asher said. "We don't know what danger is waiting in that cave."

Flora shook her head. "You're too heavy for Rose and I to pull up."

He glared at her. "I'll climb up."

"But what if you can't?" Flora asked. "I should go."

"You've never even seen the ocean before today, Flora," Rose said. "We can't have an uninformed or fear-based decision being made down there." She looked at Asher. "I can do this. I need you to trust me."

Asher closed his eyes and blew out a long breath before opening them again. "We won't be able to help you when you're down there."

"Just be there to pull me up. I can take care of the rest."

He narrowed his eyes at her, as if wanting to argue further, but nodded. She smiled as she pulled me to my feet.

"Come on, we're almost there," she said. "We'll be done in no time."

Rose

I tied the ropes around myself in a makeshift climbing harness. I checked that the rope was anchored securely to a tree at the top of the cliff, directly over the cave. The cold air rolling off the water chapped my lips as I took a deep breath.

Nothing to worry about. I've done this before. Not without a real harness or an experienced climbing buddy, but I'll be fine—right?

"Do you have your flashlight?" Blaine asked. He was following me around, nervously checking my knots to make sure they were secure.

"Yep."

"And your inhaler?"

"Right here." I patted my pocket.

I didn't think I would need it—the air in Silaris was so much easier for me to breathe—but I always kept it close. Blaine nodded and I backed up to the edge of the cliff. I pulled the rope tight, preparing to go over.

"Wait." Asher paused his frustrated pacing to approach me. He put his hands on either side of my face and a growl rumbled from him. "May your hunt be fruitful. Please be careful."

"I will."

He searched my eyes for a few seconds, then let go and stepped away. I leaned back on the rope until I was perpendicular to the rock and began my descent. Blaine looked like he was going to be sick as I dropped out of his sightline, but Flora and Asher poked their heads over the side to watch me pick my way down the uneven surface. Blaine's expression after he tried looking over the cliff had ripped a hole in my chest. It reminded me of the fear I felt every time someone touched me after that terrible day. I didn't want anyone to ever have to feel that way, so it was no problem at the time to volunteer. Now, however, I was second guessing my resolve.

The rappel down was simple and I felt no fear dangling high above the ocean. It was the cave waiting below that worried me. I wondered if I should link my mind with Asher's so my friends could know what was happening, but I quickly discarded the idea. I would work better without the distraction.

The rappel line brought me down beside the mouth of the cave. I must have miscalculated where to tie my anchor. Once I was level with the opening, I sidestepped several feet to peer inside. I didn't see any wild creatures waiting to eat me, so I stepped onto the landing and loosened my grip on the rope, stretching my fingers. I clicked on the flashlight I'd clipped to my belt loop and did a cursory search of the cave.

Rough stone walls surrounded me, still damp from the ocean spray below. The tide had been going out during our journey here—years spent around the ocean made you notice those sorts of things—and I couldn't be here when it began to rise. The rocks were slippery with algal growth. One wrong step and I could slip and hit my head. If I concussed myself down here and the tide filled the cave, I would drown. I peered into the darkness—there was no way my rope would be long enough to go very deep.

I grimaced—Asher was not going to like this.

I stepped out of my harness and secured it on a rock jutting from the wall before entering the cave without a lifeline. The sound of the waves outside faded as I walked, replaced with the echoing plink of dripping water. The air went from smelling of fresh ocean spray to the stale smell of isolation and decomposing sea creatures. The remains of several fish, both large and small, scattered the rocky ground. This confirmed the tide would make it up to this point. I quickened my pace.

Hiking boots were great for trails, but they weren't my ideal shoe for spelunking. I slipped on my third rock, this time earning a gash on my palm from grabbing a sharp ledge for balance. I hissed at the pain, but pushed it from my mind. My friends were counting on me. I was tempted to take my shoes off and go barefoot, but I cringed at the idea of slicing my feet on a rock and then having to walk all the way home. How did this slippery algae grow in such a dark cave, anyway? Didn't it need light? Maybe it fed off of whatever magic was placed here. It may have even been cultivated as an obstacle to keep people from venturing too far into this cave by accident.

I walked carefully along the uneven ground for several minutes, though it felt like it took much longer. The cave was spacious, other than a few sections where I was forced to squeeze through narrow gaps. I was grateful I wasn't claustrophobic. After one particularly tight opening, I emerged into an underground cavern. It reminded me of the one in the Howling Peaks, only smaller. The cavern rose several meters above me in a rough dome. In the center stood a pedestal surrounded by dark, placid water. The pedestal held a glowing blue gemstone.

I paused, remembering the striations of glowing yellow rock Asher showed me. I clicked the button on my flashlight, throwing the cave into an oppressive darkness, and waited. The only sounds were my breaths and the slow drip of blood from my hand onto the damp ground. I grimaced and wiped my palm on my jeans. Moments later, the veins of minerals in the rock began to glow a magnificent electric blue. The colored light reflected in the glassy water, creating an effect that I wished I had the artistic ability to recreate. After a few seconds of letting my eyes adjust to the glow, I could see better than I could with the flashlight, so I left it off and clipped it back to my belt. I bent down to remove my boots, noting a shell on the ground etched with the same glowing blue lines. I slid the shell into my pocket and took a moment to admire the view before wading into the dark water.

As my bare foot broke the still surface of the chilly water, whispering sounded behind my back. I spun, but there was nothing there. The voices kept whispering behind me, like they moved when I did. I took a steadying breath and took another step toward the pedestal.

I couldn't make out the words, but the whispering got louder as I approached the blue Argem. They put my teeth on edge. The freezing water got deeper. I was only halfway to the stone and it was already up to my waist. I shivered at the thought of going any deeper—and probably at the cold—as I trudged on. I needed to hurry. My body could only withstand so much of this temperature before shutting down. The first thing we learned in boating school was cold water pulls out your body heat much faster than cold air. I only had minutes to get the stone and get out.

The voices were louder now as I went chest deep into the water. I could make out their words if I focused, eerie and feminine.

Are you here for safety?

Are you here for wealth?

Are you here for power?

"N-no," I forced out between numb lips. I moved my arms in a swimming motion to propel myself forward faster. I was so close to the pedestal, maybe I wouldn't have to actually swim.

What do you want?

Why are you here?

Who are you?

A step from the stone, the ground sank out from underneath me, plunging me under the surface. Darkness closed in around me and cold water forced the air from my lungs. Even with my eyes open, I saw nothing but the black void around me. I tried to swim up, following my air bubbles, but no matter how hard I swam, I didn't move. Through my panic, I felt the voices in my head, sifting through my recent memories.

Before I could slam my mental shields up, something solid hit my feet and forced me up through the water column. I gasped my first breath when I crashed through the surface, an arm's length away from the blue Argem. The voices were silent. After a brief hesitation, I reached out and grabbed the stone with numb hands. My blood smeared the stone, but I didn't feel any pain. A flash of warmth spread through me, and I heard a different voice echo through my mind. A rough, deep voice.

Hurry, little sister. You don't have much time.

I zipped the stone in my jacket pocket as I fled. My swimming turned to running when I felt solid ground beneath my bare feet. My gasps echoed through the quiet cavern and water splashed around me in my mad dash for the exit. I scrambled through the narrow opening and over the slippery rocks along the passageway.

The sense of urgency to flee—to escape this dark cave—was overwhelming. Was I panicking? That was a sure way to break my ankle. I tried to collect my scattered thoughts. Why was I running? I started to slow.

Faster! That sense of urgency struck again. *Flee this place!*

I darted forward when I heard a loud crack behind me. I glanced back to see a glow emanating from the tunnel. Red-hot magma flowed out of a crack in the wall, coming right for me. The temperature of the cave rose instantly. The dampness on the walls sizzled as it turned to steam. I slipped and sliced my knee on a sharp rock but scrambled back to my feet. Pain radiated from my soles as I ran over jagged rocks, but I ignored it, pushing myself faster. More cracks sounded from behind me, but I didn't look back. I didn't have time.

I rounded a sharp corner and saw the pale blue sky through the mouth of the cave. A relieved sob ripped its way up my throat. I barely grabbed the rope when the voice shouted at me again.

Jump!

I obeyed, using my forward momentum to swing myself from the cave's mouth. Frigid wind sliced through my wet clothing and bit into my skin. I rotated in the air as I swung and got a final glimpse of the cave. Magma—lava, my cold-shocked brain supplied, now that it surfaced—already flowed out the opening. It hissed like an angry snake as it hit the churning water below.

I slammed into the side of the cliff and cried out as pain lanced through my shoulder. My fingers spasmed and I lost my grip on the rope. I dropped several feet down the cliff before my frozen hands reacted, clutching tighter and halting my descent. I risked a glance down. The frayed end of my lifeline dangled not far below me. If I lost my grip again, I would plummet into the ocean. No one ever answered my question about the sea monsters.

"Rose!" The shout came from the top of the cliff.

I looked up. Smears of blood coated the rope above me. Where had . . . ?

Rope burn. My brain told me from somewhere far away. Why was it so hard to think? Why was I so cold?

"Just hold on, Rose, we've almost got you up!" The voice was closer this time. Those were my friends up there, just a few feet away. What were they doing? Why was I holding this rope? It stung my hands. I started to let go.

Hold on, little sister.

I listened to the voice. I trusted it. I held on until hands grabbed me. The last of my strength fled as I was hauled over the edge onto the safety of the packed dirt. Pine needles scraped and stuck to my damp skin as my vision faded to black.

Twenty-Two

WHEN THE FIRST CRACK reverberated through the ground, I sprang to my feet. Flora jumped up from where she was meditating, and Asher broke from his relentless pacing to scramble to the edge of the cliff. My stomach flipped as they leaned over, scanning below for any movement.

"Do you see anything?" I felt useless.

"No," Flora said, not taking her eyes from below.

Asher glared down, silent. The tension in the air was palpable as we listened to the ground crack underneath us. I knew Rose could handle getting the Argem, but if she got hurt down there, it would be my fault. Scenarios played out in my head. Rose plummeting into the ocean. Rose trapped in a narrow cavern. Rose crushed in a cave-in.

All I could do was wait. I held the rope like a vice, ready to do . . . something. Anything. Not knowing what was going on was incredibly frustrating. I couldn't even look over the cliff's edge without getting lightheaded. I was supposed to be this world's hero, but what kind of hero let their fears control them?

Flora's gasp was my only warning. I planted my feet and tightened my grip just in time to feel the jerk of Rose's weight on the rope. Asher snatched the line with a grimace and reeled her in. I felt the Argem's power grow stronger—she did it! She got the stone!

"Rose!" Flora shouted. She glanced back at me and lowered her voice. "She doesn't look great. I don't know if she can hold on long."

What? No. She got the Argem. She's fine. She has to be fine.

Asher moved so fast his hands blurred. I abandoned the rope—no help at the moment, anyway—and crawled toward the edge of the cliff.

"Just hold on, Rose, we've almost got you up!" Flora shouted again.

I made it to the edge of the cliff and peered over just as Rose came into reach. She was soaking wet and shivering. Her dark hair whipped in the wind, tangling in strands around her face. The rope above her was stained with bright red blood where she must have slid. Her hands were so slick with blood, I was amazed she could even hold on.

Asher reached down to grab Rose's jacket a millisecond before she went limp. I swallowed hard and reached over the edge. I took hold of her right arm at the same moment Flora gripped her left. The three of us hauled her up to safety, then I scrambled away from the ledge on hands and knees.

Asher scooped up Rose's unconscious form and darted into the forest, out of the near-constant wind. I hurried after him, unsure how to help, as he collapsed with her bundled in his lap. The water from her soaked body leached into his clothes as he pushed wet hair away from her face with trembling fingers.

Rose was so pale she looked blue. Her pallor contrasted sharply with the crimson smears of blood on her hands and bare feet. She wasn't shivering anymore, but that wasn't a good sign. When I grabbed her arm, she was ice cold.

"Flora, please, you have to—" Asher's panicked plea cut off as Flora placed glowing hands on either side of Rose's head. Flora closed her eyes and poured magic into Rose for several minutes. As I watched, color returned to Rose's skin.

I blew out a long sigh when Rose began shivering again. After another moment, Flora looked at her hands in horror and fell backwards. I caught her then lowered her to a seated position on the ground.

"That's all my magic and she isn't safe yet." Flora didn't open her eyes as she spoke, as if she didn't have the energy to do even that. "We need to get her out of those wet clothes before they freeze her again. Blaine, get some blankets and build a fire. Make it big, we need to get her warm, quickly."

I hurried off to follow her instructions. I brought them all of our sleeping bags and heaped them in a pile. Then I rushed out to gather firewood while Flora peeled off Rose's wet layers. By the time I got back, Flora was snapping at Asher to take off his shirt.

"I don't think that's a good idea," Asher said.

"It's wet, and she needs to be dry. Take it off. She'll forgive us later if she lives through tonight."

That gave me pause. I looked over to see Asher stripping off his shirt.

"Pants too," Flora ordered. Asher shook his head but complied.

"Make that fire!" she yelled at me. I jumped to obey.

By the time the fire was crackling, Flora had wrapped Asher and Rose in a mountain of blankets. Asher sat with his back propped against a tree, and Rose leaned back against him. Flora knelt before them, systematically pulling out each wounded limb to clean and treat. Rose still shivered despite being surrounded by blankets and lycan. Her lips were finally turning pink again. I reached out and grasped the exposed arm of the hand Flora was bandaging, trying to rub some of my warmth into her skin.

"Hang in there, Rose," I said to her, unsure if she could hear me. "You're gonna be okay."

Her eyes fluttered halfway open as she looked at Flora and me without focus. She tried to lift her head from where it lay on Asher's chest.

"S-stone . . . j-j-jacket."

The three of us froze at the sound of her voice. It was so weak, like an echo on the wind. If I didn't see her lips moving, I wouldn't have believed she actually spoke. We sat in stunned silence as she slid her gaze to Asher, then passed out again.

"I'm finished with the bandages." Flora's voice slurred with exhaustion. "Blaine, set up her sleeping bag close to the fire. Asher, you'll sleep next to her. I don't generate as much heat as she needs without my magic. Blaine will take your place if you get too cold."

Asher huffed and lifted Rose easily, carrying the blankets with her. He tucked her into a sleeping bag then slid in beside her. I helped zip the bag up around them and felt a sudden, sharp stab of fear. She looked so small in his arms—would she make it through the night? My gaze lifted to Asher, trapped in the sleeping bag. The same terror reflected in his expression. I covered them with another blanket and threw another log on the fire.

Flora grabbed Rose's discarded jacket. It was drenched, so she carried it to me, held at arm's length. In all my panic, I must have blocked out the feeling of the Argem nearby. Now that there was nothing else for me to do, the constant thrumming of power grew incessant.

Flora swayed. "Check the pockets."

I reached into the pocket and gasped when my hand closed around the Argem. The events in the underground cavern flashed through my mind. Weirdly, I was seeing them from the point of view of the stone. This Argem felt . . . sentient. Its voice—the one Rose heard in her mind—must have been Alaric's. I closed my eyes and put the stone to my forehead.

"Thank you."

Flora and Asher shot me confused looks. Warmth shot up my arm as I slid the Argem into my sword. I took a breath, then relayed the memory to my friends.

Rose

I woke in the dark, surrounded by a comfortable warmth. I sighed, snuggling deeper into my blankets. What was I thinking going into that freezing water? Mom was going to kill me when she found out. But wait . . . that wasn't right. My mom was dead.

Where was I? Why did my limbs hurt? I tried to make my sluggish brain work but was distracted by a puff of hot air against the back of my neck. And again. It came at regular intervals. Breathing. Someone was behind me.

Arms wrapped around me, the skin burning with an almost uncomfortable heat where it touched mine. There was a reason I should stay wrapped in those arms, but I couldn't remember. I couldn't think. I struggled to get out of the cage of blankets and flesh, but I was so tired. So weak.

To my surprise, the arms circling me loosened. I was free.

Adrenaline rocketed me to my feet. My body wracked with violent shivers as the cold night air hit my bare legs and stomach. I wrapped my arms around myself. Where the fuck were my clothes?

Right, they were soaked. I was freezing. At least I was still wearing underwear. What on Earth possessed me to jump into that icy water? Was I in shock?

It was too dark outside the ring of campfire light to take in my surroundings. Tree trunks stretched into nothingness above. My arms and legs burned. Fire ran through my veins, even as my limbs shook from the cold. I looked at my hands—they were bandaged. My bare feet were wrapped up too. When did that happen? Who . . . ?

My friends. They must have taken care of me when I needed help. I looked at the two others in our camp—one was sleeping, the other sitting near the fire. That one watched me, his eyes wide. I couldn't pull their names out of my clouded memory.

I looked back to the first man. He stood with raised palms but didn't chase after me. He wore only underwear too, but the cool night air didn't seem to bother him as he watched me. His exposed skin was covered in scars. I glanced down at myself again. My mouth went dry remembering the press of that skin against mine.

I would have blushed if I had any spare heat to do so.

"I'm sorry. I didn't want you to wake like this." The man spoke like he was trying not to spook a startled deer. "Please, come back. You're still too cold." He offered me his hand. "I'm not going to hurt you."

I swallowed. I knew he wouldn't hurt me. I wouldn't have gotten out of the blankets if I knew it was him holding me. I thought it was someone else . . . someone I never wanted to be that close to again. The world swayed—or was that just me?

"Please, Rose." He tensed. What was he afraid of? He lowered his voice to be even quieter. "I'll keep you safe."

"Asher?" I breathed.

"Yeah, little witch. It's me."

My muddled brain finally unlocked. *Of course* Asher would protect me—he promised. I wanted to run to him. I wanted him to wrap his arms around me. I wanted his warmth to chase away my shivers. I tried, but after my initial burst of fear-driven adrenaline, my legs refused to listen. I managed a single step before a particularly violent shiver sent me to my knees. I grunted as pain jolted up my thigh, and I noticed yet another bandage on my knee.

What had I done to myself?

Asher was beside me in an instant, draping a still-warm blanket around my shoulders. He tried to put his arm around me, but I flinched away. I grimaced—I knew he was trying to help me, but I couldn't stifle my stupid reaction. He pulled back, giving me space, then made a stopping motion towards the fire, where someone—the other man—now stood. My shoulders hunched and I fell into myself, making myself smaller. My thoughts were coming too slow. The figure froze then sat back down at Asher's command. Asher took a deep breath. It came out shaky. Was he cold, too?

"Can I help you back to your sleeping bag?" He knelt beside me and offered a trembling hand. When I took it, his shoulders sagged. I felt the tension leave his body and immediately felt more relaxed. I nodded through my shivers and he pulled me to my feet. When it became clear my legs weren't going to work, he scooped me into his arms. His skin was warm against mine. When he set me down on the now-cool blankets and pulled away, I whimpered. He gave me a strange look when I grabbed his arm.

"D-don't g-go," I said through a shiver. He hesitated but covered my hand with his. The warmth of it teased up my arm like a promise, cracking open the block of ice in my chest.

"Are you sure? You just ran from me."

"D-didn't r-recognize you." My teeth chattered. "Sh-sh-shock."

He raised his eyebrows at me. "You know you're in shock?"

"P-please, Asher. I'm so c-cold. I need—"

He slid into my sleeping bag before I finished my plea. I grabbed onto his warmth like a lifeline. I sank down into the blankets, hiding from the cool night air and pressing my frozen cheek into his warm chest. He didn't even flinch. I put my arms around him and pulled myself as close as I could get, feeding on his warmth like a heat-sucking vampire. Asher released a quick exhale at my touch.

"Sorry," I mumbled into him. I wasn't sure if he could hear me, but he chuckled and I felt it deep in his chest. The sound warmed me up further.

"Don't be sorry, little witch." His voice was rough as he wrapped his warm arms around me and hooked a leg over mine. "Just be warm."

I sighed as my shivering subsided and I drifted off into a dreamless sleep.

To my surprise, I woke up that morning draped over the bare chest of a lycan. How I ended up in this position, I wasn't completely sure. With the exception of the past evening being a blur, however, my brain seemed to be working properly again. Asher was still sleeping, one arm behind his head and the other draped casually over my back. I took a deep breath to calm my racing heart as I tried to figure out how to disentangle myself without waking him.

When I attempted to lift myself away from him, he reflexively squeezed me closer. His eyes snapped open, suddenly alert. My breath caught at the panic that flashed across his face, accentuated by the dark circles under his eyes. He immediately loosened his hold on me but didn't let go completely. I was hyper-aware that *a lot* of my skin was pressed against his. My entire body flushed with heat. Relief washed over his features as he scanned my face.

"Hey," he said in a rough voice.

I had to swallow before I could speak. "Hi."

"How are you feeling?"

"I'm . . . not wearing clothes." My voice was raspy.

"I'm sorry." Was he blushing? "Flora removed them. I promise I didn't look."

He handed me a water bottle from beside the sleeping bag. I took a long swallow and shivered as the cold liquid ran down my throat. His gaze never left my face as I lowered the bottle from my lips. His hand was still pressed against my back.

"Flora used all her magic just to keep you alive. After that, we were forced to resort to more basic means of warming you up. You were so cold. I swear I didn't . . ." He was rambling. "I wouldn't ever . . . I thought you . . . I'm sor—"

"Asher, I understand." I felt the sincerity rolling off him—as well as the concern and the guilt—even though his mental shield was solidly in place. "I'm not mad. I'm . . ." I bit my lip. "Grateful."

"And physically?" His thumb swept the tiniest caress over my spine. "Tell me how you feel."

I couldn't help the heat that spread to my face. "I'm pretty warm now."

Asher chuckled, the sound of stress evaporating from him. An unfamiliar warmth replaced his worry.

"Please, never stop blushing," he whispered. "I can't handle seeing you as pale as you were last night, ever again."

I shivered at the memory of that mind numbing cold—or maybe at the raw emotion in his voice. I pushed myself off of Asher, putting as much space between us as the sleeping bag allowed. "Um . . . where's my backpack?"

"Stay here, I'll get it." He slipped out into the chill morning air. I watched as he grabbed both our packs and brought them over. He set mine beside me then turned his back to pull on his own clothes.

I grabbed an outfit at random and changed inside the sleeping bag. The task was difficult thanks to my injured hands, but I eventually wiggled the clothing on. I had abandoned my hiking boots in the cave during my hasty retreat, but luckily I packed a set of sneakers. I loosened the laces enough to squeeze my bandaged feet into the shoes. A dull pain radiated from my hands and feet, but it was nothing compared to last night's pins and needles.

Asher turned back around when I unzipped the sleeping bag. I tried to stand, but it took me a few attempts to get my feet underneath me. Eventually, I resigned to taking Asher's outstretched hand to pull myself upright. Once I was up, I let go of him and walked, unsteadily, to clean myself up. When I returned to the fire, Blaine and Flora were speaking to Asher in hushed voices. When they saw me, relief erased the worry etched into their faces.

"Rose!" Blaine's voice was oddly strangled as he approached me. He opened his mouth to speak, but nothing came out. He looked exhausted. Did any of them actually sleep last night? Eventually, he found his voice. "Can I hug you?"

When I nodded, he engulfed me in a tight hug, lifting my feet off the ground for a moment before setting me down lightly. He held onto me for an entire minute. When he shuddered around me in what felt like a sob, I squeezed him back tightly.

"Hey, it's okay." I tried for a soothing voice.

"This was all my fault." He buried his face in my messy hair, muffling his words. "It should have been me in that cave."

"It wasn't your fault."

"I thought you were going to *die*." The word was accentuated by another shudder.

I pulled away to look into his red-rimmed eyes and gave him what I hoped was a consoling smile. "Blaine, you can't get rid of me that easily."

The ghost of a smile appeared on his face, but it didn't clear the haunted look from his eyes. Flora pushed in front of him before he had a chance to say anything else. She grabbed my wrists, avoiding my bandaged hands, and pulled me over to sit by the fire.

"Tell me about any discomfort," she said. "I'm out of magic, so I can't feel it."

"I'm fine." I flexed my fingers around their bandages. "I'm still a little stiff. My hands feel like they aren't quite responding as they should, but they don't hurt like they did last night."

She nodded and began to undo the bandage on my hand.

"You were going hypothermic," she said. "You're lucky you didn't lose a limb."

"Thank you for that."

"Thank Asher," she said. "He did the hard part of sleeping next to an icicle all night."

"You did a lot, too," Asher said as he sat down beside me. He handed me an already open protein bar and set another bottle of water at my feet. "Eat."

I didn't feel hungry, but I took a bite anyway. I finished the protein bar before Flora finished unwrapping the gauze around my hand. Asher handed me another, then set one beside Flora. She glanced at it but kept working.

I was halfway through the second bar when the injury on my hand was exposed. I grimaced when I looked at the wound. Several layers of skin had been torn away by the rope burn, leaving my entire palm raw. There was a deep gash running from the base of my thumb to my ring finger joint.

"We're going to have to keep these covered to keep them clean," Flora said. "When we get back to Elvanar and I can recharge my magic, I'll be able to heal you. Until then, however, I'm afraid we're stuck with your method of healing."

I wrinkled my nose, thinking of the long trek back to the Rift. I finished eating and took the water bottle as Flora cleaned out the wound with antiseptic. The burn from the chemicals was refreshing after the numbness I felt last night. When she started to rewrap my hand, I stopped her.

"This needs stitches," I said. "Can you grab the needle and thread?"

"Stitches?" Flora asked, confused. I guess it made sense that a creature with the ability to heal the worst wounds using magic wouldn't know what stitches were. Blaine must have come to the same conclusion, as he jumped up to gather the supplies.

"Do we have numbing stuff?" he asked, looking through the kit.

"I don't need it," I said. I didn't want my hands to go back to feeling numb.

He frowned at me but retrieved the sterile packet containing a threaded needle.

"I don't actually know how to do this," he said.

I gaped at him. "You're pre-med."

"Yeah, emphasis on *pre.*" He grimaced. "I won't learn how to do this until medical school."

"I've got it." I held out my hand for the pack. He handed it to me and I tore it open. The three of them watched with wide eyes as I slid the needle through my skin and tied the first knot. I gritted my teeth through the pain as I pulled the stitches tight. I tied off the last stitch and gestured for Blaine to cut the extra string. He did so, with eyebrows raised, and Flora wrapped the hand with fresh gauze.

"Wow," Blaine said. "Maybe you should be pre-med too. You've obviously done that before."

"Just a few times." I shrugged. They all stared for a beat, unsure if I was joking or not.

"Oh," Blaine exclaimed, breaking the silence, "I wonder if Loretha could heal you?"

"It would be worth asking," Flora said, moving to my other hand. "We are going to pass that way, anyway."

The rest of my wounds were superficial and didn't need to be stitched. The scratches on my feet weren't too bad, but they would be a nuisance to walk on. It would be a relief if Loretha could heal them, but I was pretty sure I could make it home, even if she couldn't.

"I might have to take you up on that offer now, Blaine," I said.

"What offer?"

"The one about the boots. I left mine down in the cave. They're probably a bit toasty now."

Blaine huffed a laugh. "We'll get you some as soon as we get home."

Twenty-Three

Blaine

I KEPT GLANCING BACK at Rose on our way to Loretha's cabin—I had to make sure she was still there. The going was slow as she stepped tenderly on her injured feet, but she didn't complain. She never complained. She smiled at me every time she caught me looking at her—it made my chest constrict. She may have forgiven me for sending her down into that cave, but I hadn't forgiven myself yet. I doubted I ever would.

My mind flashed back to the car crash fifteen years ago. I remembered the still face of the young girl in the seat beside me. She could have been sleeping when they laid her tiny body on the rough blacktop and covered her with a white sheet. She hadn't survived the initial impact. I remembered the sound of my mom's grief as she clutched me and rocked. I hadn't understood the feeling at the time. I loved my sister, but I was so young. I just didn't understand why she hadn't come home with us. I didn't understand death. The grief came later.

This time, though, when Rose was blue and barely breathing, I understood. The panic that gripped me in those initial moments ripped the air from my lungs. Even when she was safely tucked into her sleeping bag, I couldn't shake the fear that she wouldn't survive the night. That we had shared our last conversation. Our last hug. My sleep was fitful, and I woke several times just to confirm she was still breathing. I was exhausted when I woke to see Flora and Asher standing by the fire, speaking quietly to each other. When I didn't see Rose, I assumed the worst. I jumped to my feet, but by the time I made it to the two of them, Rose had walked out of the woods.

Other than the bandages, she looked almost normal. There was color in her cheeks again and she wasn't shivering. She smiled at us and some of the ice in my chest thawed.

"Rose!" My choked voice sounded too similar to my mother's wails of grief. I swallowed and ran to her, barely stopping myself from wrapping her in a hug. I was so worried. I just wanted to make sure she was really there—that my eyes weren't playing tricks on me. I wanted to tell her how much she meant to me and how scared I was, but the words lodged in my throat.

"Can I hug you?" was all I managed to say. It was enough. When she nodded, I embraced her. I hugged her like I would have hugged Eliza, if I had ever gotten the chance after that night. I was still shocked at the depth of emotion in my chest, several hours later. Every time I glanced at Rose, relief flooded me. She was still here. She was still breathing.

By mid-afternoon, I glanced back again to see Rose and Asher falling farther behind. I mentioned it to Flora, who was in the lead, and we waited while the two of them caught up.

"Do you need to take a break?" Flora asked.

Rose shook her head. "I can keep going."

"What about you, Flora?" Asher looked her over. "It can't be easy for you without your magic."

"It's nothing I can't handle," Flora scoffed.

I frowned. Flora was standing more slouched than usual. She cocked one hip, like she was favoring her left leg. Dark circles shadowed dull green eyes and her usually pink lips lost their color. Even her perfect hair frizzed and tangled around her shoulders. I was so worried about Rose, I hadn't noticed Flora was struggling.

"Are you sure, Flora? You look a little—" I snapped my mouth shut when she shot me a venomous glare. "Great! You always look great." I cleared my throat and rubbed the back of my neck. "But maybe we should take a quick break."

Flora forced her shoulders back and lifted her chin. "I'd rather get to Elvanar as soon as possible so I can replenish." She grimaced at Rose. "But we can stop, if you need. Your body is still recovering."

"Really, I'm fine." Rose said. Asher looked down at her with a frown. "I'll let you know if I need a break."

I somehow doubted that, and the look on my face probably conveyed my feelings. Rose looked like she was about to comment on my expression, but Asher interrupted before she could.

"Rose, are you hiding your pain?"

Her gaze flicked to his and her whole demeanor shifted. Her shoulders relaxed and she sighed, letting her exhaustion show momentarily. It was like watching someone take off their battle armor, shedding layers of protection that kept them safe for so long.

"I . . . I don't want to slow us down," she said. Asher raised his eyebrows at her lack of answer, but she just shrugged and looked away.

"What if I carry you? Your feet will get a break and we can keep moving."

"My feet are . . ." She was no doubt about to say 'fine,' but she trailed off when Asher cocked his head. "You can't carry me all day."

"I bet I can." He dropped to one knee on the pine needles. "One way to find out—hop on."

She almost protested, but then glanced at Flora and me. She rolled her eyes as she wove her arms around Asher's neck. He lifted her easily, gripping underneath her knees for support.

"Anything hurting?" he asked.

"N-no."

Asher sniffed the air. "Good."

Flora led the way, and I fell into step behind Asher to take up the rear guard. We traveled like that until darkness fell and we were forced to make camp. Rose had, at some point during our walk, fallen asleep, so she offered to take the first watch after dinner. We gratefully accepted, and I fell asleep shortly after laying out my sleeping bag.

The next morning, Flora helped Rose change her bandages. Flora looked thoughtfully at the wounds before wrapping them in clean dressings. At Asher's insistence, we ate a quick breakfast before continuing our journey. By my estimation, we were only a few hours' walk from Loretha's cabin. That was a few hours for me to ruminate on my failures.

"Are you okay?" Flora asked, pulling me back to the present.

"Hmm?" I looked around. The others were far enough behind that they hadn't overheard.

"You aren't acting like yourself," she said. "You know what happened to Rose wasn't your fault, right?"

"She was only down there because I couldn't get over my stupid fear."

"You're allowed to be afraid," she said. "Do you want to talk about it?"

"Not really."

She raised an eyebrow at my sulky response. I rolled my eyes. I was allowed to be normal sometimes, wasn't I? Just because I was technically an adult, didn't mean I felt like one.

I sighed. "Like I said before, it was a car crash. I was really young . . . maybe five? I don't remember, exactly. All I remember is the car hanging halfway over a bridge, my seatbelt the only thing keeping me from plummeting hundreds of feet into the water below."

"That's where your fear of heights stems from?"

"I guess." I shrugged. "I don't even remember the collision. I must have gotten a concussion or something. It . . ." I swallowed. "It killed my younger sister. Eliza. She was so young, she never really got a chance to live."

Flora reached out and took my hand. I squeezed hers in thanks.

"It's why my parents are so protective," I continued. "They already lost one kid, they didn't want to bury another. After the other day . . . I get it."

"You thought you were going to lose another sister."

I nodded, not trusting myself to speak.

"She knew the risks before she went down there."

"I know. It's just hard not to feel responsible."

"Believe me, I understand how that feels."

Yes. I glanced over at her thoughtful expression. *I bet you do.*

Rose

"Are you hurting again?" Asher pulled me from my thoughts. We had fallen several steps behind Flora and Blaine. "I could carry you."

"What? Oh, thanks, but that's okay." I blushed.

"It's really no trouble." He smiled at me, eyes amused. "If your feet hurt—"

"They don't." I cut him off. "I mean, they kind of do, but not bad. I would rather they hurt a bit. It reminds me they aren't numb. Maybe that's stupid."

"No, it makes sense."

We walked in silence for a while and I fell back into my thoughts.

"You seem distracted. What's wrong, little witch?"

"I . . . I've been thinking." I swallowed. "My parents died in a fire. A fire that didn't hurt me. What if . . . what if it was my fault? What if I caused the fire?"

"You didn't."

"How are you so sure?" I asked, shocked at his certainty.

"Loretha was pretty confident that the other day was the first time you used your magic." Asher frowned. "Were you sick after the fire?"

"I don't think so. I was dealing with a lot of grief, so I don't really remember. Then they sedated me at the hospital . . . it's all kind of a blur."

"Were you angry or frustrated that night?"

"I . . ." I hesitated, but forced myself to continue. "Yes. I was. It was the night I was . . . after that memory you saw."

Asher stiffened. He didn't say anything, but he offered me his arm for support. I took it greedily and continued.

"I snuck home that evening. I didn't want to talk to anyone. I couldn't eat. I didn't even see my parents before I went to bed. Looking back I wish . . ." I sighed and shook my head. "I was so angry at what he did to me. So disgusted with myself at what I allowed him to do to me up to that point. I was already planning to leave him. Lying in bed that night, I decided to tell my parents what happened. I was dreading that conversation. Then I woke up surrounded by flames." My voice grew very quiet, but even though he was looking ahead, I could tell Asher was listening to every word.

"The rest of it, everything that happened with—" I took a deep breath and forced out his name "—with Cal was just pushed to the background while I dealt with my parents' deaths."

"It sounds like you never got a chance to work through it."

I shook my head. "And here I am, opening the trauma firehose on you. Sorry."

"It's okay, little witch." He placed his hand on top of mine where I was clinging to his arm. "You can talk to me about anything."

"I know." I smiled up at him, surprised to find my own statement true.

"I don't know what caused that fire, but I do know it couldn't have been you. Even with your powers running wild, you would never have hurt them. You're too good."

His confidence gave me hope, but that insistent voice in my head wouldn't shut up.

Good people didn't burden everyone around them.

About a mile out from Loretha's cabin, I relented and let Asher carry me. The thought of walking any farther had my stomach sinking into my stinging feet. When her garden appeared from behind a thick patch of trees, Loretha emerged from her house. She paused when she saw us, eyes going wide. I smiled at her friendly face and waved from my perch on Asher's back.

"Cousin, this is the second time in as many visits you've been carried over my doorstep." She put her hands on her hips. "Next time you better walk through this threshold properly."

I laughed as she held open the door. Asher carried me inside and deposited me on the couch.

"I *could* have walked this time, but someone was being overprotective." I shot a good-natured glare at Asher.

"I warned you." His eyes danced with humor as he backed away to give Loretha a chance to look me over.

Loretha fussed over me like a mother hen while Flora recapped our travels for her. Loretha had unwrapped my feet and the hand with the stitches by the time Flora finished the story. She paused briefly from her examination of the wound, looking at Blaine.

"You have the Argem?" she asked.

He pulled the sword out of his sheath enough to display the blue stone. Three collected so far. Just one more to go. Loretha blinked at it a few times before focusing back on my injuries.

"Oh!" I pulled my less injured hand free and dug into my pack. I ignored the sting of pain and pulled out the shell I grabbed in the cave. It shone a pearlescent white, broken by veins of blue. "I got this for you."

Loretha was quiet as she stared at the shell in her palm. She curled her fingers around it and when she looked up, her eyes were misty.

"Thank you, cousin. This is incredibly thoughtful." Her expression hardened. "But going into that freezing water was extremely stupid."

Asher's hands curled into fists where he leaned against the hearth. Blaine rubbed the back of his neck then slumped onto the couch beside me. Flora popped a hip and crossed her arms, expression hostile.

I laughed, dissolving the tension in the room. "Yes, I know."

Loretha studied me, narrowing her eyes as if worried about my sanity. That was probably warranted.

"Sorry, you sounded just like my mom when you said that. Same inflection and everything."

"I see." Loretha's features softened. "Well, I can definitely heal these injuries, but it looks to me that you've already started healing them yourself."

"I . . . what?"

"I imagine if you hadn't been recovering from hypothermia, they would be completely healed by now."

"How did I heal myself without knowing?" I asked.

"You must have channeled the right feeling, by chance." Loretha smiled, glancing around at my friends. "I imagine you have your friends to thank for that."

"What's the feeling?"

"Well, that one is still debated between witches." Loretha took my wounded hand between hers while she was speaking. A soft glow emanated from her palms and energy jolted through me, tickling the skin around the cut as it healed. "The emotions are so close to each other, it's hard to differentiate one from the other. Some say healing comes from a feeling of safety, others say love."

She released my hand. The lingering pain was gone, and there was only a faint white line where the jagged gash had been moments prior. She moved on to my next injury as I processed her words. I felt safe with my friends the last few days, but had I felt love? I didn't speak again until she finished healing the rest of me.

"Thank you."

"Any time." She smiled. "I'm sorry I'm not able to do anything about the scars. If you made it here sooner, I might have been able to avoid them, but with how much time has passed, there's nothing I can do."

"It's alright," I said. "I can barely see them."

"Plus," Blaine chimed in, "battle scars are cool."

"Well, you can get some next time." I laughed. "I think I've had enough."

"I agree." He squeezed my shoulder. "You aren't allowed to do anything remotely dangerous anymore, no matter how badass you are."

I rolled my eyes.

We stayed with Loretha that night so I could practice my magic. When I grew too tired to conjure anything, we discussed magical theory. Darkness fell outside as we sat at her table. Fire crackled in the fireplace across the room, sending warmth around the cozy cabin. Blaine and Flora were reclining on the couch. Asher was stretched out on a blanket on the floor. They were already asleep.

"It's thought that healing comes from the feeling of safety," she said, "because the actual injury would have come about during an unsafe event. Therefore, the opposite of whatever you were feeling during the injury is what heals you. However, love is a strange emotion, magical in itself. Love heals mental wounds without magic. That leads me to believe that it could do more with magic. I personally don't know the right emotion, so I just channel both when I need to heal."

She looked over to where my friends were dozing and I followed her gaze. I smiled, admiring the peaceful faces that were too often lined with tension. They looked younger like this.

"It must have been hard on them to almost lose you." Loretha stared into the fire. "They're exhausted. Worry does that to a person, you know."

I frowned, remembering the dark shadows under all of their eyes that first morning I had woken up. Had worrying about me caused them that pain?

"Do you love them?" she asked me quietly.

"Of course I do. They're my friends."

"What about *him*?" She nodded to the sleeping lycan.

"I . . . I don't know." I definitely felt *something* for him. Was that feeling love? I wasn't sure.

A soft smile touched her lips before it turned wry.

"I expect you'll figure it out soon enough," she said, rising. "Get some sleep, Rose. You still have a long journey ahead of you."

I leapt to my feet, surprising her with a hug before she could walk away. She hugged me back without hesitation.

"Thank you," I said as I released her. "I can't tell you how happy I am to have met you."

"Me too, dear." She leaned forward and placed a kiss on my forehead. A pulse of warm energy buzzed through me. "Just some extra healing. Now get some rest."

I nodded and she retired to her room. I grabbed some of the blankets off the pile she left out for us and draped one over each of my friends. Blaine was the only one to stir when I covered him.

"Thanks, Rose," he muttered without opening his eyes.

I grabbed a few blankets for myself and hesitated by the fireplace as I decided where to sleep. Eventually, I threw a few blankets on the floor next to Asher and settled in beside him. We weren't touching, but I was close enough to feel the heat radiating from him. I didn't think I woke him when I laid down, but he shifted onto his side and put an arm around me. I tensed for a moment before letting myself relax. I assumed he moved in his sleep, so it surprised me when he spoke quietly in my ear.

"Is this okay?" His voice was so soft, I wasn't sure if he was actually awake. Thinking I may have imagined the sound, I nodded. "Verbal confirmation, please."

"Yes, it's okay," I said, laughing softly. He squeezed me once before falling asleep. I was close behind him as I lay snuggled in the blankets in the cozy cabin. It had been a long time since I felt this content. Even before my parents died, I had Cal to deal with. He had been around for years and never once made me feel this safe. On the contrary—he made me feel scared. Alone. At the time, I'd thought I was in love with him, but that wasn't love—it was isolation. I looked at Asher and sighed, comfortable. The warm feeling of safety spread from where his hand rested on my hip, radiating through me and lulling me into a deep sleep filled with dreams of wolves and wildflowers.

Blaine

Loretha hugged each of us before we left, surprising us all. Asher's shocked face was worth any discomfort I felt hugging the older woman. I managed not to laugh, but Flora still rolled her eyes when she noticed my expression.

It took us two days to get from the edge of the Howling Peaks to Loretha's cabin, so we needed to get moving if we were going to make it home before school on Monday. We planned to risk traveling through the desert this time. Asher was concerned his former pack would be waiting for us if we went back through the mountains. He wasn't worried about Cora and Toreth, but claimed he didn't have a chance against their alpha. I doubted that. Asher was just as large as any of the alphas I saw in Alaric's memories—even larger than some. I didn't complain, though. The trip through the desert would be faster, and I was ready to get home and sleep in a real bed.

We walked late into the evening and only stopped to set up camp when I almost walked directly into one of those sentient gray pools. Asher had pulled me away in time, but after that, Flora deemed it too dark for Rose and I to continue safely.

When the sun came up the next morning, we found ourselves in a contaminated section of the forest. The fog was thick around us, significantly diminishing our visibility and dampening the usual morning chorus.

"I should have realized," Flora said, as we hiked. "The sounds of the forest are so muted here."

"Was it like this last night?" Asher asked. "Even in the dark, we should have noticed."

"You think it's expanding?" I asked.

"I don't—" Asher cut off, staring into the forest to our left. His eyes narrowed and he maneuvered himself between Rose and whatever he was staring at. The motion made me draw my sword. "Flora, do you hear that?"

"Yes," she breathed, drawing her sword, as well, "but I'm blind without my magic. I don't know what it is."

"Neither do I." He sniffed the air. "It smells . . . wrong."

We waited there, poised and ready to defend ourselves. I peered into the forest, but I couldn't see anything moving. The stillness was unsettling after hearing the constant chatter of wildlife in the background for the past week. My patience was wearing thin when Asher finally spoke up.

"I think it's gone." He didn't relax.

"Let's keep moving," Flora said. "Stay quiet and stay alert."

We didn't catch any sign of the creature for the next few hours, though Asher made us pause every so often to listen. We came abruptly to the boundary between the Hiraeth Pines and the desert. The pines were dense enough that we didn't see the barren land until we almost stumbled into it. The fog stopped suddenly at the border, as if contained to the Hiraeth Pines by a magical shield. Standing in the center of the boundary line, directly in our path, was a woman.

She wore a black cloak that flowed from her shoulders to the ground. Her midnight black hair cascaded down her shoulders, almost merging with her cloak to form a hood. Slender, pointed ears poked out between the strands as she stared down the line of the border, apparently unconcerned with how exposed she was. Behind her was sand-swept desert, stretching as far as I could see.

"That has to be the Defector," Flora murmured.

"If she hasn't seen us," I whispered, "maybe we can double back and get around her."

"That thing is back," Asher snarled. He glared into the forest behind us. "More than one of them."

As he said the words, a rattling noise reverberated from the fog. It reminded me of a rattlesnake from those nature documentaries I loved. Several other rattles sounded nearby. I couldn't see more than an occasional flash of silver scales through the fog. The creatures cornered us against the edge of the boundary. There was no turning back now, unless we wanted to fight an unknown creature with an enemy at our backs. We were trapped.

"I know you're there." The Defector's voice was soft and musical. It stirred something in my memory. "It's time we finally meet."

"What do we do?" Rose asked. My mind kicked into strategy mode.

"If she wants to talk," I said, "then we talk. Those creatures probably won't leave the territory." And if they did, I would wager the Defector wouldn't let them attack until she said her piece. "I'd rather face her at full strength than after a battle, anyway."

"We're not at full strength," Flora hissed. Her knuckles were white against her sword.

"No," I said, "but she doesn't know that."

I'm not sure what she saw in me, but whatever it was made her face harden with resolve. She nodded. Asher still glared into the woods. Rose had her sword raised beside him. She glanced back and forth between the woods and the Defector, unsure which was the greater danger.

"Ready?" I asked them. Asher looked to Rose and tapped his temple. She pressed her lips into a thin line, then they nodded in unison. "Then let's go."

I feigned confidence and gripped the hilt of my sword as I walked toward the lone elf. My friends followed close behind. When I stopped several feet from the Defector, they stepped up beside me, one by one. A platoon ready for battle. I had to admit, we made a rather striking display of solidarity.

"Have no fear," the strange elf said. Her eyes swirled a milky white with tiny black pinpricks in the centers. Her lips tilted up in a polite smile, but her eyes stayed cold. "My pets will not harm you."

Of course those creatures belonged to her.

"You're the Defector, I presume?" I kept my voice calm and level, even though my heart thundered in my chest.

"Am I the 'Defector'?" She scoffed. "Those elders are so dramatic. Young man, you may call me Mika."

I didn't speak, just watched her warily. From the Council's description, I expected an evil, terrible creature. This was just . . . a woman. One who felt somehow familiar, at that.

"Don't worry," Mika said, looking each of us over. "I'm not *actually* evil. Having a different viewpoint than the Council only brands you as such."

"What do you mean, a different viewpoint?" Flora sneered. "You *murdered* people."

"Poor youngling," Mika tsked. "You don't even realize the depth of the lies you've been fed. I've never killed anyone, unlike your Council." Her lip curled. "They deserve death for taking my husband and daughter from me."

There was a silence as we processed what she said.

"Oh, did they not tell you that part?" Mika asked. "Of course not, it wouldn't place them in a good light. They care so much for appearances."

"A child? The Council would never . . ." Flora trailed off, frowning. The gears worked in her mind. She could accept the Council's actions were harmful to people of other races, but to accept them killing elves?

"Tensia would have been about your age now." Mika's eyes narrowed further on Flora.

"Why would they do that?" I asked, drawing Mika's attention.

"Power, perhaps? Control, maybe? I don't know. You would have to ask them. I didn't stick around long after my daughter's death. I left to grieve and to heal. I made my own paradise, far from the scheming of that wretched Council and their simpering sycophants. A place where I could discover the truth and make my own choices.

"That's why I'm here," she continued. "I know they've tasked you to destroy me. I don't hold that against you—you don't know any alternative to obeying. They spin their pretty lies so well, it's hard not to be ensnared by their words. I am offering you a different path. Join me. Experience my world. You may come to find that the Council isn't as all-knowing as they pretend. Seeing the four of you working together . . ." She looked into each of my friends' eyes before continuing. "I think you will like my Utopia as much as I do.

"I concede you have no reason to believe me. Currently, you just have my word over that of the Council. Perhaps I can give you a . . . gift of sorts. A bit of the truth I have come to discover in my research. Proof of my good will toward you."

Mika's cold gaze drifted over each of my friends, before coming to rest on Asher. Her lips turned up in a tight smile.

"You have been told that lycanthropy is a disease brought about by the magics in this land. While that is not untrue, its source is a bit more sinister than a naturally occurring illness." Mika shook her head, long black hair flowing around her shoulders as she did so. "Your species is not a sickness, child, but a curse laid upon you by the elves of old."

I watched from the corner of my eye as Asher tried not to react to the statement. Nonetheless, I saw his eyes narrow at the elf. My mind raced through the consequences of the statement. If what she said was true . . .

What else had they lied about?

"Feel free to discuss among yourselves. Confirm the truth in my words. I expect your answer next time we meet. Until then—" she opened her hand and a shadow sprang forth. Before I could even flinch, it enveloped us. The taste of pennies coated my mouth. I reached out to my friends but felt nothing in the darkness. After a timeless moment that dragged on for an eternity, the darkness receded.

I forced my eyes open, shielding them against the bright sunlight, and looked around—we were still in the boundary, but we had definitely moved. The deciduous trees of Elvanar towered over us like gods. Flora, Rose, and Asher were beside me, shielding their own eyes from the sudden light. Somehow, we made it across the desert without taking a single step inside.

"What the hell was that?" Asher growled.

"It . . ." Flora shivered. "It wasn't like the magic I use. I didn't like it."

"It felt a lot like Toreth's magic," Rose wrapped her arms around herself. Asher put a comforting hand on her back.

"Come on." I spat the copper taste from my mouth and glanced back into the desert before heading for the familiar trees. "Let's get out of here."

Twenty-Four

Blaine

THE INSTANT WE LEFT the infected swath of forest, Flora excused herself to recharge her magic. The rest of us set up camp and the fire was crackling happily by the time Flora joined us. She brought with her an assortment of berries from some bushes nearby, promising they were safe to eat. She was lighter on her feet, like being without her magic made her physically heavier.

Asher caught us some small game, which I was helping to skin and prepare. As I placed the finished pieces of meat in a pile, Rose threw them on the small cook pan over the fire. We had developed an efficient system over the past week, and dinner was ready within the hour. Soon we were eating our meal directly out of the still hot pan.

"These animals are far too docile." Asher grimaced as he took a bite of said animal. "Hunting them is no fun at all."

"You're complaining about an easy hunt?" Flora asked. "I would think it a nice change after the scarcity of game in the mountains."

"It was nice at first. Hunting for nonexistent food isn't fun either." He scowled at a piece of meat. "It's just . . . too easy. I almost feel bad catching them. It's like . . . they don't know the rules of nature. Some of them don't even run. It makes it feel less like a hunt and more like slaughter." He sighed as he popped the meat into his mouth.

"Well," I said, still chewing my food, "I, for one, appreciate the speed at which dinner was caught and prepared."

Asher smirked at me. It faded quickly and his eyes went unfocused as he stared into the woods.

"Are you okay?" Rose placed her hand on his forearm.

Asher frowned. He opened his mouth to speak—then he suddenly relaxed. He blinked and cocked his head, listening to something on the wind.

"Do you hear that?" he asked no one in particular. I glanced at Flora, who was the only one with hearing as good as Asher's. She sat cross-legged with her eyes closed, swaying back and forth.

"No, but I feel something," Rose said. "Something magical. It feels . . . good, actually."

"It *does* feel good."

I couldn't feel anything, but I wasn't particularly magically inclined. Rose stood up, reaching to throw another log on the fire, but Asher pulled her down into his lap.

"What are you doing?" She laughed at him. In answer, he wrapped his arms around her and nuzzled his nose into her neck. "Don't you want a fire?"

Asher muttered something I couldn't hear, prompting Rose to close her eyes and lean into him. That companionship, that closeness . . . it looked nice. I wanted it. Without thinking, I reached out and took Rose's hand. She didn't flinch or tense when I touched her. For some reason, a voice in the back of my head found that odd. I raised her hand and was just about to press my lips to it when Asher's growl froze me in place. I met his gaze over Rose's shoulder and read the blatant challenge in it. The pure animal look on his face shook me from whatever spell I was under. I dropped Rose's arm like it was infectious.

What was I doing? I shook my head to clear it. Part of me was weirded out by my impulse, but another part wasn't sure why I stopped—it urged me to rise to Asher's challenge.

"Sorry." I didn't know who I was apologizing to, but Asher's eyes cleared and he pulled back sharply from Rose. When she looked at him, there was confusion written on her face—but no fear. No reservation.

"Flora," Asher shuddered. His gaze bored into Rose like he needed her to breathe. "What is that music?"

Flora stopped swaying. The relaxed smile faded from her lips as she took in our tension. She narrowed her clouded eyes, thoughtful.

"Oh," she said after a moment. "I've been in your world for so long, I lost track of time." An innocent smile blossomed across her face. "It must be the Revival Celebration. Oh, I'm so glad we didn't miss it."

"What does it do?" Asher asked, roughly. Rose placed her hand on his chest and tried to lean closer, but he held her away. The brief thought that I should give them privacy flitted from my mind. I didn't feel the need to avert my eyes. Why would I? There was no shame here.

"What does what do?" Flora asked airily, eyes drifting closed again.

"The *song*, Flora," Asher growled as he reached up to tangle his hand through Rose's hair. "What is it?"

I didn't hear any music, but Flora started to sway again.

"The Song of Rejuvenation." She spoke the words in a melody that had Asher shaking. "We sing it to bring life to the forest. It makes flowers bloom and animal populations flourish."

Asher laughed but there was no humor to it.

"Leave it to the elves to control the reproduction of other species," he muttered.

I blinked. "So essentially you're singing, like . . . an aphrodisiac to the animals?" It was a weird thought, but I found myself relaxing.

"Not *just* the animals," Flora said. "It's for us, as well. My people have trouble conceiving. The song helps."

I cocked my head and studied her. That was a very open statement. Flora was typically more secretive about her race. I watched as she sighed deeply and lay on her back in the grass, giving herself over to the music.

"You humans are such prudes," she said in that same, ethereal melody. "Just enjoy the ride."

"Except I'm not exactly human," Asher growled. "The wolf part of me *really* wants to take control. Rose, I need you to shield us."

Rose obviously struggled to focus on Asher's words. She reached up to skim her fingertips along his jaw. He shivered.

"Relax, bro." I leaned back on my elbows. "College is all about experiences, right?"

Gracefully, Flora got to her feet and floated over to me. She was more beautiful than ever. More inhuman, too. Her eyes glowed green in the dimming light and her perfect lips curled into a lazy smile.

"If you want a real experience, come with me." She offered me her slender hand.

I took it without hesitation and let her pull me into the woods. There was laughter in her voice as she started to sing. The words were familiar, but they didn't fully resonate in my brain. Abruptly, Flora paused. She looked back the way we had come, confusion crossing her perfect features. Her green eyes smoldered and her lips twisted to the side like they did when she was unsure. I was distracted by the movement. What could she be thinking about? My only thoughts were of touching those soft, pink lips. Of feeling them press against mine. Possibly other parts of me as well.

I leaned toward her, but she put her hands on either side of my temples. Awareness washed over me like cold water down my spine. I gasped at the abrupt change in my mental state.

"I've temporarily blocked the song from your mind." Flora cocked her head to the side. "I can't hold it away for long, but I'll respect whatever you say in this moment, while your mind is clear. Are you sure you want to participate?"

I blinked at Flora as clarity settled into my mind. Did I hear her correctly? Was she actually asking if I wanted to have sex?

That sounded like a dream come true. But . . . I couldn't sleep with her, right? Flora was my friend. I didn't want to make things weird in our group. Sex ruined friendships. I didn't want to be *that guy*. Even though I had been admiring Flora for months now, I couldn't ask her to do that.

She was still so close, her green eyes alight with magic or the light of the forest or . . . maybe lust? I wasn't sure. The desire to press my lips against hers was still there, even protected from the spell as I was. The desire to press every part of myself against her. To remove every barrier between us, mental and physical.

My attraction hadn't come from this spell—I knew that. Flora was magnetic. I was drawn to her from day one, as much as I tried to hide it. I didn't want to come off as some creep by hitting on her, even despite my temptation to tell her she was the most gorgeous thing I had ever seen.

I was perfectly fine just being friends, if that's what she wanted. But now she stood before me, as beautiful and ephemeral as the forest around her, glowing like some sort of god. I wouldn't have asked her, but since *she* was the one offering . . .

"Yes," I answered her. "Very much so."

Flora laughed and let the magic rush back into my mind. As I chased her through the trees, I finally heard the music.

Rose

Asher's molten gold eyes burned into mine. His strong arm wrapped around my waist, holding me on his lap. I wanted—no, I *needed* to touch him. I ran my fingers through his silky hair and a low growl rumbled from his chest. His thumb caressed the sensitive skin of my neck, sending electricity shooting all the way to my toes.

A tiny moan escaped my lips and he shuddered. His touch was intoxicating. I tried to lean into him—to press myself closer—but his grip moved to my shoulder and tightened. He held me away with one arm, while holding me close with the other. He possessed so much power over me, but I felt safe. I was totally and completely—

"Give him a real choice, Flora," Asher growled.

Cold jealousy flashed through me. How dare he say *her* name while holding me like this? Tiny pellets of hail fell around us. The ice melted as it hit him, leaving perfect drops of water on his tan skin. The frozen crystals stuck in his dark lashes, making his eyes burn hotter in contrast. Even through the sudden shift in weather, his gaze never left mine.

Asher's unwavering attention tamped down my jealousy better than any words. As quickly as it started, the localized hailstorm ceased. That urge to lean into him flared again. I rubbed my thumb across his bottom lip, wiping away a half-melted hailstone.

"My name should be the only one on your lips," I breathed.

"Rose." He groaned and his fingers dug into my skin.

Yes.

"Rose, focus." His urgent tone cleared some of the fog from my mind. "Shield us."

"But . . . I hurt you last time."

"It's just you and me. I can't—" He shuddered beneath me and his hands tightened. "Please try. I can't take much more of this."

He was trembling. What was wrong? I tried to think but my mind was fuzzy. That music was so distracting. So were his eyes. And his hands. And his lips.

"Shield us, little witch. Or at least shield yourself before you hear the music."

Too late. The elven music flowed through my mind like a raging river, twisting through my thoughts so swiftly I could hardly concentrate on his words.

"I trust you." His words were laced with a lupine whine. "Please."

His plea finally broke through the fog. His fear crashed into me like cold water.

I threw my arms around his neck and pulled him close to me before summoning my shield. Instantly, the music ceased, along with the other sounds of the forest. As soon as my shield cut us off from the elven magic, Asher sagged against me. My whole body heated as my brain started working again, but I didn't dare loosen my grip on him.

What was I thinking? I wasn't one for public displays of affection. I wasn't one for affection at all. I knew I was attracted to Asher, so I wasn't completely surprised the magic amplified those feelings . . . but had I really almost let *Blaine* kiss me? I shivered. He was like my brother—I'd have to scrub that arm as soon as possible.

"I'm sorry." Asher tried to release me, but I clutched him tighter.

"Don't be sorry." My voice was huskier than I expected. "You did nothing wrong. Are you okay?"

He nodded against me then tightened his hold.

"I'm better. I can still feel the magic, but it's manageable now that I can't hear that song."

I knew what he meant. I could think clearly now, but the way he looked at me earlier—like I was the most important thing in the world to him—was still vivid in my memory. I took a deep breath to settle myself and rein in my wild feelings. It was the spell. He only looked at me that way because of the spell. I knew he cared about me, but it wasn't like that.

Was it?

"How long can you hold the shield?" he asked.

"We'll find out together," I said. He huffed a laugh and I smiled at the sound. After a moment's hesitation, I asked, "What were you so afraid of?"

"I . . . I didn't want to do something you would regret tomorrow."

"Why would I regret it?" I whispered.

"Rose." His soft voice sent tingles down my spine. "I'm trying so hard to gain your trust. I refuse to do anything to risk that."

"What if I wanted you to keep going?" I whispered. I felt him stop breathing. He pulled back to look at me, eyes thoughtful. After a moment, he shook his head.

"No," he said firmly.

Oh. I looked away as shame swept through me, turning my stomach. What was I thinking? I wasn't a lycan. Was it weird for him that I was a witch? Maybe . . . maybe my past really was too much for him to deal with. I blinked rapidly to dispel the sudden pressure I felt behind my eyes at the rejection. He tipped my chin back toward him with a finger and sighed.

"Not *tonight*, little witch. Please don't look like that. Just because you want it right now, with the magic still lingering around us, doesn't mean you actually want it. That you actually want *me*." His hand splayed back across my neck and I couldn't help but lean into him, even after his rejection. He took a shaky breath. "I'm trying so hard to be good and not to give in to this stupid spell. That dejected look on your face is breaking me. Please, just . . ." He closed his eyes and rested his forehead against mine. "Ask me tomorrow. I will do *anything* you ask of me tomorrow. I just want to be sure it's *you* asking, not this spell. I don't want to take something from you that you aren't ready to give."

"That's . . ." My breath caught. He was resisting because the spell was messing with my mind. He said 'no' because I couldn't make an unbiased decision. He was actively *not* taking advantage of me. How broken was I that I didn't realize that from the start? Warmth blossomed in my chest. "That's . . . amazing. You're amazing."

He smiled and shook his head. His thumb grazed along my neck to my collar bone, sparks jittering along my skin in its wake.

"I am barely decent," he corrected me. "Anyone truly amazing would let go of you and move as far away as possible." I tightened my hold on him and he laughed. The sound was warm and sweet. "Don't worry, I'm not that strong."

I closed my eyes and relaxed, enjoying the feel of his fingers on my skin. After a few minutes of silence, I voiced the question that was on my mind since the fog cleared. I wasn't sure how I managed the courage, but I was willing to bet the residual effects of the spell helped.

"Is this . . . is this what it feels like for normal people?"

"What do you mean by normal people?" he asked, fingers never pausing in their lazy motion.

"I mean people who haven't been . . . through the experience I've been through," I said. His fingers stilled on my neck. "I've never felt like this before. I've never really *wanted* to be touched, but tonight . . ." I took a deep breath and laid my hand over his. I didn't want him to pull away. "There's this feeling . . . this *need*. It's unsettling, but wonderful. Is that how you feel all the time?" I opened my eyes to see him staring at me. He wore a soft, gentle smile, and his gaze dipped to my lips. I blushed.

"Not all the time." His smile deepened and he reached up to brush my warm cheek with his thumb. "As much as I appreciate your blushes, you don't have to be embarrassed. I do feel that way a lot. Especially when you're around, little witch."

"I . . . really?"

"*Especially* when you talk about wanting to be touched."

I blushed deeper at the intensity in his gaze.

"Let's just make it through tonight, okay?" he said. "We just talk. No firsts of any kind."

"What if I never feel like this again?"

"You will, little witch. I'll make sure of it."

We sat like that, tangled in each other's arms for hours. We spoke all night, sharing our wildest dreams and our deepest fears. Asher kept me awake by pointing out constellations and talking about wolf lore, while I kept us shielded from the elven magic. When we felt it was finally safe to do so, I dropped my shield. The first rays of sunlight were just starting to filter through the trees. The usual cacophony of songbirds was muted, as if they too stayed awake all night. Asher pulled a sleeping bag around us and I settled against him on the ground. Exhausted, we immediately fell asleep in each other's arms.

Blaine

I woke to the sun directly overhead and shielded my eyes. Flora shifted beside me, cuddling deeper into my arms. She smelled of citrus and lavender. Momentarily stunned, I could only stare as the events from last night crashed back into my head. We still weren't wearing any clothes—only using my jacket as a blanket. I swallowed as I replayed last night over and over again in my mind.

The spell definitely lowered some inhibitions. My mind was fuzzy on some of the details, like I drank too much and sections of my memory blacked out. At the time, however, I knew what

I was doing. Or, well, Alaric had known. I was pleased to find that, as inexperienced as I was in that particular area, I had access to some of my past life's experiences. I ran my fingers over the soft skin of Flora's back and watched the goosebumps form. She definitely liked it when I—

"We should probably get back to Rose and her puppy," Flora hummed, interrupting my thoughts. "I hope they had fun last night. They'd both benefit from working out some tension."

"Should we maybe talk about what we did last night, first?"

She tilted her head up to look at me. "Do you regret having sex?"

"Not at all."

"Good."

She pushed off me to stand. The residual heat of her delicate hand on my bare chest was a brand that remained long after the contact was gone. She took her time to dress, gathering the articles of clothing that I had tossed haphazardly to the ground around us last night. I drank in every part of her slender form as she did so.

"I thought you were into girls," I blurted.

Smooth, Blaine.

"I'm into everyone." Flora shrugged. She was so beautiful, the view was captivating. I tried not to gawk—she was my friend, after all, not some romantic conquest—but she was curvier than I previously realized. Her flawless pale skin glowed in the morning light. She was just . . . perfect. Even after last night, I couldn't get enough. Would she let me peel off the clothes she just put on? "Especially if it's only sex."

Her offhand comment twisted my gut. "Only . . ."

"Don't misunderstand, Blaine. It was great—surprisingly so—but you're not my typical partner. I mean, you're human."

"Right." *It was only sex. Nothing more. Just the spell.*

The thought gripped my chest like a vice, but I buried the feeling down deep. Flora ran her hands through her hair to dislodge the leaves tangled there before tossing my clothes at me. She smirked, noticing my stare.

"Are you going to get dressed?" she asked.

I blinked at her, then pulled on my clothes. We made our way back to the campsite in silence, because for once, I couldn't find any words to say. When we arrived, the fire had smoldered into ash. Rose and Asher were still asleep. They cuddled together much the same as Flora and I had been, except they were tucked into a sleeping bag. And clothed.

I pushed thoughts about their evening from my mind—it wasn't any of my business. I grimaced at the memory of what I tried to do to Rose last night. Why would I try to kiss her? Sure, she was beautiful, but I thought of her as a sister—didn't I?

Yes. It was just the spell.

Flora threw a few logs onto the fire and the two of us waited for our friends to wake. When the fire was crackling away, Asher stirred. He raised his head to look at us, then looked down to the sleeping girl using him as a pillow. Obviously trapped, he lowered his head back to the ground to wait for Rose to wake. Dark circles ringed his eyes, like he hadn't slept much. I trained my gaze back on the fire, forcibly cutting off that train of thought. My eyes probably didn't look much better than his. I rubbed my face with my hands.

"How far are we from the Rift?" I asked under my breath. I didn't want to disturb Rose. At least one of us should be well rested.

"Only a few hours' walk," Flora matched my volume. "We could be on Earth by tonight if you want. Though, we still have another day until we are due to be back."

"Maybe we should sleep here another night," I said. "I'm exhausted."

Asher chuckled from where he lay, and I shot him a glare.

"Shut up, Asher," I said. "You look as tired as I feel."

"Different reasons, I can assure you," he said. Rose stirred at his words but settled when he stroked her back. "Was that song a one-night thing?"

"Yeah," Flora said. "Tonight will be a festival to celebrate the children, since they wouldn't have been allowed to partake in last night's activities. Performances and face painting, that sort of stuff. Nothing like last night."

Part of me was disappointed at that, but I shook myself out of it. Of course I wanted a repeat of last night, but I didn't know if my heart could take it. Especially knowing it hadn't meant anything to Flora.

"Maybe we should go to that," Rose said from the sleeping bag. I didn't realize she was awake and listening.

"Well, good morning," Asher said to her. "How long have you been awake?"

"A while." She sighed deeply. "But I was comfortable."

The smile that Asher gave her was so intimate, I had to look away.

"We could go to the festival," Flora said thoughtfully.

"You sure you want to show us off?" I was surprised she was willing to bring a human, a witch and a lycan to an elven festival.

"After last night, no one will have the energy to realize you aren't elves." She looked down at her hands. "Plus, I think Asher is right. We shouldn't be hiding the fact that the territories are no longer isolated."

"What about your Council?" Asher asked, obviously surprised that Flora had admitted he was right.

"The Council can suck it," she spat. I raised my brows at her phrasing. College was a terrible influence on her language. "Especially if what the Defector—what *Mika*—said was true. If they killed her family, how can we trust them?" She hugged her knees to her chest. "If we can't trust the Council, who can we trust?"

Her bleak expression made my chest tighten. I reached out and took her hand. I wasn't sure where Flora and I were in regards to each other after last night, but that didn't matter. I was always going to be here for her. I would always be her friend.

"We trust each other," I said, looking into her uncertain eyes. I looked at Rose and Asher, still in the single sleeping bag. "We learn as much as we can, then we make a decision together." I looked back at Flora, who was staring at me thoughtfully. "We don't have to trust anyone else, but we trust each other."

Flora nodded and looked at her hands. Her blonde hair hung around her like a curtain. My hand itched to pull it back and reveal her face, but I refrained. When she looked back up, her features had hardened.

"Okay," she said, "let's go."

After a quick dunk in a nearby river to clean up, we packed and set off toward Trehilm while the sun was directly overhead. As we walked, I measured my steps so they brought me beside Rose. I opened my mouth to speak and she glanced at me. The blush that filled her cheeks when she looked away withered the words on my tongue. Well, I guess she remembered what I had almost done last night.

"Hey . . ." I tried again after clearing my throat. "I'm sorry about last night. I didn't mean to . . . I shouldn't have . . ." I sighed. "I'm sorry. I wasn't thinking."

"I know," she said, still not looking at me. "It was just the magic. It's okay, Blaine."

"It's not okay if I made you uncomfortable."

"I didn't exactly tell you to stop," she said, dryly.

"You shouldn't have to tell me to stop." I glanced back at Asher, who had dropped back to give us some privacy. He was still watching with his ever-thoughtful expression. "I shouldn't have done it in the first place."

"How about this . . ." Rose said, pulling my attention back to her. "I'll forgive you if we promise never to talk about it again. Ever."

"Deal." I extended my fist to her and she tapped it lightly with her own.

We walked for a few hours through the wilderness before coming upon the first signs of civilization. When Flora revealed the treehouses to Asher, he gaped openly. I forgot he wasn't with us the last time we came to the elf city, and I enjoyed watching how similar his reaction was to ours. Whereas I was overwhelmed with the excitement of discovering a new world, his face held a tinge of sadness. As the sun set, we entered the city proper. Lanterns were lit and swarms of colorful fireflies danced above our heads, casting a rainbow of light on the festival-goers below.

"I can see why you think the lycans are barbarians," Asher said to Flora, a strange tone in his voice. "Compared to this, we are."

"No, you aren't." Flora looked at him sharply. "We just got lucky. We used magic to create this entire city. Without magic, we are nothing."

I almost missed a step. The words were almost exactly opposite the argument she and Asher had only days ago. He didn't say anything as we made our way to the area I recognized as the market square. The booths had been transformed with colorful decorations. Flowers of every color and shape lined the fabrics and birds swooped and sang, even in the growing darkness, as hundreds of elves meandered through the streets.

A group of children, looking to be around ten years of age, burst out of one tent and made a beeline for another. There were maybe seven of them, but they were moving so fast, zipping in and out of the adults on the street, that I couldn't tell for sure. One girl, smaller than the rest, bumped into a man. She stumbled backwards before he reached out and caught her. She stood still long enough for me to notice the two blonde braids running along her head were adorned with the same flowers that bloomed all around us. She bobbed a quick curtsy to the man and was once again zooming away after her friends.

"Flora?" A voice called from a few booths away, pulling my attention from the group of children. A tall man with violet eyes and jet-black hair approached. He looked to be only a few years older than us.

His face broke into a wide smile, transforming his features from fearsome to admirable. Jealousy shot through me as a similar smile broke out on Flora's face, and she launched herself at the man. He picked her up easily and swung her around in a hug. "I was hoping you would come home for the festival," he said with a laugh, setting her back on her feet. "Hello, my flower. I've missed you."

"I missed you, too," she said, still smiling. "These are my friends." She grabbed his hand and pulled him over to us. A weight settled onto my chest. The unexpected rush of jealousy caught me off-guard, and I focused to keep the emotion off my face. "Blaine, Rose, and Asher." She pointed to each one of us in turn. Then she gestured to the tall, dark man. "This is my father."

My jealousy was swiftly replaced by confusion. Even with Alaric's memories, I could not figure out how to estimate the ages of elves.

"Pleasure to meet you, friends of Flora." The man scrutinized us. His eyes lingered on me and I grew cold. Did he know what Flora and I had done last night? That was impossible, right? I stifled my relieved sigh when his eyes left me and narrowed on Asher. I had the feeling Flora's dad knew exactly who—and what—we were.

Typically, I was the first to make the polite introductions, but I was too overwhelmed to form intelligible words. After one look at my stunned face, Rose stepped forward to speak to the intimidating man. Asher hovered close behind her, ready to snatch her away at any sign of trouble. I couldn't blame Asher for his unease—the elf was staring daggers at him. It seemed the man was deciding if Asher was a threat worth dispatching. A charge filled the air around us as each sized up the other.

"It's a pleasure to meet you, too, sir," Rose said with the sweet smile she could conjure in an instant. The man's gaze reluctantly left Asher and settled on her. He cocked his head to the side and the pre-battle charge dissipated as he studied her.

"Please, call me Ebb," he said, then smiled. "You keep fascinating friends, my flower. I look forward to learning more about each of you, but for now, please, enjoy the festivities. I have some business to take care of."

"You're leaving?" Flora's face fell.

"Unfortunately." He smiled ruefully. "I will be home tomorrow. You know where to find me. I expect a visit from you soon." She nodded, and he took her face in his hands, placing a light kiss on her forehead. "Until then, may the Forest watch over you."

He nodded to each of us, then slipped away into the growing darkness. After a few steps, I lost him in the crowd. Flora deflated as he disappeared, but she turned back to us with a smile.

"That . . . was your dad?" I asked, stunned.

"Yeah."

"Did he know that we . . . ?" I trailed off with a glance to our friends. "You know."

"How would he know that? Better yet, why would he care?" She smirked at me, then rolled her eyes. "You humans are such prudes."

"You two look nothing alike," Asher said. Rose elbowed him lightly in the side and shook her head. He blinked at her. "Was that rude?"

"Yes," Rose said the same moment Flora said "No."

I chuckled.

"I've been told I look a lot like my mother." Flora's smile turned sad. "She died when I was very young."

"I'm sorry to hear that," Asher said. His expression turned thoughtful. I wondered if he was drawing comparisons to his own life.

"Come on," Flora said, gesturing back toward the festival. "Let's go get something to eat."

Rose

Flora grabbed Blaine's hand and pulled him toward the food vendors. Asher started to follow, but I slowed.

"Hey, Asher?"

"Yes?" He stopped walking.

"About last night . . ." My eyes dropped from his and I had to swallow before continuing. "You were right about . . . about not wanting to . . ." I took a deep breath. Why was this so hard to talk about? "Thank you for stopping us from . . . doing anything we'd regret this morning."

I crossed my arms in front of myself as the silence stretched between us. I couldn't meet his gaze. I wasn't sure I could handle what I'd find in them.

A gentle finger under my chin lifted my head. My stomach churned with dread. I bit my lip and braced for disappointment. Anger. Betrayal.

His eyebrows pulled together. "I will do everything in my power to keep you safe."

Something like electricity buzzed in my chest. I believed him. I trusted the man standing before me. After last night's events, I was certain he wouldn't hurt me. He could have done anything to me last night . . . I had *asked* him to . . .

My cheeks burned as I thought about my bold words from last night. Asher must have sensed my thoughts because his lips turned up into a sly smile. His fingers slid to cup my neck and his thumb skimmed my cheekbone.

"Although . . . what I said last night still stands. Ask me again tonight and I will *happily* oblige."

"I-I don't think I'm quite ready for that." My gaze dropped to the ground. I couldn't look at him without seeing the heat behind his gaze. Or without thinking of some of the things I wanted to do last night. He lowered his hand.

"That's okay," he said. "You've already given me more than I deserve. Are you hungry?"

I nodded, a little dazed at the quick shift in conversation.

"Let's go get some food." He draped his arm around my shoulder, steering me after Flora and Blaine. I leaned into him and smiled. I didn't feel the slightest desire to pull away from his touch.

The area with the food tents was teeming with activity. The tantalizing aroma of meats and roasted vegetables filled the air. Some foods were recognizable to me, others were far from it.

Baskets of spiky yellow fruit were everywhere. The rinds were so thick they had to be cut with long, serrated knives. Large, purple spheres hung in bunches like oversized grapes. As I watched, an elf took one of the spheres from the bundle and peeled off the skin before taking a bite of the red flesh inside. Jars of different types of honeys, syrups, and preserves lined the stalls, free for anyone to sample. Descriptions of their contents were displayed on tidy note cards before them.

We found Flora and Blaine ordering food. Blaine handed us each some kind of meat on a stick while Flora paid the vendor. I sniffed the charred meat. Its sweet scent made my mouth water. Blaine was already devouring his, so I took a bite. The mix of sweet and savory flavors was delicious.

"All this sugar ruins the quail," Asher said with a grimace. He took another bite of the meat anyway.

"I think it's delicious," Blaine said through a full mouth. "How can you tell it's quail?"

"Birds have a distinct flavor to them," Asher said. "Can't you taste it?"

"Meat tastes like meat to me." Blaine's face lit up with a goofy grin. "Why? Does it taste *fowl* to you?"

I snorted a laugh and Flora rolled her eyes.

Flora led us to another tent where they were coating balls of fried dough in a thin layer of honey. They called the little donuts 'poufitos' and served them with a light dusting of sugar. Flora ordered a dozen for us to share and paid the vendor. We ate the flaky, sugary-sweet pastry while we meandered around the festival.

We separated a bit as we walked through the artist tents, admiring the paintings and other creations lining the walls. There were lanterns made of palm fronds woven into patterns meant to cast the light. Ceramic kitchenware lovingly carved with intricate details of forest life hung from display racks. There were little figurines of people and animals made of glass or grown from flowers. Everyday household items turned to beautiful decorations when crafted by these elven artists.

I paused to study an overhead view of a landscape painted on a very flat piece of shale. The rolling fields were being tilled by a horse-drawn plow far below the artist's perspective. In the distance, little houses with purple thatched roofs looked like they belonged in a medieval village. The houses were arranged around a large castle with tall spires.

I lost myself in the painting. It was well crafted. The fantastical elements mixed with the ordinary just enough to feel real.

"I see you are admiring my most recent work."

I jumped to find a tall elf beside me. His long platinum hair swayed around his pointed ears as he looked at me. I thought I saw a flash of confusion in his face, but it was quickly overshadowed by a kind smile.

"I apologize for startling you." His voice was musical, like so many other elves we met, but there was a coarseness to the sound that stood out against the pure tones of the others. "Share with me your thoughts?"

"It's beautiful," I said. "Everything here is beautiful."

"Yes, I know." He gave me a gracious smile. "But this painting caught your attention. Why?"

"I—I don't know."

The artist lifted his focus to something behind me. His pale eyebrows raised over gray eyes, but his tone remained the same. "What draws you here, brother wolf?"

Asher met my gaze when I looked over my shoulder at him. I watched him give the painting a cursory glance before focusing on the artist.

"Uh . . ." The term caught Asher off guard. "It's an intriguing viewpoint. I've never seen anything like it."

The artist nodded and studied his painting. Asher used the opportunity to inspect the elf. I thought I even saw him sniff at the air.

"Indeed, I imagine this is how the mighty dragons of old viewed us," the artist said, wistfully. "Flying high above the world on those powerful wings. Untouchable to the tiny creatures below."

The artist gazed into the painting, lost in thought. He said nothing else, almost like he forgot we were there. Asher shot me a bewildered look behind the artist's back and I tried not to laugh. I nodded to the door and we made a quiet exit.

As we navigated through the artist's tents, we met up again with Flora and Blaine. Gasps and cheers sounded from farther down the aisle, so we made our way in that direction. We reached an opening to find a small crowd gathered around a roped-off area. In the center of the empty space stood Jallix, the blacksmith's apprentice, sword in hand. As we approached, a small child tossed one of the strange purple fruits in the air toward Jallix. With a quick flick of his wrist, Jallix cleanly cut the fruit in half with the sword. The gathered children laughed and cheered in delight while Jallix handed the sliced piece of fruit back to the child. The young elf took a bite and stepped away so the next child could throw their piece of fruit at Jallix. It was an odd game, but the children seemed to really enjoy it.

Jallix noticed us and nodded a greeting in our direction before turning to the next child. The next piece of fruit was cut from the air just as efficiently as the first.

"Flora?" The high-pitched voice drew my attention away from the strange display of swordsmanship. I looked around to see a familiar girl hurrying toward us.

"Hello, Tisha." Flora's features went blank.

"What are you doing here?" Tisha asked in a hushed voice. When she took in the rest of us, her mouth pressed into a thin line. "Blight, Flora, why would you bring *them* here?"

"Excuse me?" Flora asked in a cool voice.

"Don't be like that." Tisha shook her head in obvious annoyance, causing her dark red hair to sway around her sharp cheekbones. "We may have had our differences in the past," she glanced at us before lowering her voice, "but I don't want to see you get hurt."

"What do you mean?" Flora's tone warmed a little in response to Tisha's words. "Why would I be hurt?"

Tisha looked around at the faces of the many elves passing by. It was obvious she wanted to say something but didn't want to be overheard.

"With my placement near the Council, you know I have access to . . . certain sensitive information." Tisha's lips tightened into a line. "People have been disappearing recently."

Blaine, Asher, and I shared a glance at that. Was the spreading evil causing people to disappear? Was Mika taking people? What was going on?

Tisha stepped close and threw her arms around Flora's neck. Clearly surprised by the sudden embrace, Flora awkwardly returned the hug. I saw Flora's brows knit together as Tisha whispered something into her ear. After a few seconds, Tisha let go. She backed away a few steps before slipping into the crowd without another word.

I felt Asher's mind brush against my own, so I opened my shield to let him in.

She told Flora not to put faith in the Council, he said to me through the link. *And not to let them see us here.*

I raised my eyebrows at him. Could he really hear that well? He glanced at me sideways and gave a small nod.

Flora watched the retreating figure for several heartbeats. She placed a hand over her heart then shook her head.

"I think," she said to us, "we need to pay my father a visit. It's time we get some answers about Mika and the Council."

Twenty-Five

Blaine

WE SNUCK FROM THE festival just as the singing began, pure voices rising over the cacophony of the crowd. As we slipped away, I glanced behind us to see fireflies swarming in the sky. The ethereal singing coaxed them into images, giving life to the story I expected was being told to the festival goers. I would have liked to stay and watch, but it wasn't worth the possible danger that awaited there.

We had one more night in Silaris before we would be missed at home, so we camped at our usual site near the Rift. After barely sleeping the night before, we all crashed hard. I passed out before we could even discuss setting a watch. We woke early, wanting to make our way to Ebb's house before too many people were awake to notice us.

We climbed the steps that curved around the large tree, and Flora knocked on a door set into the bark. The door was tall and narrow, with elegant curves instead of the hard corners I was used to seeing. Ebb's violet eyes were punctuated by dark circles as he answered the door, but he smiled warmly when he saw his daughter. Ebb's look of delight at seeing Flora dimmed upon seeing the rest of us, but he gestured us all inside.

"Make yourselves comfortable," Ebb said. He disappeared through an archway in a wall that blended seamlessly into the floor and ceiling.

The room was small but cozy. The wall curved inward, following the outline of the tree trunk. As there was only one door on this level of the tree, I suspected Ebb owned the entire floor. That was interesting. Most of the homes we saw in Trehilm contained at least three entrances on each level. As a healer, Ebb must have been compensated well.

Several chairs decorated in colorful leaf patterns scattered the room. A large desk sat in one corner, papers strewn across its smooth top. A hearth on the far wall contained a smokeless, crackling fire. The mantle above the hearth was cluttered with random knick-knacks.

I approached one of the chairs to find it upholstered with different types of leaves woven together. I sat gingerly, expecting the material to be delicate—the last thing I wanted to do was come into someone's home and destroy their furniture. I waited for the rip, but the material held strong. I suspected magic had something to do with it.

Rose sat in the chair beside me, Asher taking up guard behind her. Flora walked over to the hearth to stare into the fire. She smiled fondly at a few of the items on the mantle. To me they looked like meaningless trinkets, but to her they were obviously important. Ebb came back into the room carrying a tray of mugs. Flora helped her father distribute the tea before taking a mug into her own hands. Ebb took a seat at the chair behind the desk and smiled at us.

"To what do I owe this visit?" he asked. "Not that you need a reason to visit, my flower. Your faces just look . . . grave."

"We received a strange warning." Flora hesitated as her speech pattern automatically flipped into something more formal. "At last night's festival, we were warned not to put our faith in the Council. Not to let them realize we attended."

"Who would warn of such a thing?" Ebb asked, surprised. The question was light—innocent—but Flora didn't betray Tisha's name to her father.

"A friend."

"Be cautious, Flora," Ebb said, only a hint of reproach in his still light voice. "The Council does not take kindly to dissent."

His eyes swept over me, Rose, and Asher. There was a steeliness in them, like he blamed us for this conversation. Perhaps he was right. Flora wouldn't have doubted the Council before we put those thoughts into her mind. I was proud she was thinking for herself—no one should blindly follow another.

"Oh, of course not," Flora said, waving off the conversation. She caught Ebb's glance at us. She apparently decided it wasn't wise to push him on that subject while we were here. "I wouldn't dream of that."

Ebb nodded and his smile grew relieved as she dropped the subject.

"Good," he said. "You do not want to earn the Council's ire."

I couldn't tell if the words were meant as a warning or a threat. Furniture creaked as Asher's grip tightened on the back of Rose's chair.

Flora, however, smiled and nodded. "I assume you know of our quest?"

"I do."

"Did you know Mika and her husband?" Flora asked, conversationally.

The smile slipped from Ebb's face and he blinked at Flora, momentarily speechless. His tired eyes seemed to not want to open right away. He left the festival early. Where had he been all night?

"I did," Ebb said.

"What about their child?"

There was a beat of silence as he stared at Flora.

"Yes." There was an odd catch to his voice. Flora must have heard it too, because she cocked her head to the side.

"So there really was a child?" When Ebb didn't speak, Flora asked, "Can you tell us how her husband died, exactly?"

He gave Flora a long, measured look. "It was said Mika's darkness poisoned Dorian's heart until it could no longer beat."

"Yes," Flora said, "but what were his symptoms? There must have been others."

"Let me think . . . it was so long ago." Ebb rubbed his tired eyes. "He grew irritable at first. His limbs started responding slowly to his commands. His fingers and toes turned black. Soon after that, his heart just . . . stopped fighting."

I grimaced at the thought of the slow decline in health. Give me a quick death in battle any day over that sort of torture.

Flora, however, stiffened. She glanced at something on the mantle before focusing back on her father, staring at him in disbelief.

"His fingers turned black, then his heart stopped?" she asked.

"Yes, it was quite unexpected as . . ." Ebb trailed off as Flora plucked a vial from the mantle. His shoulders sagged. "Ah."

"The rare appleberry," Flora said, inspecting the vial in her hands. It looked like it contained dried apple seeds. "Found only along our northernmost border, will give similar symptoms, will it not?"

"You have quite the memory, my flower. I hoped you had forgotten that particular piece of information."

"I'm not likely to forget about a rare plant that can so easily stop one's heart." Flora's eyes narrowed. "Especially one whose seeds have been in our home my entire life. I never asked why you kept poison on the mantle."

The two of them stared each other down while I exchanged wide-eyed glances with Rose and Asher. This conversation had taken a turn into dangerous territory. I wasn't sure if we should be here, but like it or not, we were stuck now.

"Did you kill Dorian?" Flora asked her father.

Ebb's gaze drifted to the vial in her hand as he answered.

"I had my orders from the Council. I followed them."

Flora gasped. "You killed that child?"

"I *saved* that child!" Ebb bellowed, leaning forward over the desk and slamming his fist down on its surface. "I couldn't let a child grow up in that house, tainted by that evil. It would have destroyed her."

"You saved . . ." Flora exhaled sharply. Perhaps she was relieved that her father drew the line at killing a defenseless child, but her eyes narrowed. "Who? She would have been my age . . . I would know her . . . who is she?"

"You don't know her," Ebb said with a wave of his hand. "We sent her to live in the east to keep her as far from danger as possible."

"He's lying," Asher said quietly. They were the first words he had spoken since we arrived. Flora and Ebb both glanced at him, the latter with a sneer.

Weeks ago, Flora wouldn't have trusted Asher, but we had been through so much in such a short time. We had all changed. We had all grown. I could almost see the memory of our promise flash across her eyes.

We trust each other.

"You are going to believe this mongrel over me?" Ebb whirled back to Flora.

My temper flared at the derogatory term. Asher had done nothing to this man, and Ebb still pulled out the racial slurs. I had hoped today's elves were better than those in Alaric's time. I was quickly losing that hope with the turn of this conversation. I wanted to snarl along with Asher at the injustice of it all, but I didn't have a chance.

"*Don't* call him that," Rose spat.

She didn't back down—didn't even flinch when Ebb's hard violet gaze skewered her. Rose glared right back at him as the room grew hot with her anger. Hesitantly, Asher placed his hand on Rose's shoulder. When she looked back at him, he gave her a small, grateful smile. The unnatural heat instantly disappeared from the room. Ebb had no idea how close he was to losing his treehouse in a blaze of Rose's anger.

"Who is she?" Flora asked again, drawing Ebb's attention back to herself.

Mastering himself once again, Ebb leaned back in his chair. He kept his mouth shut and held Flora's angry gaze with one of his own. I could almost see the gears working in Flora's mind. The puzzle she was putting together. Between one blink and the next, her bright green eyes glistened with moisture as she glared at Ebb.

"You never talk about her. About my mother." Flora's tears threatened to spill from her eyes, but they stayed in place—probably through sheer willpower. "I thought it was because it was too painful for you but . . . why have I never seen a likeness of her?" Her voice was rough. "Do I even look like her?"

Ebb held her gaze for a moment longer before dropping his violet eyes to the ground.

"No." He sighed, causing Flora to shudder. "You look more like your father. Like Dorian."

The vial of appleberry seeds fell from her hand and shattered on the floor, scattering the deadly poison everywhere. Tears rolled down Flora's cheeks as she backed away from the man before her. She shook her head and fled out the front door. I was up and following her before I realized I was moving.

"Flora, wait!" Ebb's plea was ignored. She was already running.

I followed Flora for half a mile and only caught up when she stopped. Her back was to me and her hand clutched the nearest tree for support. She was gasping for breath, although the run through the woods was too short to have winded her. I took a moment to catch my own breath before approaching her.

"Flora?" I wasn't sure if she heard my approach and I didn't want to startle her. Not after everything she had just gone through. She was already trembling.

"Is . . . that even . . . my name?" she choked out between gasps.

She sank to her knees, one hand pressed to her chest, the other still clutching the tree. I knelt on the soft grass beside her and placed what I hoped was a comforting hand on her back. I didn't know what I could say to help her, so I didn't speak. I just stayed with her. Just as she had once stayed with me when Alaric's memories grew too painful.

I stayed there as her gasps turned into sobs. Eventually, she leaned into me. I wrapped my arms around her while she cried. She felt so small as her tears soaked the front of my shirt—so breakable. She hiccupped against me, trying to draw air into her lungs through the weight of her grief. I held her tightly, trying to keep her together through the strength of my arms alone.

I held her until the sobs subsided. Until her gasps turned into regular breaths. Until the tears stopped flowing. Even then, she didn't pull away.

"I don't know who I am anymore." Flora's muffled voice drifted to me sometime later.

"This doesn't change who you are, Flora." My voice was rough, like I was the one crying. "You are still one of the strongest and most beautiful people I know. You are kind, caring, and a great friend. Who your parents are doesn't change that."

"He lied to me." Her voice was so soft I could barely hear it.

"I know. I'm so sorry."

"I'm alone."

"You are *not* alone," I said, surprising myself with the intensity of my tone. "You have me, Flora. You have us. You will never be alone."

"You're going to *die*." Her voice broke on the word and she was sobbing again. "In one hundred years, you are going to grow old and die. You're going to die and leave me here, all alone. I . . . I don't want you to leave me."

Shit.

I had no words to say to comfort her. She was right. I couldn't believe I hadn't realized it before. Flora would live for centuries—long beyond me. Even if I miraculously made it through this quest in one piece, I was still a slave to my human lifespan. Even Alaric couldn't figure out how to fend off time. Her relentless despair brought tears to my own eyes.

"I'm here right now," I said with conviction. It was all I could promise.

Rose

"Please." Ebb stopped me by placing a hand on my shoulder. I tensed and Asher's lip curled into a snarl. "Please tell her . . . it was all for her. For her safety. I love her as my own. I always have and always will."

Asher growled a warning at Ebb, but I just took the elf's hand, deftly removing it from my shoulder in the process.

"I will. Just . . . give her some time." I dropped his hand and walked out the door. Asher stayed behind me, keeping himself between me and danger as we descended the steps into the forest. I paused when I got to the bottom, unsure where to go. Asher pointed me in the direction of some broken branches. I nodded my thanks to him and we set off at a march.

"He killed her father and then took his place," Asher said to me when we were far enough away to be out of earshot. "I don't know if *time* will be enough for her to forgive him."

"I don't know either." I sighed. "But that's not for us to decide."

We walked for a while in silence before Asher drew me to a stop. He was looking ahead with furrowed brows.

"I hear them up ahead," he said. "She's . . . upset. Blaine is with her. Should we continue or wait for them here?"

"Let's wait," I said. "I know I don't like an audience when I'm upset."

"I've seen you upset," he said, cocking his head as I settled down against a tree.

"Well, you're different."

"Oh?" He raised a brow, then settled in next to me.

I scooted closer. "You know you are."

He put his arm around me in response.

"Thank you," Asher breathed. He stared into the distance, lost in thought.

"For what?"

"For defending me back there." He looked at me. There was something in his eyes I couldn't quite place. Some emotion I couldn't understand. "No one has ever . . . I'm not used to . . ."

He trailed off. I blinked up at him as he swallowed and tried again.

"Thank you, Rose." His smile was the most vulnerable expression I had ever seen.

"You're welcome, Asher."

I wanted to say more—something to fit the weight of the moment between us. To tell him how much I would do for him and how thankful I was he had come into my life. To tell him how I was never going to be able to pay him back for saving me. How I would never be able to thank him enough . . . but none of the words I thought sounded right. Nothing was good enough. Not for him.

Then the moment passed. His smile turned wry and amusement danced in his golden eyes.

"I really thought you were going to burn that elf where he stood for what he called me."

"I didn't mean to." I rested my head on Asher's shoulder and let my eyes drift shut. "I would hate to hurt someone Flora cares about . . . but I definitely would have torched him if he attacked you."

Asher's arm tightened around me as he chuckled. I felt a light pressure on my hair that could have been his lips, but I didn't dare open my eyes to confirm. I couldn't keep the smile from my face as a rush of warmth went through me. Safe. I felt so safe with Asher. How did he do that to me?

"So protective," he whispered into my hair. I didn't even have the energy to roll my eyes at the comment as I slipped into the strange space between waking and sleeping. The warmth he provided was pulling me deeper and deeper into oblivion.

"You're worth it," I managed to mutter.

"You are incredible, little witch." The words were so soft, I might have dreamt them.

I don't know how long I slept. Asher squeezed my shoulder and I woke to see Blaine and Flora appear from the trees. I scrambled to my feet and rushed over. I threw my arms around Flora, then pulled away and studied her. Her eyes were rimmed in red, but they were dry.

"Are you okay?" I asked.

"No." She attempted to smile. "But I will be."

"We're here for you, whatever you need," Asher said from behind me. I hadn't heard him approach, but I somehow knew he would be there.

She nodded to him in thanks. I squeezed her shoulders once before letting go and stepping away.

"I know we have a lot to discuss. I know we still need to get the last Argem," she said, exhaustion heavy in her voice, "but, I think I would like to go back to Earth. I just . . . I need to process."

"Well then, let's go home," Blaine said. "We can take a few days to plan what we want to do next."

"Yeah," I agreed. "We'll figure it out, together."

"We can't make any big trips until over winter break anyway," Blaine said. "We have plenty of time to figure things out."

Flora nodded and smiled at each of us. She glanced back toward Ebb's house once, before taking a deep breath and turning away from the only family she ever knew.

It was a quiet journey back to the Rift. We walked together in pairs—Blaine and Flora took the lead while Asher and I followed close behind. Blaine offered his arm to Flora and they walked close together. Gathering my courage, I reached out and took Asher's hand. Heat blossomed in my cheeks as he intertwined his fingers with mine.

When the Rift finally came into view, Asher and Flora both tensed. I looked around to see what was wrong, but I didn't notice anything out of the ordinary. I followed Asher's line of sight, but there was no movement or—

There! A shadow shifted amongst the trees.

"Who's there?" Flora called to the shadow. "Reveal yourself!"

Asher used our intertwined hands to pull me behind him as Elder Rhisler coalesced before us. The green ceremonial robes blended in with the surrounding forest, but the vining gold circlet atop his silver hair glimmered in the late morning sun. His gray eyes roved over us before locking on Flora.

"Head Elder?" Flora tried to stand up straighter—to pull herself together—but I could still see the slump in her usually proud shoulders. "Wh-what is it you are doing here?"

"Looking for you, youngling." The elder took a step closer. "We have urgent need of you in Trehilm. Please, come with me."

He gestured for Flora to join him, but she hesitated, looking at Blaine.

"Your companions may depart. This is an internal matter. It is not for human ears," the elder said.

"Is this about our quest?" Flora asked. "Shouldn't the Veritace be included in those discussions?"

"You question me?"

Flora flinched but held her tongue.

"Fascinating." The elder frowned. "I received word you may have uncovered some . . . sensitive information. I hoped it would not have such a grievous effect on your loyalties."

Flora visibly tensed. Blaine placed a hand on his sword. I just blinked at the imposing elf. How did the Council find out so quickly? Would Ebb have told them? That . . . that didn't make any sense.

"Already, you are questioning the decisions of the Council." Rhisler shook his head solemnly. "How long will it take for you to turn on us, completely? I told them we should have taken care of this dreadful business when you were a child. It would have been . . . cleaner."

"Head Elder, I don't understand . . ." Flora trailed off.

"Do not be troubled, youngling." Elder Rhisler smiled tightly. "I will remedy our mistake."

He lunged. Blue lightning erupted from his fingers and darted toward Flora at incredible speed. Asher—even with speed magic—barely had time to pull me away before the lightning struck.

Asher shouldn't have worried—Blaine deflected the blow with Peacekeeper. He used the same maneuver he had in the Harmony Chamber on our first trip here. Unlike that time, however, his expression wasn't one of shock or fear.

It was anger.

"We aren't going to be that easy to bury, Rhisler," Blaine hissed through clenched teeth.

Electricity crackled around the elder like a forcefield. A politician's smile touched his shrewd lips.

"Pardon me, Veritace, but there is no need for you to interfere. I must remove this youngling from your group," Elder Rhisler said in a chagrined tone—no more distressed than a waiter that mixed up our order. "We will find you a new, better guide."

"Why?" Blaine scoffed.

"She has been deemed unsuitable for the task."

"She's more than suitable."

From where Asher and I stood, I could see Flora glance at Blaine with wide eyes before they settled back on Rhisler.

"That is not your decision to make, *Veritace*." The elf somehow made the honorific sound like an insult.

"Yeah, I think it is."

"You understand," Rhisler raised a slender eyebrow, "it would be easy enough to kill you and wait for the next reincarnation to come along."

"You can't!" I shouted. Asher tightened his grip—ready to whisk me away—as Rhisler inspected me. Disdain warped the elf's features when his cold, grey eyes fell on us. "W-What about the Defector? I thought you were in a hurry to stop her."

"You humans age so quickly." The elf raised his brow. "Waiting another few decades would be worth avoiding the risk this youngling brings. I can already see the evil growing in her. Before long, she will be just like her mother."

"You can't have Flora," Blaine said in a tone that didn't invite further argument. "She's with us now."

"If that's your final decision, Veritace, I will accept it on behalf of the Council."

A bolt of lightning flashed from his hand toward Blaine.

Blaine deflected the magic again, but the sudden attack jolted Flora from her shock. She made a quick, flicking motion with her hands and a strong gust of wind picked up around us. The wind grabbed up leaves from the ground and pulled foliage from the trees, before shifting to twist around Flora like a tornado. The wind circled Flora like a shield—the forest itself protecting her.

She was the embodiment of her forest god as the wind lifted her hair into a halo atop her head. Her green eyes glowed with an otherworldly light as she stepped forward. Tendrils of leaf-filled wind flicked out around her like whips. Goosebumps formed across my skin at the elven power, so different from mine. Magic crackled and popped around me as the bolts of lightning met Flora's wind.

Flora could defend herself, but she couldn't attack. Rhisler's magic was too fast—too powerful. Every so often, a blue light of energy would strike at Blaine, and Flora would send out a whip to deflect it. She was using too much energy. I didn't know how long she could last against the older elf.

Asher released me and shifted into his wolf form in a quick flurry of motion. He leapt toward the elder with a snarl. Without glancing at the giant wolf, Rhisler shot a bolt of blue magic at him. The lightning moved too fast for me to even think about putting up my shield. Time slowed for me as the magic pierced Asher's chest. To my eyes, he froze mid-bound, every muscle in his body tense as the electricity coursed through him.

Time resumed as he crumpled to the ground.

"No!" I screamed as he went down.

My hair whipped around my face as I threw myself to the ground beside the limp wolf. The smell of burnt hair filled my nostrils as my fingers clenched into the thick fur of his neck, feeling for his heartbeat. Where did you even look for a pulse on a wolf?

"No no no no . . ." I couldn't stop the words from tumbling off my lips over and over again.

I could feel my panic rising, shutting out any thoughts other than those of the too-still form before me. Only when I felt Asher tremble beneath my fingers could I breathe again. Tears blurred my vision as I looked up at Rhisler. He stared down at me with contempt as I clung to Asher. He clicked his tongue at my display, then turned away. I wasn't a threat to him.

Or, so he thought—he didn't know about my powers.

Blaine

Asher fell.

Asher—the strongest member of our group—fucking fell. Was he dead? No. He couldn't be. But what if he was?

My fault. It was all my fault. My chest tightened. I asked him to come with us. He was only here because of me—his *savior*. What kind of savior couldn't protect the people he cared about?

My heart stopped as Rose threw herself over the fallen wolf. She shot a venomous glare up at Rhisler. If he laid a finger on her, I would—

What would I do? What *could* I do? I sure as hell couldn't outrun a lightning strike. I couldn't protect her from Rhisler. I was going to watch her die. My heart pounded in my chest, and heat flushed through my body. The elves were going to kill her, just like they killed Alora.

It was happening again.

No, not the elves—one corrupt elf. I shook myself—now was not the time to fall into Alaric's memories. I tightened my grip on Peacekeeper. He would not get away with hurting my friends.

"Blaine!" Flora's scream came as a gust of wind-made-solid collided with a bolt of lightning only inches from my face. I stumbled back a step, gasping. Flora just saved my life.

Pay attention, Blaine. Time to be the hero you're supposed to be.

Rhisler advanced on Flora, forcing her backward. He summoned several bolts of lightning at once, but they were all deflected by Flora's protective tornado. She wielded her magic like a god, but I saw when she faltered. She stumbled over uneven ground and her magic weakened for a millisecond. Rhisler took full advantage. He pushed more energy into his attacks, lightning becoming larger and more erratic. Blue sparks began to weave their way inside Flora's gusts.

How do I help her?

Would I survive stepping between dueling elves? If Flora couldn't fend him off with her magic, how was I going to fare with only a sword? I'd probably end up like Asher.

I dared a glance at my friends, and Rose's gaze snapped up to mine. My breath caught at the agony scrawled all over her tearstained face. She was so pale, and her breaths came in heaving gasps. I watched as a dissociative haze clouded her eyes. If she slipped back into how she was before—that lifeless husk of a person—that would be my fault, too. Instead of falling into shock, her pain shifted into rage. An icy calm settled over me, along with a realization.

I forced my focus back to Rhisler. I gritted my teeth and fell into a guard position. He wouldn't harm anyone else. Not while I still lived.

I attacked.

Peacekeeper arced through the air, singing for Rhisler 's blood. Lightning crackled around me, cascading from the main bolt and fizzling in haphazard lines. Peacekeeper's draconic magic allowed me to block the lightning. Instinct told me where to step to avoid the stray electric bolts that branched out, grasping at me with volatile fingers.

Sweat dripped from my forehead, stinging my eyes. Static energy crackled the air around me, and the hair on my arms and legs stood on end. My biceps and thighs burned from the forced precision of my parries. Burning ozone filled my nostrils, and my fingers tingled. I fought for every step as I inched closer to Rhisler.

He wasn't even giving me his full attention. One hand was still stretched out to berate Flora, while the other pummeled me with electricity.

I needed to go faster. Flora's magic wasn't limitless—she couldn't hold out forever. Peacekeeper blurred in my hands as I pushed myself harder. I was tired and growing sloppy. Instinct told me I needed to slow down and conserve energy. Instead, I took a risky step forward. I recognized my mistake immediately—I overextended. My muscles quivered, and my legs stalled beneath me. I couldn't move fast enough.

Blue light filled my vision.

Rose

Rhisler shot four simultaneous bolts of magic at Blaine. Exhausted as he was, Blaine wasn't able to deflect all of them. He fumbled and was hit.

Twice.

Peacekeeper flew from his hand, spinning out of reach. It skidded to a halt in the green grass as Blaine fell to his knees, then collapsed. I stopped breathing.

"Blaine!" Flora screamed.

The tornado flared around her, doubling in size. She changed the course of her magic, abandoning her defense and channeling everything toward Blaine. The wind carried with it a pale green light that surrounded his motionless body. She was trying to heal him.

"Please, please, please." My shaking fingers dug into Asher's fur as I begged. I begged Flora. I begged the forest god. I begged the stars. I begged anyone who would listen. Asher was only hit once and was barely alive. Blaine had been struck twice. From where I sat, I couldn't see him breathing.

The light winked out and the magic dissipated, just as Blaine took a sudden, rasping breath. I watched as Flora fell to one knee. She must have used all her power to heal him. I blinked through my tears to watch as Elder Rhisler strode toward her on unhurried steps. She looked up at him and her features twisted in betrayal.

"Don't hurt them," Flora pleaded. "They shouldn't be punished for what I am. It has nothing to do with them. Please."

The elder stopped over her and tilted his head to one side.

"Their survival depends on their response to your death."

Flora's gaze swept around one last time. She looked into my eyes and I felt a tap on my mental shields. A branch tapping lightly against a window. I didn't know how, but I knew it was Flora. I opened a pocket for her immediately.

Don't fight him, she said into my mind. *You can still make it home if you don't fight him.*

I shook my head. Flora shot me a sad smile through her exhaustion. Her gaze fell to where I clutched Asher. She frowned, her regret filling my mind. When Flora looked at Blaine, anguish twisted her expression. An unbearable sorrow rocked through our connection. Guilt. Blaine's eyes were still shut tight. He was curled on his side, gasping. It looked like every breath hurt, but he was alive.

May the Forest watch over you all.

"No!" I screamed again. She cut off our connection and glared up at Rhisler.

Rhisler raised his hand and pointed his palm toward Flora's heart. She didn't flinch. She didn't seem scared, just resigned to her fate.

"We should have killed you that night. At least I get the chance to rectify that mistake," Rhisler said with cold detachment.

No. This can't happen. Could I shield her? Where was my shield? Where was my feeling of isolation? Why couldn't I find it?

Shock. I had to be in shock. Again. That was inconvenient. Maybe I couldn't force magic that required complex feelings. Frustration though—and anger. I *always* had access to anger.

Flames roared to life around me. Good, now I just had to . . . what? I could summon flames, but I couldn't do anything with them. I couldn't use them as a weapon. I couldn't control them. Except . . .

No one else would die.

Rage swept through me. My fire jumped to my fingertips—past my fingertips. Fountains of flame cascaded out of me in all directions. I jumped away from Asher to avoid hurting him, though my magic didn't touch him. The grass and trees around me weren't so fortunate. I left charred footprints behind me as I ran at Rhisler.

For a split second, Rhisler's eyes bulged. Then his features melted into cruel distaste. He looked me up and down, measuring my power as I charged. Deciding how much trouble I would be.

It infuriated me.

I threw out my hands and shot fire at the elder, bathing him in heat and liquid flame. I screamed out my anger. My grief. My rage. I screamed until there was nothing left in me.

Ten seconds.

Twenty.

I couldn't think of anything else. Only of how this man hurt my friends.

My fire flickered out and I fell to my knees. I was so tired and my head felt like it was about to split open. Tears stung my eyes and I closed them. I didn't want to see the burnt husk of an elf. I didn't want to see what my anger had done—who else it had killed.

"I must say, that was unexpected."

Impossible. I opened my eyes. Rhisler stared at me with his head cocked. He was standing at ease before Flora, not a single silver hair out of place.

My flames hadn't even touched him.

Shame hunched my shoulders. Defeat had me slumping to the ground. I lost control and sent all my magic at this man, yet I still couldn't even touch him. I couldn't stop him.

With a flick of his wrist, he sent me flying backward.

I landed hard and the impact stole my breath. I didn't get up. Instead, I crawled to Asher and cried into his fur. If we were going to die, at least we would die together.

Rhisler watched me crawl. "It astounds me that our ancestors lost a war to these weak creatures."

"They're stronger than you know," Flora hissed.

"Hmm." Rhisler raised his hand. Electric blue bolts of magic shot from his palm and connected with Flora. I screamed as the magic wracked through her. Her small body arched backwards until her spine looked like it would snap. Her mouth contorted in a silent scream, her eyes closed tight against the pain.

I didn't want to watch, but I couldn't look away. Just looking at the bright lightning shot a stab of pain through my temples, thanks to my excessive magic use. I was drained. Not a hint of my power remained. I was utterly useless and my friends were paying the price.

Flora was dying.

The lightning stopped. I watched in horror as Flora crumpled to the ground. Was that it? Was she dead? Did life leave a person so quickly?

Was I next?

I tore my gaze from Flora to look at the elder. I expected him to point his palm in my direction next—but he didn't turn. Rhisler's silver eyes widened where he stood, and a dark patch spread down the chest of his green robes. His hands flew to his neck. In the sudden silence of the forest, a gurgling sounded from his throat.

A glittering, blood-soaked blade protruded from his neck.

When Ristler fell to his knees, a shadowed figure appeared behind him. The shadows pulled back from the figure's face, revealing dark hair, a strong jaw, and violet eyes.

Ebb.

Ebb's expression was murderous. He looked from Flora's still form to the elder staring up at him in shock. His face didn't change as he listened to the pleading gurgles coming from Rhisler.

"Was this the Council's decision, or yours?" Ebb asked, voice as dark as a moonless night. When Rhisler didn't answer—not that he could with a knife obstructing his windpipe—Ebb focused hard on the elder. "Ah, good. You acted without the Council's knowledge. That makes this easier."

The gurgling cut off as Ebb reached down and swiftly jerked the knife from Rhisler's ruined throat. The wet crunch of metal against bone made me retch. I looked away as blood gushed from the elf's neck and he fell to the ground.

Dead.

Ebb's knife tumbled from his fingers. He ran to Flora and dropped to his knees beside her. He scooped her up and hugged her against himself, hands radiating an eerie violet light that soon encased her entire body.

"I'm sorry, flower," he murmured over Flora's limp body. "I should have been here sooner. I should have told you everything. I'm so sorry."

I sobbed when Flora gasped awake. She took in her surroundings—me crouched over Asher, Blaine huddled on the ground, the dead elder—before noticing who held her. She scrambled away from Ebb on shaky limbs, cutting off his healing magic.

"You killed him?" Flora whispered in disbelief.

"Flora, I—"

"I'm fine!" Panic laced her voice. She looked at Ebb's hands then pointed at Blaine and Asher. "Heal them!"

Ebb tilted his head to the side and furrowed his brow.

"I'll heal," she said, "but I'm out of magic and my friends are gravely injured. Please!"

Ebb nodded and got to his feet. Glancing between the human on the ground and the giant wolf in my arms, Ebb sighed. He walked to Blaine first, placing a hand on his shoulder. Blaine's rasps gradually softened as the violet light spread over him. Eventually, Blaine opened his eyes and Ebb stepped back.

Flora rushed to Blaine as he pushed himself to a sitting position. She wrapped her arms around him, burying her face in his neck. Ebb walked over to me and crouched down on the other side of Asher. I looked into Ebb's eyes and could read nothing in the hard gaze. Could I trust him with Asher's safety?

"Are you injured?" he asked.

I had a splitting headache and there was a twinge in my knee from landing weird, but it was nothing I couldn't handle. I wouldn't take any healing magic before Asher. I shook my head.

"Then I suggest you release the wolf so I can work."

Letting go of Asher was the hardest thing I'd ever done.

After healing Blaine and Asher back to consciousness, Ebb stayed with us while Flora replenished her power. Ebb frowned when Flora stayed within view as she sat to meditate, but he didn't say a word about it. He had to know privacy wasn't worth her safety.

If one of the Council of Elders had the idea to attack us, another might try too.

"I assume we won't be welcome in Trihelm once word gets around we played a role in killing the head elder," Blaine mused as we sat around a crackling campfire at our usual campsite near the Rift.

"No one will hear of what happened here today," Ebb promised. "I have ways of covering up this type of incident."

That was believable. Ebb had already disposed of Rhisler's body and removed all trace he had been here in the time it took for my shaky hands to build a fire.

"I guess we know how people are disappearing," Asher growled. I squeezed his hand. I hadn't been able to let go of it since he shifted back into his human form. Not after almost losing him.

"Perhaps." Ebb's eyes narrowed in thought. "I agree the Council has the ability to make people disappear, but what would be their motivation?"

Blaine scoffed. "They just tried to kill Flora because she discovered something they didn't want anyone to know. I'm sure they have plenty of secrets they want to keep hidden." He pushed his curls away from his face. "I really need to find that last Argem."

We lapsed into silence.

When Flora finally stood and made her way to us, she looked healthier. She had a blush on her cheeks and a spring in her step again. That spring faltered when she saw Ebb.

"I can't talk to you," Flora said. "Not yet."

Ebb flinched from her words, but he nodded.

"When you're ready . . . if you're ever ready . . . you know where to find me."

Flora nodded, looking at the ground.

"I love you." He strode into the forest without waiting for a response.

When he was out of sight, Flora sagged. She ran her fingers through her perfect hair like she was ready to pull it out. She sat down hard on the log beside Blaine and put her head in her hands.

"I'm sorry, everyone," she said. "I should have never brought you here."

"None of this is your fault." Blaine put his arm around her and pulled her into a hug.

She gave a derisive laugh.

"It's not," he repeated. "I firmly believe we're meant to be here together. Nothing you did could have kept us away."

I reached out to take one of Flora's hands with my free one. When she looked up at me, I saw so many questions brimming in her unshed tears. Questions I didn't have the answers to.

"We don't blame you for any of this," I said. It was the only thing I could think of to comfort her. She blinked, and the tears slipped down her cheeks.

"You three should go get some rest," Asher said.

I looked back at him then down to our still clasped hands. I knew he was right, but I wasn't ready to let go of him yet. I wasn't ready to let go of any of them yet. I wanted to stay in this instant forever, all of us connected to each other by touch.

But Flora was already pulling her hand from mine.

"Are you going to be okay here?" I asked. Asher would be by himself, with no way to contact us if he needed help.

"I've been fine on my own for a while now." He smiled wryly. "I'll survive a few hours alone."

Just don't stay away too long, if you can help it. His words floated through my mind.

I wouldn't dream of it.

His smile turned warm as he stood, pulling me into a standing position. Before I could talk myself out of it, I pulled him into a hug. He was still for a heartbeat before wrapping his arms around me.

"Be safe over there, little witch."

I smiled and nodded against him. "You be safe over here."

"Always am."

When I stepped out of Asher's arms, he was smiling. Blaine was already standing. He had one hand outstretched to where Flora still sat on the log.

"What do you say, Flora?" he asked. "Ready to go?"

"Yes." She wiped her eyes and looked toward the Rift. She reached up and took Blaine's outstretched hand. "Let's go home."

Epilogue

Asher

S HE WAS HUGGING ME.

Rose was hugging *me*.

I was frozen in shock for a moment before my brain started working again and I wrapped my arms around her. I kept my touch gentle, though it was difficult not to lift her up and squeeze her into me. I wanted to hold her here forever. Where she would be safe. Warm. Protected.

Mine.

I shook the thought from my head. She didn't truly want me, even if she had said as much during that stupid song. That had just been the spell.

"Be safe over there, little witch," I pleaded. I felt her nod against my chest.

"You be safe over here." Her voice wavered. Was she worried about me? I smiled at the absurdity of the thought.

"Always am."

When she pulled away, her warmth lingered. I looked down to where her small hand still clutched mine and tried to squash the warmth that blossomed through my chest at the sight. I could still feel the phantom press of her body against mine.

"What do you say, Flora?" Blaine asked, interrupting my thoughts. "Ready to go?"

"Yes," Flora's voice was tight. Clipped. I could smell the misery wafting off her as Blaine hauled her to her feet. "Let's go home."

Home.

The word sliced through the warmth in my chest like a claw through flesh. It was a place I could never go. A place I would never ask Rose to give up. Not for me.

Flora was first through the Rift. She didn't say goodbye but I couldn't blame her for that. I understood wanting to be alone.

Blaine clapped a hand on my shoulder and flashed the confident smile that came so easily to him.

"Thanks for all your help, bro," he said. "I don't know what we would have done without you."

I wasn't sure how to respond to that.

"Don't get too bored without us here." He let go of me and walked toward the Rift.

"Being bored sounds like a luxury," I said.

He laughed as he disappeared.

I looked down at Rose. She was still clasping my hand tightly, reluctant to let go.

"We'll be back as soon as we can." She looked up at me with sparkling blue eyes. She opened her mouth to say more, then pressed her lips together. She didn't pull her hand from mine. A tentative hope warmed my chest, urging me toward recklessness.

"I know." Slowly, I lifted our clasped hands. I watched her carefully as I leaned down, giving her plenty of time to pull away. She didn't. I dipped my head to brush a light kiss on her knuckles. "I'll be here."

When I looked at her again, she nodded. Her cheeks had flushed a deep red and she was biting her lip. The movement was . . . distracting. I wanted to reach out and—

Stop. Not mine.

I released her hand and forced mine to stay at my sides. She stepped toward the Rift. Rose looked back at me, soft pink lips lifted up into one of those perfect smiles. The sight ripped my own smile to the surface.

I watched the Rift reach out and wrap itself around her. The churning vortex mocked me. Not only could I not hold her the way it did—the way I longed to—but it barred me from traveling to her home. I couldn't follow her to the other side. I couldn't protect her.

I was useless.

The Rift obscured her, and then she was gone. The smile fell from my face.

"Be safe, little witch," I repeated to the empty forest.

Despite the healing I'd just received, my right shoulder gave a sharp twinge of pain.

Flora

Wisps of color dissipated as the kitchen formed around me.

I anticipated it but still wrinkled my nose when the noxious smell hit my nostrils. Poison permeated the air here, even inside. It always took me a moment to establish my magical mask—to weave the air into something breathable. I sent my thanks to the Forest for allowing me the magic to breathe easily.

Hopefully They could hear me from here.

I stepped away from the Rift—away from the vibrant forest of my childhood—and further into the lifeless house. I took in the familiar white cabinets and the stained wooden countertop. The noisy appliances and the harsh overhead lights. I glanced through the dirty window to the hazy, polluted streets outside. The shock of coming to Earth after spending time in Silaris was always difficult. The whole house—this entire world—screamed of death.

Even the plant life here felt less *alive*. It was hard to admire beauty in the dull petals of a flower pulling nutrients from pollution-ridden soil. It was hard to listen to the labored rasps of trees struggling to survive in this smog-filled world.

Earth wasn't like Elvanar. This wasn't the land where I could commune with the Forest. Where I could close my eyes and listen to the trees sing for hours. Where I could sing, too, and be part of their conversation. Where the animals weren't afraid of me. Where I could breathe without constantly using magic.

Where I was born.
Where I was stolen.
Where I was lied to.

I thought back to my earliest memory and an image formed in my mind. Bars surrounded me. A slender face masked in shadow loomed overhead. The warmth of magic surrounded me and songbirds circled slowly above. Was that the night I was abducted?

Perhaps it was only a dream.

"Flora?"

I jumped at the sound of Blaine's voice. I didn't realize he came through the Rift already. Rose, too. They were both staring at me, concerned. How long had I been standing here? I shook my head to clear it.

"Yes?"

"Are you okay?" His tone made me think he was repeating the words.

I don't know.

"Are you?" My voice wavered slightly, but I didn't think Blaine or Rose had the hearing to detect it. "You almost died today."

The image of Blaine lying on the ground, not breathing, would haunt my dreams. He had befriended me. He had traveled to new, dangerous lands with me. He had fought for me. He had comforted me—even loved me.

Then he almost died for me. All of his pain and suffering over the last few weeks . . . it was entirely my fault.

"I . . ." He paused. "I feel fine. Totally healed."

I looked at Rose. "And you?"

Rose glanced at Blaine then back at me. She nodded, but a wrinkle formed between her brows as she frowned. She reminded me of Tisha when she wore that expression. They had a lot in common. They were both always worrying—always neglecting themselves to benefit others.

"Flora—" Rose started, but I interrupted before she could say something that would no doubt make me cry. I was tired of crying.

"Good." I turned away. "I'm going to bed. Get home safely."

Without another word, I walked to my room. I locked the door behind me before curling up on my bed. I grabbed the closest pillow and hugged it against my chest. I closed my eyes and listened.

Blaine and Rose spoke quietly for a few moments. They gathered their things. I heard the front door open and close. Car doors slammed shut. Blaine's car roared to life, the radio blasting for half a second before he could turn the volume down. I heard the tires crunch against the pavement as he pulled away from the curb. The regular thrumming of the engine grew softer and softer as he drove away. Soon, I couldn't differentiate the sound of his car from the cacophony of machines and alien creatures that sounded throughout the night here. Every night.

My friends had left. My fath—no . . . *Ebb* had lied. My father was dead. My mother didn't know I was alive.

I had to think.

I recalled my memory of Mika. It was difficult to believe we met only days ago. She was so intimidating. Regal, the backdrop of golden sand in rolling dunes behind her. Beautiful, if you ignored her eyes.

I shivered at the recollection of those milky-white irises. They were cold. Calculating. The eyes of someone who closed herself off from the world, never expecting to be open again. Someone who would always be alone.

Is that my future too?

I looked *nothing* like her. Then again, Ebb said I looked like Dorian. What did he look like? Could I find a portrait of him in one of the libraries? It wasn't uncommon for people to commission portraits of their families.

Did Dorian still have living family out there? Did . . . did *I*?

I squashed the thought as soon as it surfaced. I didn't want to think about that—didn't even want to hope. Hope was dangerous. Hope made the pain so much worse when it inevitably crashed down around you.

The quest, I told myself. *Focus on the quest.*

We had one more Argem to get. The Council may have lied to us about Mika, but they were right about the stones—they held important memories. Blaine needed to remember everything. It was crucial he be prepared for . . . whatever happened next. Silaris was still in danger. The evil was still spreading. I saw the sand—the lifeless desert—with my own eyes.

I hugged my pillow tighter. I may have a personal crisis to work through, but I couldn't let Elvanar be destroyed. I wouldn't let the music of life be silenced. I wouldn't let any more of Silaris turn to sand. We would get that last Argem from the humans and we would get the rest of Alaric's memories. Then . . . we would figure it out.

The four of us. Together.

Acknowledgements

Thank you for reading Falling through Fire. Publishing a book is a team effort, and I couldn't have done it without all my supporters. This includes my editors, early readers, artists, fellow authors, friends and family.

Special thanks to developmental editor Jennah Saisquoi for reading this story a fraction of the amount of times I have, but still more than any one person should. To cover designer Sara Copes for putting up with my last minute design shenanigans. To Daniel for giving me the courage to start typing before I believed in myself. Without you, this story would have never been written.

I love you all.

About the Author

Leah Lore is a fantasy and science fiction author from southwest Ohio. An avid reader from a young age, she was constantly daydreaming stories to escape reality. When not writing, Leah can be found at the stable with her unicorn, hiking in the woods with her partner and their rescue dog, or cuddling on the couch with her cats and a good book.

Leah was a finalist in the 2024 NYCMidnight Short Story Challenge and her short stories have been published in several anthologies. Leah writes character-driven adventures with an emphasis on mental health and self-worth. She has a MS in biology from Wright State University. Her education and love of nature have been pivotal elements of creating beautiful yet realistic worlds brimming with magic. Follow Leah's progress on her newsletter, website, and social media: https://linktr.ee/leahlore

linktr.ee/Le
ahLore

Also by Leah

Novellas:
Contact Initiative

Anthologies:
No Good Dead – Hidden Villains: Criminals
To the Stars – Kaleidoscope Hearts Volume 6
Sky's the Limit – Kaleidoscope Hearts Volume 7